CROWN OF BLOOD AND BONE

• CURSED KINGDOM •

CROWN OF BLOOD AND BONE

CURSED KINGDOM BOOK ONE

Cover and Interior Design by We Got You Covered Book Design

WWW.WEGOTYOUCOVEREDBOOKDESIGN.COM

ISBN (paperback): 978-1-7383322-1-2
ISBN (hardcover): 978-1-7383322-0-5

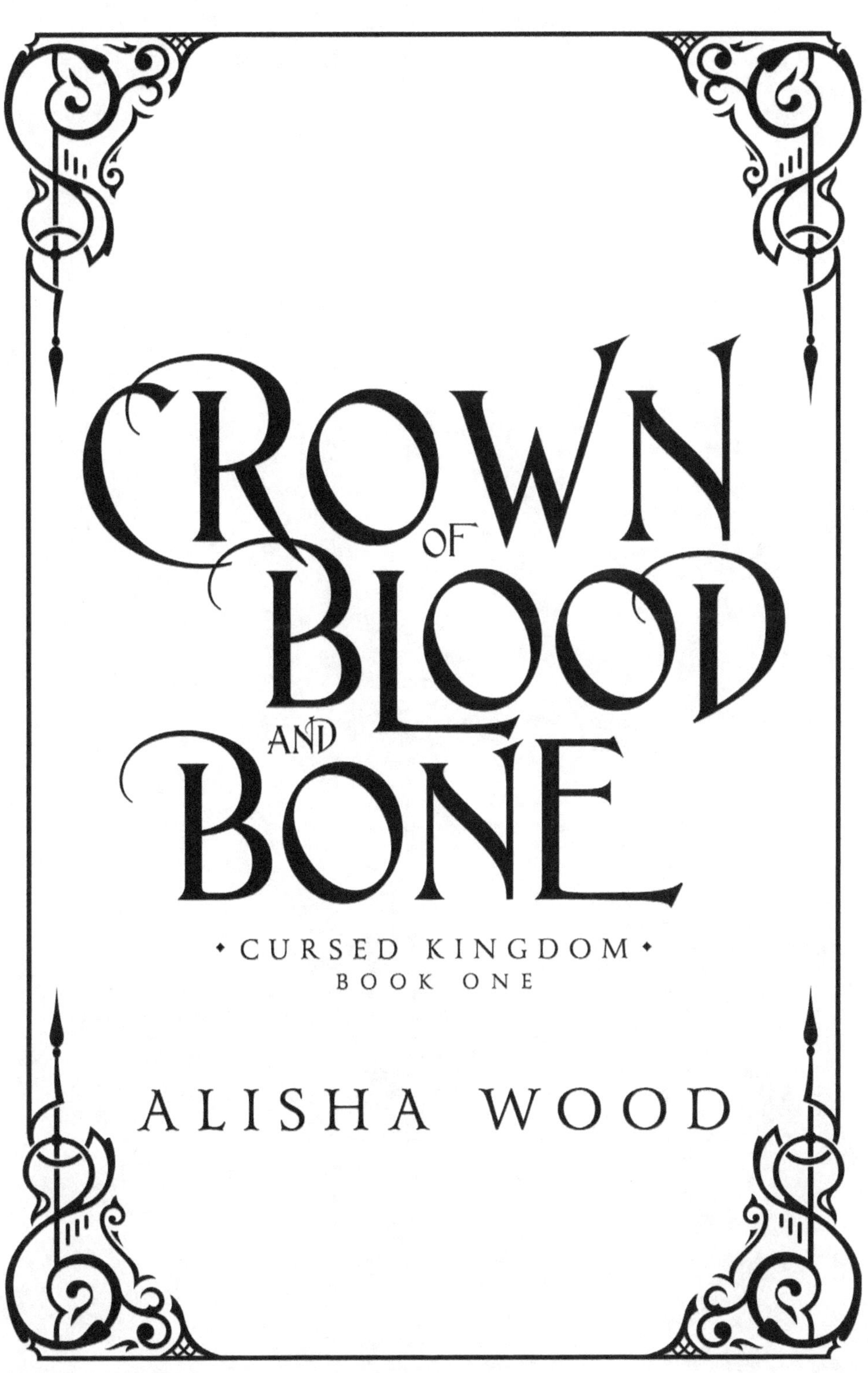

CROWN
OF
BLOOD
AND
BONE
• CURSED KINGDOM •
BOOK ONE
ALISHA WOOD

For Evan,
for always believing in me.

CONTENT WARNING

The following is a list of potential triggers you will find in this book:

- Self harm & mutilation (on page, for magic use)
- Death of a parental figure (off page)
- Mention of deceased parents (off page, historical)
- Death of a sibling (on page)
- Death of an infant (off page, historical)
- Murder (on page)
- Grief, guilt, depression, panic attacks
- Violence, blood, gore, mild language

For a full list of trigger & content warnings,
please visit my website:

WWW.ALISHAWOOD.COM

ONE

A R I

The look on Merlin's face turns feral as he backs me across the small clearing, each step slow and measured. The heel of my boot snags on a root and I stumble. His arm darts out to balance me before I can fall, and the glint in his green-gold eyes turns hungry—predatory—causing my breath to catch in my throat.

His grip loosens, his hand turning feather-light on my skin, leaving a trail of lightning in its wake. My chest tightens, and his eyes flash with the same heat I feel coursing through my body at his touch.

"Stop toying with me," I grit through my teeth, forcing myself to focus on the mage in front of me.

He backs slowly across the little clearing, muscles flexing with the effort of restraint. His dark, midnight hair is still damp from our morning swim, curling at the edges and blown unruly from the wind. It makes him look younger, more like the twenty-five-year-old he appears to be and less like the immortal he actually is.

"Where's the fun in that?" He smirks, taking a step back, watching me over the tip of his sword. "Disarmed or blood drawn?"

"Do you really wish to see what happens if you draw blood?" It's hard to sound intimidating when your opponent knows all your secrets.

"Do you really think it would make a difference?" His smile is lazy and infuriating.

"Disarmed," I say. "No magic today."

"As you wish."

He lunges then, wielding his sword with the type of precision that can only come with centuries of practice, immediately putting me on the defensive. We dance around the clearing in chaotic harmony—me retreating, him advancing, neither of us actually managing to disarm the other.

The longer it draws out, the tighter his focus gets. As if between one breath and the next, what we're doing shifts from a fun training exercise to a competition he has to win. By the time he's backed me against a tree— an unfortunate misstep on my part—there's no trace of warmth left on his face. His grin is more animalistic than human, and entirely triumphant.

We're locked in a bind, our blades crossed between us, and in this moment, it would be far easier to draw blood than disarm, but neither of us dare to change the rules mid-fight.

"Yield." His breath is warm on my face.

"Never."

"Ari." He arches an expectant brow.

"Merlin." My voice is taunting.

A small smile lifts up one corner of his mouth, and he shakes his head slightly. "How will you get out?"

"Not by yielding…" I grunt.

He snorts, and there's a hint of affection in his eyes. "I'm stronger than you, taller than you, and I have you pinned. How will you get out?" he asks again.

My mind flits through the options, discarding each of them until there's only one left. I could try to feint an attack, or I could try to get out from between him and the tree. I could even try to get his legs out from underneath him, but at this range, there's only one way I'm going to disarm him.

Without giving him any more time to consider my actions, I pull my arm back just enough to lower it and lean forward. His sword arm shoots out to the side to avoid slicing into me half a moment before my lips crash into his.

In the space between heartbeats, he's kissing me back, and now he's pushing me up against the tree for an entirely different reason.

His body fits against mine perfectly, as if we were moulded for each other—or from each other. His mouth is warm and hungry, leaving a trail of kisses across my jaw and down my neck. His hand slides up my body and into my hair, holding me firmly in place as he leaves a trail of goosebumps across my skin. He stops at the hollow of my throat, biting gently, and I can feel the desire growing in him, just as clearly as I can see it in his eyes.

That look is all it takes—all it ever takes. My hands tug at the hem of his tunic, pulling it from the waistband of his pants. A shadow crosses over his face, and then he takes a slow, deliberate step back, putting unwanted space between us.

He looks disheveled, but he also looks victorious.

Confusion wrinkles my brow, my mind not able to catch up fast enough.

His eyelids flutter closed, and he pulls in a shaky breath before regaining his composure. A slow smirk spreads across his face before he glances at the ground between us. My eyes follow his, and I swear under my breath.

On the ground, next to my feet, is the sword I hadn't even realised I'd dropped.

"You almost beat me today," Merlin says absently. We're lying in a tangle of limbs, hidden to the rest of the world by the tall grass swaying around us.

He's toying with the end of my braid, rolling it between his fingertips, the pale colour of my hair a nice contrast to the deep tan of his hands. His eyes are intent upon my face, and gone is the fierce determination of before, replaced with the quiet contentment of familiarity.

It's bittersweet knowing that I'll see less of him for a while—until Penn leaves to hunt again.

"Aye." I wave a hand in his direction. "So much for my distraction tactics."

"Oh, they would've worked, had you not let go when you did." He smirks. "I was one moan away from dropping my own sword."

"Don't tease me." I smile easily at him. There's no bitterness over my loss earlier; Merlin often beats me.

"I wouldn't dream of it," he says, leaning in to kiss me. It's soft and gentle, and holds none of the hunger from before.

The afternoon is unseasonably balmy, the sun rapidly warming the valley around us. The sky is an endless blue without a cloud in sight, and the valley itself is lush and thriving. The bright green of springtime and the promise of early blooms speckle the grasses in whites and yellows, soft purples and deep reds.

We come here often when Merlin visits.

It's just a valley—just a grassy slope at the base of a mountain, splitting the forest like a stone in a river. An unremarkable expanse of land, but to us, it's *our* unremarkable expanse of land.

We spend our days here, like this—caught up in the moment, and lost in each other. To each other, we are but a distraction, and this valley is our place to be distracted.

A low rumble like the beginning of an afternoon storm spreads through the valley, catching me off guard and pulling me from my thoughts.

There's something different about it—something wrong. It feels *off,* somehow.

"That doesn't make any sense," I mutter under my breath, eyeing the sky and pulling myself into a sitting position.

Merlin sits and wraps his arm around me, pulling me close and trailing his mouth along the base of my neck.

A second rumble follows closely after the first, causing the hair at the back of my neck to stand on end, and then before I can fully comprehend what that sound means, I'm hopping from foot to foot, stuffing my feet back into my boots. Allowing myself half a moment to regain my composure, I take off at a sprint.

My mind focuses as I run, shutting everything else out and narrowing to one singular thought: find the dragon.

I run as fast as my human feet will carry me, wishing once again for my own set of wings.

The valley is quickly replaced with forest, racing by in a blur. Tree branches snag at my hair and face, replacing the distractions from only a moment ago. The sting on my cheek is little more than an annoyance, though I can feel the blood lining the cuts all the same.

I know this forest.

I grew up in these woods.

I can run these trails blindfolded.

Yet for all my familiarity with the land, it seems to take forever to cover any real ground.

The normality of the forest shifts from pines to willows, and birches to lilacs. The scent of the blossoming trees is delicious and inviting as I continue to make my way deeper into the forest, completely at odds with the growing unease in my chest.

When my home finally comes into view, I slow, skittering to a stop and surveying the scene before me. Many of the trees have been damaged or torn from the ground, lying erratic and broken. I call out to him, shouting his name repeatedly.

On the other side of all the destruction lies our cave—hundreds of years old and carved into the mountainside. The mouth is large and shadowed, moss covering most of the surrounding rocks, vines of ivy growing wild and untouched for decades.

But there is no movement within the cave, and something tells me that if I ventured inside, I would find it empty.

The spring blooms are more vibrant here than in the valley, and constantly enchanted to perfection. A siphon intended to take the edge off; to maintain a level of balance with my magic.

A wide array of flowers sprout up in clusters between the trees—infinite variations of colours, both muted and vibrant, all surrounded by a hundred shades of green; bright, and dark, and faded alike—all of it trampled.

I struggle to grasp what could have happened, and the destruction both concerns yet intrigues me.

Now that I've had a moment to catch my breath, my other senses are starting to pick up on things, like the lack of sounds—bird, or bug, or any other forest dweller, for that matter. The air seems different, too—charged, almost, and slightly metallic.

The sun catches on something just up the path, momentarily blinding me. An irritated hiss escapes my lips as I blink away the sharpness.

Cautiously, I tiptoe towards the foreign metal heap awaiting me. I still haven't decided if this is an elaborate yet unexpected training lesson or not by the time I get close enough to make out the distinct shape of a human.

It coughs and sputters, and then it spits up an unfortunate amount of bright red blood all over the nearest fern. A twinge of fear prickles under my skin, but I force myself to keep walking, ignoring the rising panic in my chest.

Penn would not bring a human here just to harm it, nor would he leave it behind and expect me to do so. Dragons have little time or use for humans, let alone deign to torture one. They neither like nor trust humans, which makes the fact that Penn agreed to raise me both unexpected and extraordinary.

I'm close enough to the human now that I can tell it's a man, and he's badly injured. A sword and shield lay forgotten at his side. But if this man is not here because of Penn, then he is not meant to be here—especially when I cannot seem to find Penn, himself.

If the man wore a helmet, it is nowhere to be seen. Instead, dark coppery hair sticks to his forehead, coated in sweat, dirt, and smears of blood. Dull brown eyes struggle to focus, while slow, ragged breaths attempt to fill his lungs.

The man coughs again, more blood spilling from his mouth. His brows furrow when he finally sees me, his eyes growing more doubtful with every passing second.

"What are you doing here?" I ask, nudging him with my foot.

His armour creeks in protest. There are puncture marks on his breastplate, deep gouges that no doubt extend into the flesh and body beyond.

"How is this p—"

"Why have you come here?" I demand, cutting off his wheezing words and growing angrier as the silence stretches on. The rising panic has my heart hammering tenfold in my chest. "Tell me!"

His mouth forms the shape of what looks like an apology, but no sound comes out. Pointing to the east, I follow his line of sight past the immediate destruction. A continued line of uprooted and overturned trees forms a pathway of immeasurable disarray. Gashes of scorched earth still smoulder in thick, deep lines across the greenery.

"*Penn.*" His name is little more than a whisper on my lips.

I glance back to the man at my feet for only a second, but it's enough to know that he's dead. Uneasiness ripples through me at the sight of him, but I shove it down and take off again, pausing only long enough to grab his discarded sword.

TWO

ARI

I follow a scattered trail of opalescent blood through what remains of the forest surrounding our home. There is no clear route—any that had existed are now destroyed—and I have to jump over, crawl under, or climb around the chaos, which slows my progress immensely.

A screech louder than a thousand ravens fills the air before it turns into a deep, guttural roar. My knees wobble with the vibrations, and my stomach sinks, heart hammering wildly in my ribcage.

Another deep rumble has my feet doubling their pace, flying over debris, and I don't dare stop, even when wayward branches leave sharp trails of blood across my cheeks and arms.

I hear you, I promise.

The sound of shouting voices finally filters in over the sound of my own raging heartbeat, and I barely have time to register the scene in front of me before I come crashing to a halt. The entirety of my momentum takes me—and the armour-clad human in front of me—easily to the ground.

"What the hell—" The human groans, shock and confusion evident in his tone.

I roll off him with a thud, gasping for breath, greedily trying to suck air back into my lungs.

"A maiden? Here?" A thick layer of uncertainty coats his voice. He's not quite a man yet, and although youth still clings to his features, he can only be a few years older than me. His hair is gold like the sun, his eyes blue like a lake, and even under his armour I can tell he has more muscle than he knows what to do with. Hovering over me now, and unsure with what to do next, he asks, "Where did you come from?"

I try to speak but can only wheeze, eyes squeezing shut as I swallow down a thick lump of tangy saliva.

"Are you alright?" he asks breathlessly. My eyes snap open, meeting his own with an annoyed glare.

The sound like rumbling thunder is so much louder now that I'm right in front of him. As I roll onto my side, the thick, heavy ropes wrapped around Penn's neck and wings catch my eye. A strangled sob escapes my lips as I hoist myself onto my knees, then my feet, still trying to even out my breathing.

"I don't think you should stand—"

"Shut up." I spit a mouthful of blood at his feet, gingerly touching the deep cut on the inside of my cheek with my tongue.

"You're bleeding—" he protests, gesturing to the recent, shallow cuts on my arms and face.

"Aye, that's what happens when you're a girl," I snap, turning toward Penn.

The human makes the mistake of reaching out to stop me, a firm hand wrapping around my elbow. My eyes land on his hand, his fingers locked securely around my arm, and I cannot stop the angry, frustrated growl that leaves my mouth. I lash out with my free hand, shoving against his chest. Stumbling back a step, he lets go of me with a look somewhere between shock and fear etched onto his face.

"Oi!" he shouts, anger seeping into his tone. "What's your problem?"

With my arm now free, I continue to make my way toward Penn

without sparing him another glance, ignoring the other two men staring dumbfounded at the scene I've just created. Both of them hold loose rope ends in their hands.

Penn's gaze is so intently focused on my face that my heart nearly skips a beat. He looks equal parts fearsome predator and furious parent.

The only thing I care about is that he's still alive.

His neck is tied down, pinning his face to the destroyed forest floor, thick plumes of smoke drifting from his nostrils. One wing is bent at an impossible angle under the strain of the ropes, and the other has a tear in it longer than the entire length of my body. He must have other injuries because I followed a decent trail of his blood here, but I can't seem to find anything obvious at first glance.

My heart crumbles at the site of him. Hot, furious tears threaten to spill from my eyes. Swallowing down a lump of emotion, I grit my teeth and reach for one of the ropes closest to me.

My hands are but a hair's width from him when something strong and solid snakes around my waist, yanking me backward. Penn cries out, angry or afraid, I cannot tell, but the sound is near deafening.

"What are you doing?" the same boy from before shouts in my ear. "Are you crazy?"

"She might be," one of the others says indifferently.

"Let me go!" I seethe, writhing in his iron grip.

"Somehow, I don't think that's a good idea." He chuckles, backing up several steps without releasing his hold on me.

"I didn't ask what you think," I snarl at him. Each step he takes farther away from Penn has my anger twisting into pure rage.

"The dragon will kill you," he argues, his breath uncomfortably warm on my face.

"I said, let me go!" I twist so that our faces are mere inches apart, my breathing quick and sporadic. Determined blue eyes bore into mine, unyielding and unafraid. "I will not hesitate to kill you."

"Tristan," he says, voice even, "do we know who this maiden belongs to?"

"I am no maiden," I scoff, still struggling to free myself from his grasp, pushing and shoving at his chest and arms. This time, it's useless. There isn't enough space between us, and he anticipates what I will do to free myself of his grip. His arm is like an iron shackle around my waist. "And I belong to no one."

"A lady, then?" he asks, tilting his head to one side.

An exasperated hiss escapes my lips.

"Right." He arches an eyebrow, intrigued. "If you are not a maiden and you are not a lady, then what are you?"

Penn must shift his weight, thrashing under his restraints because the ground rumbles and once again I find myself tangled in a heap with my captor.

Before I can disentangle myself, his hand closes around my wrist. This time, I cannot stop the tears from falling, a heavy sigh hitching in my throat.

"You weep for the dragon?" he murmurs, his face full of disbelief.

"Please," I beg, "let me go to him."

"Does he belong to you? Or"—he pauses for a moment, considering—"you to him?"

"Aye." I laugh solemnly at the absurdity of the question. "Something like that."

Slowly, he releases me, even going so far as to pull me to my feet before nodding in Penn's direction.

A sob of relief escapes my lips as I crash into the side of Penn's neck, my fingers dancing over his iridescent crimson scales. "Shh." I try to make soothing sounds, but they come out broken and strangled. "It's okay, I'm here now." He leans into me, almost imperceptibly, and my heart lurches. "I've got you."

His eyes momentarily dart over my shoulder, searching for something behind me. Absently, I shake my head. "He's not here," I murmur. "He didn't come." I can't tell if the dilation of his pupil means this pleases or annoys him.

My gaze travels slowly over the surrounding area, searching for what I need. After a moment, it settles on one of the other men—on the short dagger at his hip.

"You," I growl in his direction. "Tristan, is it?"

He looks a little worse for wear. There's a rigidness to his stance, something about the way it seems to cause him pain to breathe that makes me wonder if he's broken a rib. There's a nasty cut along his forearm, and the early shadows of a black eye starting to take form. He neither flinches nor breaks eye contact, and I welcome the challenge—it gives me something to focus my anger on.

"Well?" I snap, impatient. "Is that your name, yes or no?"

"Aye," he says, entirely unfazed.

"Great, give me your dagger." I gesture toward the small blade with one hand, keeping the other firmly planted on Penn's neck.

"No, absolutely not!" the third man says, bristling at my demand. He looks mostly uninjured, although his overall appearance is rather disheveled. Perhaps his self-preservation instincts are greater than that of his comrades. "I will not allow you to release him."

"Then by all means, cut him free yourself!" I shout, my voice edging on panic now.

"Absolutely not!" he says again, more forcefully this time. "Garreth is dead because of that dragon. The last thing we're going to let you do is let him go."

"Your friend died because you tried to slay a dragon…" Tilting my head to peer at him more closely, I stifle a laugh at the irony. "So, it's okay for the dragon to die, but not one of you?"

His face turns a livid shade of red. He takes a step toward me and Tristan stops him, one hand tight around his arm. "She's right," he says softly.

Ripping his arm out of Tristan's grasp, the knight rounds on him. "You can't be serious? You can't honestly mean to let her—"

"Here," the first boy says, pushing past the others. Penn snarls at his approach, and he flinches, though he does not back away.

"You might be braver than is wise," I say, staring at him evenly. Between us, he holds out his hand, offering the sword I dropped when I first arrived.

"Some would say bravery is a noble—"

"I don't care," I say, snatching the sword and setting to work, methodically cutting my way through the ropes.

I can hear them shouting behind me—arguing over one another, deciding whether or not to let me free the dragon. They say it so cavalierly, as if that is all he is: a dragon. They argue as if it is their decision to make at all.

"I can't reach," I murmur to Penn. He shifts, leaning to the side and repositioning his back leg so I can climb atop it and continue cutting.

The men shout in alarm now—both for my safety and to question my sanity—their voices incessantly nagging in the back of my head.

"Would you shut up?" I yell, throwing an irate glare over my shoulder.

Once I've cut the last of the ropes on this wing, they slide to the ground, coiling into messy piles beside him. Penn gingerly extends his wing, furiously eyeing the tear up the middle of it.

"Never mind that now," I say distractedly. "I'll mend it later. Let me free you first." His growl is deep and I can't help rolling my eyes. "We both know letting it mend itself will take far longer than if you'd just let me do it."

"Is she talking to the dragon?" Tristan asks incredulously.

"I thought I told you lot to shut up?" I say, pointing the sword in his direction as I round the bulk of Penn and begin cutting the ropes on his other wing. It doesn't take nearly as long as the first one, and when I'm finished, he shakes his torso, wings loosely flapping with the movement.

"That's how you tore your wing, isn't it?" I ask him, kneeling by his head. "You tried to fly."

His eyelids flutter closed in triplicate.

I lift one of the ropes atop his neck, but before I can cut it, the first boy comes questionably close to us again, his stupidity making me pause to regard him.

"Before you let him go…" His voice trails off, his tone wary.

I merely stare at him while he searches for the right words. When they don't come, irritation mixed with exhaustion gets the best of me. "Well?" I demand.

"Maybe you should reconsider?" he offers, but even he doesn't sound confident in his suggestion. Behind him, one of the knights snorts in derision.

"Do you have any idea what you've done?" I say to him, relishing in the way my hostility continues to surprise him. "Any of you?" I round on his companions, levelling them with every ounce of aggression I can muster. "Do you realise that even if I don't die trying to save his life, he's going to have to kill you for coming here? For what you've done? For what you now know?"

"Silence."

The solitary word is ancient and heavy with authority. I do as I'm told, biting my tongue for good measure.

The three of them stare between Penn and myself as if they've just seen someone rise from the dead.

After a brief moment of strained silence, when nobody dares to move a muscle, let alone breathe too loudly, my gaze moves over the three of them, taking in the blades and bows, the steel and armour.

"How'd you manage to capture him, anyway?" I ask, aiming for nonchalance as I turn back to Penn and the last of the ropes pinning his neck down.

For a moment, none of them say anything, but eventually, the one called Tristan opens his mouth. "I am relatively skilled with a bow," he says evenly. "After he was injured, I was able to pin him down with ropes coated in dragon's bane—"

"Dragon's bane?" I ask, momentarily fumbling the sword in my hand. My eyes widen before finding his over my shoulder.

"Aye." He nods. "It's a—"

"I know what it is," I snarl, turning to glare at him properly. "Are you insane?"

"It's not toxic to humans. You'll be fine."

My jaw clenches hard enough to ache. "I just told you I know what it is." Pushing the words through gritted teeth, I ask, "How much did you use? How much of it was on the ropes?"

His momentary silence has my heart dropping into my stomach. When he confirms my suspicions, it feels as if the ground shifts beneath my feet. "Enough to kill him, if exposed long enough."

Turning back to Penn, I quickly and methodically work on cutting away the rest of the ropes. Once he's free, he slowly rises to his full height, towering far above us. His massive body shimmers in the late morning sun.

Twisting his head back and forth as if to crack his neck, he returns to my level and nuzzles against my torso. I wrap my arms around as much of his thick neck as I can, and let the tears flow freely now.

A comforting sound rumbles in his throat, coaxing a singular, tired laugh from me.

"It's okay," I murmur into his scales. "I'll fix it."

He shakes his head, beginning to pull away from my embrace.

"It's not your decision," I say angrily, swallowing down the lump in my throat. Hot tears leave tracks down my cheeks but I make no move to wipe them away.

He leans into me once more, and my eyelids grow heavy with fatigue now that the adrenaline has begun to fade, even though I now know that I'm nowhere near done what I need to do.

I speak quietly to him in the language of dragons, telling him of my plan, and his head rears back in opposition.

"You must let me," I say, stung by his refusal and unable to keep the desperation from my tone. "You cannot stop me, Penn."

Again, his eyelids flutter closed. After a long moment, he concedes, nestling into the ground and gently elongating his torn wing before me.

"Trust me," I whisper.

"You two are seeing this, right?" the third knight says skeptically. "She's talking to the—"

"Shut up," Tristan murmurs.

I turn to them, my body tired and aching, the adrenaline now fading, again eyeing the small dagger at Tristan's hip. Without voicing my request, he slowly and wordlessly walks over to us, removes the blade from its sheath and hands it to me. His eyes never leave my face, the scrutiny nearly uncomfortable.

Heaving a deep sigh and flipping the blade once in my hand, I dig the point into my left palm, wincing and gritting my teeth against the pain as the blood immediately begins to pool. Ignoring the startled sounds coming from the three of them, I carve a deep line into the flesh of my palm, squeezing my fingers tightly over the bloody mess.

I glance at the knight in front of me, take in the tight scrunch of his brows and the way his lips are slightly parted as he stares at my hand, wondering if he knows what I'm about to do—if he's going to try to stop me.

He can try, I suppose, but short of killing me, there's little he could do to interfere now.

He doesn't, though. Instead, he retreats back to the others, giving me space. My eyelids drift shut as the spell pulls itself from my lips easily.

Placing my bloodied hand on Penn's wing, the leathery tissue beneath my palm, coated in my blood and humming with the healing spell, begins to knit itself together, painstakingly slow.

I study the wing as it heals itself, the wing I know like the back of my hand—its veins and webbing and membranous tissue that are as familiar as if it were my own limb.

When it's finally mended, I pull my hand away, glancing at my palm. While my magic has been healing Penn, it's also been healing my wounds. Now, the slice I made only a handful of moments ago is little more than a raised pink line across my palm, sticky with drying blood.

With a heavy sigh, I drag Tristan's blade across my palm once more, reopening the wound before tossing the dagger to the ground.

Placing my bloody hand on Penn's torso, I pull in a deep, shaky breath and begin chanting under my breath, trying to reverse the effects of the dragon's bane.

I stand there for a long time, swaying unevenly on my feet before I can feel my magic deplete itself.

I am not a mage.

My magic is not endless.

If Merlin were here, he would scold me for using nearly every last drop—but for Penn, I would give it all.

Black spots dance at the edge of my vision as the world tilts on its axis.

I sway as consciousness leaves me like the low tide leaving the shore.

I fall, but I do not remember hitting the ground.

THREE

LANCELOT

I thought she might be some form of tree nymph, or maybe even one of the forest folk—between the unnatural paleness to both her hair and skin, and the undeterred fierceness in her eyes. Bits of purple flowers, leaves, and broken twigs adorn her braid, for all the world making her look like a wrathful little wildflower.

And then she bared her teeth, hissing at me, and spoke the dead language of dragons.

Now I can only stare at her, utterly and completely mesmerised. At least Tristan and Perci look just as astonished as I feel.

As a child, my mother often told me that all magic has a price, and it must always be paid. Her voice dances through my mind, as clearly as if she were standing before me, and it takes everything in me to ignore the pain and resentment building in my chest—to not let it grow into more than I can handle right now.

Blood, I realise disturbingly, is what this girl is using as payment for the magic she wields. She's offering up her blood in order to save the dragon. A dragon who seems to care for her, oddly enough, especially for a species that cares about nothing but themselves. My mind races as it tries to decipher what series of events could've led these two to one another.

The words float from her lips in a language I have no hope of understanding. Truthfully, I didn't even know that any other species could learn their language, although this sounds a bit different than before—smoother and less guttural. But whatever she's saying—whatever she's doing—it's mending the wing.

"Is she healing the dragon?" Tristan's disbelief mirrors my own.

A weird mixture of shock, awe, and annoyance fill my chest. It took a lot of energy to get the dragon subdued, and she's effectively just undone everything with a slice of her hand and some pretty words.

And, for some reason, we're letting her.

The three of us seem frozen in place, watching this most unusual girl use magic to save a dragon. Magic that's use is very much forbidden in this kingdom, by anyone, but especially anyone not born with the power.

I have an incredibly limited knowledge of magic, except for whatever I've managed to learn from my mother and her stories of Merlin over the years. There are few people I hate more than Merlin, and fewer still who know of our acquaintance—if you can call it that.

I may not know much about magic, but I somehow don't think she's strong enough to—

She sways on her feet, her head dropping to the side a bit, and I lunge, catching her just before she hits the ground.

The dragon cries out in a deafening roar. Tristan and Perci jump back, out of fear and self-preservation, to distance themselves in case it attacks again, but I can only stare at the girl.

Not a nymph or one of the forest folk, and she doesn't have the telltale markings of a mage. She claims to be neither a maiden nor a lady, so then what is she? Or better yet, *who* is she?

Her eyes frantically dart back and forth beneath closed lids. The cuts she'd sustained prior to finding us have healed, though the blood is only just beginning to dry. Her lips twitch as if she's still trying to utter the spell, but I cannot make out any words.

My whole body goes rigid as the dragon's face appears inches from my own, a giant blazing golden eye, roughly the size of my head, locked on her face.

My hands shake as I lower her to the ground, gentler than I would have thought I could manage, but I'm certainly not going to risk being eaten or disemboweled for mishandling her. Whoever she is, she's important to this dragon.

The cut on her hand looks half healed, still slick with blood. Tristan's dagger lies discarded and forgotten a few feet away from us, and I reach for it slowly. The dragon bristles, and a growl like the clash of thunderclouds comes from deep within it.

"Easy," I say quietly, placing my other hand up between us in what I hope is a peaceful gesture, tossing the blade back towards Tristan. Unlatching my breastplate and shucking it over my head, I try my best to keep my movements slow and nonthreatening.

"What the hell is he doing?" I hear Perci ask.

I ignore him, tearing a long, thick strip from my undershirt, holding it up for the dragon to see before gesturing toward her hand.

Again, the dragon bristles, baring his teeth in a menacing grimace. I will my fingers to stop shaking long enough to bandage her wounded palm.

It releases a sound I can only assume resembles impatience while my fingers re-tie the last knot for the third time. Nervous beads of sweat form along my forehead, neck, and all down my back. Breathing in slowly and not daring to look at it again, I murmur, "I'm not going to hurt her."

"You must go now."

The blood turns to ice in my veins—the haunting, ancient voice unsettles me to my core. "You speak the common tongue?" I ask, still avoiding eye contact.

"I speak many languages."

The girl stirs at the sound of his voice, her head lolling back and forth in my lap. "Did you teach her?"

The dragon equivalent of a sigh rumbles out of his chest. "You have done enough damage here today. Leave before you can do any more."

I huff, anger mingling with residual fear. "You're just as much to blame as we are!"

It happens so fast I don't even see it coming.

There's a slight pressure at my hip and then the girl is on her feet, having silently drawn my own sword, the tip of the blade now held to the base of my throat. I am unable to comprehend what just happened fast enough to get a word out before she curls her lip in a snarl, glaring at the three of us.

"He told you to leave." The ferocity in her tone, her eyes, and the way in which she grips the sword send an odd mixture of shivers throughout my body. "I would not linger, if I were you."

Tristan wavers, uncertainty etched in every inch of his body beside me, but Perci practically trips over himself in his haste to put some distance between him and the girl with the dragon.

I cannot seem to stand, let alone make my feet move.

"Is this you being brave again?" she asks, still sounding angry, but there seems to be a hint of intrigue to her tone now. "I would not suggest it."

"Who are you?" I ask, unable to stop myself. It's the wrong question. Any chance at a conversation, no matter how small, dissipates before my eyes, an invisible door slamming shut on the curiosity in her eyes, leaving only cold fury behind.

Whether the dragon can sense her emotions or is just ready to be rid of us, I cannot tell. Lifting his head to the sky, his chest swells before an enormous, scorching stream of fire erupts from his mouth, the air filling with the acrid smell of brimstone. When his eyes meet mine again, the glare he levels at us is made entirely of nightmares.

"Time to go, Lance!" Tristan shouts, sounding farther away than I should be comfortable with.

My eyes linger on the sword in her hand—my family's crest engraved on the pommel—before flicking to her ice-cold eyes. My feet make the involuntary choice to back up, and I struggle not to trip over the debris.

Following after Tristan, who looks reasonably uncomfortable but is waiting for me impatiently up ahead, we turn and run back the way we came, Perci already far ahead of us.

In the heat of the moment, while running from the raging dragon, it didn't occur to me the damage we were inflicting upon the forest here, and a tiny pang of guilt pokes at my chest.

That guilt grows and blooms into full-on shame when I see the body lying broken and abandoned. Garreth lies in a drying pool of his own blood, the dark colour a stark contrast to the bright greenery beneath.

Perci kneels beside his brother, reciting the final prayer. Tears fall from his eyes, landing on Garreth's face. We failed in our mission today, and it has cost us in more ways than one—and a large part of me wonders if what happened here is going to end up costing Tristan and me our friendship with Perci, too.

"This is my fault," I say, feeling both emotionally and physically drained.

"No, it's not—"

"You're damn right it is!" Perci snaps, cutting Tristan off and rising to his feet. He stalks over to me, shoving me hard. I realise as his gloves come into contact with my chest that I left my breastplate back there, surely now as lost to me as my father's sword.

"Enough!" Tristan shouts, wedging himself between us and pushing Perci back a step. "What's done is done. Nobody was forced to come here. We all knew what we signed up for when we decided to do this."

Perci looks away, chest heaving.

"We are all responsible for the events that unfolded today," Tristan says, the harshness fading from his voice. "Let's just find the horses and go home."

We both nod in compliance before Perci goes rigid, eyes focused in the direction we came from.

Materialising from the midst of the destruction, the girl seems to float in and out of view between the trees, walking toward us.

I'm surprised to see that she's alone.

The three of us exchange a series of uneasy looks, my heartbeat doubling in my chest. Something heavy and distinctly metal is thrown over one shoulder with something long tucked under the opposite arm.

She looks equally frightening and ethereal—like something resurrected from the darker side of magic. An eerily calm expression sits on her face, considering everything that just happened.

"We're leaving," Tristan says when she stops a few paces away.

She nods absently, depositing two swords and a breastplate at her feet. "Your horses will have startled and run off," she says matter-of-factly. "They do not like dragons."

"Aye." He nods. "I gathered as much."

"I'm sorry about your companion," she says, eyes flicking toward the fallen knight behind us. Her jaw clenches slightly, but no other emotion betrays what she's thinking.

Tristan nods, inhaling deeply through his nose. "I'm sorry about your forest."

Perci rounds on him, an incredulous look on his face, betrayal burning in his eyes, but she neither seems to notice nor care. Her eyes bore into Tristan's, the intensity making me flinch, unable to imagine how he's not physically squirming under her endless gaze. In fact, he seems to be studying her just as intently.

Her mouth twitches as if she can't decide if she wants to say something else or not, until she eventually heaves a sigh, her eyes heavy with reluctance. "This way," she says, resigned, turning to the west and walking in the opposite direction from where we came.

We stand motionless for a moment before Tristan takes the first steps to follow after her.

He's braver than I often give him credit for.

The better part of an hour passes before we find the horses, all four of them grazing on a grassy knoll by a crystal-clear stream.

We followed her wordlessly, away from the ruin left by our battle, winding our way through a dense section of forest, through a steep valley and over half a dozen hills before ending up here.

Sometime throughout the last hour, she's managed to free her hair of its collected flora fragments, leaving the broken remnants of flowers, leaves, and twigs in her wake.

Veering away from us, she treks downstream a dozen or so paces before kneeling beside the water and scrubbing the dried blood from her now un-bandaged hand.

A heavy silence has settled over us, and by the time she returns a few moments later, we still haven't said a word.

Speaking clearly and with little emotion, she looks at Tristan as she says, "Thank you for the use of your dagger. You'll want to clean off the blood before it rusts." Glancing at Perci, she says, "You may return to collect your companion and any belongings you've left behind, and then you must leave." When her eyes find mine, the pale green colour freezes me in place. "Thank you for tending to my wound, though it was rather unnecessary," she says, dipping her head just a little.

I open my mouth to say something, but she turns away before anything comes out. Tristan shrugs, grabbing the reins of his mare and following after her. Perci trails close behind, his and Garreth's horses in tow. My own mare comes up behind me, gently nudging my shoulder before we, too, fall in line.

We've just re-entered the forest when the horses begin to act up. Their ears anxiously twitch from side to side and their steps falter, becoming unsure. The girl's head swivels furiously, looking all around us for the unseen threat.

"Is something the matter?" Tristan asks, his voice steady but cautious.

"We should not tarry," she calls over her shoulder, quickening her pace.

"Is there something in the forest?"

"Do not focus on the forest," she says without stopping. "Focus on the path ahead."

"Are we in danger?" Tristan asks her, one hand tightening on his mare's reins, the other making its way to the bow strapped across his back.

"A dragon may be the biggest monster in this forest, but it is not the only one," she says, turning to regard him for a moment. "Whether or not you're actually in danger is of little consequence. The biggest mistake you can make now is provoking it." Her lips twitch into a grimace, and surprisingly, her tone softens as she continues. "It can drive you mad, the things you'll see in the spaces between the trees. Shadows darker than they should be, movement closer than it ought to be. Danger is everywhere, but it's only dangerous if it thinks you care. Most of these creatures in this forest are simply curious—and a little nosey. Most, but not all."

Perci mumbles something I can't make out under his breath.

She glances at him briefly, her face remaining devoid of any emotion, though she cannot hide the uncertain flicker in her eye as she says again, "We should not tarry."

Fortunately, whatever luck the universe has to offer finds us through the woods without any further incident. Idly, I wonder if we should have blindly followed her into the forest in the first place, especially after what we tried to do to her dragon.

She could have taken us anywhere.

As we get closer to the cave, the heaviness of our silence seems to disperse, only to be replaced with a deep sadness. Tristan and I lift Garreth onto his horse, pausing to close his eyes. Perci ties the mare's reins to his own saddle before mounting and kicking off without a word.

Silently, the girl watches them go, her face impassive.

Pausing with one foot in the stirrup, Tristan turns to her, mouth open as if to say something, but shakes his head when he sees her face. Climbing atop his horse, he nods at her once, offering her a tight-lipped ghost of a smile which she returns, much to my surprise.

I find myself wondering how often she's come across humans in her life. How long has she lived here? How long has she been with the dragon? *Why* is she with a dragon?

Taking a hesitant step towards her, I halt when she takes a step back, keeping the distance between us. My mouth opens and closes half a dozen times, different questions forming on my tongue but none of them managing to slip free.

"Are you having a fit?" she asks, brows furrowing.

"I have so many questions," I say, the words seeming to trip over themselves, coming out in a rush.

"I should assume so," she says, arching an eyebrow.

"Leave it alone, Lance," Tristan warns, an unusual sternness to his voice.

"But I—"

"I said leave it alone!" he snaps, raising his voice at me for the first time in a long time and startling his horse in the process.

"Aye," I concede, climbing into the saddle. "Okay." He nudges his horse into motion, pausing once to glance over his shoulder at her, that same intensity from before in his gaze as he studies her. After a moment, he nudges his horse's flank again and they depart at an eager trot.

Her eyes find mine, an unasked question barely hidden in their measured indifference.

"Maybe, one day, I'll see you—"

"I shouldn't hope so," she says evenly, no hint of a smile left on her face.

Releasing a small, defeated sigh, I nod, tugging on my horse's reins.

"Oh, and Lance?" An odd sensation ripples through my veins as she says my name, unfamiliar yet somehow oddly satisfying. There's a lilt to her voice that catches my attention—an edge that makes me uneasy. I meet her eyes over my shoulder. "It would not be wise to return."

FOUR

A R I

"They're gone," I announce, approaching the mouth of the cave. "I watched them ride south until they disappeared into the horizon."

In truth, I watched for a long while after that, too. By the time I stood and stretched out my aching muscles, the sun had almost completed its descent, a hundred shades of orange filling the cloudless sky.

I had quickly followed after the knights on silent feet through the forest, taking a shortcut to a raised outcropping of rocks that would give me an uninterrupted view of their retreat once they cleared the forest. Now, back at the cave, and seeing the destruction of the forest surrounding it again, my stomach clenches, bile rising to my throat.

I shouldn't have followed them…and I definitely shouldn't have helped them. But curiosity got the better of me, and the sooner they were out of our forest and far from our home, the better.

"Penn?" I call into the darkness of the cave, kicking at the rocky earth with the toe of my boot.

The ground rumbles, knocking my knees together.

"Penn, are you angry with me?" I ask when he still doesn't properly acknowledge me.

Uncertainty fills my heart at his rejection.

While anger isn't out of character for him, it's rare for him to get angry with me. Merlin? Always. Bax? Sometimes. But me? Never.

Even when I was eight and pestered him relentlessly for months on end to let me raise chickens, he only huffed a black cloud of smoke into the air, sighing dramatically when he finally agreed. Or, when I demanded he teach me how to fly, even though he kept telling me he could not do so because I did not have wings, he simply watched me jump out of trees for the better part of a month until I broke my arm and finally gave up.

And when I brought Merlin home for the first time, explaining to Penn the deal I'd made with a mage to teach me how to use magic… Then, he'd simply glared at the pair of us, nostrils flaring, before turning and stomping back into the cave.

Now, I take a deep breath and a hesitant step forward, forcing my feet to carry me into the darkness. Even without a torch, my feet know every inch of this cave, confidently carrying me to my destination.

After a moment, a large eye opens, faintly reflecting the dying light from outside the cave. It's the muted colour of sunshine, flecked with amber and gold, a thick black slash down the centre.

A heavy sigh releases a puff of warm air from his snout, chasing the early evening chill from my skin. Another handful of steps removes the last of the distance between us, and I'm surprised to find his scales are clammy under my hand. "Are you alright?" I ask slowly.

"I'm fine, little dragon." He sounds the opposite of fine.

"Penn, what's wrong?" I press, failing to keep the concern from my voice. "What can I do?"

"I need you to find me some yarrow leaves," he says after a moment, a caution in his tone that doesn't normally dwell there.

"Are you still injured?" I ask carefully, refusing to allow the panic I felt only a few hours ago take hold again. "Where?" I ask, rubbing circles into my forehead. The effects of using so much magic earlier still throbs behind my eyelids. Too much—I'd used too much magic and lost consciousness. Merlin would be furious, but Penn… It could have cost him his life.

Had I not passed out when I did, it could've cost me my life as well.

"I couldn't see the wound when I was mending your wing and trying to siphon out the poison from the dragon's bane. I didn't know where else to direct the magic," I say as the image of opalescent blood splattered across the mossy floor of the forest fills my head. "You…you're still bleeding?"

"Do not worry, little dragon," he murmurs. "Some crushed yarrow will set things right."

Leaning forward, I rest my forehead against the side of his face, placing a gentle kiss just beside his eye. "I'll be back as soon as I can."

I leave the cave at a sprint, not stopping until my feet reach one of the oldest parts of the forest. I don't often come this way—only when I need to replenish my supply of certain healing plants and now, today, to help those men find their horses. Undeterred by the near run-in with the dyad of dryads this afternoon, I set about looking for yarrow and silverweed, goldenrod and horsetail—anything I can think of that will help stop the bleeding, all the while keeping my eyes and ears open for any sign of their return.

Penn should be healed by now, or at the very least well on his way. Perhaps I did not get all of the poison, or perhaps the effects still linger?

In my haste, I didn't think to grab a torch, and what's left of the sunset does little to help me, but years of foraging this part of the forest for herbs and roots to aid with healing has given me the knowledge of where to find what I need quickly. By the time I emerge from the trees with an armful of plants, the sun has completely set, the moon slowly creeping into the sky as the first clusters of stars come to life.

Guilt slowly starts to set in, making my stomach turn. If I had gone there to replenish my stores this morning like I was supposed to—before Merlin showed up with his distractions—I wouldn't have wasted so much time just now.

The veins within the mountain rock—spelled luminous long before I can remember—provide decent enough light to see by, but I light a candle upon entering my makeshift workshop anyway, gathering what I need to make a salve for Penn's wounds.

Yanking the stems from the calendula flowers and dropping them in a large stone mortar, it only takes a few minutes after adding a mixture of yarrow leaves and goldenrod roots to form a thick, sticky paste.

My eyes dart around the various ledges and makeshift shelves lining the stone walls of the small room. A dozen or so clusters of dried herbs and spices line the wall closest to me, with twice as many bundles of fresh herbs and medicinal flowers cluttering the ledges in unorganised disarray. A mortar and pestle sit on the sole wooden table, along with a bowl of water, a sharp knife, and a pile of torn cloth in various sizes.

Bright green leaves accompanying small white petals surrounding large yellow centres catch my eye, and I grab a fistful, crushing the entirety of the feverfew plants into the salve.

Memories of Merlin this morning float through my mind as I work—the distraction not unwelcome. He was erratic and disarming, yet almost volatile. He'd surprised me in the valley, like he usually does, intercepting me on my way to the river. He'd joined me for a swim, and then we'd sparred until we were both panting and sweaty. We'd spent a good chunk of the morning that way, but he'd seemed distracted…and giddy…and entirely like himself, I suppose. He eats, breathes, and sleeps chaos. Today was no different.

And yet, something felt off about it all. The same but different somehow. It's not that he didn't question my hasty departure, or even that he didn't come back to the cave with me—he avoids Penn whenever he can—but something nagging at the back of my mind has unease rippling through my veins.

Heaving a heavy sigh and finally satisfied with my concoction, I waste no more time, retracing my steps through the cave until I reach Penn.

Penn is sound asleep and snoring softly when I return.

Having brought the candle and the mortar, I place everything down on a large rock nearly half my height then silently tread over to the sleeping dragon and press my palm to the end of his snout.

Sluggish eyelids open to reveal an iris of molten gold and a black vertical pupil thicker than my arm. "Little dragon," he purrs.

I stare at the ancient dragon before me and can't help smiling. "Show me where you're hurt."

To my surprise, he does so without hesitation or complaint. Rolling onto his side, he lifts his front arm, exposing an impressively long slash, the blood barely clotted and the edges only just beginning to heal.

"Oh, Penn." I sigh, scooping a large handful of salve with one hand. "I'm so sorry."

"What do you have to be sorry about?" His voice is deep and thick with sleep.

"If I had come sooner, maybe I could have…" My voice trails off, another thought occurring to me. "If I hadn't gone off this morning to—"

"Do not be foolish, Ari." He snorts, his tone indifferent.

"Why did they come?" I ask, the only question I've been truly unable to ignore since they left.

"I do not know"—he sighs—"but I do not like it." After a long moment of contented silence, he adds, "They could have killed you…or worse."

I scoff, nearly choking on a laugh. "I'd like to see them try."

"They were knights of the king's army—"

"I don't care who they are or where they come from," I snarl.

He lets me finish applying the salve in silence, giving me a moment to collect myself. I'm almost convinced he's fallen back asleep when he finally speaks again, his words burrowing deep into my core. "I killed a human today."

"I know," I whisper. The knight's vacant brown eyes flash in my mind, but I shove the image away, focusing on Penn.

"I did not mean to."

"I know." I assure him, placing a gentle hand on the side of his neck.

He hesitates, letting the silence grow heavy. "The one with the dagger wounded me, so I sat on him."

The words he said are so at odds with the cavalier way he said them that it takes me a moment to fully understand. "You what?"

"I just wanted to squish him a little—incapacitate him until I could get the others under control."

"You sat on Tristan?" My hand flies to my mouth, and I can't help laughing. The sound is loud, and harsh, and a little wild as it echoes through the cave.

Penn's mouth twists into the smallest of smiles before dropping again. "The other one attacked me out of retaliation, and it just…happened so fast."

"It was an accident, Penn. Defending yourself doesn't make you a monster."

He makes a sound somewhere between a growl and a snort and then changes the subject. "Did you have another dream last night?"

"Aye." I huff, wiping my hands on the leg of my pants. "How did you get the blood in my cup?"

"I had Merlin dry some and add it to your tea stores the last time he came to collect," he says unapologetically. "I know the poppy's milk only helps you so much, but we both know why you need to ingest my blood, regardless of the side effects."

"You're not the one who has to deal with the side effects, though," I say, offering him a pointed look and a lopsided smirk.

"Yes, but today was a reminder of why you must take it, little dragon. Never forget what it does for you—what it offers you."

"I know." I sigh. "Honestly, I should have known before the cup ever touched my lips." I can almost smell the intimate familiarity of it, the herbal notes in the tea and the citrusy scent of the poppy's milk—a little sweet, a little poison—and underneath all that, a hint of dragon's blood. The same way I've been drinking it for well over a decade. "You know what your blood does to me." I glare at him half-heartedly, pursing my lips. "I do not care for those infuriating, nonsensical dreams, Penn."

"I know, little dragon," he says, "and yet, I will not apologise." He tilts his head to one side curiously. "What did you see?"

"Nothing, really. A blur of images, like always." I sigh again, frustrated.

"Tell me." He settles in, curled up like a cat, tucking his tail in close. I crawl over his good arm, nestling in-between it and his chest, his wing wrapping around me like a warm blanket.

"I saw Merlin. Well, his eyes."

"Are you sure it was him?" Penn tries valiantly to stifle a yawn.

"Aye." I nod, nestling farther into his warmth. "They might be a defining feature of the mages, but they were definitely his eyes." I'd know his specific shade of green-gold anywhere—distracting, mesmerising, and unmistakable; perfect at hiding the mischief beneath.

Penn says nothing, so I continue, exhaling deeply. "The sword."

"In Camelot?" he asks, intrigued. I don't often see that sword.

"Aye." I yawn, letting my eyes fall closed. "And Nhimue. At least, I think it was her… It's been a long time since last we met."

"Anything else?" he prods.

"The serpent medallion." My hand drifts to the outline of the warm metal beneath my shirt.

Again, he says nothing.

"Did you see his sword, Penn? The engraving on the pommel?" I ask, exhaustion from the events of the day fully setting in now.

"I did not need to see the sword to recognise the bloodline it belongs to."

"What do you think it all means?" I ask, not for the first time.

"I do not know," he says. "For now, we rest."

Snuggling in even more, I rest my cheek against his crimson scales, letting sleep take over.

FIVE

ARI

It takes the better part of a month to clean up the mess left behind by the knights. If I hadn't nearly drained the entirety of my magic, I could've done it in half the time.

Despite Penn insisting I take extra doses of dragon's blood to help speed things along, my magic still takes time to replenish. Even more so when I'm consistently using it to return the forest to its proper state, causing the process to be both slow and draining.

Penn, now fully healed, has left again to hunt. He was hesitant to leave me alone after what happened, but after several arguments and my constant nagging that he needed to regain his strength, he relented.

The only part of the destruction I haven't been able to erase yet is the place where the knight died. I can barely stand to return to the spot, much less stay there long enough to wield my magic.

I know I could leave that small part of the forest alone and let it regrow on its own, but that doesn't feel right. I didn't know the knight's name, and the others took his body when they left, but some tightening *thing* in my chest urges me to do more.

Sometimes, when I close my eyes at night, the image of him haunts me. His brown eyes, dulling with the last fading moments of life… I've seen many things, but I have never seen someone die. On those nights, the sound of his slow, ragged breaths keeps me awake long after the moon has reached its apex, and if I do manage to sleep, it's never for long.

Despite what happened, despite why he came, he deserves to be remembered in this forest. He deserves a marker for the place he took his final breaths. He deserves to leave some indication to the world that he'd stood and fought, even if he'd lost. Even if no one who loved him ever knows it exists.

It's what I would want, if the situation were reversed.

We deserve the reminder, too—Penn and I—of how close we are to Camelot, and just how quickly things can change when you least expect it. When you get too comfortable.

Wiping slick palms on my pants, I force myself to take a steadying breath and head for the last piece of ruined forest.

The blood is gone, washed away by the rain weeks ago and long since soaked into the earth. Idly, I wonder if a blood flower will sprout in its place. They're a rare sight, the circumstances of their creation a bit complicated, but it wouldn't surprise me to find one here this time next year.

Images of that day flash through my mind like strikes of lightning— little tiny instances from those handful of moments, frozen in perfect clarity for me to relive again and again.

The confusion—and doubt—etched into his face.

The sweat, dirt, and smears of blood coating every inch of him.

The silent apology and the shaky hand pointing toward our comrades.

But was it mine or his that he intended me to find? Was I meant to help or intervene?

Or perhaps he was simply trying to do one final, helpful deed in his dying moments. Either way, his death was a needless accident, and he deserves to be honoured in some small way.

Turning in a slow circle, it only takes a moment to find what I'm looking for: a medium-sized boulder, half covered in moss and lichen. I push, and pull, and use my hands to dig away the earth around it until it comes free of its home.

By the time I've managed to roll it to the spot where the knight died, I'm sweating, panting, and covered in dirt. I stare at it for a long time, unable to do anything else. After what seems like an eternity, I pull the dagger free of the sheath on my waistband and begin carving.

In the middle of the boulder, on the side facing me, I carve three runes—one for peace, one for protection, and one for courage—hoping they'll serve him well in the next life. Other than that, I leave the rest of the stone empty. I don't remember if they spoke of him in front of me or not, but if I ever learn his name, I'll come back and add that, too.

I decide not to fix the remnants of the damage immediately surrounding the boulder. The forest can heal and rebuild itself in whatever way it chooses.

"You're early." I groan, sitting up quickly and glaring at the mage before me. "And you startled me."

The air still shimmers where he'd manifested himself into the valley only a moment ago, the accompanying surge of static washing over my skin like a gentle wave. A deceptively charming grin lifts up one side of his mouth, his enchanting eyes gleaming in the afternoon sun. "Where's the dragon?" he asks casually.

"Hunting." I settle back onto my elbows, tilting my head toward the space beside me.

Gracefully, he lowers himself onto the grass, nodding absently. "I heard you ran into a bit of trouble a few weeks back."

"You did?" I ask, eyebrows raising in surprise.

"Ari," he chides, "I hear everything. You should know that by now."

I roll my eyes at Merlin, which only makes his grin grow wider. "And where have you been, then? It's been nearly a month since I've last seen you."

But all he says is, "Away."

After a few moments of silence, each of us nestled comfortably into the grassy hillside, surveying the vast green valley around us, I murmur, "I didn't know when I'd see you next." Eyeing him sidelong, I add, quieter, "But I wasn't expecting you today."

"Yes, well"—he sighs theatrically, grinning playfully at me over his shoulder—"here I am."

"I don't have what you're looking for," I say unsympathetically, lifting one shoulder in a half-shrug. "You know as well as I do that it doesn't keep well."

"How bold of you to presume what it is I came here for, dear Ari." His smile turns impish and the gleam in his eye makes me arch a brow in his direction.

"I don't think I have it in me to do a lesson today," I say absently, "but if you've come for—"

"Unfortunately, that is also not what brings me here today." Though his smile turns feral, immediately contradicting his words.

"Then why have you come?"

"Why do you not wish for a lesson today?" he counters.

I hadn't wanted to tell Merlin how completely I'd burned myself out after saving Penn, but there wasn't any point in lying to him either. "That trouble you mentioned… It took a lot out of me."

"I imagine it did," he says, pursing his lips, eyes losing focus. "It's actually why I've come today."

"It is?" I ask, confused.

"Aye, I've come to have a conversation."

"Aren't we already having one?" I ask, arching an eyebrow at him again.

His grin widens. "You're always such a pleasure, did you know that?"

He stands and begins to pace back and forth. The sun is warm and inviting today after several weeks of constant rain, and a cool refreshing breeze compliments the coming bloom of spring. The forest is finally coming alive after a long, cold winter.

Granted, the area directly surrounding my home always looks like spring at its best, but that's because I enchant it to be that way. A constant siphon of magic to take the edge off—and to practice control.

I was not born with the gift of magic, and so maintaining the balance within my body does not come as easily to me as it would a mage. Magic is a foreign entity to my body, and so, if I do not use it often, or use enough of it, it starts to negatively affect me.

On the other hand, if I use too much of it, it can leave me nearly catatonic—which is what happened after the last of the adrenaline and sheer determination wore off after saving Penn.

I slept for nearly three days, only rousing enough to drink small sips of water.

Dragon's blood—the very thing I assumed Merlin was here to collect today and his payment for teaching me magic—helps take the edge off the side effects magic creates within my body, and since Penn has always insisted I learn as many ways to protect and provide for myself as possible, he's been willing to provide me with a constant supply. His contribution to Merlin was considerably more hesitant.

Taking his blood when I don't need it, however, also has a somewhat negative affect on me, giving me nearly prophetic dreams—or night terrors, depending.

It took us years to learn what types of magic suited me best—which were easiest to call upon and summon, and which took the least amount of sacrifice from me to be wielded. Those who wield magic often excel in one or two areas, like healing or protection, spells or elixirs, though Merlin seems to have mastered them all.

Regardless of the type, all magic requires payment. For me, it's blood.

Merlin almost stopped our lessons when he finally realised what it would cost me to be able to use magic, but I was far too obsessed at that point and swore to him that, if he abandoned me, I would simply find another mage to teach me.

He'd liked that idea even less.

And so began our journey of trial and error into my education of magic wielding.

"Tell me," he says now, pausing in front of me, eyeing me curiously, "did you know any of the knights who showed up here a few weeks ago?"

Immediately, I feel defensive, which is not something I often feel around Merlin. I open my mouth to reply, but he continues on before I get a chance.

"Of course, you don't." He shrugs one shoulder, tilting his head to the side. "You only know me and the dragon."

I glare at him, confusion trailing his words as they sink in. Although they sound condescending, his tone does not.

"I believe it's created a bit of a mess… You see, the one who died—well, to put it bluntly, his friends aren't very happy."

"He's only dead because *they* attacked Penn." My face flushes with anger as the memory of that day returns in full force, the image of his vacant eyes vivid in my mind.

"Yes, but the knight is dead," Merlin says evenly, "and the dragon is not."

"You don't expect me to feel bad about what hap—"

"No." He laughs a loud, breathy sound. "No, I do not. But they want revenge, Ari. And considering that only one of the knights died, that means the ones who survived know the way back here." The way he points it out—as if I'd be unable to connect the dots on my own—sets my teeth on edge.

"What are you saying?" I grind out, my jaw clenching and unclenching around the words, a hiss barely contained behind my teeth.

"What I'm saying is that you need help." He shrugs once more, stuffing his hands in his pockets. It makes him look boyish and unimposing—two things I know to be untrue.

"And I suppose you're here to offer it to me?" I ask, annoyed at his overall indifference to the whole situation.

He nods, grinning impishly again, and I wonder if any of those smiles are ever truly genuine, or if they're only ever full of secrets. "For a price, as usual."

He is nothing if not consistent.

"What is it that you want?" I ask. It's not a question, not really. He knows exactly what he wants, and there will be no bargaining. There never is.

"You know me so well." His tone is airy and mocking.

"You didn't answer my question." The indifference in my voice is forced, my level of anger rising quickly.

"A favour."

"A what?"

"You know what a favour is, Ari," he says, pursing his lips. "Something I can"—he hesitates on the word—"*request* of you at any time, no questions asked."

"This seems wildly out of *my* favour." I groan, pushing off the ground to stand in front of him.

"Yes, well"—he seems to mull my words over, his eyes doing a slow perusal down my body and back up again—"the way I see it, either you can take the deal or you can wait and see what happens." One corner of his mouth twitches upward. "Fate and all that."

"Why must everything come at a price between us?" I ask quietly. "Why can things not just be done to simply help one another?"

It's not the first time I've found myself questioning his motives. I believe he cares about me—to some extent—but I also believe he is so stuck in his ways that he'll never change. So driven by his need for control that he cannot let go, even for a moment—not even with me.

"I think there's plenty we do to help one another, Ari." He smirks.

We stare at each other for a long moment. Ignoring his innuendo, I sigh. "What exactly are you offering me?"

"I can conceal the cave so that they cannot find it, no matter how hard they try," he says, arching an eyebrow in silent question. "I think that could be of great use to you."

I narrow my eyes at him, trying to find the trick in his offer. Magic always has a price, but is this worth an unnamed debt I will have no choice but to fulfil?

If they cannot find the cave, then we have somewhere safe to be.

If we have somewhere safe to be, then they cannot find us.

If they cannot find us, then they cannot attack Penn again.

Heaving a sigh and rolling my eyes in defeat, I offer him my scarred left hand. His eyes seem to glow in triumph as he takes my hand into his, pulling a small dagger from his belt.

"I, Merlin, will conceal the cave belonging to the young miss Ari and the dragon Penn at the expense of one currently unnamed favour." He slices the blade across his palm in one fluid motion before doing the same to mine. "Do you agree?"

I wince, clenching my jaw and hissing at the pain. "I do."

His hand wraps around my own, our blood mingling with the magical deal promised between us. "I'll even throw in a little extra something for you on the side." His lips twitch upward again, his fingers tightly squeezing mine. "If any of the knights of Camelot happen to find themselves in your woods, this scar will alert you to their presence. Do you accept?"

"Aye," I say unevenly. "I do."

"As I said before…" He releases my hand and places the dagger back in his belt, a depraved sort of smile lifting up the corners of his mouth now. "Always a pleasure, Ari." But there's an odd sort of disingenuousness to his tone that makes the hair at the base of my neck stand on end.

SIX

LANCELOT

"I say we kill the dragon," Bors de Ganis, captain of the king's army, boasts to the entirety of the tavern, ale sloshing over the side of his mug as he gestures widely to the room. "A life for a life."

A responding chorus of "Aye" fills the room, as it always does.

It's been over a month since we returned from that cave in the woods. Over a month since we laid Garreth to rest, but still the rage and grief weighs heavily on the knights of Camelot.

Perci has barely spoken to me since our return. Seeking out the dragon was Garreth's idea, led by the notion of more than a centuries worth of gold hidden deep within that cave. It might have been Garreth's idea, and it certainly didn't take much to convince me to join him, but Perci and Tristan only came along because I pushed for it.

The journey back was long and silent, weighed heavy with anger and mourning. Even the horses were irritable and on edge by the time we returned to the castle.

"This lot can't take on a dragon," Kay groans, eyeing Bors disapprovingly. "They can barely get through their bloody training without complaining."

"Would you not have Garreth avenged, then?" Bors seethes, glaring at Kay. When he gets no reply, Bors turns to the rest of our table, zeroing in on our silence and overall lack of support. "And what about the rest of you? Would you not have Garreth's life repaid with that of the dragon who took it?"

"Come off it, Captain," Tristan warns, shifting in his seat. He's usually the one to talk down the crowd once they've decided on revenge, having always been a voice of reason among the brashest and foolhardiest of knights.

"You were there"—Bors sneers—"and you let him die—"

"Aye, I was there!" Tristan raises his voice. Jumping to his feet, his chair clatters to the floor behind him. "And you were not. Do not speak to me of matters you know nothing about."

Despite why we were there, Garreth died trying to save Tristan—intervening when the dragon had him pinned beneath his massive body—and that guilt weighs heavily on him. His hazel eyes are nearly black in the low light of the oil lamps, and his chest heaves with the effort of restraining himself.

A hush falls over the tavern, the red-rimmed eyes of those who've had too much to drink shifting back and forth between Bors and Tristan as he slowly picks up his chair and sits back down. Nearly every night ends up like this. The knights gather in the tavern to remember Garreth, to mourn him, and someone always suggests revenge. Killing the dragon is the only answer.

But none of them were there. None of them know how hard it was for us to even subdue and capture him—how much dragon's bane Tristan had soaked the ropes in beforehand…and how much it cost us to acquire it in the first place.

None of them know how easily that girl undid what was so hard for us to achieve.

Bors all but growls, turning his attention back to those at his table, chugging the rest of his drink.

"I don't think I've ever heard you lose your temper like that," Perci says, eyeing Tristan sidelong. "Didn't know you had it in you." A slow, half-smile spreads across Perci's face as he lifts his mug to Tristan, effectively diminishing the tension.

We cheers, finishing the remnants of our ale in silence.

"I won't go back," Perci says finally, any trace of amusement gone from his face. "I can't."

Garreth's death was harder on him than the rest of us. If I had any real siblings—any true-born brothers aside from the ones I've gained through knighthood—I don't imagine anything would ease the pain of losing them, least of all returning to the place where they died so brutally.

"Aye." Tristan nods solemnly. "I'd rather set off on a witch hunt to find the Holy Grail than return there."

"Aye." I snort. But even as I agree with them, I know it's not true. The smile fades from my lips as the truth settles in: I would return in a heartbeat. I ache to return there. In truth, I've thought of little else since we left.

I have so many questions.

So many questions that will never have answers.

She must be human—there's no other explanation. As far as I'm aware, there has never been a mage born without dark hair and green-gold eyes. She is far too tall to be one of the little folk, and she does not bare the markings of nature like the three races of nymphs do. And although I've never seen one, something tells me she isn't one of the forest folk like I'd initially thought, either.

So, what is a human doing protecting a dragon, and how did they even come to be together? Furthermore, how does a human know how to use magic, let alone something as nefarious and archaic as blood magic?

"Lance?" Tristan's voice breaks my reverie. The raised eyebrows and expectant expression on his face tell me I've missed something in my daze.

"What?" I ask, looking between him, Perci, and Kay.

"Do you think it's real?" Kay asks slowly. "The Holy Grail?"

"You're still going on about that?" I exhale a laugh. "Yeah, I suppose so.

I have no reason to believe otherwise."

"Where d'you reckon it is?" he asks, signalling the barkeep for another round.

"They say no one's ever seen it before, but that would defeat the purpose of all the secrecy then, wouldn't it?"

"You're distracted," Tristan grumbles. "You're distracted and you're being sloppy." Irritation rolls off him in waves. "Pay attention."

"Lay off it, Tris." I sigh.

He's right—we both know he is—and yet, it's the last thing I want to hear right now.

"Should've had one less drink last night, eh, Lance?" Perci croons from my left, giving me the urge to shove my fist down his throat.

The whine of metal on metal rings through my bones, pulsing behind my eyes. The training field is full of paired-up swordsmen, each one more hungover than the last.

Things got a little too heated for comfort in the tavern last night, no thanks to Bors. He's going to be a real problem if he doesn't drop this revenge endeavour for Garreth soon.

In all truth, it doesn't even make sense how hard he's pushing for this. Bors is the captain of the king's army; Garreth was a foot soldier. I get wanting retribution, I do, but there has to be more to it for him than revenge for a fallen soldier. He doesn't see us as equals—he never has and never will. So, if it's not truly about vengeance, then it must simply be that he wants the bragging rights of taking down a dragon.

The only reason we were even able to get the dragon tied up in the first place was because the poisoned ropes weakened him enough for us to get the upper-hand. Whether or not we managed to have the element of surprise, after we failed so spectacularly, I doubt either one of them will likely get caught unawares again. The dragon or the girl.

The grip on my sword loosens, faltering at the thought of going back there. At the possibility of seeing her again.

Infatuation—that's what Tristan's been calling it. *"You're too infatuated for your own good,"* he keeps saying. *"Nothing good will come of this, Lance. Leave it alone."*

Using my distraction to his advantage, he moves without warning or apology. I'm unable to block the attack in time, and the wide arc of his blade connects with my forearm, slicing through the leather bracer and into the skin beneath impressively.

At first, there is nothing. Then the pain comes, followed closely by warm, sticky blood, welling up and sliding down my arm beneath the leather and dripping onto the earth below.

"Shit," he breathes, sheathing his sword. I drop my own, opening and closing my hand in an attempt to ease the stinging.

Tristan lets out a low whistle as he comes to stand before me, taking my arm and inspecting the wound. "To be fair, you should've seen it coming," he says quietly, then, "We ought to go see a healer."

I nod, pausing to grab my sword, the serpent pommel like a beacon in the dirt. At once, I'm flooded with images, flashing so quickly they're almost impossible to decipher. Stories and memories, dreams and delusions. What once was and might have been. What should have been and won't ever be.

This sword is both a blessing and a curse. It's the only thing I have left of my father, and I wield it out of duty—out of loyalty to my family.

Even if my father was branded a traitor and murdered for treason.

As quickly as they come, the images pass, and I sheath the sword with a sigh, still flexing and clenching my hand as the blood flows from the wound.

Tristan tears a strip of fabric from his tunic, wrapping it around my forearm. "Sorry." He shrugs, smiling sheepishly. "I did warn you, though."

"It's fine." I nod tightly, returning the smile half-heartedly.

The training field is outside the city walls, which makes the closest healer one of the locals instead of Morgana or someone else from the castle.

I follow Tristan through the cobblestone streets, and when I finally realise where he's headed, a petulant moan escapes my lips. "You're not seriously taking me to see Vera, are you?"

"She's the closest healer," he says matter-of-factly over his shoulder, "and easily the best one in the kingdom."

"I don't know what it is, but there's something unsettling about her." I groan, unfazed by how childish I sound.

"I'll never understand why you're so bothered by her." He sighs. "You grew up—"

"I know very well where I grew up, Tristan." It comes out harsher than I intended, but it doesn't seem to bother him either way.

"She'll sew up your arm and we'll be on our way in no time. Quit moaning."

We make our way through Camelot quickly, winding through several narrow alleys to save time.

While the castle sits at the heart of Camelot, the apothecary lies in the outside ring of the surrounding city, nestled somewhere between the wealthy and the struggling. The very best of everything, according to Arthur, is closest to the castle—the best butcher, the best mason, the best iron workers. Aside from the staff employed within his walls, the wealthiest and best of their trades form a tight circle surrounding the castle.

But charging the most doesn't make you the best. Arthur doesn't spend enough time walking the streets of his own kingdom to be able to confidently declare who is superior at anything.

Thankfully, the most frivolous of the lords and ladies who kept court with Uther have dissipated over the years, due in no small part to Arthur's utter lack of tolerance of them. If they do not serve a real purpose to the crown prince, they do not end up staying long at court. Those who merely wish to keep their title and do as they are told stick to their estates.

And those who wish to live their lives freely and keep to themselves hide in plain sight.

It doesn't take long at all to reach Vera's, but the blood has soaked through the makeshift bandage Tristan tied around my arm by the time we arrive.

As the apothecary comes into view, a lump begins to form in my throat. I've been inside a handful of times, each time just as uncomfortable as the one before.

In spite of my upbringing, I do not trust mages.

Because of my upbringing, I do not trust mages.

The gnarled wooden door inches open just as Tristan's hand rises to knock, and the familiar smell of burning sage wafts out to greet us. Glancing over his shoulder, he merely raises his brows at me before entering. Heaving a sigh and refraining from rolling my eyes, I follow after him.

If the prince or his uncle ever caught Vera using magic so freely, they'd burn her in the town square simply for the fun of it.

Tristan wouldn't be so indifferent about it, then.

Magic has been forbidden in Camelot since the day the last Uther was crowned king. Arthur seems more tolerant of the mages than his father was, considering one lives in his castle and shares his mother's blood—but even Morgana doesn't get to use her magic without limitation.

Again, my mind wanders to the girl with the dragon—of the ancient language she spoke and the spell she used to weave his wing back together.

All magic is forbidden—blood magic above all else. Having caused the death of Queen Igraine, even the mention of it has seen people thrown in the dungeons—by both Arthur and his father.

And yet, she'd used it so freely…summoned it so easily…

Idly, I wonder, not for the first time since meeting her, who trained her? It's doubtful that a dragon could teach her to maintain such control, and I don't even think they have the same kind of magic.

No…her magic is that of the mages. Raw, chaotic, and bordering on the very edges of balance.

Tristan clears his throat, staring at me expectantly, and I realise that I've been standing on the threshold, entirely lost to my thoughts.

The front room of the apothecary is cozy, but there's enough room for us to occupy it comfortably without being in each other's faces. An old work table lines one wall, an empty mortar and pestle in the centre. The opposite wall has floor-to-ceiling shelves, decorated with more plants than I would ever be able to identify. The front wall of the store is almost entirely made of windows, save for the gnarled wooden door, and opposite that sits a curtain obscuring anything else from view.

Vera steps into the front room, tugging the curtain closed behind her and drying her hands on her apron. "Knights," she says by way of greeting. She smiles easily at Tristan before her piercing gaze turns to me.

Her eyes unnerve me, always assessing and absorbing, seeming to see things that others don't. The unique colour accentuates her nearly black hair and sun-bronzed skin. Whichever far away land she came from must have been warm.

Something unwelcome slithers down my spine the longer she maintains eye contact, causing the hairs to prickle at the back of my neck. Some instinctual thing inside me sets off warning bells in my head like war horns, only vexing me further.

Perhaps she merely delights in my discomfort.

I was raised around some of the gentler types of magic, but it does not make me trust her any easier. I'm not afraid of magic, I'm not uncomfortable around it, but my dislike and distrust of mages is so deeply rooted into my history—into my very core—that it's hard to look past. Even for a friend of a friend.

Which makes Vera's almost romantic accent disconcerting as the words roll off her tongue when she asks, "What may I do for you today?" She finally looks away to eye the pair of us from head to toe.

I hold out my arm—willing it not to tremble—and the blood-soaked bandage in answer.

"A few stitches, if it's no trouble," Tristan says, smiling at her playfully.

"No trouble at all." Tilting her head toward the curtain, she tugs it open and gestures for us to follow her through it.

The back room of the apothecary is much larger than the front one, nearly triple the size. A small window sits beside a small door that looks as if it leads into a garden beyond, with a wash basin beneath the window and a small cabinet housing pots and plates just beside it. A tight staircase disappears into the shadows to the right.

The rest of the walls are covered in shelves, crammed with all manner of plants and herbs and bundles of flower—both living and dried. Jars and vials of powders and liquids, baskets of cloth, and candles—the latter on every surface, ledge, windowsill, and even the floor.

In the centre of the room is a large, circular table. It, too, like everything else in the shop, is made of old, knotted wood. A fat, fluffy ginger cat is sleeping soundly on top of it.

The smell of extinguished candles, dried herbs, and something…spicy, lingers in the air.

"Have a seat." Vera nods to the stools tucked under the table, then to the cat. "Though, I would advise you not to disturb Ector."

I do as she asks, laying my arm on the table in front of me and unbuckling the bracer. Tristan takes up post by the back door, arms folded loosely across his chest.

Hovering over me and peeling away the ruined leather and scrap of cloth, Vera studies the wound intently. "The cut is deep but clean. It will heal nicely." She stares at me pointedly for a moment, then adds, "Do not undo my hard work by ripping open the stitches."

I nod, swallowing dryly.

She flits around the room, collecting various things and organising them on the table, humming distractedly under her breath.

She looks only a few years older than myself and has never been caught doing anything remotely unsavoury. As far as she tells it, she fled a dying land and a tyrant ruler, seeking a fresh start and the luxury of keeping to herself.

I really don't have a reason not to trust her, but I can't seem to allow myself to lower my guard around her, either. It's the eyes. The unnatural and unsettling colour combination is both a lure and a warning all at once.

Vera's presence alone doesn't bother me, and by all rights, she's the least troublesome mage around. But there's something about their type of magic—perhaps it's lack of limitations compared to other magic-wielding species—that makes it hard for me to trust them outright. Makes it hard to disassociate her from the rest of them, knowing what they can do. What they've done.

What *he* has done.

Perhaps it's only because the one mage I wish to locate is the one who keeps alluding me. The one I need to break the curse and return the freedom he so callously stole...

Finally, Vera sits down next to me and pulls my hand toward her, gingerly probing the gash.

Her eyes lift to meet mine, the barest hint of an apologetic smile on her lips. "This is going to hurt a bit."

SEVEN

ARI

"Again," Penn bellows, his voice ringing out like thunder across the field. The sun is finally warming the earth and drying the forest after nearly a week of gloom and rain.

Rolling my eyes and neck simultaneously, I swing the sword, rotating the hilt in my hand to adopt an offensive stance.

"The line of kings in Kent began with Hengest and has thus been unbroken in succession for five generations."

As I recite Britain's royal lineages, I work my way through the dance of sword play—slashing and striking, blocking and deflecting—manoeuvres memorised long ago.

It's ineffective to train by myself like this and, often, it feels like I'm simply twirling a sword around a field. I much prefer when Merlin agrees to spar with me, either by fist or by sword.

I open my mouth to continue, but Penn quickly interrupts with, "Left hand, in Latin." I switch the sword to the opposite hand, sliding my feet to match my new position, and continue in Latin.

"The line of kings in Wessex started with Cerdic, then his son Cynric, the Hound King, followed by Ceawlin. Ceol defeated his uncle in battle and replaced him, denying the throne to the rightful heir. Though, if he should die before his son comes of age, Ceawlin's son Ceolwulf will take over."

"Dragon," Penn says in his own native tongue, exhaling a thick plume of black smoke through his nostrils.

"Northumbria is the newest kingdom," I say, switching languages again. "Brutally claimed on the far side of the northern mountains and held onto through a considerable amount of bloodshed. Aethelfrith is the first king and, so far, still managing to hold onto his crown. Although, not without difficulty."

Bracing my hands on my knees, I pause to catch my breath before continuing.

"His vicious commander has helped lead him to several victories defending their borders from the Vikings they ousted from the land he now claims as his own. But there is great unrest in his kingdom, and many seek to usurp him. Without any children of his own, he has sent his only niece to seek a marriage alliance with a southern kingdom to reinforce both his allies and his claim as king."

Sheathing my sword and dropping it to the ground, I beginning a series of stretches to alleviate the tight muscles in my back and neck.

"You're forgetting one," he says—both a warning and a challenge.

"Camelot"—I sigh, grunting and wincing around the strain in my muscles—"started with Uther and has been ruled by eight Uthers since. Arthur will be the tenth king of Camelot when he comes of age later this summer."

"Good," Penn says, shaking out the stiffness in his own limbs from sitting for too long. Dropping one shoulder low to the ground, he waits until I am situated upon his back before straightening up again.

"We are both aware that I know all this…" I mutter, scowling at the back of his large, crimson head.

"And yet, I ask you to recite it, anyway." He exhales another thick puff of smoke, pushing off the ground. "Why?"

"Because you like to bore me with tedious lessons in history, languages, and etiquette." I grip the edges of his scales tightly as his wings flap for a moment, gaining momentum before pushing down forcefully and launching us into the sky.

The moment we're airborne, my stomach lurches in the most delicious way. I crave this feeling when I go too long without it. The only thing I have ever wanted—and neither been brave nor stupid enough to spell myself a pair of—is wings.

"I make you recite it so that you will not forget it," he growls, wings now fully extended as we glide through the clouds. "It is good to know the history of the lands you live in."

"Aye." I nestle into his back. "I suppose it is."

After the yellow grass of the trampled field and the green trees of the forests give way to the deep blue of the ocean, I sit upright, arms extended at my sides as if I, too, have wings. My hair trails behind me in a long braid, and tears sting my eyes as we race through the sky.

"Hold on, little dragon." Penn laughs, a deep booming sound.

"I have no doubts that you would catch me if I fell," I shout above the wind, unable to hide the smile in my voice.

"I will always catch you, little dragon."

He gives no warning before dipping downward, diving toward the glittering surface of the water. A scream of pure delight rips from my throat as I cling to his scales for purchase, my hair whipping wildly in the wind behind me.

When he straightens again, a hair's breadth from the surface, a contented bliss fills my chest.

"I wish you wouldn't leave again so soon," I call above the howling wind.

"Do not fret. I'll be back as soon as I can." He climbs upward again, soaring towards the clouds.

"Perhaps I could come with you this time."

"If I was going for any reason other than to hunt, you know I would bring you. But we both know you do not like to witness what that looks like."

"I know." I nestle into him again, breathing in the scent of brimstone, smoke, and home.

The iridescent crimson scales of his neck are warm on my cheek and beneath my hands. After a while, the comfort and familiarity of flying with him lulls me to sleep.

In the largest cavern within the cave, Penn is curled up like a cat on a nest of dragonstones. They glow a soft blue and emanate an inviting warmth, like a dragon-sized stone from the bottom of a hearth. It's *just* too warm to the touch for my inept human skin, so, instead, I perch on a ledge half a dozen feet off the ground and enjoy the radiating warmth from a distance.

He's been sleeping on and off since we returned from this morning's lesson, and I alternate between reading aloud and in my head depending on his current conscious state.

He's been sleeping a lot lately, even for a dragon. I think the dragon's bane took far more out of him than he let on, but he refuses to let me use any more magic to try to help him. When he's here, he barely lets me wander more than a stone's throw from the cave, I suspect out of fear of being blindsided again, so I've had to resort to sneaking away while he's unconscious.

Since the attack, he's only gone hunting nearby, wary of traveling too far. But our forest does not hold much that can sustain him long term, and now, he's finally grown too irritable on the meagre hunts to postpone going properly for any longer.

He leaves tomorrow for a real hunt, and already he's lectured me twice today on safety precautions while he's away. Stubborn dragon. I am quite capable of—

My left hand erupts in pain, catching me entirely off guard. I fumble for the book as it falls from my hand, a thick volume of a dead language, now discarded and forgotten on the ground below.

A hiss slides through my teeth as a burning sensation spreads through my palm.

"Ari?" Penn's voice is both near and far, and full of worry. "What is it?"

Gripping my left hand in my right, I try to massage the skin around the most recent scar that adorns my palm in hopes of ebbing away the pain.

"It's nothing," I say through gritted teeth, hopping off the ledge and bracing myself against the stone wall of the cavern.

"It does not seem like nothing, little dragon," he says, concern laced through his words. He shifts to look at me better, the dragonstones trembling with his movements.

It occurs to me as the pain in my hand continues to intensify, that I probably should have told him of this latest deal with Merlin. It also occurs to me that, if he felt I was in danger, he would only postpone his departure longer—something neither of our sanities could truly handle. He needs to eat properly—to hunt something that can sustain him for longer—and I need the freedom to wander the forest again, uninhibited.

"It's only a minor inconvenience." I struggle to keep my voice steady, even more so to meet his gaze. Guilt chases the lie as it leaves my lips, leaving a sour taste in my mouth.

He eyes me warily. Big, bright yellow orbs like golden sunshine that seem to stare right through me.

"It's okay," I assure him. "I'm fine."

Staggering to my feet, I turn to leave, making my way from the depths of our home, cautiously aware of the doubtful eyes watching me go.

As I make my way through the forest, clenching my hand against the burning sensation, I cannot help but wonder which knight I will find.

The one who was quick to depart and quicker still to thwart my efforts at saving Penn? The one who offered me his blade, with a curious gaze that perhaps sees much more than he lets on? Or, the one who is far too audacious for his own good and seems to have nothing in the way of self-preservation skills?

Or, most worrisome of all, perhaps they've all returned together, seeking retribution for their fallen brother.

EIGHT

LANCELOT

There's no warning before the cold sting of metal touches my collarbone, at last alerting me to her presence.

I've been wandering around the forest for the better part of the day, foolishly hoping to find my way back to that cave.

"What are you doing here?" she hisses in my ear.

A drop of fear rolls down my spine, unnerving me despite its anticipation. Her blade presses into my throat when I swallow.

"Speak," she growls.

"I have questions," I say, embarrassed at the lack of nerve in my tone. I had gone over what I wanted to say several times on the ride here, but none of those conversations had started like this.

"I told you not to come back here." She remains behind me, still unseen. My eyes dart around the trees in front of us, looking for any indication that she might not be alone, but I neither heard the dragon's approach nor see him now, and the smell of smoke and fire remains thankfully absent.

"I hoped that might be more of a suggestion than an actual command." I hazard a laugh.

"I assure you, it was not." The blade disappears from my neck, and I find myself mildly surprised that I seem to be standing here relatively unscathed.

I don't move. I don't speak. I barely even breathe.

Whatever mercy she's decided to grant me, whatever trust she's conceded to me—no matter how small—I don't dare risk it.

"You shouldn't have come here," she says, more quietly and less angrily than before.

"I came alone," I offer, keeping my voice steady and even. "It's just me."

"I'm well aware of how brave you think you are, but I didn't realise you were exceedingly stupid, too." Her words bite, but there's no real harshness to them.

"Bravery aside, I don't believe you're going to hurt me," I say, slowly turning to face her. "At the very least, you aren't going to kill me."

"What makes you so sure?" She cocks her head to the side and it makes her look predatory, yet somehow, she looks just as peculiar and out of place as before—just as beautifully bizarre as the last time she stood before me.

She takes a handful of steps back now that I'm facing her, keeping a healthy distance between us.

Her pale, ivory hair is braided and tossed over one shoulder, falling nearly to her waist. Her muted green eyes are cool and reserved; there's nothing warm or inviting about them. A thick silver chain disappears into the collar of her plain tunic, a bow and quiver are slung over one shoulder, and a long, well-cared-for dagger is clenched in one fist.

"Because if you were going to kill me"—I shrug, making a point of looking at each of her weapons before meeting her intense gaze again—"you would have done so without ever revealing yourself to me."

"That's fair." She tucks the dagger into the belt around her hips. "Though, it doesn't mean you should have returned."

"I have questions," I say again, as if that justifies my presence here today—as if it justifies pulling double guard duty for two weeks to make sure I had a clear window of time to escape the kingdom while Tristan and Perci were busy and could neither stop me nor follow me here.

"Why do you deem yourself worthy of answers?"

"Why do you deem yourself worthy of remaining a mystery?" I counter before I can stop myself.

Her brows slowly drift upward, a quizzical sort of smirk lifting one side of her mouth. She stares at me for a long moment, assessing me, weighing the options.

I cock an eyebrow and offer a genuine smile, hoping she deigns to humour me and not just leave me standing here alone in the forest.

"Fine, but your questions are not without conditions," she says, the hesitant smile disappearing as she shakes her head.

"Of course. Name them."

"You may ask whatever you like, but I make no promise to answer."

"Okay," I say, nodding hesitantly.

"The only reason I'm indulging you is because I have some questions of my own."

"Okay. Is that all?"

She nods, then pauses in thought. "If I say we need to leave, it would be best to assume it's a life-or-death situation. Lingering does not bode well in this forest."

"What lurks in this forest that you're so afraid of?" I ask, brows furrowing. "You have a dragon and you can use magic…"

"Currently, a pair of nomadic dryads," she answers, glancing around the trees. "Evil, vengeful creatures that I'd rather not cross paths with if not entirely necessary."

"Is that what spooked the horses that day in the forest?"

"Yes."

"Do they not normally live here?"

"No." She shakes her head once. "They draw their power from oak trees—something this part of the forest is intentionally devoid of."

I gesture to the fallen tree beside us, and she perches atop it gracefully but remains alert. When I move to sit down next to her, she jumps to her feet and puts a considerable amount of distance between us—more than she had before.

Loosing a sigh and trying not to be offended, I move across the small clearing to lean against the base of a large tree instead.

A silence not entirely uncomfortable falls over us as I study the forest around us, and, eventually, she moves back to the fallen tree, sitting down hesitantly.

Busying myself with taking in our surroundings, I realise I have to trust that she has no reason to lie about something ominous dwelling here. Nothing strikes me as particularly menacing, but to me, the forest just looks very old and very green. Besides, the horses were not spooked by her, and we all definitely felt *something* that day in the woods. Hopefully, wherever the dryads are, they stay well enough away from us today.

"Is that from using magic?" I ask, nodding to the myriad scars on her hand, unsure why I landed on that as my first real question.

For a moment, she only stares at me without breaking her silence.

Glancing at her sidelong, I add, "I noticed them when you sat down. Some of them look fresh, and you've been opening and closing your hand as if it's bothering you. I figured it was as good a place to start as any."

She stares at me, eyes darting back and forth between my own. Her hesitance is answer enough, so when she says, "Cuts always itch while they heal," I just nod.

Rolling up the sleeve of my tunic, I hold my arm out toward her. "Aye, they do."

"Trip with a sword in your hand?" she asks with just a hint of mirth, eyeing the long slash on my forearm.

Unable to stop the smile that spreads across my face, I nod. "Something like that." The fine stitching Vera had done would leave far less of a scar than if I'd done it myself.

"What do you hope to gain by coming here with your questions?" she asks, any trace of humour now gone from her voice.

"Knowledge," I say quickly. "The truth."

"About what?" There's an edge to her tone now, sharp like the tip of a dagger.

"About the girl living in the middle of nowhere with a dragon for a pet," I say honestly, shrugging. "Every single part of that sentence is bizarre and intriguing."

"He's not my pet," she says angrily.

"Your captor, then?" I'm only half-joking.

"He raised me," she says dismissively.

"You might see that as an answer, but I'm afraid it only gives me more questions."

"Whether or not it invokes more questions is not my concern. It's the truth."

"Do you have a name?" I ask, holding her pale green gaze.

"I do," she replies, a hint of amusement creeping back into her voice.

"Are you going to tell me what it is?"

"You didn't ask what it was, only if I had one." The mischief in her tone has its intended effect. Everything she says to me is an enigma. Every sentence, every word leaves me wanting to know more.

"May I know your name?" I ask, grinning widely.

"You may not." She snorts. Looking away, she seems to momentarily lose herself in the trees. "Not today, at least."

"Do you intend to see me again, then?" I press, surprised.

Instead of answering me, she shifts on the fallen tree, tucking one leg beneath her and changes the subject.

"Which king do you serve?" Her tone is soft, but her movements are quick as she pulls the dagger from her belt and snaps off a nearby branch roughly the size of her forearm. Using the blade to peel away the dead bark, she gives the impression that she's indifferent to my answer—or perhaps my presence—though the lines of tension in her body directly contradict that.

The way she asks seems more like she's seeking verification and less like it's an actual question.

"King Uther of Camelot," I say tightly, though without hesitation. To my knowledge, this part of the forest is still within Camelot's borders, so I do not fear declaring my allegiance in front of her.

"But he is not king anymore," she muses, still gazing at the trees.

"Aye. May he rest in peace."

She asks, "What of his heir?" but something about the question feels off, although I can't quite place why.

"Prince Arthur? What of him?"

"What do you make of him?"

"He's still just a boy, regardless of his bravado."

"He could have you hanged for that."

"Do you intend to tell him?" I ask, already knowing the answer.

Again, she chooses silence over answering me.

"Why did you come here," she asks, "before?"

I flinch, though I don't think she notices as she still isn't looking at me. I've been dreading this question the most.

"Truthfully, it started out as a bit of fun—a wild idea, born by whispers of an almighty dragon and an incomparable treasure."

"You came here for gold?" Her eyes grow wide, then narrow.

"Not all of us wish to be indebted to the crown," I murmur—a half truth.

"And you assumed killing a dragon granted you the right to his riches?" she snaps, anger flaring, her words rumbling out one after another. "What if he had none? Not all dragons do, you know. What if you came all this way and killed him for nothing?" she demands, jumping to her feet. Her sudden fury catches me off guard, her rebuke tightening my chest and filling it with shame.

"I—" I pull in a deep breath, shaking my head. "I don't know."

"You are far less intelligent than you think you are," she spits, slowly returning to the log.

Warmth blooms on my cheeks. Her admonishment turns my stomach, and embarrassment floods my veins.

When she speaks again, the anger has left her voice, though a hardness remains. "Going after a dragon's treasure is just about the dumbest thing you could do."

I nod, searching for a way to change the subject again.

Stretching my legs out in front of me, I ask, "How many languages do you speak?"

She laughs a singular, humourless laugh. "Most of them."

"I don't even know what that means." An exasperated sigh forces its way through my lips as I run my hand through my hair, scratching absently at the back of my head.

I look up at her, surprised to find her staring back at me. She hesitates for a moment, an array of uncertainty dancing across her features. "Do you truly wish to know?" she asks, peering down at me.

"If you wish to tell me," I say honestly, leaning my head back against the tree.

"English, Latin, Greek, and Gaelic…conversational Norse…" She ticks them off on her fingers, one at a time, as she speaks. "Nyad, Dryad, a bit of broken Mountain Troll…" She scrunches up half her face, one eye squinting and the other nearly rolling to the back of her head. "A handful of dead languages, enough Little Folk to get by, and enough Gnome to know that I have no desire to associate with gnomes."

"You—" I bolt upright, turning to stare at her, mouth agape, sure that I've misheard her. "What?"

"Horrid little creatures." She shivers, shaking her head. "The last time I tried to catch one, it left me paralysed for nearly three days."

"How could you possibly know so many languages?" I fail to hide the incredulity from my voice.

"I've had a lot of time, many books to read, and incredibly patient teachers." Her voice is nonchalant as she folds her legs beneath her once more. It seems at odds with her demeanour. Unsure, almost.

"You were paralysed by a gnome?"

"He bit me," she says, holding a finger out in my direction as if that settles the matter entirely.

I lean back against the trunk again and we sit in silence for a while, but I find myself periodically checking to see if she's still there. I have no doubts that she could vanish without so much as a whisper if she wished to.

Eventually, I pluck up enough courage to ask another question. "Have you been alone here all this time?"

"I have never been alone." Her answer is both quick and firm.

"I mean besides the dragon," I amend gently, shifting to face her better.

She seems to mull over her answer for a moment. "We had chickens for a time." She smiles absently. "They fancied Penn—followed him around from dawn until dusk. It drove him mad."

"Where are your parents?" I ask, knowing I shouldn't but unable to stop myself all the same. Who would leave their child to be raised by a dragon? Was she abandoned? Stolen? Cursed? The moment the words leave my mouth, I regret asking the question. "Do you have any family at all?"

An angry flush spreads up her neck and cheeks. "My parents are exactly where they're meant to be. I've never had need nor want of any other family than the one I've got. *Penn is my family.*" She says it with such conviction that I don't doubt she feels any differently.

"I'm sorry," I say, hoping it sounds as sincere as it's meant to. "What are the dead languages?" I ask after a moment, in hopes of changing the subject back to one she'll actually talk about. "And why are they dead?"

She avoids my gaze for a while, her jaw working furiously. Finally, after it's been so long that I don't believe she intends to answer any more of my questions, she says, "I only know three of them, but I'm sure there are more."

I raise an eyebrow but otherwise remain silent.

"Dragon, Elvish, and that of the Forest Folk." Jaw still clenching, she adds, "They're called dead languages because either no one is left to speak them—like the Elves—or there are not enough of a species left for it to be a commonly known language—like Dragon and the Forest Folk."

"Can I tell you something silly?" I ask, not waiting for an answer before continuing, not giving her a chance to end the conversation just yet. "When I first saw you that day in the woods, I thought you might be one of them—the forest folk." I chuckle now at the memory.

"Don't be absurd," she scoffs. "You would never find one of the forest folk in the company of a dragon."

I laugh despite myself. I have never met someone so complex and simple at the same time. I don't even think she understands how incredibly rare and uncommon it is for someone to know three or four languages, let alone more than a dozen.

"Did Penn teach you all those languages?" I ask, pleased to be able to put a name to at least one of them. It's not implausible; dragons are ancient and know more about anything than any human could ever hope to, I'm sure.

"No," she says slowly. My eyes flick to her pale green ones, which are distant and unfocused. "I had a tutor for a while, and I've known Merlin for many, many years. The three of them taught me just about everything I know."

I don't know which part I find more surprising—and fascinating. The fact that someone else has known she was here all this time and willingly came here to tutor her within such close proximity to a dragon, or that she knows Merlin.

Before I can focus on that, I ask, "Just about?"

A slow, sly grin lifts up both sides of her mouth as she says, "Some things can only be learned through exposure."

Unsure what to make of that, I settle on what initially snagged my interest, letting the full weight of its implications settle over me. "You know Merlin?"

"Aye." She nods. "I do."

"Not many people can say they have that honour."

"Not many would call it an honour." She snorts. "Any who would surely haven't spent much time in his company."

Another moment of silence falls over us. Not wanting to press it further for now, I decide to change the subject again.

"What happened to your tutor?" I ask finally.

"I don't know," she says quietly. "He stopped coming to see me shortly after my tenth birthday."

"He wasn't afraid of Penn?"

"He's the one who brought me to Penn." She meets my gaze steadily.

"Wait, what?" I ask, sitting upright again.

Getting to her feet gracefully, she simply shakes her head.

Following suit, I rise to my feet as well. Her eyes take me in from head to toe before her jaw tightens once more. "I meant what I said before." She continues to stare at me evenly. "It's not wise for you to return here, and while I cannot stop you, I certainly do not encourage it."

Without another word, she turns and walks away, slipping into the sanctuary of the forest almost immediately.

Willow, the brown mare gifted to me by my father shortly before he was wrongfully murdered for treason, is grazing blissfully when I return. She's exactly where I left her, as I knew she would be. She whinnies as I approach, then again when I stroke her velvety face.

The majority of the ride home is spent contemplating everything the strange girl said—and everything she didn't.

Idly, and not for the first time, I wonder what her name is, mentally running through all the monikers I can think of.

I wonder if it's even in a language I can understand, all things considered.

The more time that passes since the day we tried to slay the dragon—*Penn*—the guiltier I feel, and surprisingly not just because of Garreth, either. Regardless of why we pursued the idea in the first place…so much of what we did that day was ill-fated.

We were unprepared, and we suffered greatly because of it.

The loss of Garreth still weighs heavily among the knights, as I assume it will for quite some time. Perci's still barely speaking to us, although he hasn't asked to be moved from the room he shares with Tristan and myself, either.

Even knowing what I now know, and disregarding the girl's personal relationship with the beast, I can't help wondering how many knights it would take to accomplish what we could not—what we might have, if she hadn't shown up. Even though we managed to capture him, it never truly felt like we were going to succeed.

Would she defend the dragon if there were an army of knights there for his head and his riches?

Her admonishment still stings, the embarrassment returning tenfold.

"You came here for gold?"

"Not all of us wish to be indebted to the crown."

I had never said those words to anyone other than Garreth, Tristan, and Perci before, not even my own family.

But it was true. I am far more indebted to the crown and the arrogant prince who sits upon the throne than almost any other knight—besides Tristan, perhaps—and in more ways than gold.

I let my mind wander, succumbing to the enigma that is the dragon girl. Again, I can't help wondering where her parents are...and *who* they are. Even if they're dead, it seems as if she's spent her entire life here with the dragon...

But where is she from? Who brought her to him in the first place, and why did they stop coming to see her?

And Merlin...

Notoriously elusive and a striker of impossible deals...

How did the dragon girl come to know the most powerful mage in existence?

"Not many people can say they have that honour." In truth, it was a test to glimpse the dynamic of their relationship and to see just how loyal she may be to him. Either he's simply a means to an end, or he's since burned whatever bridge was formed between them.

And yet...very few humans can say they've spent any significant time with a mage, let alone Merlin himself.

Except, perhaps, Tristan.

Then again, I'm almost positive very few humans can say they've spent any significant time with a dragon, either.

The girl isn't the first magical person I've encountered, not by a long shot, but she's certainly the most interesting. Tristan would tell me that I'm too obsessed with her, too *infatuated*. But it's intoxicating. It's thrilling and wild, and...addicting. Everything she tells me is merely a crumb when I crave a feast, a drop of water in the ocean of curiosities surrounding her. Camelot is full of good and decent people, hard-working and kind, but none of them hold a torch to the eccentricities and oddities that she offers.

She keeps saying it would not be wise to return, and yet, I know without a doubt, that I will do exactly that.

NINE

A R I

Twice now, I have told Lance not to come back, and yet, little more than a week after our second encounter, he seems to have found himself here once again.

After the burning sensation had carved its way across my hand, it took a little more than an hour to track him to the river that cuts through the southernmost part of the forest.

One leg is stretched out on the riverbank in front of him, the other bent at the knee with his arm wrapped lazily around it. He seems content to just sit in the rain and throw rocks in the water, but considering how deep he's come into the forest, it's no coincidence that he's here.

The sound of rain—a light *pitter-patter* making its way through the canopy of trees—masks any sound as I make my way toward him. If he's aware of my arrival, he shows no signs of it.

"Why have you returned?" The sound of my voice causes him to startle, though only a little.

He turns to glance at me over his shoulder, blue eyes bright with excitement. "I had more questions," he says sheepishly, ignoring the rain that soaks his hair and clothes.

"Of course, you did." I sigh. "Only, I do not think you understand the risks you are bringing upon both of us by coming back here—again."

"Is there really that much harm that can come from us talking?" he asks earnestly.

"I do not wish to tempt fate, knight. Something you seem hellbent on doing."

"I don't really know what to tell you"—he shrugs, slowly rising to his feet—"but I don't think I can stop coming here."

"Perhaps you should try."

"I don't want to." There's something about the way he says it—softer, yet full of raw emotion—and something in his expression that makes me pause, like a deer unsure if it should flee or not. Unsure whether or not it was a predator that spooked it in the first place.

"What do you want?" I ask quietly, barely audible above the gentle rain and muted sounds of the forest.

"To get to know you."

"Why?" I breathe.

"Why not?" He cracks a slow, genuine smile and it lights up his whole face.

Deep down, I know that entertaining this is a bad idea. I know that once I open this door between us, this gateway from his world to mine, it will not be easy to close again.

And yet, I can't help being curious.

"Where is your horse?" I ask. His eyebrows shoot up and then furrow, the question clearly surprising him. "You did not walk here from Camelot, so where is your horse?" I ask again.

"She's wary of the woods," he says slowly, eyes scanning our surroundings. "She's grazing near the southern edge."

"You shouldn't leave her alone, not in this forest. Not even on its edge." I nod downstream with my head where the water is shallow enough to reveal an easy path across. "Come, let's go find her. You can ask your questions as we walk."

Lance simultaneously surprises and confuses me. His personality, so at odds with itself, leaves me wanting to know more—to understand him. The need to do so becomes almost tangible, a curiosity that simmers and burns within me in the time between his visits.

He comes to see me three more times in the next month.

Sometimes, he only stays for an hour or two, and sometimes, it's nearly the whole day. With each new time that he comes to see me, the desire to figure out what makes up all the little pieces of *him* turns into an itch that cannot be scratched, no matter how hard I try.

So, reluctantly, I stop trying.

Before long, I'm asking just as many questions as he is, and while neither of us seem too keen on talking about our families, nothing else seems to be off-limits.

He tells me what it was like becoming a knight, and how he didn't truly feel like he fit in until he met Perci, and then Tristan a few years later. He tells me of his first battle—a skirmish on the borders of Camelot and Kent, and how despite Camelot being victorious, the men they lost that day affected him deeply.

I tell him about growing up in the forest and being raised by Penn. About the trials and errors of learning magic, and of being taught by someone who is far too impatient for an immortal with nothing but time on his hands.

He seems particularly interested when I talk about magic and Merlin— especially Merlin. I'm careful with what I say, to not give too much away. The mage's business is his own, as is his reputation. I neither defend nor dispute it, nor do I care to.

As a knight, Lance seems oddly reserved in his affections for the former king, yet proud of the kingdom he's been tasked to protect. Though, if his flippant remarks are anything to go by, there is certainly no love lost between him and Arthur. He's quick to belittle the prince, and even quicker to criticise his choices, yet it is the prince's uncle, Gawain, who rules as Lord Regent until Arthur's eighteenth name day.

As a man—well, almost a man—he is carefree and lighthearted. He smiles easily, laughs loudly, and is absolutely brimming with questions. His interest and eagerness know no bounds, the quest for answers nearly insatiable.

If I'm being honest with myself, it's refreshing. The few relationships I've had throughout my life have all had a purpose. Penn's duty has been to protect and raise me, to prepare me for the future and anything it may throw at me. Bax, my tutor, taught me to indulge in my interests, to be passionate, and to never lose sight of things that are important to me. And Merlin has helped me grow and understand my magic, as well as to never be afraid to ask for help, so long as I understand the cost.

But with Lance…the lack of purpose is what makes it most appealing. We're simply exploring the pieces that make us who we are with no goal in sight. We're enjoying each other's company and seeing things from the other's perspective. There's no ulterior motive, no goal to be obtained, no game to be won. It's just…*fun*.

He laughs now, pulling me from my reverie. The sound is contagious, pulling a softer version from my own lips.

"I like spending time with you…" There's a weighted pause, his eyes intent upon my face as he asks, "Will you finally tell me your name today?"

"Ari."

"Ari," he says slowly, testing it. Tasting it. "Is that short for something?"

"Most definitely."

He gives me an exasperated smile. "I like spending time with you, Ari."

He reaches up to tuck an errant lock of hair behind my ear, his fingers lingering on my neck for one heartbeat, then another.

My chest tightens, and when my eyes drop to his mouth, I can't help wondering if kissing him would be the same as kissing Merlin… Or if it would be an entirely different sort of adventure.

I shouldn't be feeling this way, and now that I've let him in, now that I've let him get close, I don't know how to back up—to rebuild the wall and put some space between us.

I don't know what will happen if I don't.

And, more importantly, I don't know if I want to.

"What if the humans aren't so bad?"

"I've never led you to believe that humans are bad, little dragon." Penn flaps his wings gently, stretching the muscles along his spine and shoulders after a long morning curled up in a tight ball. On either side of him, the trees shudder with the gusts created by the movement. "I've only ever said they are dangerous."

"But I'm a human." I take one last look at the contents of my bag, ensuring I've grabbed enough of the plants we've come this far north for.

"And you are dangerous." He snorts, eyeing me with a look that dares me to challenge him. I open my mouth to do exactly that when he says, "Never forget that it was humans who took everything from me—and would have done the same to you."

"Bax saved me," I argue, arching an eyebrow at him. "And he brought me to you."

The closest thing to a smile that a dragon can manage spreads across Penn's face. "That he did, and I am thankful for it every day."

His head nuzzles against my torso and I wrap my arms around either side of his snout. "As am I," I murmur, placing a kiss upon smooth crimson scales. "I love you."

"I will love you always," he replies in Dragon, all harsh hisses and sharp clicks. His eyes drift closed in triplicate and we simply stand there for a moment, letting the weight of his words sink in. In this life, I have another handful of decades at best, but he will be alive long after I have left this world, and no amount of time that I have with him will ever be enough.

Eventually, he pulls back and lowers his body to make it easier for me to climb onto his back. Once I'm situated, he pushes off the ground and we soar into the sky.

We left before sunrise this morning, utilising a break in the rain to do as much flying as possible while remaining dry. Penn is miserable when he's wet.

Now, we stay low, rising and falling with the ever-changing elevation and hugging the treetops to avoid the storm clouds gathering overhead. More than once, we've come a little too close for comfort to an unexpected bolt of lightning.

With neither of us feeling the need to shout above the roar of the wind, the trip home is mostly silent. Though, I can't stop replaying his words over and over in my head, nor can I ignore the wistful tears they bring to my eyes.

"I will love you always."

TEN

ARI

When Merlin finds me outside the cave the next day, I'm torn, my thoughts caught between Lance and what Penn said about humans being dangerous. Lance makes me feel light and airy, and he fills me up with this absurd, giddy sort of delight, like I'm feeding off his enthusiastic energy. And yet…

Humans and their malicious, greedy nature is why Penn and I are both in the situation we're in. It's why he has no mate and was forced to flee his home. It's why I was raised by a dragon instead of my birth parents. It's why we've lived this life together—here, in the forest, away from humans.

Lance is dangerous because I let my guard down around him. Because I trust him, despite how and why we first met. Because he makes me feel things that only Merlin has ever made me feel. And I know that despite it all, I'm still looking forward to the next time that burning sensation takes root in my hand.

Merlin clears his throat, regaining my attention. He stands before me, slightly annoyed at my distraction, the sun casting him in a warm, golden hue that makes the freckles splattered across his cheeks and nose stand out like dark little constellations.

"My head's just not in it today." I sigh, fists clenching and unclenching distractedly.

"Your thoughts are preoccupied. Come, let us clear your mind."

He leads me northwest, through the forest and into the deep, grassy valley beyond. I follow him wordlessly, still lost to my thoughts.

It's been two months since the knights of Camelot attacked Penn. Three weeks since my last near-encounter with the dryads. Penn's wounds have long since healed, and his wing is in perfect condition. The cut on my hand from Merlin's bargain is little more than a line of scar tissue.

As promised by Merlin, Lance hasn't been able to find his way back to the cave, so I've never had to worry about Penn finding out that he's been coming to see me. I'm fully taking advantage of the fact that he can't simply follow me on foot through the trees, and trusts me enough not to try to find me from the sky.

If Merlin has somehow learned that I've been spending time with one of the knights, he hasn't said anything during our time together. We haven't spoken about them, or Camelot since the day he offered the deal to conceal the cave.

Yet…I can't shake the feeling that I'm missing something.

"You ought to heal that," Merlin says, staring pointedly at the fresh cuts on my hand, startling me from my reverie. "The forest grows restless these days. Many things would follow the scent of your blood far and wide."

"I… It's fine," I say absently, holding my fist to my chest. I'd been trying to reverse the affects of venom this morning, something we haven't gone over since my last gnome-induced-paralysis.

One side of his mouth lifts up, a singular soft chuckle escaping his lips. "Here," he says, holding his hand out toward me, "let me."

I lay my hand in his, staring at the multitude of scars covering my palm. The skin is both smooth and rigid, with years and years of scar tissue built up under the surface. In the centre—thanks to today's lesson—a fresh cut stretches from thumb to pinky, no longer bleeding but bright red and angry-looking nonetheless.

Slowly, he brushes his thumb over the cut. It tingles and itches as it begins knitting itself back together. I have to fight the urge not to clench my fist to ease the discomfort.

He uses my hand to tug me to the ground, and we nestle into our usual spot among the hillside. The long grasses mostly hide us from view, not that there's anything particularly nefarious in the valley to be hiding from, let alone anything I would be afraid of with Merlin at my side.

The wind is cold today, and neither of us had anticipated leaving the relative safety of the forest. Both of us sit with our hands tucked beneath our arms, puffing little clouds of air out in front of us, but it's not until my teeth start chattering that he produces a large, thickly woven blanket, materialising it out of thin air.

The valley momentarily distorts in front of me, the air shimmering with the use of his magic.

We settle into the blanket, lying back fully and sticking close for warmth. All afternoon, we watch the clouds pass by overhead, listening to the sounds of the forest—the shrill cry of a hawk, the *tap tap tap* of a woodpecker, the wind whistling through the trees, and the distant, soft tinkering of the little folk. The wildflowers peppering the valley have begun blooming in earnest; their combined scents are heady and intoxicating as they float along the late spring breeze.

We lie there for hours, in the most comfortable, contented form of silence.

This is my favourite time spent with Merlin. I love magic lessons—even when it hurts and it takes everything out of me. I love sparring with him—when he lets me win, and even when he doesn't. I love learning about faraway places he's been to, the people he's met, and the unsavoury bargains he's struck.

I even love the deal Penn and I made with him the day I found him in the woods.

When Bax used to visit me, he'd bring clothes and books with him. When he stopped, Merlin started. Over the years, he brought other things, too—weapons and spices and anything I couldn't have gotten on my own. He didn't have to do that—it wasn't part of the deal—but he did so all the same.

But it's days like this, the quiet moments spent doing absolutely nothing, that are my favourite.

Secretly, I think they're his favourite, too.

He's constantly on the move, striking bargains and generally getting up to no good. He makes trouble for people, then benefits doubly from providing them with the only way out. He lies and tricks and deceives to get what he wants.

He is a mage.

He is immortal.

He is untouchable.

And he makes no apologies for any of it.

He neither asks me for forgiveness nor expects me to make excuses for his actions. It's none of my business what he does—it doesn't affect me or my life with Penn. But we are two lonely people who found a common ground; when the days get long and things get hard, he comes and seeks solace in the silence of my company—and I am happy to give it. He provides me with a respite from the monotony of lessons with Penn, and the inane mundanity of my simple everyday life.

We are friends. Sometimes more, sometimes less. But always, we are there when the other needs it.

After a few hours, his breathing eventually grows deeper. A small smile touches my lips, but I do not wake him.

I spend the rest of the day warm and sheltered from the wind, nestled close to Merlin, watching clouds drift by overhead, and listening to the grasses slithering around us. When the sky grows dark and the first of the stars begin to dot the sky, I finally let my eyes drift shut, too.

When I wake a few hours later, it's jarring and disorienting. At first, it feels as if Merlin is on top of me, pinning me to the ground. The weight on my chest is crushing, making it hard to breathe. By the time my eyes are open and focused and fully taking in our surroundings, a soft hiss leaves my lips.

"Merlin!" I scream his name as best I can, struggling against the weight of my restraints. Cursing under my breath, I twist and turn, squirming to free myself from the roots wrapping around my body.

"*Shhhhhh, hush now,*" the dryad closest to me purrs in a lyrical sort of singsong voice.

"*Let him sleep,*" the other croons, one word bleeding into the next like leaves rustling in the wind.

Their voices are everywhere, both one and many, echoing around the valley and rattling through my head. Their lips do not move, yet their words whisper in my ear as if they are next to me.

It is both disconcerting and unsettling.

"Merlin!" He lies beside me, pinned and motionless, the blanket nowhere to be found.

I need to keep them distracted, keep them talking, and keep their attention away from him. If he's not awake—if he cannot rouse—then I need to get us out of this.

"What have you done to him?" I ask, my breath coming in short bursts.

They smile in tandem, rows of fangs gleaming at me in the moonlight, every tooth ending in a deadly sharp point.

Swallowing down a lump of mixed emotions—fear, dread, anxiety—I force my mind to slow, to focus on what needs to be done.

The roots protruding from the ground slowly wrap tighter around me. My hands are pinned to my sides, but there is always a dagger on my belt. I just need to get it.

"We did nothing," the first one lies, gliding towards me. Its bark-like skin catches shadows thrown by the moonlight, keeping half its face in shadow.

"Then why isn't he waking?" I demand, forcing myself to maintain eye contact.

Their bodies are distinctly feminine, though I do not believe them to be strictly male or female but something in-between. Tall and slender limbed with a slight curve of the chest, they have long, wispy hair that floats in the wind, and large, depthless eyes which now regard me intently.

"They call it the eternal slumber," the second one says, bending down to push the dark hair from Merlin's eyes. *"Soon, he will not be able to wake up."*

"And then what?" I snap, gaining both their attention.

"And then we eat him," the second one answers, tilting its head to one side.

Fear shifts to rage, causing a visceral reaction in my chest. My hand is on the dagger, but I don't have the room I need to pull it out. I have no other way of cutting the roots, but all I know is that I must keep their focus on me.

"What did you do to him?" I demand again, eyes frantically darting between Merlin and the dryads.

"Just a kiss," the second one says, smiling to reveal the rows of sharp teeth again. Revulsion shoots through me and I have to suppress a shudder.

The roots binding me tighten, and my hand slips on the blade. A hiss escapes my lips as the pain momentarily distracts me. Panicked and angry, I say, "I thought you said—"

"We lied," the first one interrupts with a grin, crouching down in front of me. Its face is mere inches from mine, its endless eyes staring directly

into my soul.

"You shouldn't have done that," I whisper, a hint of a smile in my voice.

A deep crease forms between its brows, eyes boring into my own.

I dig my fingers into the earth beneath me, letting my blood soak into the dirt and roots, and then I smile in earnest.

I whisper a spell in Latin, and the dryad goes up in flames. It roars and flails as the fire engulfs it.

"What have you done?" the second one shrieks, a high-pitched wail that threatens to rupture my eardrums.

Whatever magic was used on Merlin is broken by the dryads' deafening screams. Immediately, he begins struggling against the roots that hold him to the hillside, alarm evident in every inch of his face. I allow myself only a heartbeat to look at him—to make sure he's okay.

By the time the last of the dryads' binds burn away from me, the first of the creatures has fallen immobile at my feet. The second lunges at me, and it takes everything in me not to panic. To stay my hand until the last possible second.

My hand, now gripped tightly around the hilt of the dagger, lifts to plunge it into the dryad's throat. The hateful words it had been uttering are now forgotten as its fingers flutter to the wound, grasping for the blade as I use all my strength to carve a line across the base of its neck.

I yank the dagger out and flinch as black blood sprays my face, watching as this dryad crumbles beside the other.

Once my ears stop ringing, I realise that Merlin—still struggling—is shouting my name, over and over again. He's in such a panic that he hasn't even managed to free himself yet.

"I'm okay," I murmur, staring at the fallen creatures before me.

There's a bright flash of light, and then he's beside me, cursing under his breath, hands flitting over my arms and legs. Vaguely, I notice they're shaking as they assess me for injuries I don't possess.

"What happened?" he demands, momentarily satisfied that I'm not hurt.

"I fell asleep," I whisper, finally meeting his gaze.

His intense, green-gold eyes dart back and forth between my own, a multitude of emotions held within them. He swallows visibly then lifts my hand up between us. I watch as he heals the cuts on my fingers where my hand was wrapped around the blade. Pulling my hand to his mouth, his eyes drift closed as he kisses my knuckles.

"Why were they trying to kill you?" I ask, my voice shaking.

"I assume they wish to possess my magic," he rasps.

When he opens his eyes again, all the emotion from before is replaced with detached indifference.

An hour after daybreak, the sky turns bleak. The bright blue promise of a new day—and an escape from last night's horrors—is replaced with ominous cloud cover. The sky holds the threat of rain, and the air is still chilled as it winds through the valley.

Thunder rumbles and crashes in the distance just beyond the valley. A light mist clings to the edges of the surrounding forest, shrouding everything in an extra layer of gloom.

My mood is both solemn and somber.

After torching the other dryad's body, Merlin set out to find the source of their powers. The forest directly surrounding my home is intentionally devoid of oak trees, something both Merlin and Penn have continued to make sure of over the years, but that doesn't mean the rest of the forest covering the mountain range is free of them, too.

I didn't offer to go with, and he didn't ask me to join him.

Sometimes, I don't fully understand the dynamics of our relationship.

Sometimes, he's kind and comforting.

Sometimes, he's calculating and vindictive.

I never know which version I'm going to get of him, and, over the years, I've learned how to handle all of them. But last night, he looked truly afraid—something I have never seen in him before.

Merlin is quick to guard his emotions, rarely letting anyone truly see him out of fear of them using those emotions against him or having some kind of edge over him. He looked as scared as I felt, and then it was as if he just shut it off, completely unbothered by how close to death we had just been.

And then he left.

I can't stop seeing the look in his eyes when he woke up; it plays over and over in my head, on a continuous loop. Him struggling, panicked and afraid. It haunts me the whole way home.

The forest is eerily silent as I make my way back to the cave. Most of the animals seem to have fled with the arrival of the dryads, and all of the mythical inhabitants tend to disappear when Merlin is around.

They generally keep to themselves—the mountain trolls stick to the rocky cliffs of the northern mountain range; the nyads stick to their streams and lakes; the dryads *usually* stick to the comfort of their oak trees; the little folk and the gnomes run freely but unseen through the underbrush of the forest.

As for everything else… The elves have long been gone from this earth. There are so few dragons left that we rarely come across another one, and because of the mutual hatred between the two species, I've only ever met one of the forest folk.

But if there's one thing the entirety of the magical creatures of the realm can agree on, it's the general dislike and distrust of mages.

The fact that the dryads were so bold last night unsettles me to my core.

ELEVEN

A R I

Nearly two days later, Merlin returns, surprising me in a small clearing on my way back from the river. I expect him to share his findings in regards to the oak trees he'd been in search of or any other information about the dryads. Instead, he merely stares at me, his expression unreadable.

"Merlin?" His name is as much a greeting as a question. Thunder cracks loudly above and lightning flashes across the sky.

Penn is due back later today, and I want to be at the cave when he returns, but seeing Merlin in his current state gives me pause. An uncomfortable tingling feeling raises the hairs at the back of my neck.

His trousers are filthy and torn, and his tunic is stained with blood— mine, the dryads, and I suspect some of his own. His hair is disheveled, his complexion pale, the skin beneath his eyes a deep purple.

"Are you alright?" I ask warily. "You look as if you haven't slept since…" My words trail off, but the rest of my sentence hangs between us.

"I haven't," he says, voice low and raspy.

"Come to the cave, let me make you some tea. You can rest for a while—"

"There was a nest of them," he says distractedly, "only a hundred leagues from here." His eyes stare at the ground before my feet, unseeing. Remembering.

"You tracked them so far?" I ask cautiously.

His eyes snap to mine, and I flinch. "So far?" he asks, a hard edge to his tone. "That's far too close for comfort for a nest that size, Ari."

This version of him is new to me, unknown. The wildness in his eyes and the general disarray of his presence is unsettling, sending a spike of terror running through me. I do not move for fear of triggering something in him, some response I do not have time to anticipate.

"I encountered more along the way," he says quietly, not breaking eye contact. "There were dozens… I followed them to their nest, and then I destroyed the ancient part of the forest they infected with their malice."

"Merlin…" I don't know how to respond to that. I know of where he speaks; even Penn would not let me venture there. And he… "Surely, you wish to rest?"

"What I wish," he says slowly, taking a careful step toward me, then another until he closes the distance between us and gently drops his forehead against mine, all but whispering his next words, "is for you to distract me."

I hesitate for only a moment before bringing my hands to either side of his face. He shudders at my touch, then leans into it, chest heaving. I wait, smoothing my thumbs over his cheeks in gentle strokes, until he opens his eyes again. My heart lurches, and the uneasy apprehension I'd felt a moment ago dissipates, melting into something else entirely. The colours of his eyes thread together so intricately, the hues bleeding together so beautifully…

The desire burning there—the need—nearly undoes me.

There are only two ways Merlin ever wishes to be distracted, and I am willing to give him both. Right now, he is teetering on the edge, all but begging me to pull him back.

So, I do.

My lips crash into his with the desperation of too much time spent apart. My hands roam greedily, alternating between tugging his hair and pulling him closer. His hands flit over me in a frenzy, clinging to my waist one moment, threading through my hair the next.

I tug his ruined shirt over his head, our lips only breaking apart for a moment. He groans, the sound nearly pained as it rumbles from his throat. His lips move away from mine, his mouth alternating between biting and sucking its way down to my collarbone.

"Speaking of distractions…" Merlin says airily, lips still warm on my throat. I freeze, my hands stilling on the muscles in his back. He leans back, and though his face is unreadable, his demeanour is far too rigid to be indifferent. His barely contained wrath is still visible in every line of his body.

"Yes…?"

"How are the knights of Camelot these days? Or…is it only the one knight?"

I know it's a stupid question before the words ever leave my lips, but I ask it all the same. "How did you know?"

"Honestly, Ari." He releases a small sigh, arching a conspicuous brow at me.

Was Lance telling people in Camelot that he'd come to see me? Had he told anyone else how to find us? Just because they couldn't find the cave didn't mean they couldn't show up in the forest. And if they were willing to wait us out…if they were close enough to see Penn take flight…sooner or later, they would find us. We can't hide forever.

"I don't care if you choose to entertain yourself with some boy knight in my absence. My ego is not so fragile that a few secret rendezvous in the forest would send me into a jealous spin."

He's feigning nonchalance, but there's a tightness to his shoulders and a hard set to his jaw.

"So, if you know precisely what's been happening, why even bother with pretence? Why not just outright ask what you wish to ask?”

“Because I do not care how you choose to pass the time when I am gone, Ari. I just didn’t want you to think I didn’t know.” He shrugs. “We’ve never been ones to over complicate things. I know who you are, and I know what we mean to each other.” His eyes dance with the type of assurance that can only come from years of familiarity.

“Merlin, I—“

The haunted look from his arrival creeps back into his gaze, devouring anything else I was going to say.

“Nowhere is too far, Ari. No number of enemies is too great. There is nothing I wouldn’t do to keep you safe.” Then, softer, “There isn’t *anything* I wouldn’t do for you.”

His forehead drops to mine once more, though this time our lips do not meet in the middle. He grazes my cheek with the back of his knuckles, a soft smile playing at his mouth.

Chuckling once to himself, he expels a quick breath. Then, inhaling deeply, he lifts each arm up and over his shoulders, reaching behind himself to unsheathe a weapon I know he does not wear. The air shimmers, distorting the trees behind him, and there’s a twinge of static—a metallic tang in the air as he pulls two swords from the pocket of space he keeps things in, manifesting them into shaky hands.

“I still find myself in need of a distraction.” He inhales deeply again, and his breath is a warm rush on my face as he slowly pushes the air back out. Hands now lowered, the swords form a sort of cage on either side of me.

My eyes dart back and forth between his, my chest barely rising with shallow breaths as we stay locked in this moment. A series of lightning strikes touch down somewhere in the distance, visible only for a second as they depart from the clouds, lost to the height of the forest surrounding us. Thunder echoes wildly through the mountain range.

His brows tug together, just for a moment, and then he angles an arm in a way that offers me one of the swords.

I stare at him for another charged moment, then accept the blade, nodding.

A third rumble of thunder surrounds us, deep and low.

"Do not go easy on me," he whispers.

"I wouldn't dare," I reply, one corner of my mouth twitching upward as I back up to put some space between us.

His eyes glow with the next flash of lightning, and then he strikes.

The clouds open up, and rain begins to fall the moment our blades clash. He moves swiftly, each strike harder and faster than the one before. He uses precision and purpose, and he shows no restraint—no intention of yielding. It takes everything in me to keep up, to block his blows and stay on the defensive.

He seeks a way to let his frustrations out and I can give him that. Though, I can't help wondering how easy it would be for him if he were truly trying to kill me. Merlin is old—though I don't know how old, exactly—and has many, many years of swordplay on me.

We dance around the clearing in chaotic harmony. Rain rolls off his bare chest in rivulets, weighs my clothes down, and drips into our eyes. The longer we spar, the more tired he gets and the more even his breathing becomes. I can see the change happen in him gradually—the rage fading to resolve— then, finally, his shoulders relax and he truly begins to enjoy himself.

After that, I match him blow for blow.

Before long, he's on the defensive, a wicked gleam in his eye. He's having fun now, and that was always my goal.

"Challenge me," he growls, his smile feral.

My grin matches his, and I block his next attack but do not deflect it. The whine of metal rings in my ears, and I welcome it. He moves to pull his sword away, and I wrap my other hand around the blade, embracing the flash of pain.

I cry out, and he falters, surprised.

His eyes travel to the edge of his sword where my blood coats the blade, and his smile turns devious.

"You think you can best me with magic?" he calls dubiously, retreating a few paces across the clearing. Sweat dots his forehead, mixed with rain, and his bare chest heaves with the exhilaration. Rotating the sword in his hand, he levels the tip with my heart and waits.

His stance leaves him wide open, but I see it for the trap that it is. Hissing through the pain, I let the blood well up into my clenched fist. Pulling three steadying breaths into my lungs, and ignoring the shaking in my hands, I charge him.

He expects me to exploit this weakness, and I let him think that I plan to. I run straight at him, sword arcing through the air with the intention of striking him, but, at the last second, I dive, sliding past him and slicing into the meat and flesh of his thigh instead.

He curses loudly and drops to the ground, hands already working to heal the wound.

Using his momentary distraction to my advantage, I dig my fingers into the earth—much the same way I did with the dryad. My limbs ache, sweat slides down my back, and my breath comes heavily. Propped up against my sword with one hand, I let the blood from the other flow into the earth and merge with the rain-soaked soil. Feeling for the natural currents in the ground, I send my magic toward them, muttering a spell under my breath.

Merlin whirls on me, agitation and appreciation mixed in equal measure across his features. "What are you going to do?"

"Run," I breathe. His brows furrow deeply and then the ground begins to shake. Yanking my hand and my sword from the soil in tandem, I sprint towards the forest as fast as I can.

The ground in the clearing fissures, leaving a giant gap in its wake. Whether Merlin got to safety or not is of little concern to me; he can protect himself. Instead, I focus on running until the ground stops shaking.

When it does, I crash to my knees, panting hard.

After hiking through the forest all morning, an extended sparring match, and then a substantial surge of magic, I am left utterly exhausted.

"Well done." Merlin steps out of the trees, clapping. "Truly, you surprised me."

"I know," I pant, smiling up at him.

"What made you think to use my weapon for your own gain?" he asks.

"You'd know what I was doing if I used my own blade," I say, chest still heaving. "Using yours gave me the element of surprise."

He crouches down in the mud a few feet before me but says nothing.

Lightning cracks across the sky again, but the storm seems to have lost its rage.

After a moment, I meet his eyes and whisper, "It's how I broke free."

I don't have to elaborate, the flash in his eyes tells me he understands.

"Well," he says, swallowing visibly, "don't think you'll be able to use that on me twice." I smile at him, and he returns it half-heartedly. The pair of swords—one in his hand, one at my feet—vanish before my eyes, just as easily as he'd manifested them.

He moves until he's directly in front of me, our breaths mingling in the small space between us.

"Thank you for the distraction," he says quietly. I nod, breaking eye contact, but his hand finds my cheek, turning my gaze back towards his.

His eyes dart back and forth between mine—searching, though I do not pretend to know for what. Leaning in, he places a gentle kiss on my forehead.

"I'm sorry for falling asleep," I whisper. He pulls back, brows furrowing ever so slightly, and then he looks away, releasing a heavy sigh.

Standing abruptly, the air shimmers around him, distorting the trees again.

One second, he's there, and the next, he's gone.

TWELVE
LANCELOT

"Stop fidgeting," Tristan scolds without so much as glancing at me. "People have been beheaded for less."

We stand on the side of the stone dais, waiting for the lord regent to wrangle Arthur out of whatever miserable state he's found himself in today and deliver his speech to the people.

Most of the town square is currently empty, save for a few children playing with wooden swords while their mothers look on.

"He's not here to see me fidget, Tris," I mumble, shifting my weight from foot to foot. "We don't even need to be here yet. Bors is only punishing us."

A dozen guards, including us, have been stationed around the dais since daybreak. The same dozen guards the captain of the king's army has lost wagers to in the tavern over the last month.

"We're here to ensure there is no threat to Arthur when he arrives," Tristan says automatically.

"There *is* no threat." I groan under my breath. "The only threat to Arthur is himself."

"True as that may be, this is still our job, Lance."

We wait for another hour before the square starts to fill up, people shielding their eyes from the blinding sun—a welcome reprieve from the consistent rain we've had over the past few weeks. The air warms quickly, and with all the extra bodies in the square soon the temperature becomes uncomfortable inside my armour.

Before long, Lady Guinevere arrives, somehow managing to simultaneously fit in and stand out. Immediately, the people are infatuated with her, waving and smiling and tossing flowers at her feet.

Her blonde hair is pulled away from her face with severe braids, long curls spilling down her back. Gold rings are woven into the plaits, matching the dainty circlet she wears across her brow and the half-dozen little hoops she has pierced along one ear.

Her dress is a deep burgundy with bits of gold, tight at the top and flowing at the bottom. She looks every bit the royal but more a northerner than someone who hopes to rule alongside Arthur one day.

"Stop staring." I nudge Tristan with a smirk. "People have been beheaded for less."

"I'm not staring," he hisses.

"Everyone else is." I snort. "She's pretty."

"She is a wolf in a pretty dress," he murmurs, disgust evident in his tone.

Not long after, a disgruntled-looking Arthur arrives with the lord regent and royal advisor in tow. His trousers are wrinkled, and his tunic and doublet were hastily thrown on and clearly not inspected by a page. Though he wears a belt, there is no sword at his hip. The sneer on his face matches the coldness in his eyes, offsetting the brightness of the colour. A crown so black it appears depthless sits askew atop his ruby-red hair.

He does not so much as look at Lady Guinevere before stepping onto the dais.

If she is slighted by this, she does not show it.

"People of Camelot," Arthur says, loud and confident. "Welcome."

The people clap, a murmur of unearned awe and approval rolling through the crowd. He could stand before them eating a turkey leg and they would undoubtedly applaud.

"As you well know, a very important time is nearly upon us," he continues. "In a few months' time, my name day will arrive, and, with it, my coronation."

They applaud, cheers and whistles coming from all over.

"I would like to announce a festival in honour of all that awaits us." He gestures to the square and the vendors lining the perimeter. "A month of festivities, food and drink, dancing and music, and, of course, a tournament."

At the back of the dais, the lord regent leans toward the royal advisor, whispering something behind his hand. Their distraction lasts for only a moment, but it does not go unnoticed by either myself or Lady Guinevere, who regards them with cool indifference.

"The grand prize for whoever shall win my tournament is the title of King's Champion and one wish—anything you like and, if it's within my power, I shall grant it for you. Be it eternal glory, endless ale, or anything in-between."

A low murmur rustles through the crowd, causing some of the knights closest to them to shift, hands settling on the swords at their hips.

"Anyone may enter, but it is not for the faint of heart. And for those of you lucky enough, you may even get a round in the ring with me."

Again, the lord regent leans toward the royal advisor, a tense, inaudible conversation passing between them behind Arthur.

"What a bold declaration," Tristan mutters beside me.

I nod. "What a bold declaration, indeed."

"I think you should enter," Perci says around a mouthful of food. He's finally talking to us normally and consistently again.

"I think you should chew and swallow," Tristan says, grimacing across the table at him.

"I think we should all enter," Kay pipes in, glancing around the table. Torr and Graham nod in agreement.

The tavern is full of knights after shift change, mugs of ale and plates of food at every table. The singular barmaid is running around frantically, trying to keep up with all the orders. The noise is loud but not so much so that we can't hear each other speak.

"I don't know," Tristan says, draining the last of his ale. "I'm far better with a bow than a sword these days."

"We both know that's not true," I say with a laugh. "You may be less practiced with a sword now than you were before, but you still bested me recently." I smirk, showing off the now-healed scar on my forearm. "And besides, Bors will surely be competing."

"Aye," Perci says, tipping his mug toward Tristan.

"So, you'll be competing, then?" Tristan challenges, rounding on me.

"There are far better things I would rather do than gain Arthur's approval," I mutter.

"*Prince Arthur,*" Torr corrects, a heavy silence settling upon the table. Everyone shifts in their seats, but Torr holds my stare, a slight raise to one eyebrow.

The barmaid returns with another round, oblivious to the silent tension.

"Aye," I concede after she leaves, "*Prince Arthur.*"

Beside me, Tristan tenses, waiting for Torr to say something else. When it seems as if he won't, Tristan raises his mug to the rest of the table.

"To the tournament," he says. "May the best knight win." Each of us lift our mug to his, repeating the sentiment.

When the barmaid rushes past again, Perci stops her with a gentle hand on her elbow. She glances at his fingers for only a second before they quickly release her. She nods to him, eyebrow lifting expectantly, and he orders another round of dinner: roasted quail, buttered potatoes, and steamed carrots.

"Will you joust?" Graham asks no one in particular, looking at each of us around the table.

"Nah," Tristan says. Perci and I both shake our heads.

"Maybe," Kay offers, lifting one shoulder. Beside him, Torr nods.

"I intend to knock Bors off his high horse this year," Kay grumbles, eyes flashing over the rim of his mug. He throws it back, downing the contents in one long breath.

He still favours his shoulder after last years' match against Bors left it dislocated when he was thrown from his horse. It took him months to be able to wield his sword one-handed again.

After several more rounds, Kay, Torr, and Graham pay their tab and call it a night, claiming early guard duty tomorrow.

As Perci wanders over to the bar to order another round for the three of us, Tristan moves to sit across from me, eyeing me disapprovingly.

"I'm too drunk for one of your lectures, Tris." I sigh, staring at a rather large gouge in the old wooden table.

"Aye, and yer gonna get one anyway," he says, anger lacing through his tone. "What's the matter with yeh?"

A small smile tugs at my lips. His northern accent always comes out when he's been drinking, no matter how hard he tries to hide it.

"What's your problem now?" I ask, sinking back into my chair.

"Yer gonna get yerself into a lot o' trouble one o' these days"—he drops a fist on the table, the sound surprisingly loud in the tavern—"walkin' around with yer *'Arthur'* this an' *'Arthur'* that. You serve him," he says forcefully. "You live in his kingdom. Don' be a damned fool."

"Oh, come off it—"

"No, you come off it!" He slams his hand onto the table again, glaring at me. "You walk around here like somebody owes you somethin', Lancelot, but they don't. Get yer head on straight before yeh lose it."

Perci rejoins us, sliding hesitantly into a chair next to Tristan. "Everyone alright?"

"Aye," we say in unison, layers of drunken anger in one singular response.

"Right…" Perci says hesitantly.

Shouts and jeers rise up from the far side of the tavern. A dozen or so knights crowd around a table, but Bors' voice carries well enough to know he's the focus of their attention. The words "dragon" and "forest" filter through the din, sending an uneasy tingle down my spine.

"They're plannin' somethin'," Tristan murmurs, eyeing me cautiously, his anger from before now redirected. "I don't like it."

My mind wanders to Ari—to the enigma that is the girl in the forest. Her features flash through my mind, and I'm nearly overcome with a sense of yearning—to see her again, to make her smile, and laugh, and roll her eyes at me.

As if he can read my thoughts, Tristan demands my attention once more with that northern drunken drawl. "Yeh haven't done anythin' stupid, have yeh, Lance?"

"No," I lie, forcing myself to meet his steady gaze. Hazel eyes squint at me in the dimness of the tavern. Swallowing down a lump in my throat, I ask, "Why d'you reckon I've done something stupid?"

"'Cause if anyone o' us were to do somethin' stupid, it'd be you."

"He has a point," Perci says dryly.

"What are you accusing me of, exactly?"

"Not accusin' yeh o' nothin'," Tristan says evenly. "Just makin' sure is all."

The next few days are heavy with unrest and the underlying tension in the kingdom is palpable. Sometimes, it's nearly suffocating.

Bors' nightly speeches turn near riotous. The knights grow angrier, more vengeful. Tristan is on edge all the time, unsure of whether or not he should challenge them or say nothing at all.

Although Perci seems to have forgiven us, he spends more time than ever at Garreth's grave, grieving the brother he lost too soon.

Sometimes, I catch him and Tristan in whispered conversations that seem to die out when I approach, but I try not to let it bother me. If Tristan's found a way to help him cope, it's not my place to interfere.

Unfortunately, Tristan was right, and it seems that Bors and his men are indeed planning something, but none of us can get close enough to his inner circle to find out what it is. They know we oppose their revenge plan, so they've thoroughly excluded us from it.

Rain continues to assault the kingdom, day in and day out—an omen in disguise, no doubt. The more days that pass, the more the tension builds, and so too does my urge to return to the forest to see Ari again.

It's been far too long since I last returned, and the restless feeling taking root in my veins is making me jittery.

A slew of questions I still have flood my mind, but only a few stand out above the rest. Who are her parents? Where did she come from? Why was she taken in the first place?

She's been very open about a lot of things and just as eager to ask me questions in return. But we don't talk about her family, so I don't expect to get those answers yet.

And the only other thing she guards almost as fiercely as the topic of her parents…is the topic of Merlin.

She admitted that he taught her magic, and that there was a lot of trial and error to learning how to wield it. I'm sure that's something that can only be mastered over a long period of time…so, just how close to Merlin is she, exactly?

THIRTEEN

ARI

"You're distracted." Penn sounds more worried than upset.

"Sorry," I mutter half-heartedly.

"What troubles you, little dragon?" He rises from the bed of dragonstone, the soft blue of the stones glowing vibrantly against his pale underbelly. "Did something happen while I was away?"

I glance at him and a soft, humourless chuckle escaping my lips, but I can't bring myself to say anything.

His tail twitches impatiently before he adds nonchalantly, "I flew over the old parts of the forest upon my return…"

When I continue to say nothing, he prods me further. "Leagues of scorched earth, blackened and smouldering as if struck by a thousand bolts of lightning—or a dragon hoard, which we both know is impossible." His eyes narrow slightly, the pupils dilating as they assess me. "It looked as if something had exploded. As if a plague of fury had been unleashed upon the area."

My breath hitches in my throat.

Merlin's face flashes in my mind. His stare had been vacant and unseeing, his voice haunted as he asked for a distraction.

"What happened while I was away, Ari?" Penn asks gently.

I hadn't yet told him of what happened with Merlin—of the dryads' attack and Merlin's extermination of their nest. Of course, he'd seen it upon his return—a scar that big on the earth wouldn't be easily missed from the sky.

His use of my real name and not the affectionate one is what pulls the truth from my lips.

"I ran into that pair of dryads," I say quietly, feeling small next to him and the enormity of the cavern. "The same ones who've been lingering lately."

"Why didn't you tell me?" he asks, voice neutral.

"Because it had been taken care of."

"What did Merlin do—"

"Merlin did nothing," I bite back, unable to control the flash of anger and guilt. "I took care of them myself."

"You did not burn the forest down." It's not a question, so I do not answer, though I have to look away from the intensity of his gaze. It makes me fidget, my hands opening and closing at my sides.

"Merlin destroyed their home," he says after a moment. The only sounds breaking the silence are a distant echo of a water drip somewhere within the cave, the slow steady exhale of Penn's breathing, and the rapid beating of my heart. "Why would he do that?"

"You shall have to ask him yourself"—I huff, looking at the ground—"for he did not deign to tell me."

"Little dragon," Penn rumbles, calling me on my lie.

My jaw clenches as the memory of Merlin—distraught, and disheveled, and full of despair—resurfaces. Sighing, I return my gaze to Penn's patiently waiting one.

"Merlin came for a lesson, but my head wasn't in it. We went to the valley, and he fell asleep. He's been gone so much lately, and he seemed so…tired. I didn't want to wake him." I sigh, pulling in a shuddering breath. "But then I fell asleep, too, and when I awoke, the dryads had captured us and…" As I tell him what happened, I force my voice to take on a confidence I do not feel—assurance for the dragon who expects me to think of everything before I do anything, especially when he's away. "I used my magic to save us, and now, they're dead."

He opens his mouth but says nothing. Penn rarely weighs in on the complexities of my relationship with Merlin, though I know it guilts him from time to time for allowing the mage into my life. In all fairness, I don't think even Penn's warnings would have kept me from him back then. He was far too enticing, far too…alluring.

He still is.

Bax had always been a constant in my childhood, but Merlin is the first person I remember actually meeting. He manifested into the clearing right before my eyes when I was a child.

He didn't lure me into trusting him, and he didn't lie to make me feel comfortable around him. From the very beginning, he showed me exactly who and what he was. What he could do.

Not the dark, devious, deceptive things I know he's capable of now, but he explained to me that he was a mage, that he could use magic, and then he showed me what I thought was the most amazing thing I would ever see.

He'd simply plucked a blade of grass from the earth and turned it into the most beautiful flower without blinking an eye—a pale pink peony in perfect bloom. He'd woven the stem into my braid and told me I looked like a princess.

And then he'd asked me what I wanted most in the world.

"A friend," six-year-old me had said.

"Then friends we shall be," he'd responded.

At that point, I had never really seen Penn angry before. But when I brought Merlin back to him and introduced the mage as my new friend—even as a child—I could tell Penn was furious.

"This is Merlin," I'd said. *"He's my friend."*

The pair of them had just stood there staring at each other until I got bored, placed a gentle kiss on the tip of Penn's nose, and returned to Merlin's side.

"Come on." I'd slipped my small fingers into his, tugging insistently on his hand. *"You promised to teach me magic."*

Usually, when he arrived, he was still in his normal state—his current state. Mid-twenties and fully grown into his body. Beautiful green-gold eyes, tan skin with a splattering of freckles across his nose and cheeks, and midnight hair that falls in thick, unruly waves.

But once he'd seen how much I loved magic, he seemed delighted to transform in front of me, infatuated with the pure joy it brought me. Sometimes, he would appear as a younger version of himself, wide-eyed with gangly limbs. Sometimes, he would appear as a mirror image of myself— with or without the effects of dragon's blood affecting my appearance.

That one unsettled me a little—to see what I would look like if not for the price magic had placed on my life. The same, but also very different. That version of me had more freckles than I'd ever be able to count, red hair where mine is nearly colourless, bright eyes where mine are dull— although Merlin could never truly shed the colour of his eyes. The colours that mark him as a mage.

"Are you okay?" Penn asks, pulling me from the memory.

Other than a few since-healed cuts and bruises, no physical reminders remain from that night, but I know that's not what he means. "Aye," I murmur, nodding slowly.

"You've never taken a life before," he says carefully.

"We both know that's not true," I say, glancing up at him.

Something shifts in his gaze, the sunshine glow turning molten for a moment. "You've never taken a life *like that* before," he amends, "with magic…or for someone else."

"I know—"

Something outside the cave catches his attention—some faraway sound I cannot hear. The sudden jerk of his head to better hear it has the rest of the words dying on my lips.

Whatever the distraction, it holds his attention steady. After a moment, he moves through the cave toward the main entrance.

"Penn?" I call out, but he doesn't answer me.

I follow after him hesitantly, unsure of what's drawn him outside. Pushing a curtain of weeping ivy out of my way, I stand beside him and survey the immediate forest around us.

"What is it, Penn?" I ask, brows furrowed.

"Nothing to worry about." He stretches his wings, extending them fully in the open air. "I was wondering if you might fetch some bark from the white willow trees?"

"I—aye, of course," I say, stumbling over the sudden change of topic. "Are you in pain?"

"Just my old bones giving me a bit of trouble," he teases, nuzzling his face up to my torso.

"Of course," I say again, kissing his cheek gently.

The dryads may not be in the forest anymore, but I still return to the cave to arm myself with a bow and quiver of arrows, tucking a dagger into my belt and a smaller blade into a boot for good measure.

Briefly, I touch the skin-warmed chain around my neck, ensuring it remains hidden and protected by the collar of my soft white shirt. Tucking the shirt into fitted black trousers, and slipping on worn leather boots, I quickly and deftly re-braid my hair, knotting the ends to secure it.

Snatching a woven basket from my workshop, I head back outside.

Penn is still occupying the small clearing just outside the mouth of the cave, now curled up and nestled in the sun just as he was on the dragonstone before.

"You look like a cat," I laugh, heading in the direction of the white willows.

He stares at me with the blankest expression he can muster before snorting two big puffs of black smoke from his nose, pretending to be offended.

"I'll be back before nightfall," I call to him, grinning and waving as I head into the woods.

"Be careful," he replies, not bothering to lift his head. When I'm almost out of eyesight, he adds in his native tongue, "I love you, little dragon."

The rain is light, though still persistent as I make my way through the forest.

It's been weeks of rain, ever since Merlin left to destroy the rest of the dryads. Sometimes, full-blown storms. Other times, just a drizzle, but always raining.

The ground is slick, and I have to catch myself often, using tree trunks and low-hanging branches to regain my balance.

Cutting the bark from the trees is much harder than harvesting a plant. Between the rain and the chill in my fingers, I manage not to draw any blood, but the dagger slips often—

Until it slips from my hand altogether.

I curse under my breath, equal parts annoyed and intrigued. Just like every other time this has happened, pain rips across the width of my left palm. The burning sensation is far more intense this time, fully consuming my thoughts.

With the fistful of willow bark now forgotten and abandoned at my feet, I rise and follow my gut back toward the edge of the forest.

FOURTEEN

ARI

Drawing and nocking an arrow, I keep the tip of the shaft facing the forest floor as I begin my search for Lance.

It takes a while to find him; he's much farther west than the last time he came here. I trek through the woods and past the valley, nearly to the shores of Lake Umbra before finding him.

He sits upon a large, fallen tree, crunching on a bright red apple. The rain doesn't seem to bother him, though it still comes down in earnest.

It looks as if he's come unarmed this time—or, at the very least, he's left his armour with his horse. Where the mare is, I cannot say, making that two things I know I've advised him against.

Despite the little thrill that surges through me at seeing him again, I'm still wondering if he's too brave or too stupid for his own good when he bites off another chunk of the apple. The fruit is unseasonably early for this time of year, and the sound seems to ring through the forest, reverberating off the trees. It sounds like the destruction of a hundred dead leaves, fallen and forgotten on the ground before an early snowfall. He seems completely unfazed, entirely unaware of just how loud he is in a place like this.

A slow grin spreads across my face as I lift the bow, drawing the string back to the edge of my mouth.

Inhale.

Exhale.

Release.

Lance freezes, momentarily stunned.

Twenty yards from where I stand, give or take, the remains of his apple are pinned to a birch tree, juice dripping down the bark.

Wordlessly, he gets up and crosses over to the apple, yanking the arrow from the tree. When he returns to see me standing next to the log he'd just vacated, his eyes are still wide but they're wild with amusement.

"Did my apple offend you in some way, m'lady?" He raises an eyebrow, offering me the arrow.

"Not as much as your return, I'm afraid." I take it, wiping the fruit from the shaft and returning it to my quiver, securing the bow over my shoulder once more, then add, "And don't call me that."

His smile falters, but he recovers quickly when he sees the grin I'm fighting. He gestures to the fallen tree beside us and I waver. Not because I don't want to spend time with him today, but because if Penn truly is in any pain, I want to return to him as quickly as possible.

"I don't have a lot of time today," I say hesitantly.

"If I came all this way only to see you for a moment, it would still be enough."

My eyes narrow despite the warmth I feel crawling up my neck. "Aye, well, a moment might be all you get."

His smile turns luminous. "Then consider me content."

I snort, shaking my head, perching on the log beside him. Idly, I clench and flex my left hand at my side, the pain still sharp and vivid.

He tracks the movement, his eyebrows twitching together before he asks, "Are you going to tell me what Ari is short for today?"

"I doubt it."

He chuckles despite my answer.

"Is Lance short for something?" I counter.

"Most definitely." He beams, using my own words against me. "Sir Lancelot of the Lake, at your service," he says with a flourish and a bow.

"A knight from a lake?" I ask, running through a mental list of any nearby or noteworthy lakes. There are only two in our part of the forest, but that doesn't mean either hold any significance for him.

"It's a long story," he says, his smile turning toward embarrassment. "But my name honours both my parents."

"That's a very sweet sentiment, Sir Lancelot." The engraving on the pommel of his sword, the one that signifies his bloodline, flashes through my mind. Absently, I reach for the medallion tucked beneath my tunic, but I jerk my hand away before it can make contact. If Lance notices, he says nothing.

"Please, don't start using my full name now." He chuckles, rubbing the back of his neck. "If you won't tell me your full name, will you at least tell me how you came to be raised by a dragon?"

Shaking my head, I release a short, breathy huff. "I've answered this question already."

"Not really. You told me you were raised by the dragon, and that your tutor brought you to him."

"What else is there to tell?" I ask, one eyebrow inching upward.

"The rest of the story?" He laughs incredulously.

"The rest of the story does not matter. The details are irrelevant."

"The details are hardly irrelevant..." he says, voice trailing off. When he seems to understand that I won't tell him any more, he says, "Okay, fine." Hands clapping together once, he asks, "How *does* a human learn to use magic?"

I take a moment to answer his question, considering the best way to word it without warranting an onslaught of questions in return. I need to get back to Penn soon.

"It takes years to be able to teach your body to summon magic if born without the ability."

"But what a gift," he murmurs under his breath.

"I would not be so quick to call it a gift," I mutter with a slight shake of my head. My eyes wander from the young knight, lazily soaking in the whimsy of the forest around us. The charm of the twin pines, split near the root to grow into two separate trees yet sharing one base. The richness of the spring-green canopy overhead. The scent of rain, heightening that of the spring blossoms—snake's head and hyacinth, crocus and lily of the valley, and all the lilac trees almost done with their blooms.

"Magic is both a blessing and a curse, and to those who wield it honestly, more often than not, it is a tangled web of morally questionable decisions." I sigh, returning my gaze to his—bright blue, focused, and intent. "Those of us who put ourselves through the torture of learning it are much more cautious than those who are born with it. Magic is ambiguous, and it always comes with a cost."

"What price do you pay to be able to use it?" he asks carefully. The space between us is charged, full of tension, intrigue, and something else.

The way he asks the question makes me think he already knows the answer, having seen me summon it with his own eyes, but I answer him nonetheless. "Blood," I say. "My price to summon magic and use spells must be paid with blood."

He nods, the space between his brows creasing as he asks, "So, learning to use magic has limits, then? You cannot drain your body of blood, so you must only be able to conjure up so much magic before you reach your limits?"

"Of course, it does. The gods did not grant me the ability to use it. I took it for myself. If there were no limits, there would be no rules, and without rules, magic would be utterly chaotic. Anyone who could use it would have free reign, and—"

"You took it for yourself, but, surely, someone planted the idea in your head." He arches a brow. "You say it takes years to teach your body how to summon magic, but you can't be older than me, which means you've been learning since you were a child."

"Aye."

"Did the dragon want you to learn?"

"No." A quick, loud laugh bursts from my chest. "It was most definitely not his idea."

"Your tutor, then?" There's an edge to the question, something I can't quite place.

"I asked Merlin to teach me."

Something flashes in his eyes, gone before I can figure out what it might've been. His brows pull together, and his jaw clenches as his eyes glaze over with some thought or memory. But after a moment, he says in a normal, if not airy, tone, "Such an illusive mage."

"Aye." Something tightens in my chest as I nod. "I suppose."

"Why did he train you to use magic? Most men cannot even get an audience with him, and yet, he had a hand in raising you."

"He didn't raise me," I say, almost angrily. Over the years, Merlin has done many things for me, with me, and to me, but neither of us would ever say he raised me.

"But why did *he* teach you magic?" Lance presses on. "Why not a different mage?"

The direction of his questioning confuses me, but I answer honestly.

"Mages in general are not as common as most people think, and most of them are established somewhere—not galavanting around the forest with nothing but time on their hands."

"Merlin lives in the forest with you?"

"He doesn't live *with* me," I clarify, easing myself off the large log.

His eyes track my movements, and he puts his hands up between us. "I'm sorry," he says quickly. "I just—no one knows anything about Merlin, and you seem close to him. It's hard not to get a little carried away."

I nod but remain standing.

"So, Merlin taught you magic. Did he determine the price as well?" he muses, sounding equal parts surprised and agitated.

"No, that comes through trial and error." My right thumb rubs circles into the palm of my left hand, massaging years of scars and damaged tissue marring the smooth surface. I hold my palm out to him, which he examines from his place on the log, leaning forward to look at it better. It still burns in his presence, which makes me feel surprisingly vulnerable.

Immediately, I regret showing it to him. Before I can pull away, a gentle, calloused finger begins tracing the lines. His face is indifferent, masked and devoid of emotions, but his eyes show everything.

A hiss escapes my lips, and I yank my hand away, cradling it against my chest.

"Did I hurt you?" he asks, both alarmed and skeptical.

Reflexively, I open and close my hand, eyeing the scars. Pain sears my palm like a hot brand. It never subsides in his presence, but, usually, the pain is not so blinding.

My breaths come in quick, uncertain bursts.

"Ari"—he leans forward even more, a hand outstretched toward me—"talk to me. What's going on?"

I stare at him for a moment, replaying everything—the day we met and all his visits since then—in my head as a sick feeling of dread begins to unfurl in my chest.

"You never asked how I knew you were in the woods," I force through gritted teeth. Shock and confusion slide over his features, replacing the careful indifference from before. "Every time you've come to see me, I've found you, and yet, you've never asked how I even knew you were here in the first place."

He opens and closes his mouth several times before finally asking, "How?"

"After your first visit, I made sure I would not be caught by surprise again. I made sure, if any of you returned, I would know as soon as you crossed the border into our home."

"What did you do?" he whispers, hand still hovering between us, the fear in his eyes abundant.

"I made a bargain to ensure the safety of my family," I say, unable to keep the anger from my voice. Again, I show him my palm, and his eyes land on the plethora of healed cuts. "A way to warn me should anyone come looking for us again."

"Does it hurt you?"

"The entire time I am in your presence, so long as we are in these woods, my hand burns. From the moment you arrive until the moment you leave."

"I didn't know, I'm s—"

"I do not seek your sympathies," I say, silencing his apologies. "What I wish to know is what changed? Why is the pain nearly unbearable now when we've been sitting here for—"

"If any of the knights of Camelot happen to find themselves in your woods, this scar will alert you to their presence."

Merlin's words flash through my head and the rest of my sentence dies on my lips.

If any of the knights of Camelot...

I feel the blood drain from my face as I sway on my feet.

"You tricked me." It comes out as a whisper—or maybe I only say it in my head. Regardless, I do not give him the chance to respond.

My feet are moving as fast as they can, carrying me through the woods and towards my home before I've fully comprehended exactly what is happening.

Had I not been so distracted before—so enamoured at the thought of seeing the knight again—I might've seen Penn's ruse for what it was.

FIFTEEN

LANCELOT

"*You tricked me,*" she whispers, her voice barely audible.

And then, she takes off, launching herself through the forest and sprinting down a path I cannot see, far faster than I would have thought imaginable in this weather.

It takes me a moment to regain my composure. The rough bark tears at my hand as I leap from the fallen tree, but I don't give myself a chance to second-guess what I'm doing. It takes several heartbeats to steady myself, and then it takes all of my stamina to keep her within my line of sight.

"You never asked how I knew you were in the woods. Every time you've come to see me, I've found you, and yet, you've never asked how I even knew you were here in the first place."

She made a bargain—with Merlin, no doubt—because she knew I would come back. How anyone would willingly put themselves in his debt is beyond me…and yet, she did it because of me…

The thought weighs like lead in my stomach.

Unless, by some obscure and improbable miracle, there are two Merlin's, I cannot imagine ever striking a deal with him. In fact, the only thing I would ever do if I came across Merlin is run him through with my father's sword.

I cannot even begin to fathom the dynamics of her relationships—with Merlin or the dragon. She's told me so little over our visits—enough to paint a vague picture but in no real detail. I do not understand, so, instead of trying, I just run.

I chase after her, led by the sole instinct to protect her from whatever is about to play out before us. Whatever has her spooked, whatever she thinks I've done, it cannot be good. I can only pray that she is mistaken, and hope that she'll come back to me again.

It takes everything in me to keep up to her, to keep her within my sights. She flies through the trees as if she has wings; her feet barely seem to touch the ground.

"Did I hurt you?"

A low-hanging branch catches her by surprise, but she does not falter when a line of red appears across her cheek, nor does she slow when the needles of an unruly pine snag at her hair.

"You tricked me."

I don't know what she meant; I only ever wanted answers and conversation—an opportunity to befriend the girl in the forest who was raised by a dragon. If I'm being honest, perhaps, one day more.

My lungs are on fire. Each breath burns more than the last. The stitch in my side is unbearable, but I push through it. I push through all of it because if I don't I'll lose her, and then I'll never be able to find her in this maze of trees.

Every tree looks the same, passing by in a blurry haze. Smudges of dark, splatters of light. The forest floor is overgrown with grass and clover.

Everything is green.

Everything is wet.

Even in the relative cover of the forest, rain still pelts my cheeks.

My thoughts narrow, diminishing to focus only on what I need to do to keep myself from tripping.

Inhale. Don't stop running.

Exhale. Jump over roots.

Inhale. Duck under branches.

Exhale. Don't lose her.

Repeat.

My thoughts are so focused for so long that by the time we exit the forest, I barely have time to stop myself from crashing directly into her.

I have to throw myself to the side, slamming into the ground, effectively winding myself. My ears are ringing. The weight in my chest is immeasurable. My lungs are on fire. The pressure is unyielding. Everything feels disconnected.

Vaguely, I am aware of someone screaming.

As the ringing fades, the screaming becomes nearly deafening.

In the background, the clanging of metal is unmistakable.

As oxygen finally starts to make its way into my lungs and my surroundings begin to sort themselves out, I become acutely aware that the screaming is more of a shrill wailing, bordering on deranged and animalistic.

Ari stands immobile, mouth open in horror, eyes vacant. She doesn't even look winded.

I turn to see what has her so deathly still, and my blood turns to lead, every limb weighing me down, rooting me to the spot.

Her words rip through my heart like an arrow, piercing me to my core.

"I made sure I would not be caught by surprise again. I made sure, if any of you returned, I would know as soon as you crossed the border into our home."

"I made a bargain to ensure the safety of my family."

"The entire time I am in your presence, so long as we are in these woods, my hand burns."

"You tricked me."

I retch, emptying the contents of my stomach.

"Ari." I breathe her name, still rooted to the spot. "No… I never—"

She turns to me, pure loathing in her eyes.

Her eyelids flicker, and though they mingle with the rain, tears stream down the sides of her face.

"It's not what you think—I never… I didn't… I have nothing to do with this…"

But she's not listening to me. I don't think she could hear me even if she wanted to, and I certainly don't think she wants to.

The air is thick with a tangy sort of sweetness—spicy and oddly alluring.

My stomach turns, and I retch again.

There's blood everywhere. The sheer amount of it is overwhelming. It coats the exterior of the cave, the mossy floor of the forest. It's splattered across dozens of trees.

Despite the scene before us, the blood itself catches me off guard. It's disarmingly beautiful—opaque and shiny, as if a thousand stars glisten from within the milky liquid.

I can hear them shouting now. The knights. Arguing over what to take and what to leave behind as they loot the cave. Deciding what's most valuable, deciding what they can carry.

She moves then, seeming to come to her senses, gliding like a wraith into darkness. Her feet carry her across the clearing toward the chaos in front of us. Slowly at first, then she's running again.

The closest knight has his back to her. How he didn't hear her screams, I do not know, but he never stood a chance.

By the time I register what she's done, she's already yanking her dagger from where she buried it in his neck.

There's a squelching sound as he chokes on his own blood, a soft thud as his knees hit the ground before the rest of him crumples onto the grass.

She's taken down two more knights effortlessly before someone shouts a warning, finally noticing her presence.

There are so many of them, easily three dozen seasoned and well-tested knights of the king's army. None of them, of course, wearing Camelot's coat of arms. None of them here on official business.

Idly, I wonder if Arthur even knows they're here.

I can't stop replaying those three words in my head—a continuous, torturous, haunting loop.

"You tricked me.

She thinks I led them here.

"You tricked me."

She thinks I tried to befriend her, only to stab her in the back.

"You tricked me."

She thinks I distracted her so they could kill the dragon.

"You tricked me."

Shrieking a battle cry that sends shivers down my spine, she swings the stolen sword in her hand, decapitating the knight in front of her.

SIXTEEN

ARI

Arrows litter the ground, sticking out of the earth at odd angles. There's a staggering number of them, whole and splintered and broken alike. They puncture the membraneous tissue of his wings and mar the webbing of veins within.

He couldn't have taken flight, even if he'd wanted to.

The rain has washed away some of the blood, but remnants of it are everywhere. On the rocks and the trees, the grass and the flowers. What should be shining and opalescent and strangely beautiful to look at is now dull and diluted in a pool around his body.

The layers of crimson scales he wears like armour have lost their iridescence.

The fire within him, the very thing that makes him magnificent, has faded.

"I'll be back before nightfall."

He lies there, motionless. Not breathing. No longer living.

His head, severed clean from his—

He'd known.

He'd known, and he'd sent me away.

He'd heard them from inside the cave…

"I love you, little dragon."

Why didn't we take to the skies? Why send me away? Why stay and risk fighting if he knew they were coming?

My breath comes in erratic bursts, and my hands shake uncontrollably at my sides. Lightning dances in my veins as my magic begs to be summoned, but I am unable to process anything beyond the horrific truth laid before me.

Penn is dead.

I don't understand. I don't understand any of it. How this happened. How they found us. How they managed to kill him.

I don't remember deciding to move, much less attack, but when the first knight hits the ground, a sick sort of satisfaction settles over me. The gurgling sound of him choking on his own blood, gasping for air, and the finality of the thud as his body hits the ground provides me with the briefest flicker of relief.

But it is only momentary and fleeting, and it does not last nearly long enough.

I have to force my eyes away from Penn's lifeless body—force away the onslaught of memories that threaten to bring me to my knees before I can even begin to enact my vengeance. Scattered fragments of images flash through my mind as the rain continues to pour from the sky and my feet continue to propel me forward.

Penn's bright red wings spread wide as we soar over the open ocean.

Penn stomping through the clearing, trailed by a trio of chickens.

Penn sheltering me from the rain with his wing.

Penn curled up on the dragonstone, snoring softly.

Methodically, I work my way through the knights who've invaded my woods—the murderers in my home.

The next knight drops easier than the first, both the noise of the storm and the speed of my rage giving me the upper-hand.

The third turns in time to see my blood-splattered face, shouting to his comrades. Beyond that, he barely has a chance to scream, let alone stop me.

The others have noticed me by now, so I grab the sword from the knight I've just felled, still clenched tightly in his fist. I test the weight of it, adjust to it. It's a good sword. Well made. It feels a bit awkward against the constant burning of my palm, but I let the pain fuel my rage.

The knight closest to me underestimates my abilities, now that I've traded the dagger for a weapon of size. He does not stop to defend himself, and when he rushes me, I release a primal sort of sound from deep within.

I can nearly taste the vengeance—feel it in my bones, begging to be released—and hone in on it, letting it spur me forward.

One clean arc of the sword removes his head from the rest of his body. Both pieces of him fall to the ground with a thud that momentarily satiates the growing bloodlust inside me.

The next two knights rush me at once. The first knight puts all his weight into the swing of his sword, which I manage to deflect, using the momentum to bury his blade into his companion. The blade slides between the leather ties of his armour, embedding itself in his ribcage. I use his stunned distraction to pull an arrow from the quiver at my back, plunging the tip deep into his eye.

By the time he drops, I've reclaimed the arrow and loaded my bow, shooting at the knight closest to me. I have to load and fire two more arrows in quick succession before that knight drops, too.

Someone tackles me to the wet ground; he must've crept around me while I was occupied with the others. Sitting atop my chest, he keeps my arms pinned to my sides with his knees. His fist connects with my face, and pain explodes along my jaw.

He punches me again, splitting my lip, and I spit out a mouthful of bloody saliva.

He palms a blade, holding it flush against my throat.

"Don't move," he seethes. Rain falls in my eyes, and I rapidly try to blink it away.

I swallow and relish the pain as the blade cuts into the skin at the base of my neck, and offer him the most unhinged, deranged grin I can manage.

Taken aback, he stares at me in bewilderment for a moment before regaining his composure.

"I'm not afraid of you," I hiss, baring my teeth.

"You ought to be." He sneers.

A handful of knights are making their way toward us, my advantage diminishing with each step they take.

"I ought to kill you right here and now for what you've done—"

"For what *I've* done?" I laugh. It's hollow and bitter. "I suggest you do exactly that, *knight*"—I spit the word at him, along with another mouthful of tangy saliva—"because if you give me the chance, I will not hesitate to remove your head from your shoulders, too."

His fist strikes me again, black spots forming at the edges of my vision. I welcome the pain like an old friend.

"Torr, don't!"

It's the deceiver, shouting for the knight atop me to stop. Sir Lancelot of the Lake, the betrayer.

Rage replaces the momentary respite, mingling with the bloodlust still thrumming in my veins.

I growl, glaring at the knight straddling my torso. "I will kill every single one of—"

His fist collides with my jaw a fourth time, and then the weight on my chest is gone.

Lancelot lunges at the knight, shoving him off me. They roll in the grass, struggling to regain their footing.

"What the hell is the matter with you?" the other knight shouts, righting himself. "She killed six of our men! What are you even doing here, Lance?"

Two more knights step into my line of sight—one tall and lean, the other shorter and stockier.

"Aye, *Lance,*" I snarl, "what are you even doing here?"

He looks torn for a second, unsure how to proceed. He offers me a hand, but I knock it out of the way, pulling myself to my feet on my own.

Gingerly, I probe the inside of my mouth with my tongue. There's a cut on the inside of one cheek and the tangy, coppery taste of blood coats my teeth. I spit a mouthful of it at my feet, running a thumb along my split lip.

The two new knights come to stand at my side, braced and waiting to be told what to do next. The shorter, stockier one reaches for my arm, but Lancelot's hand darts out to stop him. "Don't," he says quickly. "Just… just leave her."

"Just leave her?" Torr says through gritted teeth, levelling another hateful glare my way. "Are you daft? She just—"

"Better yet," I say, interrupting him, "just let me kill *him.*" My glare slides to Lancelot.

"Ari, you don't underst—"

"Do not speak to me!" My outburst makes them both flinch. The other knights eye me skeptically, sizing me up. Collectively, they survey the scene behind me, taking in the bloodshed of their fallen brethren.

"Who is she to you, Lance?" the one called Torr says, voice angry but steady.

He stares at me for a moment, a myriad of emotions warring in his eyes.

"No one," I breathe, answering the question when he won't. My words come out strained and hoarse. "I am nothing to him."

"Then who is he to you?" Torr rounds on me, a steely glint in his eyes.

A humourless ghost of a smile plays at the edges of my lips. "He's the reason my family is dead."

SEVENTEEN

LANCELOT

The knights of Camelot are still grieving the loss of Garreth; I cannot fathom how long it will take them to get past this.

I don't know what to do…

I don't know where to go from here…

Lines have been drawn, and I'm on the wrong side of them all.

I never intended to hurt her…

I never would have led the knights here…

And she'll never believe me, no matter what I tell her.

As angry and utterly shaken as I am by the loss of my friends…I understand why she did it. I understand, at least to some degree, the level of despair she must be feeling—the pure loathing and unchecked rage coursing through her right now.

A humourless smile lifts the edges of her lips as she says, "He's the reason my family is dead."

My blood runs cold, the air leaving my lungs in a single, pained exhale. Her words hit me like a physical blow.

Torr, Kay, and Graham turn to me in unison, their mouths agape.

"I don't understand," Kay mutters. "What is she talking about?"

My mouth opens and closes around a dozen different answers. None of them seem right—none of them seem fair, or like they could adequately explain the situation.

"The dragon," I finally whisper. Her throat bobs as she visibly swallows down a lump of emotion, tears lining her eyes. "The dragon was her family."

"Don't be absurd, Lancelot," Bors scoffs, pushing his way into our midst, sword in hand. "Dragons don't raise humans. They eat them."

She bares her teeth at him, barely containing the hiss on her lips.

Bors laughs—a deep, booming sound, loud and boastful—then levels a calculating stare at Ari. "You're feisty, aren't you?" He gestures to her with his sword then to the carnage behind her. "How's a little girl manage all that, hmm?"

Her nostrils flare, but she says nothing.

Her silence makes me wary.

"What are you doing all the way out here by your lonesome?" He begins pacing back and forth, but their eyes never leave each other. Each of them regards the other calculatingly, sizing one another up.

I'm almost embarrassed by the relief I feel that her rage is no longer solely directed at me.

"What d'you reckon we ought to do with you now?" Each of his questions bothers me more than the last, but what I feel is nothing in comparison to the visible fury building in Ari.

Bors nods at Graham, who moves to restrain her arms again. She moves so fast I barely track it—

Driving her elbow upward and into his nose, she draws his sword and retreats a few paces, rotating the blade once before aiming it at Bors. Graham cries out, covering his face with his hands. Blood gushes from his nose, bright crimson against his pale skin.

Some of the other knights have started moving toward us now, drawn away from the cave by the commotion.

Bors regards her curiously for a moment, then a slow, wicked smile spreads across his face.

"Am I to assume you are the one in charge here?" Ari growls, keeping her focus on him.

"Aye, Sir Bors de Ganis, captain of the king's army."

She smirks, chuckling smugly under her breath.

"Is that amusing to you?" he asks defensively, brows pulling together to form a deep crease.

"Not in the slightest."

"You killed six of my men in cold blood," Bors says accusingly.

"Their blood wasn't cold when I killed them."

He sneers, unappreciative of her tone. Before he can lunge for her, I step into the space between them. Possibly making the dumbest decision of my life, I turn my back to her so that I am face to face with Bors.

I can feel the stares of my fellow knights, but I do not look away from Bors. "Just let her go," I say, keeping my voice low and measured.

Bors can barely suppress his amusement as he glances at the knights around us. "Looks like Lancelot's in love, boys." Bors laughs, but there's no humour to it. "A bit infatuated, are we?" he says, turning back to me.

There's that word again. *Infatuated.*

Tristan's said it a dozen times since that first day, but coming from Bors' mouth, it makes my teeth clench together.

"She's no more in the wrong here than you are, sir," I say evenly.

Something hard slams into the back of my knees, causing them to buckle then smash into the ground. Her hand grabs a fistful of my hair, painfully twisting my head to the side. "I do not need you to defend me, *knight*," she hisses into my ear, and just like the first time I sought her out, the cold metal of her blade touches my neck.

I do not move nor speak nor swallow for fear of her slicing my throat. I'm not entirely convinced she won't do it out of spite.

"Killing another knight won't win you any favours," Bors says casually.

"I do not seek the favour of a knight." She mimics his tone perfectly.

Regardless of whether or not Bors kept his revenge plan from us, he's lost too many men already today to risk gambling with my life, too—something we're all evidently aware of.

"Release him," Bors demands.

My eyes dart between the gathered knights—Torr, Kay, and Graham, who watched her slay our comrades, Bors, who is technically responsible for us all, and those who still linger far enough away to be of little threat but close enough if they should be needed.

Arthur is going to be furious—at him, at her, at me.

I cannot see her face, but she must understand the gravity of the situation. I can tell she's stalling now, trying to find a way out of the corner she's backed herself into. The corner she was forced into.

"If I let him go, will you do me the same honour?"

"You have no honour!" Graham roars, hands still held to his face.

Her grip on my hair tightens, and I wince.

"Enough," Bors snaps, growing impatient. "I cannot simply let you go, for you have committed far too great an atrocity here today." She must open her mouth to respond because Bors puts one hand up in the air to silence her. "What I can do is take you to Camelot under my protection and promise you a fair trial for your crimes."

Even if I didn't know Bors, it would be easy to see that for the trap it is.

Again, her laugh is devoid of any emotions other than rage and disbelief. "And what, pray tell, is the alternative to that glorious option?" she asks.

His eyes flick to mine for a fraction of a second then back to hers. "We kill you here and now."

A tense, charged silence falls over the six of us, weighing down on me like an anchor.

"I have a better idea," she muses, voice light and airy.

"And what's that?"

Releasing her grip on my hair, she shoves me forward. Bors, Torr, Kay, and Graham all blanch, twitching with anticipation.

Scrambling to my feet, I hold both hands out toward her, hoping the gesture appears non-threatening. Hoping it doesn't spook her into action.

My breath hitches in my throat at the sight of her. Blood covers nearly every inch of the top half of her body. The dark crimson liquid is splattered across her face, coating her lips and teeth. It's soaked into her hair and shirt—both previously white and now so dark and bloodstained they're nearly black.

Her eyes slide to mine, rooting me in place. I've stared into those eyes so many times in the last few months—dreamt of them. Dreamt of her. All I wanted was to understand her. I wanted a chance at a future with her. To come back to her cave as a friend, not an enemy. To meet the dragon properly, and, hopefully, the mage.

And now?

The gravity of the situation, and what I've most definitely lost, threatens to consume me. My knees feel weak, and my stomach feels as if I'm going to retch again.

"I told you the cost for me was blood," she says softly, her voice little more than a murmur, "but I never said it had to be mine."

Her eyelids flutter closed, her mouth moving rapidly, the words barely audible yet just loud enough to discern that they derive from a language worth fearing.

Realisation sinks in, turning the blood in my veins to ice.

"Ari, don't…" Either she doesn't hear me or she chooses not to.

I've seen what she can do when she wants to heal someone…

I don't wish to know what her magic can do if she means to avenge someone.

"Lancelot"—Bors' words are both a question and a warning—"what is she doing?"

Another line is being drawn, only this time I do not know which side I stand on. All I know is that I cannot let her unleash magic on these knights, no matter how horrible a crime they committed against her.

I dive, tackling her to the ground. It's slick from the rain, and we roll in the mud.

She barely seems to notice. Her mouth still moves, still utters whatever spell she intends to release.

With a grunt, she pushes away from me. Opening her eyes and staggering to her feet, she seems unfazed as she slowly walks toward the other knights.

I draw a dagger from my belt without thinking, pure instinct to protect them—a*nd her*—taking over. Pulling one deep breath into my lungs, I stalk after her, striking the handle of my dagger against the side of her head.

She falters, then crumples to the ground, unconscious.

EIGHTEEN

ARI

Everything hurts. I'm groggy and disoriented, and everything feels heavy. My head pounds with each beat of my heart, pulsing in my temples and behind my lids. My mouth tastes stale and tangy, my tongue thick like cotton. It takes a couple tries to swallow before doing so becomes easy again.

The side of my head feels as though someone smashed it with a rock.

Gingerly, I lift a hand to the wound, wincing as my fingers come away red and sticky.

The cold floor beneath me seeps through my clothes—now stiff and caked with dried blood—soaking into my skin and chilling me to the bone. And while the medallion remains around my neck, the small blade once tucked into my boot does not.

Opening my eyes does not improve my spirits. My surroundings prove to be as grim and bleak as I feel.

The same cold, grey stone is everywhere. The walls, floor, and ceiling are all made of it, save for one wall, which appears to be a row of floor-to-ceiling iron bars. There is absolutely nothing inside the cell except for me; not a window, a piece of straw, nor a dusty spider web.

Slowly, I push myself into a sitting position, then to my feet, my muscles protesting furiously.

Wrapping my hands around the iron bars, I welcome the icy cold that burns my hands on contact.

"Hello?" I croak.

Silence.

"Hello?" I try a bit louder, clearing my throat.

There's a scuffling sound at the end of the hallway—a shuffling of feet, perhaps.

"Is anyone there?"

Again, I am met only with silence.

Exhaling a deep breath and pushing away from the bars, I begin pacing the small space.

It doesn't take much guessing to figure out where I am; the last thing I can remember is arguing with the knights of Camelot.

As if some internal floodgate of emotion to my heart has been opened, everything hits me at once—guilt, anguish, remorse…and rage, barely subdued and simmering just beneath the surface.

A thousand memories of Penn flash before my eyes, all of them tarnished with the final one of him lying dead and broken before our home. The knights of Camelot celebrating his demise, looting our possessions…

Camelot is the last place I ever wanted to set foot, and yet, there's no doubt that's exactly where they've taken me. Though the thought hits me with such startling clarity, it's immediately replaced with dread and terror.

Along with all those feelings, the one thing that stands out above the rest is the sting of Lancelot's deception. Because of him, because I trusted him, I lost everything.

I knew he was a knight of Camelot. I knew where he came from, and yet, I kept going back to him. Every time he came to see me, I met him.

Encouraged him. Opened up to him.

He made me feel excited and alive.

And still, he betrayed me.

I have no one to blame but myself.

I have no concept of how fast or slow time is passing—there is no window to mark the daylight, no one visible to track their movements. No one comes to see me. No one offers me food or water. It could be days or it could be hours.

By the time the first set of footsteps approach, I have paced this tiny cell nearly a thousand times, give or take.

"Stand back from the door." The voice is wary, unsure—and only vaguely familiar.

The one called Perci stands on the other side of the bars, a large ring of keys in one hand. Standing behind him, Tristan and one of the knights from *after* shift their weight restlessly from foot to foot.

Idly, I wonder if that's how I'm going to measure time now. *Before* Penn died and *after*.

I stare at them, taking in every detail I possibly can.

The way Perci won't make eye contact with me, and the slight hunch in his shoulders. The way Tristan's eyes focus on my hands, as if he expects me to use magic right here and now. The way the other one can't seem to keep his facial expressions under control, cycling through a continuous torrent of emotions.

Each of them wears black trousers tucked into black boots and a black undershirt beneath a black vest with Camelot's sigil stitched across the front—one red crown on top of another with a sword down the centre to represent the once and future kings and the sword that binds them. Tristan has a bow and quiver strapped to his back. The other two carry swords at their hips.

I don't move.

I don't do anything more than blink at them.

After a moment, Perci slides a key into the lock. It clicks loudly, echoing in the small cell when the door opens wide.

For several heartbeats, he only stares at me. His brown eyes finally meet my gaze with a multitude of emotions staring back at me, but all I can see is the knight Penn killed. They have the same eyes.

"I need to restrain you…" Perci says a bit apprehensively. Dark, coppery hair falls to his shoulders, once again, almost identical to the dead knight's. He's maybe only a few years older than me, and though he stands almost a head taller than me, his frame is both slim and muscular.

"There is nothing I can do to you in my current state," I say hoarsely, still struggling to regain my composure at the unmistakable similarities between them. "You needn't fear me."

"Oh, I highly doubt that." Tristan snorts, a wry smile lifting up one side of his mouth.

I regard him for a moment, trying to decipher his words and facial expressions, but his taunting is lacklustre and feels insincere.

I'm still pondering this when Perci slowly steps into the cell, restraints in hand.

"I am unarmed," I say absently, eyeing the thick iron chains.

"And yet, I'm sure you can do plenty of damage as is." He raises one eyebrow, meeting my gaze again and daring me to dispute his claim.

I don't. Instead, I offer him my hands, and he secures the cold metal around my wrists.

They lead me down the hall, Perci in front, the other two behind. A dozen cells line each side of the corridor, all identical to mine, all empty.

They take me up three flights of stairs, Tristan steadying my elbow when my foot slips on a slick step. We briefly make eye contact over my shoulder as I nod my thanks, but then continue on as if nothing happened.

When we reach the top level of the dungeons, Perci pulls something else from his pockets: a blindfold. A black piece of cloth long enough to wrap around my head at least twice and thick enough to block out any light—or any surroundings.

I simply close my eyes and wait, expelling a long breath. He secures it over my eyes, fastening it tightly at the back of my head. His hands shake ever so slightly, and the tiniest drop of satisfaction blooms in my chest at this response.

I don't care if he fears me, and it's unlikely that he would, but the fact that he wasn't there and I still manage to cause some sort of physical reaction in him is pleasing.

"This way," Tristan says in my ear, his hand coming to rest on my elbow. Gently but firmly, he leads me through a series of corridors, the path twisting and turning in a pattern I do not bother to memorise.

I have never set foot inside Camelot; even if I managed to escape the confines of the castle, I would have no idea how to navigate the streets or escape the perimeter walls, much less anything else, without provisions and a horse. The last thing I'm going to waste my energy on is memorising the layout of the castle.

"We're here," Tristan says quietly, pulling me to a stop.

The blindfold is removed from my eyes, and it takes a moment to adjust to the brightness. Light floods the stone corridor through a wall of windows. As my eyes dart around, taking in my new surroundings, I glimpse the sun high in the sky, the weather unusually bright and subdued today.

The two new guards standing in front of me pay no attention to us. If they know anything about me at all, they either do not care or have been instructed to appear as such.

Before us stand two massive doors carved from the ebony-hued wood of the mountain ash trees. The doors themselves are countless shades of black—charcoal to slate, obsidian to sable, and everything in-between—with random touches of red here and there, highlighting tiny features.

They are intricately carved, the details endless, and extraordinary, and nearly incomprehensible. Although I could be mistaken, it looks as if they depict the story of Camelot's creation.

Hungrily, my eyes dart across their surface, devouring the stories they hold.

A magical forest—*the* forest, *my* forest. Mythical beings, many of which I recognise, some of which I do not.

And *Penn*.

My breath catches in my throat.

Surely, it could be any dragon, but its likeness to him is uncanny…and unsettling.

I shove away those thoughts before they can fully surface, seeking out other details to focus on. The fables of the Old Legends; the four witch queens and the Lady in the Lake. The twelve conquered kingdoms and the sword in the stone—all of it, laid bare before me as I've never seen before.

In the middle, running parallel down the centre seam of the doors in bright red, sits nine crowns—five on the left, four on the right. Each one is minutely different from the last, each one representing an Uther king of Camelot. The extra space on the right must be for Arthur, to be filled in upon his coronation.

"M'lady?" Tristan's voice sounds foreign and distant. He steps up beside me, and I realise that I have no recollection of moving closer to the doors, no memory of reaching my shackled hands out to touch the intricate carvings.

Slowly, my eyes slide away from the doors, landing on Tristan's— equally jarring and refreshing after being engrossed in the complex and prophetic topography of Camelot's creation. His eyes are a mix of green and brown, a lovely shade of hazel that reminds me of the forest.

He holds my gaze unflinchingly.

Behind me, someone clears their throat. Tristan blinks, and the lingering moment of wonder and curiosity is broken. "Are you ready, m'lady?" he asks quietly.

"Don't call me that," I say, shaking my head. Taking a small step away from him, I turn back to the doors and nod.

NINETEEN

ARI

The throne room is large and incredibly overwhelming. Where the cells of the dungeon and the corridor outside were made of muted grey stone, the ones that make up the throne room are as black as the door at its entrance.

Torches line the walls at even intervals, the flames flickering and dancing in their sconces. The ceiling is high, and domed, and full of shadows.

Between each torch stands a knight, their hands firmly on their weapons. A number of them saw me disarm Lancelot—*the traitor,* I correct myself— the others no doubt heard about it.

Row upon row of wooden benches line either side of the room, each of them full of people. Most look to be more knights, wearing similar ensembles to those of my escorts. Some of them look to be important—dukes or earls, perhaps, with an extra shine to the baubles that adorn their clothes.

I've never seen so many people before in my life, let alone in one room. The overall effect is a bit daunting, and the sheer number of them is hard to keep from my thoughts. In theory, I understand that large masses live in any given kingdom, but to see it first-hand is entirely different. To think that all of them have names, families, jobs… The enormity of it, the weight of it, sends a cold sweat across my skin.

At the far end of the room sits a raised dais, and to the left of it is a smaller row of benches. A fearsome-looking girl in a pretty dress leans close to the girl next to her, whispering behind a gloved hand.

Her blonde hair is done in a series of intricate braids with gold rings woven into the strands. Both the colours she wears and the way in which she styles her hair are distinctly Northumbrian, meaning she must be Aethelfrith's niece, here to secure Arthur's hand in marriage.

Considering the sheer amount of bloodshed it took to remove the Vikings from Northumbria and the rising civil unrest within his kingdom, it doesn't surprise me that Aethelfrith would send the closest thing he has to an heir far, far away.

Cocking her head to the side, she regards me curiously, as if I am a puzzle to be solved. If she feels out of place in this room full of knights and important people, she does not show it.

On any other day, I might admire her.

On the bench next to her and her companion sit a handful of older men, all dressed in the red and black of the court of Camelot.

To the right of the dais stand two knights: Sir Bors de Ganis, captain of the king's army, and Sir Lancelot of the Lake, whatever that means. One of them avoids my gaze, his eyes sweeping over the crowd impatiently. The other simply stares at me, a thousand questions burning in his gaze.

I drop my eyes immediately, fighting the fresh wave of disgust and betrayal that courses through me. *Before*, when I saw those eyes, bright and blue and full of questions, I dared to wonder what might happen. Now, I would be content to never see them again.

A blood-red rug lines the steps and platform of the dais, with two black thrones at its centre. In one sits an older man with dark hair and dark eyes, looking agitated and impatient. In the other sits a boy my age, ruby hair atop emerald eyes and a scowl made of stone.

Though they pretend not to, they both watch me with the intensity of a hawk hunting its prey as I make my way down the aisle toward them.

Still, my escorts remain at my side, delivering me to the base of the dais. Tristan stands slightly closer to me than the other two—out of bravery or stupidity, I cannot tell. Both seem to go hand-in-hand with the knights of Camelot. He seems relaxed…at ease, almost, as if he neither fears me nor finds me intimidating.

Surprisingly, I find it the tiniest bit comforting.

So far, I think I hate him the least.

The silence that falls over the room is deafening. It goes on for an uncomfortable amount of time, each passing minute making me more restless than the one before.

Arthur appears to be rather insufferable—arrogantly draped across the throne, shirt rumpled and untucked, the black crown atop his head left crooked. His face is set somewhere between a sneer and a scowl, and something tells me it looks that way often.

If this is the monarch meant to rule Camelot, I feel somewhat troubled for its people.

Idly, I wonder what his childhood was like to make him appear this way. Is he always like this, or is he merely playing at portraying something he's not?

What was it like, growing up as a prince in a kingdom? Does he have friends or only people who serve him? Perhaps, he only has people who tell him what to do.

I consider what might turn the youthful ignorance of childhood into the hostile malice he beholds today. The battle stories of him are unimpressive, yet he's won every war he's fought, conquered every kingdom that's dared to cross him.

Just like his father before him.

But is that to the credit of his uncle, who rules until he comes of age? Or is that a son taking up the mantle of his late father?

Arthur opens his mouth, and then I regret wondering anything about him at all.

"This is the girl?" he asks incredulously, looking to Captain Bors for confirmation. The big, hulking man nods once. "Incredible." Arthur's scowl turns into a wicked grin, full of loathing and contempt. "If it weren't for all the blood, I probably wouldn't believe you."

He laughs—a hollow, airy sound. Stilted laughter echoes around the room in response.

"Do you have a name, *girl?*" he says, as if disgusted that he even has to entertain this conversation.

When I say nothing, Tristan nudges my arm.

"Aye," I say, refusing to break eye contact with the prince. "Ari."

"Where do you come from, Ari?"

"The forest."

His eyes narrow at my response, but he doesn't press me further. "My captain claims that you're behind the death of a number of my men—six, to be exact." When I say nothing again, he grows angry. "Well?" he demands.

"Was there a question?" I say, brows pulling together.

"You will address him properly," the man on the throne beside him says. Lord Regent Gawain, Arthur's uncle, and the late King Uther's younger brother.

Tilting my head to the side, I say, "Was there a question, Arthur?"

The prince's face reddens to rival his hair. Another small drop of satisfaction swells in my chest.

"You will address him as *Your Highness*," Gawain amends with a huff.

"Was there a question, *Your Highness?*" I ask for a third time, barely containing a sigh.

"Did you do it?" he spits out, teeth clenched.

I nod. "Aye."

Arthur stares at me for a moment, sizing me up, taking in the bloodstained clothes and the iron shackles at my wrists.

"Tell me, do you know the names of the men you slaughtered?" His tone holds a forced casualness to it, but his jaw works furiously.

Beside me, Perci flinches.

Again, a charged and entirely uncomfortable silence settles over the throne room.

"No?" Arthur's tone turns toward condescension. Absently, my hands open and close into fists in front of me. "Then let me tell you."

He stands and begins pacing the length of the dais. "Eamon, Leland, Roe, Kipp, Bron, and Sutton." He says each name slowly, letting the weight of each loss sink in. "Not to mention the eleven men lost to the dragon, and the one before." His eyes cut briefly to Perci, who flinches again.

"And what of the loss your men bestowed upon me?" I ask, unable to contain the rage in my voice. "Where is the retribution owed to me for the loss and destruction of my family at the hands of your men?"

Beside me, Tristan tenses.

Again, Arthur turns to Bors, a question in his eyes.

"I believe she means the dragon, Your Highness, although I do not understand—"

"*The dragon?*" Arthur whirls on me, his face a mixture of shock and disbelief.

"Aye," I snap. "*The dragon.*"

This time, when he laughs, it's sincere—a loud, hearty sound that comes from deep within his belly.

"The thing is," he says, still winding down from his outburst, "you are not deserving of retribution. My men took one life, while you alone took six, and your dra—"

"But that's—"

"Do not interrupt His Highness," Gawain snarls.

Arthur glares at him sidelong before continuing. "Your dragon has taken a total of twelve lives." His emerald gaze bores into me. "Eighteen lives of my men at the cost of one life to you."

The pride and malice in his eyes beg me to respond—to try to defend myself against him.

"The way I see it," he says, resuming the lazy strides he'd been making across the dais. "You owe the kingdom of Camelot for your wrongdoings, for the pain and loss and suffering you have inflicted upon its people, and the insurmountable damage you and your *family* have inflicted upon our army."

My hands clench so tightly that my nails split the skin of my palms. The magic thrumming through my veins itches, begging to be used, but I force myself to ignore it.

He pauses in his pacing for a moment, tapping a finger thoughtfully to his mouth. "Am I forgetting something?" he asks, eyes wandering around the room. "I feel like I'm forgetting something."

His eyes land on mine again, and then shift to my hands, still balled into fists at my sides as if he knows exactly what I'm holding back.

"Oh yes, the magic!" he exclaims dramatically, clasping his hands together in front of himself. "In case you were otherwise unaware, magic is forbidden in Camelot. And, unfortunately for you, several of my knights witnessed the beginning of what I'm sure would have been a very life-costing spell for my men. Lucky for you, I'm feeling rather generous today. Considering you didn't actually summon magic, nor did you use it on my men, we'll only sentence you for the crimes you did commit, with the understanding that, should you so much as think of uttering a spell in my kingdom, it will end with your head separated from your shoulders, much like poor Bron. Do I make myself clear?"

Blinking back tears of rage, I can do no more than nod as I swallow down a thick lump of emotion.

"Good," he says, a cruel edge to the smile ghosting his lips, "and instead of killing you, I think we'll put you to good use."

"What does that—"

"A lady's maid?" he muses, ignoring my interruption, eyes flicking to the blonde girl in the pretty dress. "No, perhaps not. I should probably see my investments come to fruition…" He sighs. "The forge? You're clearly skilled with a blade, perhaps you'd excel at creating them, too." He glances around the room once more. "On second thought, I don't think having you within such close proximity to weapons would be smart. Maybe the kitchens can find some use for you. Yes, the kitchens will be best, I think."

Clearly pleased with himself, he beams at me in earnest, as if he's done me some huge favour.

"How long?" I grind out.

"I beg your pardon?" His brows furrow, but his pretentiousness remains.

"How long must I serve in the kitchens?"

He seems to ponder this for a moment. "One year for each life taken by your hand," he says.

"By my hand?" I ask, heart racing.

"Would you rather I make it for each life taken?" he counters.

I shake my head, lowering my gaze.

"Then it's settled."

TWENTY
LANCELOT

Even from here, I can see the light fade from her eyes, turning the already muted colour nearly translucent. She says nothing, accepting her punishment without further challenge or protest.

A hushed murmur falls over the crowd as Arthur reclaims his seat upon the throne, dismissing her with a wave of his hand.

"That's it?" I whisper to Bors. He ignores me, his face unreadable.

I look to Arthur and the lord regent, the royal advisor, even Lady Guinevere. I look to Tristan and Perci, Kay by their side. I look to Ari, but none of them say anything.

Just like that, the hearing is over. Her fate sealed; the punishment decided.

"Where will she stay?" I ask before thinking better of it.

Arthur's attention turns toward me, his scrutiny nearly unbearable. "I beg your pardon, Sir Lancelot?"

"Where will she stay?" I ask again. "If she is to serve in the kitchens of Camelot for the next six years, she will need somewhere to live."

One corner of his mouth lifts up, and immediately, I regret drawing attention to myself.

"She's got a perfectly good cell already." His tone is full of mockery but, alas, holds no room for negotiation.

He turns his attention back to her and, for the first time, she flinches.

"A guard will arrive to escort you to the kitchen each day, remain while you work, and then return you to your cell when the cooks decide they are done with you. If you prove yourself to be valuable and a worthy citizen of Camelot, we can renegotiate your lodgings in a few years' time."

"She's to stay in that cell for a few *years*?"

I did not intend to say the words aloud, but I must have. Arthur, Gawain, and Bors all turn hostile gazes towards me.

"I apologise, Your Highness, Lord Regent, Captain… I understand the current situation is a bit…precarious, to say the least, but, surely, you can't expect her to live long-term in the dungeons?"

"Would you suggest I place an admitted murderer in the servants' quarters?" He laughs, but there is no humour to it. "Who should be so unlucky to share a room with her, pray tell?"

Arthur's tone is a warning, but I cannot help myself. "Then perhaps you will allow some improvements to be made to her accommodations, so that she—"

"Might *I* say something?" Ari's words ring through the throne room, loud but a bit shaky. Her gaze slides to mine for a moment, effectively silencing me as she says for the second time in as many days, "I do not need you to defend me, knight."

Every set of eyes turns to her.

Beside her, Tristan shifts on his feet uneasily as she returns her impassive gaze to Arthur.

Clearing her throat, she pulls in a quick breath. "Three years, instead of six—"

"I do not think you are in a place to negotiate right now," Arthur says, staring at her incredulously.

"Three years, instead of six," she says again through gritted teeth, "and

I will remain in the dungeons the whole time. I will do what is asked of me, I will serve my time in the kitchens—or wherever you deem fit—and I will not complain, not even once. Then, after three years, you will let me leave Camelot and return to my life outside its walls."

Arthur stares at her skeptically for several heartbeats, sifting through her words.

"Furthermore," she adds, heaving a deep sigh, "if Your Highness could find the compassion for it, I would be most thankful for the occasional respite; a chance to walk the streets—escorted, of course—to take in all that Camelot has to offer." She swallows visibly. "I'm merely asking now to spare wasting your time with an appeal in the future."

"Fine." He waves a hand dismissively toward her. "Let one of your escorts know when you seek this *respite*. They can bring it to my attention and I will determine if you have earned it or not. Do we have an understanding?"

Every word is more condescending than the last, yet, still, she nods.

"Yes, Your Highness."

"Leave us," he says, turning his attention to Perci.

Wordlessly, Perci, Tristan, and Kay lead her from the throne room.

Row by row, the knights of Camelot rise and depart, a low murmur rustling through the crowd.

"You," Arthur says, levelling a cold glare in my direction. "A private word."

I nod solemnly, following him to the hidden door on the far side of the dais. As I pass by, Lady Guinevere rises from her seat. She places a soft hand on my arm, and it takes everything in me not to recoil at her touch.

"Your bravery is commendable, dear knight," she says. I can't place the tone in her voice, but it feels off somehow.

Arthur's restrained annoyance turns openly hostile at the sight of her hand on my arm.

She merely smiles and walks away, lady's maid in tow.

My footsteps echo off the stone walls.

In all my haste to catch up to Ari, I still haven't thought of what I'm going to say to her.

When I finally find them, they've made it most of the way back to her cell, descending the spiral stone staircase to the bottom level of the dungeons. Her wrists are still bound by iron shackles, but Tristan has a hand under her elbow, steadying her on the slick stones.

Perci and Kay both whirl around at my arrival, Kay hastily drawing his blade.

"Are you mad?" Perci bristles. "You're just about the last person who should be here right now."

"What? Why?" I ask, confusion taking over my thoughts.

"Let's see," he says derisively, scolding me as if I were a child. "You defended her in front of the other knights, you jumped between her and Bors, and *then* you let her take you prisoner. There's a reason Arthur refused to put you on her guard rotation, Lance."

"Please, Perc, just let me apologise."

"Leave it alone, Lance," Tristan warns me sternly. He's no longer guiding her arm, and she's no longer in my line of sight. Tristan disappears around the corner after her, but Perci and Kay continue to block my way down the stairs.

"You ought to walk away," Perci says with a disapproving shake of his head.

"Are you protecting her"—I struggle to keep my anger in check—"from me?"

"Look." Perci sighs, pinching the bridge of his nose. "I understand that you want to apologise to her, and I'm sure you even have valid reasons, but, right now, I just need you to let me do my job."

"Give me five minutes, Perci, please."

Kay says, with a defensive edge to his tone, "You shouldn't be down here." It doesn't escape my notice that his blade is still drawn.

"What do you know of it?" I round on him, anger boiling through me. "You don't even know her—"

"And you do?" Perci challenges, daring me to contradict him. Daring me to admit that I'd done the one thing he and Tristan had warned me not to do. To admit just how badly I'd messed up. "You should get out of here before you get yourself into trouble."

"You don't understand. She thinks… I didn't… I just need to apologise." I sigh, overwhelmed with mixed emotions and the need to plead my innocence.

"You're about to cross a line, Lance, and I think you've crossed enough of those already. Go back upstairs before you do something stupid."

When I make no move to leave, he heaves a heavy sigh and continues. "You of all people should understand what it feels like to lose your family, be taken from your home, and forced to live in an unfamiliar place all at the same time," he says quietly. "I just think you should cut her some slack given the circumstances, and I think you need to consider the consequences your actions will have if you—"

"I never thought you, of all people, would be sympathetic towards her." I scoff, shaking my head.

"What's that supposed to mean?"

"Do you or do you not blame her for Garreth's death?" The words taste vile in my mouth, but I cannot stop them from coming out all the same.

He stares at me for a moment, his face nearly void of emotion except for that ember of anger flickering in his eyes—the only warning sign that I might've gone too far.

"Her dragon killed my brother…and now her dragon is dead. But it doesn't make me feel any better knowing she lost someone she cares about. The notion of being 'even' isn't all it's cracked up to be, apparently, so, as far as I'm concerned, there's no bad blood left between us."

I open my mouth to respond, but he cuts me off with an air of finality to his tone. "Walk away, Lancelot."

Quiet, muffled voices come from around the corner at the base of the stairs, followed by the soft scuff of leather on stone. Perci quickly glances at Kay, and I use their momentary distraction to push past them.

Barreling down the last of the steps and rounding the corner, I come face-to-face with the tip of an arrow.

"I told you to leave it alone," Tristan says evenly. "How many times have I told you that now?" he demands, anger growing with each word. "You have no business being down here."

Behind him, Ari stands immobile. I stare at her blood-covered face over Tristan's shoulder, her pale eyes vacant and locked on his back.

Behind me, Perci and Kay grumble, swearing under their breath as they join us in the corridor.

My gaze shifts back to Tristan, darting between his eyes. "What is this, Tris? Why are you pointing an arrow at me?"

"Because you lied," he growls. "I asked you if you'd done anything stupid, and you said no."

I close my eyes for a moment, pulling a deep breath into my lungs. "Tris, I—"

"You lied," he says again, "and eighteen lives were lost. Losing Garreth was devastating enough, and now this? Not to mention what you've done to her."

"Ari…" I turn back to her, pleading. "Please, let me explain."

"I told you not to return," she whispers, eyelids fluttering. "I told you not to come back."

Tristan stands steadfast between us, his arrow still aimed directly at my face. Absently, I wonder if he'd shoot me. I wonder if, after everything we've been through together, he'd release the arrow simply because he's been tasked to guard her.

Simply because I lied to him.

If there's one thing unequivocally true about Tristan, it's his loyalty—but does his loyalty to me exceed his loyalty to the crown he serves?

In this moment, I'm not so sure.

"You don't understand," I plead, head shaking. "It's not what you think. That's not what happened—"

"He's dead because of you." Her words come out as little more than a whisper.

"No, Ari." My head is shaking back and forth, almost violently now in my desperation for her to understand. "No, I would never do that... I never told anyone..."

Her eyes remain unfocused, still staring absently at Tristan's back. Perci puts his hand on my arm, but I shrug it off. The movement catches her attention, and the lifeless vacancy of her eyes is replaced with pure loathing, hostility rolling off her in waves.

"I told you not to come back," she says again, voice echoing through the empty cells of the dungeon. "I did not wish to tempt fate."

Tristan briefly glances at her as she steps up beside him, but his arm doesn't so much as tremble.

"Bors wanted revenge for Garreth." Beside me, Perci flinches. "From the very beginning, he wanted revenge," I say quickly. "We told him to let it be, to move on. We never... I never—"

She holds up her left hand, the scarred skin illuminated by the torchlight. "I went to great lengths to protect us..." She turns her palm so it faces her, eyeing it miserably. "And you ruined everything."

"No..." It comes out as a whisper but echoes like a scream in my head.

"What is it that you want from me?" Her voice sounds as broken as she looks.

"I just want a chance to explain. I want you to understand that I had no hand in…what happened."

She's silent for a moment, studying her hand. None of the other knights say a word.

"You never listen, do you?" she asks finally, tilting her head to the side, eyes snapping to mine. "I couldn't decide before if you were brave or stupid, but now, I know the answer."

"Ari, please—"

She bares her teeth, something resembling a hiss pushing through her lips. "Twice, I told you it would not be wise to return," she says again. "I told you I did not need you to defend me, neither with your captain nor your prince." Her anger rises with each word. "Just now, each of your comrades warned you against seeking me out, and, yet, you did so anyway.

"You never listen because you believe that you know what's best. You believe that whatever you decide to do is for the good of all, but you are wrong." Her chest heaves as she inhales a deep breath. "You were wrong to defend me, and you were wrong to return."

The moment the last words leaves her lips, she lunges, grabbing me by my vest and slamming me against the wall. My teeth cut into my tongue as my head smacks against the stone, ears ringing. Her forearm pushes into my neck, obstructing my airflow.

"Because of you, I lost everything," she seethes.

Neither Perci nor Kay make a move to stop her. Perhaps, they shouldn't.

Her eyes are murderous, but I do not flinch. I do not struggle nor try to push her away.

I do not have to.

Though her ferocity may know no bounds, she is both shorter and smaller than I am and cannot over-power me by strength alone. Perhaps, that is why none of my friends bother to stop her.

If she were using magic or had a weapon, I would defend myself.

If she were using magic or had a weapon, I would at least consider defending myself…

But she does not, so, instead, I let her work through her rage.

Because she's right. We both know she is. Regardless of my intentions, her dragon is dead. And had I not returned, he might not be.

Un-nocking the arrow, Tristan takes his time returning it to the quiver and securing the bow over his shoulder. Wrapping an arm around her torso, he drags her backwards down the corridor. She screams, shouting obscenities, kicking and thrashing the whole way.

The door at the end of the hall stands open, and they disappear into her cell. After a moment, he emerges, closing the iron door firmly behind him. Perci follows after them in silence, locking the door once more.

I pull in one greedy breath after another, doubled over and leaning against the stone wall. Tristan says nothing as he storms past me and back up the spiral staircase, Kay following close behind.

"Let it go, Lance," Perci says, eyeing my neck. He sighs, tucking the keys into the inside pocket of his vest. "This isn't an ideal situation for any of us. Try not to make it any harder than it needs to be."

TWENTY-ONE

ARI

True to his word, Arthur provides no improvements to my cell, and true to mine, I don't complain. I'm given a simple change of clothes and the odd bucket of water to clean myself with, and though it's ice cold, I'm used to the frigid temperatures of the lakes and streams in the forest, so it's almost comforting. And comfort, however small and fleeting, is one thing I never thought I'd be offered here.

As promised, a knight shows up to escort me to the kitchens, keep an eye on me while I'm there, and then return me to the dungeons at the end of each day.

Usually, it's Tristan. Whether he chose this assignment or was given it, I do not know, though I suspect the former—maybe out of pity or curiosity or some combination of both. He's polite and makes small talk, but wisely, does not mention the *incident*.

A nasty, purple bruise still mars one side of his face—though it appears to have started fading now—gifted to him by me with an errant elbow when he pulled me away from the traitor-knight.

Occasionally, Perci fills in for him, but his presence is usually awkward and the conversation is stilted or nonexistent. He's clearly uncomfortable around me, though his hand no longer trembles when he secures the iron shackles around my wrists.

Another knight, the one who was *there*—both in the forest and in the dungeons after my hearing—also rotates in occasionally. I've learned that his name is Kay, though he will not speak to me, no matter how hard I try to initiate conversation. Which, if I'm being honest, isn't very hard.

I have not seen Lancelot since I attacked him, and I suspect that a great deal of thanks is owed to my escorts for that. Despite whatever their loyalties are to him as a fellow knight, they've managed to keep him at bay.

While I don't imagine I'll be able to avoid him for the next three years, for the time being, I'll take what I can get.

The kitchen is enormous and proving a bit difficult to acclimate myself to. Part of me suspects that Eadlin and Elvi—identical sisters who come from a long line of kitchen servants—keep moving things around when I'm not there. They're both short with long blonde braids, matching brown eyes, and button noses. They giggle behind my back and knock things over at my station when they pass by. They can't be more than fourteen, but no one reprimands them, so neither do I.

They do, however, seem to have taken a liking to my escorts. Their cheeks darken to a deep shade of red when Tristan smiles at them or offers them bits of conversation, and they stare hopelessly after Perci and Kay, who ignore them entirely.

Lisbeth, the greying-haired, middle-aged woman who runs the kitchen, has been polite, but only just. She says as few words as possible to me— usually only enough to give me my tasks for the day. The first month, she watched me intensely, scrutinising everything I did, aware of everything I touched. It was extremely clear she didn't trust me nor did she want me in her kitchen. But, after a few weeks of showing up on time, staying late, doing the work given to me without complaint, and not causing any problems, she began to ease up.

Eventually, she realised that my restraints were hindering my productivity, and she started ordering Tristan to remove my iron shackles so that I could work more efficiently. As we got closer to all the festivities and our workload continued to grow, I was granted access to the cold storage cellar below the kitchens and the chicken coop out back—supervised, of course.

As it turns out, Tristan has a soft spot for chickens. But watching him interact with them—naming them and talking to them as he sneaks them handfuls of dried corn when Lisbeth isn't looking—only makes me think of Penn and the chickens we had when I was a child. So, anytime I have to go out there, I do so as quickly as possible.

Taite, another of the kitchen hands, seemed meek and quiet at first, but the more time I spend in her presence, the less sure I become of that observation. She handles a knife better than anyone else in the kitchen, her movements quick and sure, and she doesn't shy away from the less savoury tasks of plucking bird feathers or gutting fish. She rarely speaks, but when she does, it's usually to demand that more of a particular herb or spice be added to something. She's good at what she does, and she's often left in charge when Lisbeth is away.

The only other person whose name I've bothered to learn is Morgana's. She isn't the only healer in the castle, but she is one of very few, and from what I've learned through the twins' whispers, she's been in service to the crown for nearly three decades—despite looking only a handful of years older than myself. I don't see her often, but, occasionally, she comes in search of herbs and flowers—primrose and lavender, sage and elderberries, milk thistle and poppy pedals. She is as beautiful and wild as the plants she seeks—long midnight hair and sun-bronzed skin with green eyes ringed in gold.

I wonder what it must be like for a mage to serve a crown that does not tolerate magic. Alternatively, I wonder if Arthur knows what she is, but, surely, he must.

For the most part, the bulk of my chores include washing dishes, and peeling and chopping vegetables, though Taite did show me how to make a spiced dough for biscuits one morning.

All things considered, I could've received a far worse punishment.

Being forced to spend the next three years in Camelot isn't ideal, but so far, it hasn't been that bad, either.

When Kay arrived to escort me from my cell this morning, I managed to hide my disappointment at the lack of conversation my day would no doubt hold. In truth, I don't know how long it's been since my sentencing, but Kay still won't speak to me. It could be weeks or months, for I do not care to keep track, but the best I get are grunts of acknowledgment.

When we arrived in the kitchen, the top half of the wooden door to the courtyard was open wide, yet the room remained hotter than normal, making it less easy to hide my disappointment. Summer is upon us; yesterday's temperature was almost unbearable, and today's is already steadily rising. The dry heat will give way to a hot summer storm later today, leaving the air thick and humid. The kitchen is muggy, Taite's brow already slick with sweat.

Morgana has already stopped by the kitchens twice this morning, her continuous presence deeply unsettling the others. Her third arrival brings a deep scowl to Lisbeth's face. She watches Morgana almost as intensely as she watches me.

After spending a lot longer than necessary browsing the collection of jars lining the shelves, Morgana turns to regard me intently. Her head tilts from one side to the other, her sharp eyes studying me openly.

"Can I help you?" I ask, speaking for the first time today.

Out of the corner of my eye, I see Lisbeth and Taite both look up at me from their respective tables.

A small smile lifts both sides of Morgana's mouth, and we continue to stare at each other for a moment.

"I wasn't convinced before," she says absently, walking toward the table I'm currently working at, "but now that you look more like a human and less like a blood-thirsty forest creature, I have no doubts." She traces an index finger down the length of the table, eyes flicking to mine as she speaks.

"No doubts about what?" The words come out warily, without any of the tenacity I'd been aiming for.

Her smile turns calculating—cold in the overbearing heat of the kitchen. "I've seen your face before."

"What is that supposed to mean?" I ask, anger quickening my words. In the corner, Kay shifts on his feet, eyeing us curiously, but ultimately, he remains in the same spot he's been in all morning, holding up the wall.

"Exactly what you think it does," she says, one eyebrow arching.

"Aye, you've seen my face before," I snap. "I've been here for a while now."

"We both know that's not what I mean." An uncomfortable tingle ripples through my veins at her words.

"Leave me alone," I hiss, glaring at her.

Her face twists a little. Whether she's used to being spoken to with open hostility or not, I don't know, but it surprises me when she sneers and says, "As you wish."

She does not come back for the rest of the week.

The countless preparations for the month of festivities are well under way. Arthur decreed a month of celebration for his eighteenth name day, including a week-long tournament to name the new king's champion, and people have been coming in from all over the kingdom.

It would be almost insulting if it weren't so ironic—the prince's prisoner and murderer of his men, tending to the finer details of his most important affairs.

The only thing any of the servants talk about—not that they talk directly to me—is the upcoming events. The tournament, Arthur's name day itself, and his coronation all make for one very busy summer. There's also his rumoured engagement to Lady Guinevere, which surely means a wedding, although nothing has been confirmed outright yet.

My days consist of chopping and pealing, drying and preserving, and mixing and prepping things for the next day. By the time I return to my cell at night, exhaustion settles in immediately, overtaking me until one of the knights comes to rouse me in the morning.

My guards no longer bring my meals to the dungeon—Lisbeth allows me to eat in the kitchen with the rest of the servants, though I suspect that change was only to get me into the kitchens earlier each day, thanks to the ever-growing workload. Usually, the knight guarding me for the day will join us, too. They rarely turn down anything Taite cooks, and although it was a bit uncomfortable for everyone at first, it seems the others have grown used to having both myself and the knights around.

Kay flirts hopelessly with Taite, much to the twins' dismay. Perci is polite to everyone, though I've learned he went through training with Lisbeth's son, so he spends most of his time talking to her. And Tristan…

Tristan is the only one who bothers to talk to me about anything other than kitchen tasks. It feels sincere on his part—the interest and the curiosity—and although I am aware that it appears I'm indifferent to his efforts, I'm not. I appreciate that he bothers to speak to me at all. I simply cannot bring myself to feel any sort of way about it.

The last knight I opened up to betrayed me.

The last knight I opened up to cost me everything.

But, despite the numbness that keeps me from fully engaging with

Tristan, he never relents.

He asks me about life in the forest and seems genuinely interested when I talk about the different uses of plants; even Lisbeth and Taite stop to listen then, though they pretend not to. We talk about the weather and what his duties are as a knight. He tells me inconsequential things about Camelot—which baker makes the best pies, which tavern serves the best ale, which apothecary never carries anything to relieve a headache, and which iron-worker fits the best horseshoes.

We talk about anything and everything that doesn't skirt too close to personal, carefully avoiding topics that would cause too much of an emotional reaction. In truth, I much prefer the days when he escorts me to the kitchens, and I'm thankful that I see him far more than I do the others.

I've not had a break from my duties, nor have I wished for one since my start in the kitchen, so the only knowledge I've gleaned from the layout of the castle is that of my route from the kitchen to my cell, though I still have no desire to learn anything else.

The constant list of chores and tasks keeps me busy, and the full day spent on my feet keeps me so tired that I do not have time to think at night. That is how I cope…by working myself into an exhausted stupor so that when I am alone, when I am surrounded by silence, I neither have the energy nor the capacity to think. To grieve. I do not have time to process, to miss or to mourn. Even my dreams are nothing but unyielding darkness, a small mercy gifted to me by my subconscious.

I simply work and sleep, savouring conversation when I get it, and allow myself nothing in-between.

TWENTY-TWO

ARI

It takes roughly three months for the numbness following Penn's death to fade enough for the anxiety to set in. Three months of forcing myself to feel nothing, of not allowing myself to acknowledge all that I've lost—all that I've ruined. Three months of going through the motions, of working myself to the point of exhaustion, only so I can pass out as soon as I return to my cell.

I don't know what's different about today, or what caused the trigger, but the moment we start descending into the dungeons, my body seems to go to war with itself.

There's been a tingle at the base of my skull, growing more insistent over the past few weeks. A twitch to my fingers that wasn't there *before.* I blamed it on physical responses my body had created to cope with having to live in a world where Penn didn't exist anymore. To cope with having to live in a world where I'd be the only one to remember him.

Merlin never cared about him, Bax is gone, and the knights would no doubt move on, twisting their memories into exaggerated tales.

My heartbeat picks up, and my hands begin to shake. My thoughts begin to spiral, and the feeling that I've somehow lost control takes over, threatening to consume me.

How could I possibly have let this happen?

How could I have been so wrong?

How did I end up here?

The one thing I seem to be able to focus on is the fact that I shouldn't be here.

Before my sentencing, I had never been locked up. I had never been forced into a cage—literal or otherwise. I've always had the freedom to roam the forest and soar through the skies, and I never realised how much I had taken growing up in the wild for granted.

I've been so numb since *that day* that I didn't notice at first, but every time I'm forced to return to my cell, something inside me cracks and splinters a little more. Today, however, the slow damage done to whatever's left of my heart and my sanity must reach a breaking point.

Today, something in me finally snaps.

It took three months for the numbness to give way to hysterics, but in those three months, Tristan had been slowly chipping away at the wall I'd built around myself since the moment I saw Penn's lifeless body. The only person in this whole kingdom who, despite what I'd done, treated me like I wasn't a monster—like I was still human. Reminding me, bit by bit, that even if I'd lost everything, I was still here.

He's been my guard nearly every day since my trial. He's grown used to me, to my general indifference and calm demeanour. So, naturally, he picks up on the change almost as quickly as I do. He eyes me warily now as we make our way down the stone steps, brows furrowed. "Are you alright?"

"I…" My chest tightens, and my breaths turn shallow. "I don't know…"

"Ari." His hand is gentle on my elbow, pulling me to a stop beside him on the landing. "What's the matter?"

"I think it's my magic," I croak out, forcing the words around whatever's lodged in my throat, making it hard to swallow and even harder to breathe. "But I don't—"

"What do you need?" Tristan says evenly. His brow is deeply creased and his eyes are full of concern.

"A siphon." A cold sweat breaks out across my skin as my thoughts continue to spiral, and my chest heaves with the effort of trying to pull in air. I haven't used magic in three months. I've never gone this long without using magic before. Nearly every day for more than a decade, I've used magic. But now...

Magic is a living, breathing thing, meant to be cohesive with its wielder. Some self-preservation instinct or survival tactic must've taken over... some silent agreement between my body and my magic to allow me a moment to feel nothing before it would force me to feel everything.

I haven't used magic in months, and now, all at once, it feels as if it's going to destroy me from the inside out. The numbness must have been keeping the magic at bay, but no longer.

"What kind of siphon?" he demands.

He doesn't glance around to make sure we won't be overheard; he knows there are no guards posted down here when I'm in the kitchen. Currently, I'm Camelot's only prisoner, and in this moment, it is only he and I in the flickering darkness of the dungeon.

I can't think—can't focus.

"Ari," Tristan snaps, eyes intent upon my face. "Tell me what you need."

"I have to use some of it, I have to—" The trembling in my hands turns to full-on convulsing. My knees buckle, and Tristan half-drags, half-carries me down the remaining steps, his pace hurried but his arms steady.

Balancing me against the wall, he leaves one hand firmly wrapped around my elbow to help support me, his voice steady as he says, "Do whatever you have to do."

The implications alone could get him hanged for treason.

"I can't... I don't... I—"

"Look at me." His other hand comes up to my chin, carefully lifting it until our eyes lock. It's neither threatening nor intimate, but it does help me focus, reigning in some of my scattered thoughts. "Take a deep breath." His voice is soothing, placating some of the jittery lightning that seems to be bouncing through my veins. "It's okay." His tone is gentle but never once does it waver. "Let me help you."

I nod, and he lets go of my chin.

"How do you siphon it?" Neither of us have broken eye contact, and, afraid that it's the only thing holding me together in this moment, I refuse to even let myself blink.

I'm sweating. My breath is shaky and uneven when I answer him, the words coming out barely coherent and no more than a mumble. "A flower."

"What?"

Shaking my head almost violently, I backtrack. "Make a flower from a blade of grass. Slow the current of the river. Lure an animal closer. Mend a broken bone. Reverse the effects of poison. Something altering, or something constant, something to—"

"You can fix broken bones?" He stares at me intently, his hazel eyes searching mine.

"Aye."

"You're sure?"

"I've done it before." I nod, blinking distractedly at him. "Once on a mountain troll and many times on myself."

He nods then, pulling in a deep breath. "Okay," he says, then again, more quietly, "Okay."

"Okay?"

"Do you trust me?"

"What?" The question catches me off guard so much so, that for a moment, I forget about the panic that had been threatening to overtake me. "No—I don't know—What?" I manage to stammer.

"Do you trust me?" he asks again, arching a brow for good measure.

"I—I guess?"

He takes my hand and leads me toward one of the cell doors, immediately reigniting the wild emotions coursing through me. "It's okay," he says slowly, releasing his hold on me.

Pulling a dagger from his belt, he hands it to me, handle first. I reach out for it, tentatively taking the blade from him. "What—"

"Just take a deep breath, Ari," he says, as he, himself, takes a deep breath.

Untying a piece of leather from his wrist, he sticks it between his teeth, clamping down on the worn, braided material.

"What are you doing?"

His eyes meet mine again, and for a heartbeat, everything else seems to fall away. The calm certainty staring back at me is as bewildering as his next words. "Use your magic to fix it."

"What?" Alarm floods my thoughts once more, but he doesn't give me time to process his words before slamming the cell door closed on his hand.

I don't think.

I don't even breathe.

At first, nothing happens, but after a heartbeat, Tristan collapses, moaning. He slumps against the iron bars, hand clutched weakly to his body. His chest rises and falls rapidly, the leather bracelet still clenched between his teeth. He's panting, and sweating, and trying very hard not to scream.

That sound—or the attempted lack of one—is what surges me back into motion.

Dropping to my knees beside him, I've barely wrapped my fingers around the blade before the sharp edge of the dagger slices through my skin, blood welling in its wake.

Vaguely, I can hear myself chanting, begging, pleading with him to "Please pass out, please pass out, please pass out," but in my head, I'm screaming at myself, *"Don't pass out, don't pass out, don't pass out."* Just because blood doesn't make me squeamish and I've reset bones before doesn't mean I *enjoy* doing it…or the heightened element of urgency attached to it now.

There's blood everywhere, and his hand is a mangled mess.

Gingerly, I reach out to pull it into my lap, noting the tremor in his broken fingers. The moment I touch him, the scrunched up, harsh lines of his face smooth as unconsciousness claims him, the faintest bit of pressure enough to push him over the edge.

Already a dark purple welt is forming across the back of his hand, and the cut on his palm is so deep that I can see past the blood and chaos to bone and sinew beneath. The urge to retch crawls up my throat, and I have to force it down, focusing only on fixing his hand. "What did you do?" I whisper, over and over again.

The incessant stinging across my palm and fingers sharpens my focus. Wrapping my bleeding hand around his, I start muttering in Latin, directing my thoughts to his mutilated hand—to mending, fixing, rebuilding.

Relief courses through me almost instantly, though, for a long moment, it still feels as if lightning *zings* through my veins, begging to be released. But, slowly, as I watch the cracks in the bones erase themselves and the skin knit itself back together, the sensation starts to dissipate.

There's a lot of blood—on him, and on me—but he's no longer bleeding, and in another moment or so, the cuts on my hand will stop as well.

Sending a final surge of magic through my hand into his, I can't help but wonder, *Why would he do that? Why would he help me like that?*

And what if I had failed?

I sit there like that for a long time, clutching his hand in my lap, fingers wrapped tightly around his. He's leaning against the wall of iron bars, head tipped back, eyes still closed. He looks so serene—so peaceful. As if any remnants of what happened no longer linger.

"I'm sorry," I whisper, but what I wish to say is, *Thank you.*

He stirs, eyes moving rapidly beneath closed lids. After a moment, his brow furrows. "What for?" he murmurs groggily.

"You're awake." Releasing a long breath, I sag against the bars with relief.

"Did I pass out?" There's an air of amusement to his tone that immediately sets me off.

"What the hell is wrong with you?" I demand, tossing his hand back at him as if it'd burned me. He eyes me unsteadily, then lifts his hand in front of his face to admire my handiwork. Almost nothing remains—no indication of his actions at all except for the angry pink scar across his palm. "What if I hadn't been able to do it? What if I hadn't been able to summon my magic? What if I hadn't—"

"But you did."

"But you couldn't have known that I—"

"But you did," he says again, more firmly this time. He chuckles, and I want to punch him. "I've seen you mend a dragon wing… Do you really think that I would have done it if I thought you wouldn't be able to fix my hand?"

"They're not even made up of the same materials!"

"Aye, but you said you've mended broken bones before. Once on a mountain troll and many times on—"

I do punch him then. My fist collides with his shoulder and he grunts, though it seems mostly out of surprise and not because I actually hurt him.

"You're an idiot."

He chuckles again, pushing himself into a better sitting position.

"Thank you." When his eyes meet mine, a bit tired but free of pain, I can't help smiling at him, even though I'm shaking my head. "Thank you," I say again. "You didn't have to do that. I don't know how to repay—"

"It's okay," he says softly. "Are you…okay now?"

I nod, letting my eyes fall closed. "I've never gone that long without using magic before. I don't know what happened… I never even thought about it after…"

"It's okay." He nods.

"I shouldn't be here," I whisper into the silence of the dungeon. The only sound is our steadying breaths and the flickering of the torches on the wall behind us. "I should be in the forest. I should be in my home. I should be with…" I have to force a shaky breath into my lungs, and then another before continuing. "I shouldn't be washing dishes and chopping vegetables. Maybe I shouldn't have reacted the way I did, but… I shouldn't be here."

"I know." His voice is still soft and calm, reassuring in the darkness.

When our eyes meet, the brown-green colour of them reminds me so intensely of the forest that it causes my chest to tighten again. "How did they know?" His brows crease, but I open my mouth again before he can respond. "How did Bors…know where to…" I can't bring myself to finish the question, but Tristan doesn't make me.

"He had Lance followed." His tone turns wary, and he clears his throat before continuing. "After your hearing, Lance confronted Bors. He was drunk, and it was stupid, but if he hadn't then we probably wouldn't have known."

Somehow, this surprises me.

Heaving a sigh, Tristan looks away, shaking his head. "Bors never understood why we didn't want revenge for Garreth. If I'm being honest… I think he really just wanted to say he took down a dragon. I don't think he cared about revenge at all; it was just easier to rally the others behind him that way. He didn't want to risk any of his own men not returning, so he hired sell swords and mercenaries—anyone with an eye for gold and a shady task, and sent them into the forest. Eventually…they found what they were looking for."

"If any of the knights of Camelot…" Merlin's words drift through my head again. But they weren't knights. That's why I didn't know. I was focused on the fact that it didn't specify any one knight, but, instead, that Merlin's wording encompassed them all. I never once considered that who it didn't include could also be a problem.

We sit in silence for a moment, each of us lost to our thoughts. Eventually, Tristan pulls himself to his feet, offering me a hand to help do the same.

"Are you sure you're alright?"

Unwilling to lie to his face, instead I deflect, saying, "You're going to have a scar. I can mend things that are broken, I can fix the damage, but I can't make it so that it never happened at all."

"I have plenty of scars already. One more won't make a difference."

When Tristan returns a short while later, it surprises me. I hadn't expected to see him until the morning. "Do they miss me so dearly in the kitchens already?"

Unlocking the door to my cell and placing a brown leather satchel at my feet, he chuckles to himself. "I figured you'd be hungry after using that much magic… And maybe you'd like a shirt that wasn't covered in blood."

"Oh," I say, blinking back my surprise. "I—thank you."

He waves away my gratitude and crouches in front of me, pulling things from the bag: a skein of water—which I immediately drain half of—a leftover bread roll from dinner, a perfectly ripe plum that instantly makes my mouth water, and what looks like a folded-up tunic.

"This is… You didn't have to do this, Tristan."

His eyes meet mine in the dimness of the dungeon, the torches casting flickering shadows across his face. "You're not the first magic-wielder I've known," he says quietly. "I know how much it can take out of you—how much it can drain you. Bringing you something to eat and a clean shirt afterward takes little effort on my part."

"You've done more than enough already." My tone is careful, hesitant. I don't know how to navigate this new layer of debt that's settled between us. What he did for me was… I don't know if I'll ever understand why he did it, but I know I'll certainly never be able to repay him.

"Now that I know how handy you are to have around, I might just have to convince the prince to let me drag you into battle as my own personal healer the next time we go to war."

"I'm sure it wouldn't take much to convince him to let you drag me into battle." I laugh humourlessly, shaking my head. "In fact, I'm sure he would delight in being rid of me so quickly."

"I don't know about that," Tristan says, pushing himself to his feet and offering a hand to help me up. "If he wanted you dead, I don't think you'd be here right now." There's a weight to his words, something about the way he says them that makes me pause. "Then again"—he snorts, pulling me to my feet—"maybe he just wants more help in the kitchen."

Handing me the folded shirt, he turns around to give me privacy. Pulling the blood-stained one off and replacing it with the soft fabric of the new one, I can't help smiling a little. It's big—too big for me—but it's light and comfortable. And it's clean.

The sleeves hang well past my hands, but I roll them up past my elbows, and the hem falls to the middle of my thighs, but I tuck it into my pants as best I can. When I inhale, it smells like Tristan.

"Did you give me your own shirt?" I can't keep the surprise from my voice.

"I'm not in the habit of stealing other people shirts." His tone is amused.

It smells sweet and a little earthy, like lily of the valley, or the way the forest smells after a quick burst of summer rain.

"Thank you," I say softly.

He turns to offer me a small smile over his shoulder. "Of course, m'lady." I glare at him, and he full-on grins.

He reaches for the dirty shirt, stuffing it in the satchel. "I'll see if I can get the stains out, but I hope you weren't too attached to this shirt..." He scratches the back of his head as his words trail off.

"It wasn't mine, anyway." His eyes snap to mine, one brow arched, so I elaborate. "Perci brought it for me after my trial. I don't even know whose it is."

"Well then." Tristan chews on his lip for a moment. "I'll see if I can get it clean so that you have a spare."

"Why?" I ask. It's only one word, but it's the only one relevant enough to encompass all the lingering questions I still have.

"Why not?" He shrugs.

After that, I make an effort to find some small, insignificant way to use my magic as often as I can. Nothing big enough that would warrant notice, but *something* all the same. Anything to alleviate the edge and to help maintain the balance once more.

In my cell, I pick at the skin around my nails until it bleeds so that I can use my magic to silence the water drip at the far end of the dungeon. To warm the stones beneath me at night, just enough to prevent chills.

When the heat in the kitchen proves too stifling, I find a knife to graze my finger against, so that I might offer those of us working there a reprieve. In the courtyard garden, several of the late-summer produce has found itself ripening early after I happened to scrape my hand against a bit of rough tree bark.

Twice, Tristan has let me repair a worn spot in his leather training armour, and once, he even let me use my magic to mitigate a headache after a night of too much drinking. He was unsuccessful in getting the blood stains out of my old shirt but, as it turns out, my magic was able to take care of that, too.

Nothing I've done should instigate any attention, but it's still a fine line to walk, considering the implications of what would happen if I get caught—for me and for Tristan.

After the day he broke his hand to help stave off the ensuing panic attack, Tristan started taking the long way back to the dungeons. We'd walk slowly, winding aimlessly through the servants' corridors on the main floor until eventually finding our way back to the staircase leading to the cells beneath the castle.

The worse it got—the feeling of being caged in, the hopelessness—the slower we walked. If Perci or Kay were my guard for multiple days in a row, once Tristan was back on my rotation, he'd find an empty corridor with large windows, and we'd simply sit there, letting the golden rays of the setting sun warm our faces.

Somehow, he knew what was happening—knew it was so much bigger than just my magic, and for his kindness, for the distractions I never knew to ask for, but needed all the same, I will be forever grateful.

TWENTY-THREE

LANCELOT

"*Let it go.*" That's all I've heard for the last three months. *"Just let it go, Lance."*

I don't want to let it go. I can't let it go. I'm too angry to let it go.

I need to make things right. I need to find a way to apologise to her. To make her understand that I had no part in… That I would never…

I never meant for this to happen. I never meant for her dragon to die or for her to be taken prisoner. Of course, I never wanted that to happen.

But I didn't know Bors was having me followed…or that he'd hired the scum of the city to go in search of the dragon. How could I have known?

Perhaps, if I had paid more attention—if I hadn't been so wrapped up in just seeing her one more time—perhaps, I might've noticed. If I hadn't been so wrapped up in making her smile, and laugh, and slowly watching her open up to me…like a flower blooming before my eyes.

Each time I saw her, she was more relaxed, more excited, more trusting.

If I had listened to Tristan and Perci… If I had stayed away… If I hadn't been so wrapped up in *her*, perhaps none of this would've happened.

There's a ruckus across the tavern, a group of off-duty knights roaring at one another over mugs of ale and whatever card game they're playing. The barmaid purses her lips, eyeing them distastefully over the plate she's drying.

Leaning back in my chair, I cross my arms and nod in her direction, signalling for another drink when she makes eye contact.

Despite the fact that I'm on my fourth round of ale, *that day* comes flooding back. It always does. No matter how much I drink to try to numb my thoughts…to try to numb the guilt…it never seems to work. It never seems to be enough.

Everything about that day was wrong. Each thing that happened was worse than the last.

Ari showing me her scarred hand and telling me about the deal she'd made to protect them—from us. Racing through the forest only to arrive too late, for the dragon to already be dead. Her cutting down knight after knight in a blind rage, the need for vengeance a living, breathing thing. Bors stepping in and declaring her prisoner, only for her to take me prisoner instead. Her lips daring to utter a spell I could not let her unleash, no matter how wronged she'd been, leaving me no choice but to knock her out in order to stop her.

The defeated look in Ari's eyes when she accepted her punishment from Arthur will haunt me forever. Other than the first time we met, when everything about her was tense, and angry, and determined, and then her apprehension upon my first return, I've only ever seen her eyes alive with laughter and excitement, or curious and wistful…

But never defeated. Never hollow. Never lifeless.

And then, Arthur's heated words after the hearing… I'd followed him through the hidden door on the far side of the dais and into the little antechamber beyond. He'd whirled on me so quickly, so indignantly, that I couldn't help flinching.

"Whatever your intentions with the prisoner, let it end now. I will not have one of my knights consorting and conspiring with a known murderer, no matter how pretty you may think she is. Whatever there was between you, whatever caused you to defend her—to step between her and your commander—let it

die with our men in that forest." His eyes had been full of loathing, but for me or her, I couldn't tell. *"Do I make myself clear?"*

And my so-called friends, not even giving me a chance to explain—a chance to make things right. I begged Perci—*begged him*—and still, he wouldn't relent. Treating me as if I had no right to be there—as if I couldn't possibly know her well enough to try to gain her forgiveness for my hand in what happened.

I've spent hours and days across weeks and months getting to know her. All of my spare time spent learning all that she would offer me. Every chance I had, spent trying to work toward something with her, trying to build something between us.

I need to find a way to apologise to her. To make her see reason. To make her understand.

"I told you to leave it alone." I can hear Tristan's self-righteous words, clear as day, even now. *"How many times have I told you that now?"*

The barmaid returns, ale sloshing over the rim as she sets it down on the table, but I barely notice. Still distracted, I huff, shaking my head back and forth, curling my lip at the memory.

Who is he to tell me no? Who is he to decide I can't speak with Ari? Who is he to point an arrow in my face and pretend it's for her benefit?

"Because you lied." Tristan's voice is a growl in my head. *"I asked you if you'd done anything stupid, and you said no."*

You never would've understood if I'd told you, I think miserably. *You never would've accepted my choices…or my feelings for her.*

I don't care if he's her primary guard. He doesn't know her, and he doesn't know how badly I need her to forgive me. What it could cost me if she doesn't.

Sighing, I take a long drink, savouring the sweet burn of the liquid as it warms my chest.

"He's dead because of you."

"I told you not to come back."

"Because of you, I lost everything."

Her words hit me like physical blows, one after the other, relentless in their assault.

I drain the remnants of my mug in one gulp. Glancing around the tavern, I find myself glaring at the rest of the knights. I've heard them whisper about me when I pass by, heard the things they say.

They don't get it. They weren't there.

And now, Bors is punishing me, too. Putting me on the worst rotations, making me responsible for the most-inept trainees.

Everyone is mourning the loss of the knights slain by Ari. Hell, half the knights are still mourning Garreth, but because I hesitated, because I put myself between them, because I defended her…

Maybe she's right, I think pathetically. *Maybe I have ruined everything.*

TWENTY-FOUR

ARI

"Are those for this evening?" The voice is both new and close, snagging my attention. It's feminine and has a distinctly northern lilt to it.

"Oh, Lady Guinevere." Taite drops into a curtsey beside me, elbowing me sharply in the ribs when I do not follow suit.

"Please," Lady Guinevere says, smiling demurely at us. "No one is looking. There is no need for formalities with me."

Slowly, Taite rises, glaring at me from the corner of her eye. "Apologies, m'lady—"

"No, no." Lady Guinevere holds up her hands, warmth spreading across her cheeks. The usual braids and gold rings adorn her side-swept hair. Her dress is a pale plum colour with gold lacework on the bodice. "Our friend here was not raised the same way we were. I do not ask her to follow an etiquette she is not accustomed to."

"As you wish, m'lady," Taite says nervously, her soft brown eyes darting from Guinevere to me. "Is there something I can assist you with?" she asks, glancing around the kitchens. She and I are the only ones here— Lisbeth and the twins left for the market hours ago, and everyone else is either busy elsewhere or off today. Perci was called away to handle something at the behest of Arthur nearly an hour ago, promising to return as quickly as he could, though Taite waved him off, saying that it wouldn't be a problem.

"There is." Guinevere smiles again, and to her credit, it seems genuine. Her accent is both charming and refreshing. Harsher than Tristan's, even though her disposition is demure. "I was wondering if we might go over the dessert menu for Prince Arthur's name day?" she asks, gesturing to the hallway. Lisbeth has a small office down the hall where she keeps her lists and orders, a large bottle of amber liquid, and a small supply of bandages and healing ointments.

"Yes, m'lady, absolutely. Lisbeth is away from the castle, but I'd be happy to go over the menu with you." Taite wipes her hands on her apron, following Lady Guinevere into the hallway.

I would consider trying to escape if I had any idea where to go once I left the kitchens, but even with our recently scenic trips back to the dungeon, Tristan has still been careful not to show me a way out. Instead, I return to the massive pile of root vegetables for tonight's stew: golden potatoes, purple carrots, and sweet onions. Several cloves of garlic, a dozen ears of corn, and half as many heads of celery now sit abandoned next to me.

The fire in the massive stone hearth crackles and spits, the air before it shimmering slightly. A surge of static in the air tingles the hair at the back of my neck, rippling over my skin. The sensation is so familiar, and yet, has somehow become foreign over the last few months that, for a moment, I can't quite place it.

"Ari?" My name is as much a question as it is a greeting. It startles me, chilling the blood in my veins and quickening the pounding in my chest. Slowly, I turn around, equally exhilarated and afraid. Exhilarated at the mere thought of leaving Camelot. Afraid that I only imagined his voice in the first place.

"Merlin?" I ask hesitantly.

For a moment, I simply stare at him, trying to convince myself that he's real. Trying to convince myself that he's actually standing in front of me, close enough to touch. Trying to convince myself that fate and coincidences are real, and that this might be the singular greatest moment of chance in my life.

Unlike the last time I saw him, today, he looks normal and healthy. His clothes are neither torn nor dirty, and his eyes—while still heavy with lifetimes of memories and problems and substance—no longer have dark purple smudges beneath them. They no longer hold the unsettling wildness that made me so uncomfortable after our scare with the dryads.

His eyes flash, green-gold and bright in the dimly lit kitchen, breaking the momentary spell of immobilisation rooting my feet to the ground.

Launching myself at him, I wrap my arms around his neck, burying my face in the space between his chin and shoulder. His arms encircle my torso tightly in response. "Always a pleasure." He chuckles into my hair.

He's real…

He's here—right now, in front of me, in the castle kitchen, in Camelot. *He's here.*

He takes a step back, holding me at arm's length, eyes roaming over me from head to toe.

"What are you doing here?" I blurt out, ignoring the tears welling in the corners of my eyes and the relief that seeps into my chest.

"I came to see you—to check on you," he says, eyes darting back and forth between my own. "Ari, I'm so sorry…"

"We have to hurry," I say, wiping my hands on my apron. My fingers reach for the strings tied behind my back. "Before anyone returns."

A shadow crosses his face, and there's a tick in his jaw as he looks away. His eyes travel around the room, landing on nothing in particular but taking it all in nonetheless.

"What is it?" I ask warily.

It's not until he refuses to meet my gaze that I understand.

When he takes another step back and makes no move to whisk us out of here, dread replaces the flutter of relief I'd felt only a moment ago.

"You've not come to take me home," I whisper.

We both know it's not a question, not really.

"I needed…" he starts, then clears his throat, swallowing visibly. "I wanted to make sure you were okay, that you were unharmed."

My eyes lose focus somewhere over his right shoulder, a thousand images flashing through my mind—the past, present, and future all rearranging simultaneously before my eyes. In one instant, after more than a decade of knowing him—trusting him—everything I thought I knew shifts.

"Do share what your definition of 'okay' and 'unharmed' are," I snap. Tears well in my eyes again, flowing freely down my cheeks now.

"Ari, I—"

"You should leave." I interrupt, still refusing to look at him. The words come out choked and bitter. "Before someone returns."

"What would you have me do?" he pleads, shifting and dipping his head, trying to get me to look at him. When I refuse to meet his eyes, his thumb and forefinger grip my chin, gently turning my face so that I have nowhere else to look. "You cannot return home, Ari. Not now, not while it's like that. Where else would you go?"

In my haste, I never even considered what it would mean for Merlin to simply remove me from the castle and return me to the cave—or what I would find upon my arrival.

Absently, somewhere in the far corners of my mind, I assumed that when I do return, after however many years of service to Arthur—providing he holds up his end of the bargain—there will be almost nothing left if, and when, I make my way back to the cave. Penn's body will be decomposed, his flesh long gone, nothing but worn and weathered bones left to remind me of my failures.

But if I were to go now, if I return home after only several months' time… I do not wish to acknowledge the horrors that would await me. "Surely, you could—"

"It would not erase the pain, Ari. It would not erase the memories so soon after it happened."

For the sheer size of the kitchen, it suddenly seems so small, the walls closing in on me from all sides.

"Then, surely, you could take me somewhere else…anywhere else. You don't even have to—" The pained look on his face has the rest of the words turning to ash in my mouth.

You don't even have to stay with me, if you don't want to. That's what I was going to say, but perhaps, he never wanted that at all. Perhaps, everything that's happened between us over the years meant something entirely different to him. Perhaps, the idea of rescuing me—of helping me escape—is the last thing he wants to be responsible for.

"I'll make a deal with you," I blurt out, desperate. If he doesn't feel the way I thought he did, then at least I still know the one thing he loves above all else. I still understand what he covets most: being in control. "I'll make a deal with you if you get me out of here."

"I'll do anything," I add weakly when he still doesn't answer. "Name your terms and I will pay the price."

His brows furrow, lips pressed together, jaw working furiously. "Ari, I—"

"You could have saved him," I whisper. My breath hitches, and I sway on my feet at the thought.

He reaches a hand out to steady me, to comfort me. I pull my arm away, bracing myself on the table instead.

"Aye," he says tightly. "If I were there."

"I tried to summon you," I murmur. "I was covered in the blood of the knights. I spilled so much of it. They thought I was going to use a spell, but I… I tried to summon you."

"I'm sorry, Ari. Truly, I am." His tone is uneven, his expression uneasy.

"I tried to summon you, but it didn't work." I swallow down a lump of emotion.

After a moment, he says, "Ari, I cannot stay…"

I nod, waving him off with a hand, already succumbing to the hopelessness seeping back into my chest. The thought of returning to my cell today after the possibility of freedom was so close, I could almost touch it…

It takes great effort to keep my hands from shaking.

"I'll return again," he says quietly. "I'll come back and—"

"That's not necessary," I say, looking up at him with fresh resolve. "I wish for no reminders of my old life."

He stares at me for a long time, a myriad of emotions flitting through his eyes. Just as my trust in him has shattered, it seems that through the duration of this conversation, something has changed for him, too.

"Who else will bring you dragon's blood?" He says it almost angrily, as if neither of us can grasp a reality in which I do not rely on either it or him. Pulling a long, thin glass vial from his pocket, he holds it out to me, the opalescent contents seeming to glow between us. "Now is not the time to consider weening yourself from it. Not when you are surrounded by those who neither trust nor accept you."

I can't help but laugh—a cold, callous sound. "It's been months, Merlin. If you were so concerned about me not having dragon's blood then what the hell took you so long to come here?" Shaking my head, I ask through gritted teeth, "If you were so concerned, then where the hell have you been?"

I snatch the vial from his hand and pocket it before either of us can change our minds.

"I do not think you understand what I'm saying," he grits back. "Your eyes are already beginning to change. Your hair will not take long to follow suit."

"I—"

The scuff of leather on stone in the hallway startles me and my attention shifts to the door leading to the hallway. The moment I look away, the hair on the back of my neck stands on end.

My head whips back to where Merlin stood a heartbeat before, the air now slightly distorted in his place. Gone is the man who could save me.

Gone is the man who could have saved my dragon—and in his place is the boy who took everything from me.

TWENTY-FIVE

LANCELOT

"Can we talk?"

"No," she says angrily, swiping her hands across her face. Tears still fall freely from her eyes.

She no longer looks like a tree nymph or one of the forest folk. Now that she's out of the forest, she looks just like one of us, though she's still a little pale. Still a wrathful little wildflower, if a bit withered.

My breath catches in my throat, both at the site of her and at the resentment in her tone. It's been months since I've seen her, and just like the first time, I can only stare, completely and utterly mesmerised.

"You're upset," I say weakly. "Some fresh air might help clear your head."

Fighting off the remnants of my third hangover this week, I was making my way to the training ring when I spotted Perci heading in the opposite direction of the kitchens. I knew he was on Ari's watch today and decided it was worth the risk of pissing him off if he found me in the kitchen when he returned, if only I could talk to her for a moment.

I've tried to see her so many times over the last several months, all to no avail. I've never made it as far as the kitchen before, as there are always guards posted at either end of the corridor. I did make it down to the second floor of the dungeon once, but then Kay hollered for back-up.

At every turn, I've failed to get close enough to see her, and now, with Arthur's new orders for anyone not absolutely necessary to be in direct contact with her to stay clear *or else…*

"I'll do anything. Name your terms and I will pay the price." That's what she said only a moment ago. I almost repeat the words to her now. *I'll do anything, just let me apologise. Let me explain. Name your terms…just give me a moment of your time.*

She sounded so sad, so defeated. Twice now, someone I hate has caused Ari to feel hopeless. Once again, the look on her face when Arthur announced her sentence flashes through my mind. Only, this time, she's crying…

Anger surges through me. Merlin was right there, talking to Ari. He was within my grasp, yet, just out of reach. If I had not stopped to listen, perhaps, I could have—

"Just go," Ari sighs, turning away from me.

She picks up a knife from the wooden table and busies herself, cutting vegetables far more aggressively than is necessary. A crisp slice followed by the loud thud echoes through the room.

"What if we don't talk?" I ask, one side of my mouth twitching upward.

I realise that I'm still standing in the doorway, awkwardly filling the frame, but I cannot bring myself to cross the threshold.

"You could have saved him."

He was right here.

"I tried to summon you."

And yet, he left her behind.

Surely, he could have taken her from Camelot and ended her misery… so why didn't he?

Why would she have summoned him that day? Did she think Merlin might be willing to go so far as to obliterate a threat to her—to her family? What else might Merlin have done for her before deciding to abandon her? Was their relationship more than she'd let on? Was it more than I'd guessed?

Somehow, the thought stings more than I'd like.

"I hardly think you could last more than a few minutes without talking," she says without turning to face me.

"I would be honoured if you would let me try."

"Do not speak to me of honour." Though it's quiet, her words hit me like a physical blow. "Just…leave me alone."

When I don't leave, she turns to face me. She's no longer crying, though her cheeks are flushed and splotchy. The bright redness of her face is a stark contrast to the paleness of the rest of her. It does nothing to compliment her features, though I dare not say as much.

"Your eyes are already beginning to change. Your hair will not take long to follow suit."

I try to study her eyes, but I cannot see what he sees in them. I haven't known her long enough to notice subtle changes, though, perhaps over time, I'd be able to pick up on them.

"Why would I go anywhere with you?"

Glancing around the otherwise empty kitchen, I swallow down what's left of my pride and say, "Because I'm offering to take you outside, and despite how much you may think you hate me right now, I'm positive that's more than anyone else in here has done for you."

Something passes over her face, something I can't quite decipher before it's gone. I study her eyes again, looking for a hint that the faded green colour has somehow changed.

"I'm not going anywhere with you if you're just going to stare at me like that the whole time." She eyes me dubiously, the scowl on her face both deep and harsh. Still, she lays down the knife and removes her apron.

"I will not look at you at all if that's what you wish," I say, knowing it's a lie. I drop into a mock bow, attempting to lighten the mood.

She glares at me wholeheartedly before crossing to the stone hearth, collecting a large, black cauldron, and returning to the table. After scooping up the piles of chopped vegetables, she pushes the cauldron toward the mostly untouched pile next to hers.

"I should probably wait for Perci"—she glances around the room uncomfortably—"though I suppose Taite can finish the rest."

"Taite can finish the rest of what?" a small but confident voice asks from behind me.

Turning toward the newcomers, I cannot hide my scowl fast enough. "Lady Guinevere." I dip my head in her direction before turning toward the brown-haired servant at her side. "And you must be Taite."

The kitchen servant has pushed past me now, making her way toward the work table Ari still stands at. They share a quick, muted conversation. Taite glares at me over Ari's shoulder several times before finally nodding and busying herself with the rest of the vegetables.

"Did you even bother to clear this with Arthur?" Ari asks warily, then her eyes slide to Guinevere and she amends, *Prince Arthur.*"

Guinevere laughs, covering her mouth at the outburst. "I meant what I said. There is no need for formalities with me."

Her words strike an uneasy chord in my chest.

Ari nods distractedly but says nothing.

"I did not, but I'll speak with him later today."

Guinevere snorts, her eyebrows quickly rising and falling. "Aye, better to beg for forgiveness than ask for permission, isn't that what they say?"

"Something like that." I nod.

Guinevere eyes us intently, a quizzical sort of expression on her face. When she realises we're both staring back at her, a warm flush spreads across her cheeks. "Ari, it's been a pleasure," she says, smiling at her, though Ari bristles a bit at the words. She turns to me with an amused expression and says, "Once again, your bravery is commendable, dear knight."

Ari watches Guinevere leave, still staring long after she's gone, brows deeply furrowed. Eventually, her gaze returns to mine, all emotion wiped from her face.

"Will you be restraining me?" she asks. It takes me a moment to realise that, of course, they've been restraining her on the way to and from the dungeon each day. Honestly, I'm surprised she isn't in shackles now.

"Will you attack any of the townsfolk?"

"No," she says, shaking her head.

"Will you attack me?"

"Probably not, although I don't like to make promises I cannot be sure to keep."

I'm almost certain there's a flash of satisfaction in her eyes, a hint of a smile on her lips—a ghost of the Ari from before.

"Are you feeling particularly murderous today?" That slight curve of her lips has me hopeful, and I grin at her in return. Despite everything that question implies, if there's even a chance of her forgiving me, I'll use whatever means necessary to obtain it.

"Not in this moment, no."

"Then I think I'll take my chances."

"As you wish," she says, adding under her breath, "though, the day is still young."

We stroll through the streets of Camelot in silence. As we walk, the overcast sky turns to rain and flashes of lightning go off in the distance, an afternoon storm raging around the castle walls.

I point out where various things are as we go but she barely seems to acknowledge them—barely seems to acknowledge me. I push on, as if she were a willing participant of this tour, showing her where the nicest butcher is and the best baker. Where the oldest blacksmith is and the cheapest tavern. I show her the stables and the cattle barn, the mill and the granary, the town market and the drinking wells.

Through it all, she only seems half interested.

"Is there anything you would *like* to see?" I ask, stopping under the awning of a small tavern, unsure where to take her next.

"Why are you showing me any of this? What do you possibly hope to gain by sharing the best secrets of the kingdom's patrons with me?" She eyes me skeptically. "You don't really believe we're going to end up friends, do you? Nothing has changed, Lancelot."

"I don't hope to gain anything." I sigh. "I just…I figured if you saw the kingdom, if you talked to some of its people, maybe you wouldn't hate it here so much." Pulling in a shallow breath, I add, "And yes, maybe I did hope we could be friends again."

"After what you did?"

"Ari, I never meant for anything to happen to P—"

"Don't say his name."

Forcing myself to meet her gaze, I nod, swallowing several times before continuing. "Then I have no other motive than that—the hope that if you don't only see the dungeon and the kitchen then it might not be so bad for you here."

I can still hold out hope that she'll forgive me one day. Time heals all wounds, and I've got three years to help her heal. Hopefully, sooner or later, Tristan and Perci will let me within more than a hundred paces of her, and perhaps, eventually, she'll even want me to come to her.

She stares at me for a long moment, brows alternating between furrowing and raising, as if she truly can't decide how to take my words.

"But I am still a prisoner," she says quietly. "I killed six of your men, and I would do it again. You cannot expect the townsfolk to accept me, let alone speak to me or wish in any way to alleviate my sentence here."

"I just thought you might like a change of scenery." I shrug.

Her eyes search mine, her head nodding slightly. "Okay."

"Okay." I offer her a small smile.

"But it changes nothing between us."

I nod again. *For now.*

"I have a request…if you're still offering." She glances at me hesitantly before continuing. "I'd like to see a healer. Preferably someone more… questionable in their practices." She swallows visibly. "But someone who can be discreet, all the same."

"Are you hurt?" I ask, unable to keep the concern from seeping into my voice. "Is something the matter?"

"No." She waves a dismissive hand between us. "No, I'm just…in need of something a bit obscure. Something I do not wish to ask for inside the castle walls."

The angry words I overheard before come floating back to me.

"Who else will bring you dragon's blood? Now is not the time to consider weening yourself from it."

Dragon's blood, that is what she seeks—and she wishes to acquire it without the aid of Merlin. It's a secret shared between us, even though she said nothing has changed.

It's an offer of trust, I realise, no matter how small. A chance at redemption. Though she did not tell me for certain what she seeks, I am confident in my guess.

"Forget it," she murmurs, turning away from me.

"No," I say quickly. "I have someone in mind."

We fall into another lapse of silence, although this one feels less uncomfortable than before.

We're currently on the opposite side of Camelot from Vera's, and it takes nearly an hour for us to return to the main town square outside the castle, with still farther to go when she stops short.

The rain is coming down in torrents now. Inwardly, I curse myself for not thinking to bring cloaks to protect us against the weather. We're both soaked, though neither of us seem likely to complain about it.

I follow her line of sight and a flash of lightning glints off metal, catching my eye. The fabled sword in the stone looks ominous in the storm.

"Is that Excalibur?"

My head whips in her direction, eyes darting wildly with confusion. "You know of the sword in the stone?" I ask, unable to hide my shock.

"Why does this surprise you?" She arches an incredulous brow at me.

"I don't know," I say honestly.

"A human raised by a dragon and taught magic by a mage is deemed acceptable, but knowledge of the sword in the stone is what surprises you most?" Her mouth twists up in a wry, almost-smirk.

"I guess I assumed that only the kingdom of Camelot was aware of its existence," I say, wincing at the ignorance of that assumption.

"I assure you, that is not the case." She shakes her head slightly.

"What do you know of it?" I ask, gesturing towards the sword.

As we make our way across the town square, rain continues to pour down on us. Lightning darts across the sky and loud booms of thunder go off in the distance like war drums.

The square is busy, even in this weather. Knights, merchants, and townsfolk alike pass around us, but most of them give us a wide berth.

"Only a little," she says, though, somehow, I don't believe that to be true. "I know that only an heir of the Uther bloodline can pull it from the stone."

"Aye, well, sort of." She eyes me expectantly, waiting for me to continue. "Only the next heir in the line of succession," I amend. "Only the true ruler of Camelot can pull the sword from the stone."

"Lucky for Arthur to be the firstborn heir, then," she says, her gaze returning to the sword. "Well"—she snorts, her face impassive—"the only heir, I suppose."

"Aye." I nod absently. "He comes from a long line of sole heirs, though there were whispers for a time that he was not the firstborn."

"What d'you mean?" She squints up at me in the rain.

I glance around the courtyard just to be safe, and though I know that no one is within ear shot of us, I lower my voice anyways. "For a long time, there were whispers of another born to King Uther and Queen Igraine—a daughter."

"There has never been a female heir to Camelot before," she says evenly. "What happened to her?"

"Aye, there has never been a female heir…Uther made sure of it." I pull in a deep, steadying breath. "They say Uther refused to have a daughter take over rule of Camelot in his stead, so he did whatever was necessary to ensure that there was no female heir."

Her face twists in horror, her revulsion almost tangible. "Are you saying that he—"

"Aye, he did," I say quickly before she can utter something treasonous so openly in the kingdom. "Queen Igraine was heartbroken. They say she didn't leave her rooms for more than a year."

"They say this, but do they know for sure? Who is *they*? And who can be sure that it was him, and not something else that took the life of their firstborn?" Her questions come out as little more than a whisper, sending a chill down my spine.

I glance around to make sure we're still not within earshot of anyone. "My father is the one who dealt with the baby—after," I say solemnly. "When it was rumoured Queen Igraine was with child again, there was so much secrecy that hardly anyone knew at all until Arthur was already born."

"Why was Uther so against having a firstborn daughter? What truly would be the harm in having a female ruler? Unless Aethelfirth is able to produce an heir, Lady Guinevere is next in line to take the throne of Northumbria when he dies."

"None, I'd imagine." I shrug. "But he was stubborn and set in his ways. Uther was not a kind man, and for all of Arthur's faults, a great deal of them can be attributed to his father."

She says nothing for a few moments, though lost to her thoughts or the beauty of the sword, I cannot tell. The rain has lightened a little but still falls persistently from the sky.

The longer the silence wears on, the more I feel the need to fill it with tidbits of information, to share the whispers and rumours, the theories and bits of hearsay spoken over the years.

"I think," I say warily, "that a large part of it had to do with his resentment toward Igraine's firstborn."

"She had another child?" Ari asks, brows pulling in.

A small smile lifts the edge of my mouth. When she doesn't know or understand something, her forehead wrinkles, brows pulling together so tightly that a little indent forms between them, as if the most important thing in that moment is puzzling out why she might not have known that information in the first place, more so than the information itself.

"Aye, she did." I nod. "She was married before she came to Camelot and courted by Uther. She bore a child—a daughter—and a magical one at that."

"I beg your pardon?"

"I'm sure you've seen her skulking about the hallways by now." I sigh, waving dismissively toward the castle. "Morgana is Arthur's half-sister."

TWENTY-SIX

ARI

"Are you positive?" I ask, trying and failing to grasp what he said. Somehow, in all my lessons and studies on the royal families, I've never heard this before.

"Aye." Lancelot shifts on his feet, looking entirely uncomfortable. "I'm positive."

My head is shaking, my body physically unable to grasp the information. Morgana, a mage, is Arthur's half-sister, and yet, magic is forbidden in Camelot. Why would he force her to live like that, even after Uther's death? And why would she stay here? "Are you sure?" I ask again, unable to stop myself.

"Morgana is Arthur's half-sister," he says again. His shoulders lift almost helplessly.

"Do you know how rare that is? Do you understand how uncommon it is for a mage to be born in this age?"

"I...no?" he says, bashful. "But, by your reaction, I assume very uncommon?"

"There are only a handful of mages whose names I've even heard, and only one I've actually met face to face—well, two, now, I suppose." I pull in a quick breath, releasing it in a puff of air.

My anger at Merlin from earlier today is suddenly replaced with dozens of questions. If anyone would have the answers, it would be him. Did he know she was here all this time? Has he met her? Has he trained her? Can she even use her magic, living in a kingdom where that is forbidden?

The sting of how easily he abandoned me is still fresh, but in this moment, the desire for answers outweighs that betrayal.

"I would assume it's about as rare and uncommon as someone magical giving birth to a human," Lancelot says quietly. Nervous energy radiates off him in waves.

"I don't understand," I say, brows furrowing.

"Not here." He shakes his head. Leading me away from Excalibur and the busyness of the town square, we slowly begin to make our way through the streets of Camelot again.

"I told you before that my namesake was a long story," he says after a moment, eyeing me sidelong.

"Lancelot of the Lake." I nod, echoing his words from before. "I remember."

"My father was a knight in the king's army, loyal to Uther and the blood crown—"

"Why do you call it the blood crown?" I interrupt him before thinking better of it.

"The name started as all stories do, I suppose—with whispers and rumours," he says wryly. "Over the years, many invaders have tried to take the kingdom by force. I believe it was the fifth, maybe the sixth Uther who was slain in his own throne room… The assassin took the crown for himself but mysteriously died before he could place it upon his brow. Some believe the crown is cursed; others believe a mage had a hand in its creation. Either way, legends say that only a true heir of Uther's bloodline can wear it upon their head. No one else has been brave enough to try." He shrugs. "Never mind the countless kingdoms Camelot has laid to bloodshed over the years."

"Hmm," I grunt, letting his words sink in.

The blood crown. It seems to fit with everything I know of Camelot and the surrounding kingdoms, though I've never heard it called by that name before. It has a nice ring to it, foreboding and ominous.

"So," he continues, recapturing my attention. "My father was a knight of Camelot for many years, but never took a wife—"

"Maybe he needn't have taken one," I say dryly, interrupting him again. "Maybe he need only ask."

A slow smile lifts up one side of his mouth, his blue eyes bright with amusement. "Aye." He nods. "Maybe he should have asked—but then he wouldn't have found my mother."

"Where was she?"

"Lake Umbra." He pushes out a long breath before continuing. "He was sent on a scouting mission into the ancient forest, looking for what, I do not know. His group of soldiers were ambushed, and he was seriously wounded. Dehydrated and alone, his survival instinct kicked in and he managed to drag himself to the edge of the lake, where my mother found him, straddling the line between this world and the next. She used her magic to heal the gravest of his wounds, and then spent the next several weeks healing the rest of him. By the time he was well enough to return to Camelot, his heart already belonged to her."

"Did your mother live near the lake, then?"

"Not so much near it as in it." He smirks at my confusion before adding, "My mother is a water nymph."

"A water nymph?" I ask, certain I've heard him incorrectly. "How is that possible?"

"I don't know that, either. But it is the truth, I swear it."

"Your word means nothing to me," I remind him sharply, "but I cannot imagine why you would lie about something like that. Do you see her often?"

He clears his throat, and I watch it bob above the collar of his black tunic. "Not as often as I'd like."

We're silent for a moment, and then I ask, "What's she like?"

"Beautiful," he says without hesitation. "The most beautiful thing I've ever seen." We continue down the street as the rain continues to fall down on us. "She has this pearly skin with just the barest hint of pale blue scales across her brow, down her spine, and around her wrists. Pointed ears and webbed toes. Long, colourless hair that flows past her feet and swirls in the water behind her. I've never seen anything else like it before."

As I listen to him speak of her, I wonder, just for a moment, what my own mother looked like. Though I'm sure it was somewhat similar to the way that I look, I cannot be certain.

"I've met water nymphs before. They can be…charming," I say, turning toward him and settling on a slightly more favourable term than the one I ought to use.

"She can be a real sea serpent"—he laughs—"but she has a big heart."

"Perhaps that is why your father fell in love with her?"

"It is. When he journeyed to Camelot to rejoin the kingdom, he started going by Sir Baxen of the Lake, and so, when I was knighted, I decided to honour my mother in the same way."

Sir Baxen of the Lake, with a sea serpent for a sigil.

"I've heard stories of your father," I say quietly—carefully—trying and failing to swallow down the lump forming in my throat. "I heard he was a fearsome warrior."

"He was."

"Where is she now?" I ask. "Your mother."

"Lake Umbra," he says hesitantly.

"Does she not wish to be closer to you? There are other lakes nearer to Camelot…"

"She cannot leave," he says quietly, "and I fear she is lonelier than ever."

"She cannot leave?" I mutter, puzzling through the pieces of his story. "Your mother is a water nymph...who cannot leave Lake Umbra?"

"Aye," he says solemnly.

"Your mother is Nhimue?" I ask, though I am already certain of the answer. I know her story well—Merlin himself placed that particular curse upon her.

"You know of her?" he asks, half in disbelief.

"Aye." I nod, meeting the intense scrutiny of his gaze full on, noticing for the first time that his eyes are the exact colour of Lake Umbra. "I've met her before."

"I don't..." His brows pull in, a multitude of emotions flitting across his face. "How?"

"My life has been full of magical creatures—dragons and mages and dryads and the like. You know of the many languages I speak, and yet, it still surprises you that I might know who your mother is, let alone a nymph as famous as Nhimue? Her lake resides in the very forest I call home."

"I just never thought..." He sighs. "I do not keep her a secret out of shame—I love my mother. But normal folk...they don't understand. They live in the relative safety and ignorance of their human lives, and anything that challenges or threatens that is feared or hated."

"Oh, I understand," I say, relishing the way the sudden edge in my voice makes him flinch. I had been distracted by Morgana and his parents, my anger toward him momentarily forgotten, but I can feel it creeping back in again, threatening to lash out. "If there is anyone within the confines of this kingdom's walls who understands your family and what they mean to you, it's me."

A pained expression crosses over his features, settling deep within his eyes. He looks as if he's going to beg for understanding again, although he's never actually apologised for what happened.

Whether or not he accepts the blame for everything that's led to this moment, it is his blame to bear. He is the only one who returned to the forest after the first time we met, and had he not done so—regardless of however things may have shifted between us during his visits—I would not be a prisoner of Camelot and Penn would still be alive.

I cannot bear to hear him try to explain his side of things again, so before he can even open his mouth, I turn and continue walking in the direction we'd been going.

We walk in silence for a while until a particularly colourful flower stall snags my attention. It's eccentric and whimsical; a kaleidoscope of shapes, colours, and smells. I don't know if I'm allowed to stop and check it out, but I do.

The flowers range from muted pastels to brilliant jewel tones and seem to be in varying stages of bloom. The top of the table is covered in a thick layer of soft moss, and potted vines of ivy wrap around the support beams.

Three young women peer at us from within the stall, all similar in face but different in features. "Lady Dragon," the one in the middle calls out, startling me. "Welcome."

The woman on the right has black hair woven into countless tiny braids, threaded together to make one thick rope that hangs over her shoulder. The one on the left has short, nearly-white hair that just reaches her chin, and the third one—the one who spoke—has long, flowing hair in the most brilliant shade of red. They all have the same unnerving, golden brown eyes and knowing smiles.

Beside me, Lancelot barely suppresses a groan as I step up to their table.

The one who spoke—the redhead—smiles wider. It's coy and something a little more mischievous.

"H-Hello," I say hesitantly.

"We're sorry for your loss," they say in unison, each of them dipping their head in what can only be respect, although I cannot fathom why.

Beside me, Lancelot freezes, an unnatural stillness settling over him.

"A scion from the dragon wood—"

"—raised from a promise born of dragon pride—"

"—bound by an oath made with dragon bone."

They speak in turn, each of them staring intently at me. I can feel the blood drain from my face as an unwelcome shiver slithers up my spine, prickling the hair at the back of my neck.

"Made with what?" Lancelot rasps.

None of them answer him. None of them even look at him.

My eyes drift from one girl to the next, meeting each of their otherworldly gazes, hoping they cannot sense my thinly veiled fear.

A long, tense moment passes before Lancelot reaches for my elbow, no doubt to steer me away, when the redhead speaks again.

"These are my sisters, Elaine and Elinore," she says, motioning to the two women standing beside her.

"And what am I to call you?" I ask hoarsely.

"My name is Elias, but my friends call me Elie," she says with another small dip of her chin. "Though, you may call me whatever you like, magic-blessed."

"Magic-blessed?" Lancelot whispers.

"Not magic-born," I mutter absently, unable to take my eyes off her.

"Thank you, Elie, but we're—"

"*You* may call me Elias," she snaps at Lancelot, glaring fiercely in his direction. "No knight of Camelot is a friend of mine."

If the ancient weight of that glare was aimed at me, I would flinch. Beside me, Lancelot does exactly that. Clearing his throat, he reaches for my elbow again. "We ought to keep moving."

Elaine tosses her heavy braid over her shoulder, exchanging an indecipherable look with Elinore.

"Should you consider visiting again," Elie says plainly, "you'll find that your company is most welcome here."

"Thank you," I murmur, unsure of what else to say. I'm still reeling at how they might know anything about Penn—and our history—when Lancelot finally manages to drag me from their stall.

"Don't mind them." He expels a long breath once we've turned onto the next street. "They're spinsters—"

"They're what?"

"Spinsters," he says again. "Unmarried, unwanted—"

"That's incredibly insulting," I say, bewildered.

He merely shrugs. "Their younger brother is a knight in training… A few years younger than them and considerably less…strange."

I don't bother to respond, walking the rest of the way in silence.

"There," he says eventually, pointing to the gnarled wooden door just up the lane from us. A carved star inside a crescent moon is the only indication on the outside of the shop.

"Do you trust this healer?" I ask, my steps faltering a little.

"Aye." He nods. "Vera is… Well, let's just say she's probably a lot closer to what you're used to."

I search his face for some hint of what that might mean when the door to her shop opens and Tristan steps out. Beside me, Lancelot swears under his breath.

TWENTY-SEVEN

LANCELOT

Immediately, Tristan's eyes land on us and he halts in the doorway—just for a second—before regaining his composure. He walks over to us, keeping his steps slow and deliberate, as if there's nothing unusual about running into us here.

"You're outside the castle," he says by way of greeting, eyeing Ari cautiously.

"He figured I was in need of a change of scenery." She shrugs, gesturing toward me.

"Aye, I'll bet he did." Tristan openly glares at me before turning his attention back to Ari. "What else did he figure you needed?"

For a second, they just stare at each other—some silent conversation passing between them that I'm not privy to. I've grown used to this angrier version of Tristan, but if she's taken aback at the air of hostility around him, she doesn't show it. "I asked him to take me to a healer."

"Are you alright?" he asks, visibly assessing her for injury.

"Aye, I just—"

"Did something happen?"

Shaking her head, she hesitates. "I'm in need of something I do not wish to ask Morgana for."

Nodding, he gestures toward the shop behind him. "Vera can get whatever it is you need. If she doesn't have it, she'll find it."

Ari nods without so much as looking at me before heading towards the shop. We watch her walk away without another word.

"Are you mad?" Tristan whirls on me once she's inside, eyes wild. "What are you doing out here with her?"

"Exactly as she said," I snap. "She's been confined to the dungeon and the kitchen for months."

"It's not your job to get her out of the castle for a leisurely stroll, Lancelot." He sneers, running a hand over his face. His blatant animosity sets me on edge.

"Come off it, Tris."

"No, you come off it!" He doesn't often shout, and he never used to let his anger get the better of him, but right now, he's positively livid. "She was right. You just don't listen—it's like you can't even help yourself."

"What's your problem, anyway?" I snap back at him. "You could have taken her out and done this yourself if it's such a big deal to you."

"You truly are an idiot." He sighs, squeezing his eyes shut in frustration. "The big deal is that she told you to leave her alone. She told you not to seek her out, and here you are, disregarding her wishes—*yet again*."

"She's caged up like an animal—"

"She's not your concern! Haven't you done enough?" Even after taking a moment to rein in his temper, he struggles to keep his voice low, and there's still an edge of bitterness laced through his words. "Isn't it enough that she lost her family, was taken from her home, and is now being held prisoner here? Do you truly think it necessary to tempt Arthur's patience, too?"

"Arthur can go—"

"Did you even bother to clear it with him before you just decided to take her from her duties?"

"Her duties," I scoff, glaring at him. "She's not a member of the castle staff, Tris."

"For the next three years, if she wants to stay alive, she sure as hell is. Whether you like it or not, you can't just do what you want and decide she's done work for the day. Arthur will have your head on a pike right next to hers for disobeying him. You need to be smarter than this."

We stare at each other for a moment, the rain and distant storm the only sound between us.

"I just wanted to try to make things better... I just wanted to apologise," I say eventually.

"An apology won't bring her dragon back." Eyeing Vera's shop over his shoulder, we watch the old, gnarled door click firmly shut, Ari now making her way toward us again. "She doesn't need to help you feel better about your guilt," he says slowly. "But...maybe, what she actually needs is a way out."

"A way out of what?" Ari asks by way of greeting, eyebrows raised.

"Camelot," Tristan says, glancing at me briefly, a flicker of mischief in his eyes.

"The festival in honour of Prince Arthur's eighteenth name day, the tournament to find the new king's champion, and his coronation as king of Camelot are nearly upon us," Tristan says, eyeing the tavern around us.

He'd suggested ducking in for a drink and a bit of privacy after Ari rejoined us in the street. The dark-haired barmaid had scowled at the rain water we drudged in, clenching her jaw but saying nothing at the sight of Ari. After only a moment of hesitation, she led us to a table in the back corner, well away from the other patrons—thanks to the coins Tristan pressed into her hand.

Now, a mug of ale sits in front of each of us, Ari's hands wrapped tightly around her drink. She glances around the tavern, eyeing the townsfolk, marking the exits, and following the workers.

"Aye, I'm aware." She nods, looking at both of us. "I don't mean to be blunt," she continues, one brow arched high, "but how will a party help me escape Camelot?"

Tristan glances at me. Four years worth of history between us makes it easy to understand the question in his eyes. I shrug, leaving the next move up to him. He's never approved of anything I've said in regards to Ari before—far be it for me to make a plan now.

She clears her throat pointedly, regaining our attention.

"Arthur's guard will be down, his senses dulled and his thoughts distracted. It might be the only time we could slip something past him… unnoticed," Tristan says, glancing over his shoulder.

"So, what, while he's enjoying his cake and crown, you'll sneak me out the back door?"

Tristan shrugs one shoulder, taking a long drink.

I nod, mulling over the limited options. "It would be the only time we could stage something to look like an accident…or a surprise. The only time that all the necessary eyes would be otherwise occupied."

"It won't be that easy, and I think we all know my disappearance wouldn't go unnoticed." She shakes her head, knuckles turning white around the mug. "I don't like it, and honestly, why would either of you want to risk helping me escape? You'd both be named traitors and end up losing your heads if you were caught. And," she adds tightly, "you *would* be caught."

"Maybe," Tristan muses, rubbing the back of his neck. "Maybe not. There's only one way to know for sure."

"No," Ari scoffs, glaring at each of us. "I'm not going to risk my life—or yours. Not when I can be out of here in less than three years. I'd much rather keep my head down and not draw attention to myself than flee and hope he doesn't notice or care enough to have me hunted down."

I open my mouth to argue, but she keeps going, rounding on me.

"What happens when he sends his men out in search of me? What happens when the knights of Camelot descend upon my forest once more? Where am I supposed to go? Where am I supposed to hide? What else would you have me lose?"

She scoffs again, pushing back from the table. "Do you expect me to flee to another kingdom so that I might escape Arthur's wrath? I never wanted to be a part of this one, much less a different one, and I will not spend the rest of my life looking over my shoulder."

"So, you don't even wish to try?" I demand, turning to face her fully.

"The moment Arthur realises I'm gone, he'll send Bors to hunt me down. Given what he did to—" Her eyes grow watery and she has to clear her throat, swallowing down a lump of emotion. "Given what I know of him," she tries again, her tone unsteady, "I have no doubts that Arthur would have him hunt me to every edge of this continent, and I have no desire to die by his hand."

"So, you wish to stay here?" I cannot keep the incredulity from my tone.

"Don't insult me." She huffs. "I want nothing more than to leave this place, but we both know I cannot simply disappear."

"You could…" I say slowly, my eyes falling to her hands. They fidget beneath the table now, but we all know of the magic she can wield—of the scars that line her palms to prove it.

"Magic is forbidden." Her face scrunches up dismissively, her lip curling as if the thought disgusts her.

"How would he know?" I challenge. When she lifts her eyes to meet mine, I ask, "How would he find you?"

"You forget that he has a mage living in his castle and another down the street." She shakes her head, the movement small but firm. "Just because *he* couldn't find me does not mean that they could not."

"But if you—"

"It is a different path with the same outcome." She sighs, hands balling into fists in her lap. "I would still spend the rest of my life living in fear, looking over my shoulder and waiting for the day that he finds me."

"Eventually, he would give up—"

"You cannot know that."

Tristan sighs, loosing a long breath and scrubbing a hand across his face. This conversation has gotten off-track and is seemingly going nowhere, all of us now on edge.

"Listen, what happened to you was unfair," I say quickly, hoping I can get through to her. "Regardless of your reaction and the consequent loss of our men, I can see how you believed your actions were justified."

"Unfair?" she asks, her tone rife with disbelief. *"Unfair?"* Her voice rises several octaves, and instinctually, Tristan and I both glance around the tavern to make sure no one is paying us any attention.

"Just listen—"

"So, what," she snaps, cutting me off. "You feel guilty and want to clear your conscience? Is that it?" A scowl settles across her face and she drains the rest of her ale in one gulp.

"Ari, I—"

"No, thank you."

"What?" Disbelief swells in my chest.

"I said"—she emphasises each syllable—*"no, thank you."*

"Just let us—"

"No." That single word holds so much venom—so much fury—it makes me flinch.

"Just leave it alone. Why do you even care? You don't know me. What possible reason do you have to risk treason for helping me escape?"

"Because you don't belong here, Ari," Tristan says, speaking for the first time in a while. His tone is calm and even, and when her eyes snap to his, a tense moment passes between them. Another silent conversation I have no hopes of understanding. She just stares at him, barely daring to breathe.

"I'm telling you this because I do know you, Ari," Tristan adds quietly. "I know who you are and where you come from. I know what you've lost and I know how hard it is for you to accept our help. But the fact of the matter is, you don't belong here."

She stares at him for another long moment, pale green eyes darting back and forth between his hazel ones, searching. An unwelcome tingle begins to unfurl in my chest, and I almost feel as if I'm intruding on some deeply personal moment between the two of them.

I have to tamp down the jealousy flaring in my chest and remind myself that they've spent a lot of time together over the last few months. While I've—unsuccessfully—done everything in my power to see her, he's been her guard, escorting her to and from her cell each day. Of course, he thinks he knows her.

Her eyelids blink rapidly and she looks as if she's seen a ghost, or perhaps, as if she's going to retch. She looks *afraid*.

My heart lurches for her, for the fear in her eyes, and my jealousy turns to resentment at the fact that Tristan put that fear there. Whatever his words meant, whatever he implied to get through to her, I don't like the reaction they've caused.

"I had a feeling you wouldn't want to pursue this option—wouldn't want to take the risk—and understandably so. But I wanted to present it to you all the same." A slow smirk lifts one side of his mouth. "I suggested running, but I had a back-up option for you to consider in case that one didn't win you over."

"What?" she whispers.

"Enter the tournament."

"What?" The word leaves my mouth before I can stop it.

"Enter the tournament and defeat the knights," Tristan says evenly, lifting one shoulder. "He announced to all of Camelot that the winner gets one wish—anything they like, and he will grant it. Enter the tournament and win your freedom."

TWENTY-EIGHT

A R I

My cell in the dungeons remains as cold and dark as always. The torchlight in the hallway casts flickering shadows across the walls but does little to actually illuminate the cell itself.

Perci intercepted the three of us on the way back from the tavern, looking particularly murderous. Tristan intervened before Lancelot could open his mouth to say something stupid, and before I could even try to come up with an excuse, Perci was hauling me back toward the dungeon, one hand wrapped firmly around my elbow.

He threatened to leave me without food until morning, saying it was the least I deserved for not only abandoning my post, but for entertaining Lancelot's foolishness…only to return a short while later with a tray in hand, muttering something under his breath about Arthur's fickle temper. Heaving a sigh that could rival one of Penn's, he deposited my dinner inside the door and stomped off again.

The coolness of the stones seeps through my clothes and into my skin, numbing me. I'm too distracted to use my magic for warmth today, too many thoughts warring for space in my head. Too many new pieces of information to comprehend and sift through.

We barely spoke on the way back to the castle. Tristan and Lancelot shared several loaded glances over my head that I didn't even try to decipher. Lancelot asked me once, quietly, if I'd gotten what I needed from Vera's. I didn't, but she didn't flinch when I asked for dragon's blood, either—or when I told her Lancelot would be paying for it. I figure he owes me at least that much.

She merely said she'd need a week or two to procure it, and that she'd have Tristan deliver it as soon as possible. I don't know if they're friends, or if she somehow knows he's one of the guards assigned to me, but I didn't bother to question it.

Lancelot failed to mention that she was a mage, but that might only be because he didn't know as much himself. Her eyes were a dead giveaway, but only if you know that particular colour combination is a marker of the mages. Arthur must not know what marks their race or, surely, he would not allow two mages to reside within his walls. And yet…

"Morgana is Arthur's half-sister."

I pour over the earlier conversation with Lancelot, sifting through the things he didn't think twice about sharing with me. No matter how many times I go over it, I keep coming back to the same question: Does Arthur know that Morgana is a mage?

Surely, he must.

It irritates me how much I wish to know the answer, and it irritates me further how fixated I've become on the matter. If he doesn't know that she's a mage, then what would he do if he found out? Would he exile his own half-sister? Would he change the laws surrounding magic in Camelot? Or would he simply do nothing, pretending that it does not matter?

But if he does know, then why has he not changed the laws? Why has he not lifted the ban on magic for the sake of his half-sister?

And perhaps most vexing of all is Morgana herself. If Arthur does not know that she's a mage, then why hasn't she told him? And why has she stayed in a kingdom that forbids her from using her birthright?

My mind shifts to his other sister, to the firstborn daughter of Uther and Igraine. The mere idea of what he had done to her makes me want to retch, so I force myself to think of something—*anything*—else.

Pulling myself to my feet, I pace the small cell and work the stiffness from my limbs. The tray of food catches my eye, and I crouch in front of it, assessing the meagre contents: a bit of leftover stew from tonight's dinner, a chunk of crusty bread, a skein of water.

Dipping the bread in the now-cold stew to soften it a bit, I eat and pace at the same time, pausing only for an occasional sip of water.

Eventually, Tristan's words replace the fixation on Arthur's siblings, beating through my veins like a drum. The more I pace, the more the thought becomes all-consuming, blocking everything else out.

"Enter the tournament."

I don't know how many knights will enter the tournament, but I do know my skill with a blade. I've been training with bows, and daggers, and swords for as long as I could wield them. I might not be the best, but I can hold my own.

"Defeat the knights."

The alternative isn't an option—it would be unwise to lay my freedom in the hands of a prince who may or may not be distracted enough to realise that I've slipped through his grasp. To simply hope he doesn't notice my absence when the celebrations have ended.

"Win your freedom."

If I have a chance to get out of here after only a few months, I have to take it. Regardless of the likelihood of success, Tristan's idea feels like the only option. I cannot simply hope that Arthur will forget about me, and I'm not foolish enough to risk my life on the whims and pretty words so boldly uttered—by a traitor, no less—no matter how badly he wishes for me to be free.

Draining the last of the water, I rattle the dinner tray against the iron bars until one of the night guards comes into view.

"You summoned me?" A wry smirk lifts up one side of Tristan's mouth.

"Aye." My forearms are threaded through the gaps in the bars and the cold bite of the iron stings my skin. He stands just on the other side, close enough that either of us could reach out and touch the other if we wished.

It's a challenge, I realise, and in some way, an offering. He's challenging the others' perception of me—the idea that I'm a monster, even if he's only challenging it to me. And, he's offering me his own personal credence— the notion that I'm not. It's just one more layer to the tentative trust growing between us. He still takes the long way back to my cell at the end of the day, still lets the sun warm my face as we linger in the empty corridors, still encourages me to use magic whenever necessary.

He continues to keep my secret, despite what the truth would cost him.

He knew his words would strike a chord in me today—that they would resonate so deeply with the fear and anxiety and dread that's threaded its way through my chest these last few months.

The day he broke his hand, I'd told him that I shouldn't be here. Now he's reaffirming that for me. *"Because you don't belong here."* He'd used a version of my own words against me, knowing it would get my attention—knowing it would work.

"Why?" he asks, handing me something through the bars.

"Because I hate you the least," I say with a grin, taking the skein of water from his calloused hands.

"Fair enough." His laugh is quick and easy. "Next time, you can just ask one of the night guards. You needn't startle them with all the ruckus."

"They don't pay me any attention." I shrug, taking a long drink of water and placing the skein at my feet next to the one Perci brought earlier. "I figured a lot of noise was the easiest way to go."

"What can I do for you, m'lady?"

"I asked you not to call me that," I say uncomfortably, pushing away from the bars and retreating farther into my cell and into myself.

"I'm telling you this because I do know you, Ari. I know who you are and where you come from."

The thought still rattles through me, setting my nerves on fire. In that moment, I truly believed that he did know me—all the forgotten, insignificant little things that make up my past. All the little truths I've kept at bay to ensure both my freedom and my future.

Fear and relief and something else—curiosity, maybe—settled over me like a blanket when he spoke those words, and they do again now.

I'm still undecided on the truth of it, on how much Tristan might or might not know.

And the outlandish things the sisters from the square uttered so confidently this afternoon… There's no way that Elias, Elaine, and Elinore could have known the truth of what their words implied. As far as I'm aware, the only humans Penn interacted with in almost two decades were myself and Bax.

Exhaling a deep breath and shaking my head as if to rid them from my thoughts, I let Tristan's words from earlier return me to the present.

"Enter the tournament and defeat the knights. Enter the tournament and win your freedom."

"How do I enter?" I ask, meeting his patient gaze. The torchlight casts shadows across his face, but I can still make out the change as his smile spreads to a full-on grin.

"You simply show up."

"Lisbeth will never let me out of my duties."

"Let me worry about that," he says dismissively.

"I haven't held a sword since…" I swallow down the emotions before they can overtake me. Despite everything, today was a good day. I got to be outside—really outside, not just in the courtyard garden—for the first time in months. In the rain… Walking the streets… Today, I went to my first tavern, and I saw Excalibur in person.

"I can help with that, too," he says gently.

"I still don't understand why you're helping me."

"Because it's the right thing to do." His smile is sad, if a bit wistful. "Because, you don't belong here."

A charged silence falls over us, emboldening me. I return to the wall of iron bars, once again threading my arms through the gaps, resting my forehead on the cold metal. Were it not for the shadows, I would not have the grit to say, "I am glad for the dimness of the dungeons, for I do not wish to see the pity in your eyes."

"I do not pity you." He shakes his head, brows pulling together. It feels as if he has more to say, so I give him the space to do so, silently waiting.

After a moment, he takes a small, unconscious step forward. "I have never pitied you, Ari. I feel… In some ways, I suppose I feel responsible for what happened to you. If we had never sought out the dragon in the first place…if we had never gone into the forest that day…none of this would've happened. Garreth would still be alive, and you wouldn't be locked down here. You would still have…" His words trail off, and he drops my gaze, looking away.

"Penn," I say quietly, lifting my head to look at him.

"Aye," he murmurs, shifting on his feet. "You'd still have Penn."

"You needn't be afraid to say his name." The words come out slow and hesitant, though I'm not sure why they come out at all.

He meets my eyes again, and even through the shadows, his pain is evident.

"You needn't feel guilty," I offer, shrugging one shoulder.

"But I do." His voice is small in the vast darkness of the dungeons. "You were right in thinking we'd want a clear conscience."

"It was no secret that there was a dragon in the mountains near Camelot. Anyone could have sought him out or stumbled upon the cave. Sooner or later, it was bound to happen," I say absently. "Honestly, given the number of rival kingdoms and wars over the years, I'm surprised it didn't happen sooner."

He's quiet for a moment, then pulls in a handful of deep breaths as if to steady himself, or perhaps, to prepare himself. "Did Lancelot tell you why we were in the forest that day?" His voice is so low I have to strain to hear him, even from only a few inches away. "Did he tell you why we were after the dragon?"

"Gold," I say hoarsely. "He said there were whispers of a dragon and its treasure."

"Aye." He nods. Hazel eyes meet mine again, so close with little more than a wall of iron between us. "Knights don't make a lot of money…and not all of us wish to be indebted to the crown."

"That's almost exactly what he said." I laugh, though it holds no humour.

"Maybe it's not an excuse, but it's the truth. I swore an oath to this kingdom, to protect its people—"

"To serve its king," I interject quickly.

"Aye, but he isn't king yet, is he?" There's an edge to his tone, one that I'm not used to.

"What's that supposed to mean?"

"Nothing," he mutters, squeezing his eyes shut. "Never mind."

"Tristan…"

He continues on as if I hadn't spoken. "Whether you like it or not, you still technically belong to this kingdom." I bristle at his words, but he ignores me. "You may have grown up in the forest, but that forest is still within the borders of Camelot—still within the confines of Arthur's jurisdiction. Whether or not he was right to punish you is irrelevant;

you're still a citizen of this kingdom and, therefore, someone I swore to protect."

"Is that oath worth risking your life for?"

Slowly, his eyes lift to meet mine. "It might be, if the alternative is that your magic tears this castle down, brick by brick. We both know what's going to happen if you're forced to stay in this cell for the next three years."

I don't know what to say—don't know how to dispute his accusation, so I only nod. There's a very good chance that he's right. My magic might be placated for now, but after a decade of using it for anything I wanted—using it for anything and everything—how long until warming some stones and silencing a drip is no longer enough? How long until the things I'm able to get away with no longer take the edge off?

His jaw works furiously for a moment. Resting his forehead against the bars, his eyes fall closed and he takes a handful of slow, shallow breaths. Eventually, he whispers, "You remind me of someone."

"Who?" I ask gently, though I don't know if I have the right to ask at all.

"Someone long gone." His breathing turns ragged and he adds, "That's why I want to help you. Because I couldn't help him when it mattered, when magic meant the difference between life and death."

The silence between us is deafening, broken only by the flicker of the torches and the whisper of our breaths.

"I—"

"Will you tell me about dragons?"

"What?" I ask, equally surprised and caught off guard by the question.

"Will you tell me about dragons?" he asks again, lifting his head so that his eyes meet mine.

My first instinct is to question his motivations—to wonder *why* he wants to know about dragons. But to doubt him now would be to go against everything I believe to be true about Tristan. Penn has been the only dragon within a thousand leagues of Camelot for generations, and if Tristan had truly wanted to hurt Penn, he would have returned to the forest.

As if he can sense my hesitation, he smirks, adding, "Until I met you, I'd never seen a dragon before. I knew they existed, but I'd never actually seen one. They were just a story my mother told us before bed."

"What do you want to know?"

"Anything." He shrugs. "Everything."

I stare at the wall behind him, contemplating. "The only two things I know to be true of every dragon is that they're immortal…and they mate for life."

He shifts on his feet, his hands fidgeting around the iron bars between us. "They're immortal?"

"Aye." I nod, then because I don't know how much he knows about the magical creatures of our world, I add, "They're one of three species who are, along with mages and elves."

"How old was Penn?" he asks quietly.

"Well over a thousand." My voice is little more than a hoarse whisper.

He doesn't say anything else, and for a moment, I don't think he's going to, but then he asks, "Was he your mate?" and I can't decide if the question makes me want to laugh, cry, or vomit.

There's no judgement—no condescension to his words. Just pure, honest curiosity.

"No," I say quickly, laughing once despite myself. "No, it wasn't anything like that. He raised me, he loved me, and he was protective of me, but he was a parent—not a mate. I don't even know if a dragon could be mated to a human… I don't even want to think about what that would mean, to be honest with you."

We share an awkward laugh.

"Dragons are rare, and mated pairs even more so. Hatchlings are so uncommon that when one does come along, well… I think most dragons would trade their gold…their immortality…all of it, just to keep their young safe." I pause, chuckling to myself again. "I'm sure most drakaina would even trade their mate for a hatchling."

"Drakaina?" he asks curiously.

"Female dragons."

Nodding, he asks, "Did Penn have a mate?"

"Aye, but she died long before I ever met him."

"I'm sorry," he says, voice sounding raw and raspy in the shadows of the dungeon.

"Whatever for?"

"All of it," he says, clearing his throat. "I'm sorry for all of it."

"They are not your misdoings to apologise for, Tristan. You needn't bear the weight of burdens that don't belong to you."

TWENTY-NINE

ARI

Almost a week later, Tristan, Perci, and Lancelot show up in the dungeon. There's a nervous energy about them, and as my gaze slides across them, I notice that each of their faces seems more anxious than the last.

"What—" My heartbeat picks up in my chest and a drop of fear slides down my back. Other than the day of my trial, there has only ever been one guard here to collect me. Usually Tristan, sometimes Perci, and every once in a while, Kay. I don't know if it's the collective tension or the restlessness, but I lean away from the iron bars, shrinking into the shadows.

Tristan's hands come up in front of him, as if to placate me. "We're here to help."

My eyes dart over them again, taking each of them in as I wait for the growing unease to dissipate in my chest. Eventually, I manage to find my voice. "What's going on?"

Keeping his movements slow, he reaches one hand under his cloak and pulls out a key ring. Fitting the key inside the lock, he twists, and the cell door pops open with a loud clang that echoes through the dungeon. Pushing the door all the way open, Tristan takes a step back to let me out.

My feet stay planted on the stones in the middle of my cell, my eyes once again darting between the assembled knights. It dawns on me then that they're wearing cloaks and comfortable riding gear, not their usual uniforms.

"The tournament is in little more than a week. We're going to help you train." Tristan's voice is quiet but steady, as if he can sense my hesitation.

My eyes snap to his. "The three of you are—"

"Actually"—Perci snaps, though his anger doesn't seem directed at me—"Prince Arthur explicitly said that Lancelot was not to come with us." He turns to glare at the knight in question. "Something about letting things die in the forest? Whatever that means," he grumbles, turning back to me. "But alas, Kay is away on border patrol, and so Lancelot has decided that he's coming anyway. Regardless of what anyone else has to say about it."

Of course, he did.

Beside him, Lancelot scoffs. "Sometimes, I wish you focused less on what Arthur does and doesn't approve of."

"And sometimes, I—"

"Enough." Tristan's tone is sharp, silencing the others immediately. "Argue later, we're wasting time."

"You're really going to help me?" I ask, eying the open cell door and the three knights beyond.

"Aye."

"And Arthur knows about it?" I somehow can't believe that he'd be okay with them putting a sword in my hand to help me win his tournament.

Lancelot says, "He thinks we're taking you to the river on the forests' edge."

"The river?"

"Perci may or may not have told him that you're starting to stink, and that maybe you could use a bath. He might've suggested that doing so away from the townspeople would be best, and that was the solution they came up with." He smirks, chuckling to himself. "You have to be escorted, of course, but you've been otherwise relieved of your duties today."

"You said I stink?" I turn to Perci, my tone only half-offended. Of course, I stink. I haven't had a proper bath in months. Even the shirt Tristan gave me has long since relinquished the sweet and earthy smell it once held. Now, I just smell like a combination of sweat, and flour, and rosemary.

Perci looks away so that I can't read anything in his expression, though I think I catch a hint of a smile tugging at his lips.

"It's the only way we could get a sword in your hands," Tristan amends, slightly amused.

Shaking my head, I laugh. "No shackles?" I ask, eyeing their empty hands.

"The prince never technically said you had to be restrained." Tristan meets my gaze with an arched brow.

Lancelot grins. "There are horses waiting for us in the stables, and the patrol guards have been notified that we'll be escorting you out of the castle for the day, so we shouldn't run into any trouble."

"Wouldn't the guards question why I'm not shackled?" I step out of the cell and we head toward the stairs.

"Perhaps, but it's far easier to ride a horse with free use of your hands. It's not outside the realm of believability." Lancelot shrugs. "And it's also the middle of the night, so, chances are they won't even notice."

"So, just to be clear," I say slowly, narrowing my eyes at the back of Perci's head. "You're giving me a horse, a sword, and you're taking me to the edge of the forest I grew up in?"

"Aye," Lancelot says. I can still hear the smile in his voice.

"You're giving me a weapon, a means of escape, and you're taking me somewhere that I'm exceedingly familiar with...all under the cover of darkness?"

They pause for a moment, glancing at one another.

"Do you think that's wise?" My tone is both skeptical and disbelieving.

"You're the one who said you wouldn't run," Tristan argues beside me. "You're the one who said you wouldn't live your life looking over your shoulder for fear of Bors hunting you down."

"And besides"—Lancelot's tone turns smug—"you'd have to kill all three of us before you could escape." He glances at me over his shoulder and I arch an eyebrow at him. He returns the gesture, asking, "Do you really think you could take us all on at once?"

"No, but I wouldn't need to take you all on at once."

In front of me, Perci stiffens. With one foot on the bottom step, he turns to regard me, eyes narrowed. "Oh?"

Everything about the way he's looking at me reminds me of the day he came to collect me for my hearing. The way his hands trembled just a little. The anger and the fear, mixing together with a thick layer of uncomfortable anxiety. He doesn't trust me, but he doesn't necessarily fear me, either. It's not quite respect, I don't think, but maybe something similar. The way one predator would regard another—aware of what they're capable, though not afraid.

I bare my teeth at him in what's supposed to be a smile, but probably comes off a little more aggressive. Keeping my tone nonchalant, I say, "I would take Tristan out first. Then you, and then you." I glance from Perci to Lancelot.

"Why?" Tristan asks. He doesn't seem angry or threatened that I'd kill him first, just genuinely curious.

"You're an archer." I nod to the bow strapped across his back. "I don't stand a chance of escaping if you're still alive, and since you could kill me from both near and far away, I'd be stupid to give you the chance to do either.

"I'd go for Perci next because he seems the most cautious around me, and the least likely to take risks. If he's already seen me take down Tristan, I bet he'd take all of a heartbeat to weigh his options before heading straight back to Camelot for reinforcements. I'd be lucky if he didn't have some sort of signal horn hidden in his saddle."

To his credit, Perci shrugs, seemingly un-offended as he nods in agreement.

"And why would you save me for last?" Lancelot asks, lips still curved with confidence.

"Because, even after I killed your friends, you'd still try to reason with me." His smile falters with my words. "You'd likely still believe that you could talk me down. You wouldn't run once I'd slain your friends because your arrogance won't allow you to give up on people."

His smile disappears altogether, but even straight-faced, he says, "You're right. I wouldn't give up on you."

"I know." I nod. "But it would be a waste of your time. If I had already killed the others, I wouldn't hesitate to kill you, too."

"Maybe," he says with a little of that confidence returning to his expression. "But I still care enough about you to try."

It's still dark when we arrive at the stables, sunrise a few hours off yet. Four horses wait for us, saddled and bridled and ready to go—two brown mares with white markings, a tan one with a black mane, and a white one with soft grey splatters. Tristan takes the reins of a brown mare and leads her over to me, stroking the white slash on her forehead. "Can you ride?"

"I'll make do."

"Have you ever ridden before?" Lancelot joins us, his own brown mare in tow. She nudges his head with her muzzle and he leans into her, the moment oddly charming.

"When I was younger, but it's been a while." The last horse I rode was Bax's, though he was much too big for me at the time.

Tristan holds the mare steady while I climb into the saddle, offering me the reins once I'm situated. "Alright?" he asks. I nod, and he climbs atop his own horse.

Perci briefly parted ways with us while we were still in the castle, saying he was heading to the armoury and would meet us here. He enters the stables now, armed to the teeth.

He stops in his tracks when he sees me, and his eyes dart from me to the horse beneath me and back again, the colour draining from his face. Wordlessly, and rather stiffly, he hands a pair of shortswords to Lancelot and another to Tristan. Without another glance, Perci climbs onto the last remaining horse and disappears from the stables.

Tristan clears his throat and catches my eye. "It was his brother's horse," he says quietly. "The other knight who was with us in the forest that day."

"Why choose this horse for me?"

"Happenstance," Lancelot says, glancing at Tristan warily. "An oversight on my part."

"Perhaps I shouldn't ride her?"

"It'll be fine," Lancelot says, shaking his head. "She needs the exercise."

The mare snorts beneath me, stamping her feet and growing impatient. I thread my fingers through her mane, murmuring soothing words under my breath. After a moment, she settles a little, though I can still tell she's ready to get out of the stable.

"Alright?" Tristan asks again, his mare sidling up next to mine.

"Aye." I nod. "Though I much prefer dragons."

He grins, nudging his horse's flank and leading her outside.

We ride in a comfortable silence, following the moon's descent toward the distant mountains. We cover the plains and farmlands directly surrounding Camelot in no time, the horses breaking into a canter as soon as we've cleared the castle gates and slowing only when we reach the edge of the river.

On the other side of the water, the ancient forest begins. Eventually, the land turns mountainous, the forest continuing far past the range of peaks in every direction. I know this forest. I grew up here. This forest is my home.

And yet, it feels weird to return. It feels foreign somehow—different. Or, perhaps, it's me that's changed.

Up ahead, Tristan and Perci wait near the water's edge. The mares' pants come out in big white bursts, clouds of fog that float and drift and disappear into thin air.

"Can you swim?" Tristan asks, nodding toward the river. "Just in case," he adds with a quirk of his lips.

I smirk, shaking my head. "Of course."

Perci's already easing his mare into the water, and one by one, we follow suit, allowing our horses to pick their way across the rocky riverbed. The water itself comes halfway up my shins, and I'm grateful that it does not seep over the tops of my boots.

Once on the other side, we dismount in a small clearing, removing the saddles and blankets to let them dry. Their horses wander freely nearby, grazing.

"Will they not run?" I ask, removing my mare's halter and watching her head toward the others.

"Not unless something spooks them." Lancelot winks, flashing me a quick grin. "But our blades won't startle them, no."

"Who's first?" Tristan asks, clapping his hands together and glancing between us.

THIRTY

ARI

The sound of clashing steel rings throughout the forest. We've been at it for hours. I'm sore, tired, and sweating profusely.

The sun blinked onto the horizon as we made our way across the river, and now steadily makes its ascent in the sky. The air is already warm—thick and muggy. Clouds are beginning to roll in, with the promise of afternoon rain hanging low in the sky.

Ducking just in time to miss Lancelot's blade, the steel *zings* past my head, causing the hair at the back of my neck to stand on end with the proximity.

"That was close." Perci chuckles.

At first, the serpent etched into the pommel of Lancelot's blade unsettled me. I hadn't seen it up close again since the day they trapped Penn. Absently, my hand had touched the matching, skin-warmed medallion always resting against my sternum, safely tucked beneath my tunic.

"Perc," Lancelot warns, not for the first time, "shut up."

"Don't look at him, look at me," I say, glaring at Lancelot. "If Perci wanted to draw blood, he had his chance." I wink at Perci, giving him a feral grin.

Lancelot chuckles under his breath.

"You're going easy on her," Perci calls, ignoring me completely. "The other knights aren't going to go easy on her. If anything, they'll be more ruthless just to eliminate her quickly."

"I'm happy to go up against you next if you think I'm not giving it my all," Lancelot grunts back, grinning wickedly.

I went up against Perci first, but I suspect *he* was the one going easy on me, and after a while, his patterns grew predictable and Tristan asked Lancelot to step in. So far, he's proven to be a wild card—every time I think I've got him figured out, he switches things up.

Tristan sits perched on a large boulder, observing everything. He's been explaining the rules of the tournament, who the bigger threats are, and the favoured fighting styles of the better swordsmen.

"Shift your left foot—aye, like that," Tristan says idly with a small nod. He's been giving me pointers when they get too close—how to better my stance and how to block quicker.

Penn was a good teacher—all things considered—and had Bax still been coming around over the last eight years, he no doubt would have been a huge help to my training. Merlin is probably more skilled with a blade than anyone, though my training with him was mostly just sparring for fun.

But Tristan—his input today is proving to be invaluable. He hops off the boulder, and we turn to him in unison. Gesturing absently toward the river, he says, "Grab some water."

I drop the blade and hunch over, resting my hands on my knees, panting hard.

"Come," Lancelot says, breathing just as hard. "Drink." His hand briefly touches my back as he passes by, and I flinch.

A cluster of emotion aimed at the traitor-knight knots in my chest— anger for tricking me and hatred for what happened to Penn. But also, gratitude for his part in getting me out of the castle—even if he's not supposed to be here—and something close to appreciation for helping me train. And then, of course, confusion at all the mixed emotions.

"But I still care enough about you to try."

Part of me wants to move on—I think—if only so that I don't have to hold onto this grudge anymore. But I know that I can't, that I'm not ready to forgive him and might never be. Absolving him of the blame and relinquishing my anger doesn't change what happened, and it doesn't bring Penn back. It only makes room for other emotions that I'm not yet ready to face.

The river is ice cold and extremely refreshing. I cup my hands in the crystal-clear mountain run-off, drinking greedily, splashing my arms and face, and dumping a handful down my back.

Leaving Lancelot at the river's edge, I walk back to the clearing where Tristan waits, two swords in hand. His bow and quiver were shed and discarded upon arrival, and it's weird to see him without them.

Offering me one of the blades with a calculating smile, he simply says, "Don't think," before lunging at me.

It's all I can do to stay on the defensive. He's relentless, striking forcefully and repetitively. Over and over again, his sword comes down on my own as he swings with wild precision.

"Don't think," he growls again, an edge to his voice, sweat beading along his forehead.

He's backed me entirely across the clearing, my boots now catching on the roots of old, gnarled pine trees. I go down hard, landing flat on my back. The cold touch of steel against my throat—just for a second—is quickly replaced with his hand in a silent offer to pull me to my feet.

I wrap my fingers around his, letting him pull me up. "That was…"

"You're in your head," he says, brows furrowed. "You're over-thinking it."

"Where did you learn to fight like that?" I ask, still breathless.

"Camelot is not the first kingdom to teach me how to wield a blade," he says quietly, confirming the suspicion I'd been harbouring over the last few months.

Our eyes meet briefly, but he turns away before I can ask any questions.

"Let's go again," I say, returning to the centre of the clearing. In need of keeping my hands busy, I swing the sword a few times as I walk, testing the weight of the blade and adjusting the grip of my hand on the hilt.

Perci catches my eye, one side of his mouth lifted in a half-smile. "Unsettling, isn't it?" he asks, nodding at Tristan.

"Why do you all have such different styles if you were all trained by the same captain?" I ask, eyeing each of them.

Lancelot rejoins us, clearing his throat. "Perci sticks to what he knows. His style is formed from habit and comfort, but he's good at what he does. He's solid in battle, but to a widely-trained swordsman, he has the disadvantage of being predictable." He glances at Perci briefly, but the other knight only shrugs.

"My father taught me how to fight with a blade before he died—before I joined the army."

A wave of dizziness rolls through me at the seemingly inconsequential piece of information he's just given me, but before I can even fully process it, he continues speaking, completely oblivious to the way my knees are buckling beneath me.

"He was trained under a different captain and developed his own style after many years serving in the army. I try to use a combination of what I learned from him and what we're taught in training to give me an edge."

The only thing I can focus on is that his father is dead.

Trying to recall any time he's mentioned his father, it hits me with startling clarity that Lancelot has only ever spoken of him in the past tense. I had always suspected, though I had hoped I was wrong…and yet, the realisation hits me like a lightning bolt to the chest.

My free hand grips the serpent medallion beneath my tunic, squeezing until the edges dig into my flesh, even through the fabric of my shirt.

He didn't abandon me…

He didn't choose to stop coming to see me…

Sir Baxen of the Lake—*Bax*—my tutor, my mentor, my friend…is dead.

Lancelot, entirely unaware of the war of emotions raging inside me, continues on as if nothing's changed at all. "And Tris…" he says, glancing at Tristan. "Well, he had training before he came to Camelot."

"I was trained under a ruthless commander who believed that all bloodshed should be quick and dirty; the faster you dispel an enemy, the faster you can move on to the next," he says, a flash of emotion shadowing his eyes. He regards me warily, I think, noting the rapid rise and fall of my chest as he adds, "It's why I chose to focus on archery when I came to Camelot."

I say nothing, letting this information sink in, forcing my thundering heart to return to a more subdued pace and willing my hands to stop shaking.

"Are you ready?" Tristan asks, eyebrows raised, but a different question lingers in his eyes—one that I cannot bring myself to answer.

I nod, pulling in a shaky breath.

Swinging the blade once, he slides his feet into a defensive stance, but confusion settles over me as I take in the position of his blade arm. His knees are bent, feet staggered in the dirt, but he's left his torso entirely open. His sword is held at an odd angle to the side of him, his other hand slack at his side.

"Attack me," Tristan says, dipping his chin.

I stare at him for another moment, then free my mind of all the distractions and launch myself at him across the clearing.

It dawns on me—too late—that he hasn't left himself open and defenceless at all, but allowed his sword arm the space to counter any attack that comes his way.

Inches from his face, steel clashes, ringing out through the clearing, echoing into the trees beyond. Using the momentum and my own weight against me, he pushes his blade against mine, shoving me back.

Grunting against the effort, I retreat a step and try again.

Blow after blow, he blocks me, never letting me get closer than a few inches. Never letting the edge of my blade touch his neck in the same defeat he bestowed upon me.

A weird mixture of discomfort and awe settle over me as I realise that, while I may be sufficient with a blade—and perhaps more so in a blind rage—there is so much more I have to learn, so much further I have yet to go.

Dread and doubt start to creep in, and with my freedom so close I can almost touch it, it turns out I might not have a chance of reaching it after all.

"Is that soap?" I ask, disbelief hanging on every word.

"Aye. I told Arthur you could use a bath, but I figured you might genuinely appreciate the opportunity. We haven't done much but offer you cold buckets of water, and while you don't necessarily *stink*"—Perci sniffs delicately—"you could still use a proper bath."

I nod, taking the small bar of tallow and wood ash from him gratefully. "Thank you, Perci."

He waves dismissively in the direction of said river, only a hint of repulsion on his face. "As proper as the rushing water of a frigid river can be, of course." I try and fail to repress my amusement as he adds, "There's a change of clothes for you in one of the saddle bags as well. We'll make sure you get time to yourself before we leave."

I thank him again and nod toward the edge of the clearing, gesturing for him to follow me.

Tristan and Lancelot have gone to hunt something for lunch, while Perci has stayed behind to act as my guard—in case I run, of course. It's probably for the best that it's Perci who's stayed, even if he's the most wary and least likely to talk to me. Tristan's skills with a bow are better applied to feeding us, and Lancelot would surely try to fill the silence with all the ways he didn't betray me.

Undoubtedly, he would still manage not to apologise despite the fact that even if he didn't kill the dragon himself, had he never returned to the forest at all, Penn would likely still be alive.

We scavenge the nearby brush and riverbank for berries and herbs, maybe a few root vegetables. We don't have anything to carry them in, so Perci holds the hem of his tunic out like a makeshift basket, and I fill it with wild carrots, water mint, and half a bush worth of raspberries.

"I think we have enough," he groans, dismayed.

As we get back to the clearing, Tristan returns with three pheasants and a pair of ducks, Lancelot following close behind him with an armful of twigs and branches.

"Are we safe to light a fire?" Lancelot asks.

It takes a moment before I realise that he's asking *me*. "I think so," I say, glancing around the woods beyond the clearing. "I don't know what lurks nearby, but there are enough signs of forest life around us that I do not think it an issue."

He sets to work building a fire, and Tristan plucks the feathers from the birds, while Perci and I wash the carrots and raspberries.

We eat and then we train some more. When my muscles protest and my hands begin to shake under the weight of the sword, the knights fight each other instead.

True to his word, as the sun begins its slow descent toward the mountains, Perci tells me to utilise the river while the other two are still going at it.

I thank him again and head toward the river, shedding my boots, pants, and tunic on the rocky shore.

Perci sits on the riverbank, keeping me within eyesight but allowing me the privacy to properly bathe myself.

The water is ice cold and invigorating. The tiny chunk of soap smells faintly of sage, and I use it to scrub every inch of my body—twice. It lathers nicely, and I even take the time to run my soapy hands through my hair, pausing to detangle some of the bigger knots.

When we finally return to Camelot, Perci stays in the stables while Lancelot returns the swords to the armoury, and Tristan returns me to my cell.

"Thank you for today," I say quietly, not wanting my words to echo in the dungeon.

"No thanks necessary, m'lady—" He pauses, jerking as if he'd been physically struck. "Sorry," he says quickly, "it's a force of habit."

"It's fine," I say. My footsteps slow as we near my cell, the door still open from this morning. "Can I ask you something?"

Tristan looks down at me, one eyebrow arched. "Almost anything," he says, a quick smirk flashing across his face.

"When did you leave Northumbria?"

He stills completely, eyes boring into mine. "How did you know?" he asks quietly.

"You have a bit of northern lilt—not always, but it's stronger if you're distracted or intently focused," I say, forcing myself to hold his gaze. "You have a natural tan, as if you were born to a sunnier kingdom. You all but confirmed it today when you spoke of not only your commander but his fighting style—two things I believe to be Northumbrian."

He eyes me for a moment, unsure how to proceed.

"Lancelot often makes the mistake of underestimating my knowledge of the kingdoms, simply because I was not raised in one." I shrug. "I've had a lot of time to read about the many kingdoms on this continent."

"Aye," he says absently. "I'll bet you have."

"When did you leave?" I ask again. We keep walking toward the cell but at a lazier pace than before.

"About four years ago," he says, voice thick. "Maybe a little longer now."

We walk the last little bit in silence. He hesitates before closing the cell door, the keys rattling loudly in the silence. "Can I ask you something now?" I nod, and he continues. "You knew Lancelot's father, didn't you?"

"Aye," I murmur, swallowing down a fresh lump of emotion.

"But you didn't know he was dead?"

"No," I whisper, blinking back tears, but fear forces my lips to keep moving—to change the subject before it's too late. "Will you be entering the tournament?"

"No."

"Why not? Surely, you stand a fair chance at winning."

"I have no interest in being the king's champion," he says with a snort, "and he cannot give me the only thing I would ask for. It seems pointless to enter if I have no desire to win."

I nod because I don't know what else to say.

THIRTY-ONE

LANCELOT

The castle staff has been working overtime to ensure that everything is ready for a month of celebration, and before long, the festivities arrive and the tournament is nearly underway.

Twice, when Kay was on Ari's rotation, I've gone to see her in the kitchen, urging her to reconsider entering the tournament. Not because I don't think she can win—she's just as good as most of the young soldiers I've trained with—but because I don't think Arthur will let her compete in the first place, and the last thing she needs is for his attention to refocus on her.

It's bound to return eventually. After his name day, his coronation, or his impending wedding to Guinevere. Perhaps, after the next war. In a month, a year—it doesn't matter. Eventually, he will get bored and his attention will return to her. But now, when she's only been here for a handful of months…when she still has so much time left to serve…

Arthur could declare her ungrateful to what he deems his mercy for shortening her sentence. Alternatively, he could extend her sentence… or worsen it. Or, perhaps if he was feeling particularly spiteful, he could behead her for the fun of it.

He's done so for less.

Naturally, she refuses. Both times. With a deep scowl settling over her features as she does so, hissing at me to, "Go away." The vigour with which she chopped vegetables for that days meal became increasingly more violent the longer I lingered.

"Just promise me that you'll consider my words." I'd said it under my breath, hoping she'd understand the weight of what I was asking—and the reasons.

Lisbeth and Taite had openly glared at me both times I visited Ari, their hostility evident from across the kitchen. I don't know if it's my presence they dislike, or simply someone interrupting their incredible workload. Either way, I took it as my cue to leave, rapping my knuckles on Ari's work table and catching her eyes one more time before stepping out.

Now, Perci and I are patrolling outside the perimeter wall. We walk in comfortable silence most of the time, and fill the rest with easy conversation.

"Why do you think Tris doesn't want to compete?" Perci asks, taking a bite out of an apple he bought on the way out of the city.

"He doesn't care about titles, and he sure as hell doesn't care about eternal glory or endless ale." I shrug. "So, what's the point?"

"Why are you competing?" Perci counters.

"The same reason you are." I shrug again. "I want the prize. Money...a favour...I don't know yet."

Except, I do know. I know exactly what I'll ask of Arthur when I win.

One way or another, I'm going to force Merlin to help me, and if he tries to refuse, then I'll find another way to do what I need to.

When I win, I can ask for a leave of absence. I can ask for the time, or perhaps the resources to free my mother from her lake prison. When I win, I can hunt Merlin down and have him reverse the curse, or kill him if he refuses.

"D'you think she stands a chance of winning?" Perci asks, the mention of Ari pulling me from my thoughts.

I think about it for a moment before answering. "Honestly," I say slowly, "I don't know. She can hold her own with a blade, but the competition won't be easy. It all depends who she's matched up against." He nods, and I add, "If Arthur even lets her compete at all."

"You think he won't?"

Again, I shrug. "I don't know. He has no reason to let her, and every reason not to."

"D'you think he'd honour it if she won?" His voice grows solemn, offsetting the bright afternoon sun. Something in his tone makes me think that, for whatever reason, this question has been bothering him. "D'you think he'd name her Champion?"

"I don't know," I say again, meeting his concerned, curious gaze. "Again, he has every reason not to."

"Aye." He nods. "I suppose."

We continue on silently for a few moments. Perci finishes his apple, tosses the core, and wipes his hands on his pant leg before speaking again. "D'you think he'd truly give her whatever she asked for? D'you think he'd let her go?"

"No."

He stops to look at me, his gaze full of uncertainty. A dozen more questions seem to slide across his face, but none of them make it past his lips.

Again, the same sinking feeling I've been fighting since Tristan suggested it—the same thing I tried to tell Ari just an hour ago—takes hold, burrowing deep. Arthur is never going to let her compete, and if he does, he's never going to name her Champion. He's never going to honour her win and grant her wish. He's never going to give her the freedom she desires.

Ari doesn't stand a chance, and she's only going to draw more attention to herself.

An unwelcome feeling spreads over me, coiling in my chest and sliding through my veins. The rest of our patrol is done in silence, though, for the first time in a while, it's an uneasy one.

On the first day of the tournament, Arthur gives a grand speech to kick things off. He talks of his parents, the late king and queen—how he wishes they were here to see him today, to be part of the festival, to still be with us. He even sheds a tear.

It's a beautiful speech, moving and impassioned and entirely full of shit. The only thing Arthur cares about being crowned king.

When he's done paying false-hearted tribute to his parents, he moves on to the festivities. He applauds the bards and mummers who've travelled from all over the kingdom to entertain the folks of Camelot during this celebration. He thanks the vendors for bringing their finest wares to sell. He encourages the small children to try and pull the sword from the stone, lest one of them be a secret heir of Camelot. He does this all with a giant, boisterous smile on his face. It makes him look boyish and entirely different from how I know him to be.

This is the Arthur of the people—the one who needs their support, even though he is the only one with a claim to the throne. And they eat it up, laughing and clapping and smiling up at him.

He mentions the archery targets, set up on the opposite side of the duelling rings from his stone dais, promising something special for whoever can hit the most bullseyes on the farthest target.

And then he talks about the tournament.

He covers the rules, requesting that there be no foul play. "The winner," he says, pausing for dramatic effect, looking out among the crowd, "shall be named the king's champion—an honour, and a tribute." The people clap. "Along with his new title, the winner can also ask one wish of me, and if it is within my power to do so, I will grant it."

"Anyone may enter, be he knight or farm boy or anyone in-between," Arthur continues, that same, ridiculous smile on his face. "But men be warned, this tournament is not for the faint of heart. You will be going up against the best of the best, and maybe"—he pauses for effect again—"maybe I'll even challenge someone myself."

The crowd cheers and applauds, several loud whistles ringing through the square. It's incredibly hard not to roll my eyes.

Tristan stands at the base of the dais, on guard and alert. His eyes meet mine briefly, and he actually does roll his eyes. I smirk, coughing to cover a laugh.

Gawain and Guinevere step onto the dais to join Arthur. A desk is brought out for the scribe now climbing up the stone steps of the dais, quill and parchment in hand. The scribe settles in, and Gawain calls for the tournament's competitors to declare themselves.

Captain Bors is first, unsurprisingly, to step forward and proclaim himself. Most of the top-ranking commanders and their seconds in command follow after him. Dozens of knights step forward, declaring themselves one by one—Perci, Kay, and myself included.

Farmers and stonemasons, blacksmiths and tailors alike, all step forward for a chance to win the title or the prize, perhaps both. When no one else steps forward, I allow myself a small sigh of relief—Ari didn't declare herself, and Arthur didn't deny her.

Tristan's eyes are focused somewhere behind me. He nods once and my stomach dips on instinct alone. I don't have to turn around to know that Ari is going to be pushing her way through the crowd.

"Is there anyone else who wishes to compete in the tournament?" Arthur asks, arms spread wide as if to encompass the entirety of the crowd.

I can see her now, out of my peripherals.

"Will anyone else add their name to the list of champions?"

"I will," she says.

THIRTY-TWO

ARI

"Are you sure it's okay? I know how much work there still is to be done…" I'm hesitating at the end of Lisbeth's work table, trying not to fidget.

She sighs, but it only sounds slightly annoyed. "Honestly, Ari, no offence, but you're a prisoner, and while I have no choice in the matter, I don't actually enjoy your presence in my kitchen. We all know what you'll ask for if you should win, and it's no sweat off my brow if you don't return to work at the end of the week."

I nod, dropping my gaze to the floor and turning for the door. Lisbeth's words are honest, if a bit blunt, but I don't believe they're meant to be hurtful.

She waits until I've nearly crossed the threshold before she speaks again, her voice loud and clear, stopping me in my tracks. "That being said… those knights will not be kind to you. Most knights aren't often kind to any lady—unless they want something from them. Give them hell."

A brief smile touches the corners of my lips as our eyes lock across the kitchen. Her greying hair is slipping from the tight knot at the back of her head, and sweat dots her brow. She nods once, dipping her chin as she wipes her hands on the apron tied around her waist, and then she turns back to her work without another glance.

A young knight waits for me in the hallway, nodding in acknowledgement when I approach. "Hello," he says, his voice shy. Bright blue eyes peer up at me beneath unruly blond hair. "Tristan asked me to wait for you and escort you to the square."

"Hello," I say, offering him a small smile. "What's your name?"

"Erec." He beams back at me, shifting on his feet. "You're Ari, right?"

"Aye."

"Is it true you had a dragon?" he whispers.

I nod, a sharp pang of sadness filling my chest. "Aye."

"That's incredible." His voice is full of amazement, under-toned by a hint of jealousy.

"He was, indeed." I'm smiling in earnest now, despite the tightening in my chest.

A warmth spreads across his cheeks and down his neck, and he quickly looks away, which only makes my smile grow wider. We walk side by side through the castle, Erec peeking at me out of the corner of his eye every couple of seconds.

Once, I lift my eyebrows in silent question, but his blush deepens and he simply diverts his gaze again without saying anything.

He escorts me to the town square and stays by my side as we hover at the back of the crowd. The moment I see Arthur, my nerves start to get the better of me. I try to slow my breathing, pulling in several deep, steadying breaths.

"Are you alright?" Erec asks, genuine concern in his eyes.

"Aye," I say shakily. "Just a bit nervous."

"Don't be nervous," he scoffs.

"Easy for you to say. Are you even competing?"

"No," he says quickly, shaking his head. "No way. My sisters would kill me if I ended up hurt…or the knights who hurt me. Perhaps all of us."

He grimaces, then chuckles to himself.

The distinct feeling of being watched prickles the skin on the back of my neck, causing the hair to stand on end. My eyes dart around the square—scanning the faces in the crowd, the stalls and merchants lining the square, and the shadowy corners beyond—but find nothing out of the ordinary.

Erec nudges me as Arthur starts speaking, but I don't hear the words of his speech. The only thing I can hear is the pounding of my heart, the hum of fear weaving between each beat. My insides feel jittery, as if lightning were coursing through my veins. My fingers open and close idly at my sides.

I watch as Captain Bors and his best commanders declare themselves for the tournament, along with a number of soldiers—including Perci, Kay, and Lancelot—and a few dozen of the more muscled townsfolk.

Up on the stone dais, on either side of Arthur, stands Gawain and Guinevere. The former looks equally irritable and disinterested. His dark brown hair is thinning on the top, his gut a telltale sign that he most likely hasn't had to don his armour in a while. Both the set of his mouth and his ruddy complexion only add to the impatience rolling off him as he scans the crowd before them.

Compared to the Lord Regent and the would-be king, Guinevere looks like a beacon of hope for the future and a vision of what's to come for the kingdom. Her golden hair is perfectly braided, cascading over one shoulder, and though her face exudes innocence, there's a fire in her eyes that challenges anyone to underestimate her. She's a rose, beautifully in bloom and daring anyone to grab the thorns hidden beneath the surface.

Arthur hasn't so much as glanced at her since she joined him on the dais.

Off to the side, a scribe is adding the names of all the declared to a list, scribbling hastily across the parchment.

I force a deep, shaky breath into my lungs.

There are only two ways this will go: Arthur will let me compete out of intrigue and amusement alone, or he'll throw me back in the dungeons before the tournament even begins.

Tristan catches my eye across the courtyard. He's standing guard at the base of the dais, closest to Guinevere. He nods once, mouth pressing into the ghost of a smile.

Another two less-than-steadying breaths, and my feet are moving forward, weaving my way through the gathered crowd of men, leaving Erec where we stood.

"Is there anyone else who wishes to compete in the tournament?" Arthur boasts, arms spread wide. "Will anyone else add their name to the list of champions?"

"I will," I say, stepping through the front of the crowd.

His gaze drops to me, and at first, I think he's going to laugh, but then a muscle twitches in his jaw and I'm confident he's going to toss me back in my cell.

"You wish to fight in my tournament?" he asks, eyeing me with such intensity it makes me flinch.

"Yes, Your Highness," I say, wiping sweaty palms on my pants.

"You wish to bear the title of King's Champion?" he asks, tilting his head to the side.

"Yes, Your Highness," I say again, keeping my voice even.

"You know what happens if you do not win?" He lifts one eyebrow. The blood crown sits properly atop his head today, not askew and half-forgotten like the first time I saw him. His clothes are not rumpled, and he stands with his back straight.

Today, Arthur looks every bit the future king he is.

Beside him, Guinevere's face is a mask of demure and courtly properness—except her eyes. Her eyes gleam like sapphires in the bright morning sun, contrasted against the onyx and crimson dress she wears in honour of Arthur.

It strikes me how beautiful their children will be—hair of rubies and gold, eyes of emeralds and sapphires. The term *royal jewels* will bring on a whole new meaning.

"Yes, Your Highness," I say for a third time.

He stares at me for a long moment—weighing, assessing—his scrutiny almost unbearable.

He stares at me for so long that the crowd begins to murmur, tension rolling through them like a wave. It doesn't escape my notice that those around me lean away, leaving a physical barrier of emptiness between us, but I never let myself break eye contact with Arthur, not for a second.

Finally, a slow, awful, twisted version of a smile spreads across his face. "Very well then," he says, turning to nod once at the scribe.

A breath of relief washes over me—too soon, I realise. He's letting me compete, but the malice in his eyes when he turns back to me tells me I don't have a hope in hell of winning.

THIRTY-THREE

A R I

The tournament is set up to take all week.

There are one hundred and twenty-eight competitors, each match is an elimination round, and only one person can win. Elimination is achieved when your opponent is disarmed or yields, not when blood is drawn. Many knights shared satisfied grins at this rule, nudging one another and chuckling under their breath.

Each day marks the beginning of the next round of eliminations, the final match taking place on the seventh day—Arthur's eighteenth name day.

His coronation will take place the following week—a whole different celebration.

They've set up four rings in the town square where the duels are to take place. At one end of the square is the stone dais where Arthur, the Lord Regent, the Royal Advisor, and Guinevere spend most of their time watching the matches. On the far end, targets have been set up for archery, and in the centre of it all sits Excalibur in its stone tomb.

I was surprised to learn that this was the first year Arthur had disallowed jousting. "He claims good horses are too expensive to risk injury like that," Lancelot had said on the first day, "though he's never seemed to feel that way before."

Now, vendors selling ale, hot foods, sugary sweets, and everything in-between line the sides of the square and spill into the streets, their stalls and carts hastily jammed into any available space. Every tavern door is thrown open, loud laughter, the clink of glass, and the scrape of chairs floating into the square.

Tristan isn't competing, so he acts as my personal coach, giving me pointers and reminders on the long walk to and from my cell each day.

I had beaten my first opponent easily—a young knight-in-training, barely more than fourteen and only just growing into his body. He was tall and lanky, but unconfident with his sword, and, ultimately, I disarmed him after only a few moments.

My second opponent took a bit longer—a farmer from outside the city. He was taller, had more muscles, and was relatively good with his sword. But he fought with strength, not strategy, and ultimately, I was able to disarm him, too, although I was left panting and sweaty when I did.

Today, I'm to fight Kay.

Tristan seems unfazed by this, but now that I'm going up against someone I know, the jittery jolts of lightning return to my veins. Idly, my hands open and close at my sides as I shift my weight from side to side.

My nerves threatened to get the better of me this morning, and I'd had to expel extra magic in order to get myself under control.

"You need to relax," Tristan murmurs. "It's just another duel, just another knight."

"It's Kay," I argue with a huff.

"So?" Tristan lifts a questioning eyebrow at me.

"It's different," I mumble.

"It's not." He shakes his head, scanning the crowd once before turning to face me fully. "Everyone wants the same thing—to win. He's just a knight, it's just a sword, just one more match."

I nod, though we both know I don't agree. I know the name that goes with the face this time. Beating him means something—it means more. It means I'm taking something from him, someone who hasn't necessarily been kind to me but hasn't been unkind, either.

"You're overthinking it," Tristan says, pursing his lips. "Get out of your head."

I nod because I don't know what else to do, then I re-do my braid to keep my hands busy, tying the ends so it stays secure.

Kay appears on the other side of the ring, nodding at whatever the knight beside him is saying. He looks familiar, though I don't know his name. Hopping over the perimeter fence, Kay picks up the sword on the ground and walks to the centre of the ring.

Tristan raises his arm, putting his fist in front of his face. I do the same, briefly touching our forearms together in an X before hopping over my side of the fence.

I pick up the sword waiting for me in the dirt, testing the weight of it in my hand, swinging it and adjusting my grip. I don't really need to—it's the same as the blade I used yesterday and the day before, but I do it to anyway.

"You both know the rules," the commander running this ring says, his voice loud and clear. "Elimination by disarming your opponent or forcing them to yield. No setting foot outside the ring. No foul play."

We both nod to him, then to each other.

"Get out of your head." I hear Tristan's voice from somewhere behind me, then again echoing in my thoughts. *Get out of your head.*

I roll my shoulders and lean my head far to each side, cracking my neck. Digging my left foot into the soft dirt, I bend my knees and pull in a slow, deep breath before Kay advances.

He moves slower than I'd expected, lazily making his way across the ring to me. I'm still trying to decide if he's toying with me or waiting for me to make the first move when he lunges, slashing wildly with his sword.

I have to jump back to avoid his reach.

I let the whistles and cheers from the crowd distract me for a moment, and he uses it to his advantage. He slashes again, and I don't dodge it fast enough this time. His blade slices through the meat of my left bicep, blood instantly oozing from the cut.

A hiss escapes my lips, and I have to transfer the sword to my other hand.

He lunges again, barely giving me a moment to gather myself, but I expect it this time. I dive low, ducking under his sword and use my foot to sweep his legs out from underneath him.

He hits the ground with a thud and a groan but keeps the sword tightly in his hand. Before I can do anything to pin him to the ground, his foot connects with my stomach, throwing me backwards.

Air leaves my lungs all at once, and I'm lying in the dirt, gasping for breath. We both drag ourselves to our knees, then our feet—him a little faster than me. He lunges for a third time, and it's all I can do to block him.

He's taller than I am, but I'm faster. Once my breathing has evened out a bit, I can keep up with him easily enough. He's underestimating me, I can tell, but I just need an opening.

Something in his stance shifts, irritation seeping into his features, and I let him continue to misjudge me. He hesitates, just for a second—long enough to toss a grin at his fellow knights—and I return his earlier favour, throwing my entire weight into my foot as it connects with his torso.

A groan of frustration and pent-up energy rips through me with the effort, as he hits the ground again. This time, I don't give him the chance to do anything at all, throwing myself on top of him immediately. I sit on his chest, one foot pinning down each of his arms, the edge of my blade flush with his neck.

We stare at each other for several heartbeats, both of us breathing heavily.

"Yield," I say through gritted teeth. Blood from my arm drips onto his leather chest armour, and he continues to stare at me.

I adjust my grip on the sword and he winces. He tries to dislodge his hand from beneath my foot, but decides the risk of me drawing blood at his throat is too high.

"Yield," I say again, "or I will pluck the blade from your hand."

Cursing under his breath and glaring at me, he says, "I yield." He deflates, eyes closing in defeat.

Extracting myself from him, I stand and offer him my hand. He takes it—unhappily—but he allows me to pull him to his feet all the same.

"I'm sorry," I murmur just loud enough for him to hear.

He stares at me for a moment, jaw clenching. His eyelids flutter shut, and he heaves a breath, shoulders sinking as he says, "You should get that looked at."

My gaze drops to the deep cut on my bicep. "Aye."

We walk across the ring together as the commander declares me the winner. There's no reason to stop and acknowledge it; there's no prize to be won today.

Tristan, Lancelot, and Perci are waiting for me on the other side of the fence, and the knight Kay was with before the fight, too.

"You did good," the other knight says to Kay.

"Shut up, Graham," he grumbles. Graham looks at me and shrugs.

Tristan and Lancelot congratulate me, and then we all walk away from the ring, heading toward the castle.

I nearly walk into the back of Kay, who's stopped walking directly in front of me. His shoulders are stiff, and tension radiates off him in waves. My hands fly out in front of me as I stumble, a little woozy from the blood loss and fading adrenaline. Lancelot offers his arm to steady me, and surprising both of us, I take it.

In front of Kay, Bors is standing with some of the other knights from *after*. They're laughing, I realise, just as Tristan and Lancelot both loose a curse under their breath.

"Is something funny?" I ask, confused.

Bors' face slides into view between Kay and Graham, and he gives me a smile that's not a smile at all. "I was just congratulating Kay here on his loss."

"Come off it, Captain," Tristan says, not particularly kindly.

Kay glares at Tristan over his shoulder, and my confusion only grows.

"I don't understand." My eyes dart from Bors to Tristan, but it's Kay who speaks.

"He's congratulating me on being beaten." Venom drips from his words.

"Isn't there always a winner and a loser?" I ask no one in particular.

"Technically." Bors shrugs.

"Then, why is it funny?"

"Because he lost to you." Bors sneers, grinning maliciously at the knights beside him.

"He thinks it's funny because I lost to a girl," Kay clarifies, seething.

Oh.

Oh.

"Why should that matter at all?" The anger in my tone mirrors Kay's for entirely different reasons. "Why should a girl be any worse with a sword than a boy?"

"Because these *men* aren't playing at being something they're not," Bors says indignantly. "They're knights."

"Except, that half of them aren't! Half of them are farmers and millers, horse hands and hopeful recruits. Being a knight only means you've had training with a sword. It doesn't make you better by default."

"Fine," he snarls, looking to Kay. "Then it's embarrassing that you lost to *her* specifically." Nobody says anything, but he continues anyway. "She's just a weak little girl who was raised like an animal by a beast in a cave."

If he keeps speaking, I don't hear it.

I don't think, I just launch myself at him, pushing past Kay and screaming things only Penn would understand. My nails rake down his face, blood instantly welling on his cheek.

Someone's arms wrap around my torso, quickly hauling me backward, away from Bors.

"Not here, Ari," Lancelot whispers urgently in my ear.

Bors moves to follow after us, but Tristan steps in his path. Perci and—of all people—Kay stand shoulder to shoulder with him, blocking the way.

"Captain," Tristan says sharply. "Respectfully, sir, stand down."

I don't hear what Bors says in response, but his eyes don't leave my face until Lancelot has dragged me into the castle and out of his line of sight.

THIRTY-FOUR

LANCELOT

For once, Ari doesn't fight me. She lets me drag her away from Bors, through the crowd and into the castle. I don't even realise where I'm headed until we're halfway to the barracks, with plenty of distance between us and the enraged captain, before it dawns on me that the barracks is the last place I should take her.

Turning abruptly down a small hallway, I only slow down long enough to set her on her feet.

"Before you tell me I shouldn't have done that—" she growls, feet now firmly planted on the ground, warm green eyes glaring up at me.

"I heard what he said." I clamp down on the inside of my cheeks to rein in all of the vicious things I wish to say, none of which are meant for Ari. Her lips wobble, just once, but to her credit, it's the only emotion other than anger that I've seen slip through the careful mask of indifference she's trying to wear. "I would have punched him myself if you hadn't beaten me to it."

She stares at me for a moment, a slow smile spreading across her face.

"I'm sorry he said that."

"Don't be," she says, brows furrowing. "I don't care what he thinks of me." Glancing around the hall, she asks, "Where are we?"

"I was heading toward the barracks—Tristan, Perci, and I share a room there—but now, I'm not sure we should risk going there. I can take you back to your cell, I suppose…"

She nods, eyes wandering around the corridor again. Her left hand opens and closes at her side, nervous energy evident in the set of her shoulders. She lifts her arm and holds it close to her body, the movement bringing on a fresh wave of blood and, with it, the memory of what happened in the ring.

"Come," I say, nodding toward the end of the hallway. "We can get to the infirmary from there."

She falls into step beside me, a tense silence settling over us as we wind through the corridors.

As we enter the infirmary, an apprentice rushes past, looking frazzled and exhausted. Several beds are occupied with injuries from the tournament, all of the men looking rather angry at being down here instead of out where the action is.

Morgana looks up from the wound she's tending and freezes, her green-gold eyes locked on Ari. The girls seem to be in some sort of staring contest, neither willing to look away first.

"Let's just go," Ari says to me. "I can bind this myself."

"No, you can't," I argue, confused by whatever's going on. "It needs to be stitched up."

"Am I still to leave you alone, or would you like me to bind that so you may fight again tomorrow?" Morgana says loudly, an air of disdain to her tone. I have no idea what she means or why Ari bristles beside me.

"Please," I say to Morgana. "That would be greatly appreciated."

Morgana still doesn't look at me. She simply raises her eyebrow and waits for Ari to speak.

"If it pleases you," Ari says through gritted teeth.

Morgana's eyes narrow slightly, but she gestures to an empty bed. Ari crosses the room and plops onto it, wincing.

"It's deep," she says absently, fingers probing the wound. "Nicked the muscle."

"Can you fix it?" Ari says.

Now, neither of them will look at the other. *What am I missing?*

"I can clean and stitch it"—Morgana nods, all business—"and I can give you something for the pain. But that is all I can do."

Their eyes meet briefly, a silent conversation passing between them. I stand at the end of the bed in awe. I don't know if I'm more confused, concerned, or something else altogether.

"I do not expect you to break Arthur's laws of magic use," Ari says quietly. "But I do thank you for the rest."

Morgana sets to work, tearing away what's left of Ári's sleeve and cleaning the wound. Ari hisses as the cloth comes into contact with her skin—whatever is in the water to disinfect the wound no doubt stings.

Morgana works in silence, taking her time to stitch the gash. Occasionally, she glances at Ari, studying her face. Then she catches me watching her, purses her lips, and returns to her work.

Before long, she's tying off the last of the stitches and gathering up her supplies. "I'll be back in a moment," she says to neither of us in particular before disappearing through a door at the far end of the room. She returns a moment later with a small jar in her hands.

"What is that?" Ari asks warily.

"An ointment to stave off infection and help with the pain." Morgana twists the lid open and scoops a generous amount onto her fingers, smearing it across Ari's arm.

Her shoulders drop, and her whole body deflates with a heavy exhale. "Thank you," she murmurs.

"Come back in the morning and I'll put more on before your next match," Morgana says, avoiding eye contact. And then she's gone, flitting about the room and tending to other patients again.

Hoisting herself off the bed, careful to avoid using her injured arm, Ari heaves a sigh. I follow her from the room wordlessly. "Take me to my cell." Her face is expressionless, and the words seem to use up the last of her energy.

"We can swing by the kitchen on the way," I reply. "You need to eat something first."

"Okay," is all she says.

A few hours later, after Ari has eaten and returned to her cell, it's my turn to go up against someone in the ring.

Part of me had hoped she'd be here to watch, but a bigger part of me is more concerned about her regaining some strength for her next match. There will only be eight matches tomorrow, and no matter who she goes up against, it will be a hard fight.

Today, as it turns out, Perci is to be my opponent. Neither of us are very happy about it, but there's nothing we can do. Most of the men competing only want glory and bragging rights.

I don't know what Perci would ask for if he won, I just know that I want to win more than he does. Friend or not, winning is the only way I can think of to free my mother, and if that means I have to beat Perci to do it, then so be it.

We promised no hard feelings. There has to be a winner, and there has to be a loser. No matter what happens, we're still friends, still brothers—this tournament won't change that.

So, when he lunges at me, launching himself across the ring, I know that he doesn't intend to go easy on me, and he doesn't expect me to go easy on him.

We give it our all, both of us sweaty and panting from the start. He's been training without us, it would seem, and he was definitely holding back against Ari. I can't help grinning at him, and he winks at me in return.

"Surprise," he says, all arrogance.

I let him back me in circles around the ring, tiring himself out. He may have been practicing in secret, but he's still not much of a strategist.

He fakes to one side, then attacks from the other, nearly catching an opening. He swings down hard, and I have to use both hands to block against his weight.

He pushes off, retreating a few paces before coming at me again. He swings—just a little too high—and I duck under it, leveraging my free arm between us as I spin away. My elbow connects with his nose, and blood pours down his face.

"Surprise."

He curses under his breath, then louder, spitting a mouthful of blood on the dirt. He wipes his face with the sleeve of his tunic, glaring at me. Abandoning what little strategy he was using, he lets anger take over. His swings grow wild and frantic. That was his first mistake.

His second was letting me block him without giving himself enough room to retreat. Our swords bind, and I break off by raising the hilt of my sword, and bringing my arm down quickly to trap his blade between my arm and torso.

With my own sword, now on the outside of his arm, putting pressure on his wrist, his choices are simple: let me break his wrist or yield.

Cursing under his breath, and glaring at me with more animosity than I've ever seen from him, he drops his blade and storms from the ring.

Even when Garreth died, he never looked at me like that. A drop of unease unfurls in my gut, and I watch him go, catching Tristan's eye before they disappear into the crowd.

We said no hard feelings. We both wanted to win—I just wanted it more.

I turn in a slow circle with my arms spread wide, offering the crowd a huge grin. They're cheering wildly, and friend or not, that was a good fight.

Perci and Kay are simultaneously nursing their drinks and their sour moods. Perci is also sporting one hell of a black eye.

Tristan, Graham, and I are two rounds ahead of them, refusing to let them ruin our night.

The tavern is full to the brim and then some, everyone reliving the events of the days' duels. Almost everyone is talking about Bors putting his opponent in the infirmary. Word in the tavern is that he might not make it—a farm boy from outside the wall.

The thought sickens me, as I'm pretty sure it does the rest of my companions, too. The tournament is supposed to be fun, if not a little bloody, but nobody is supposed to die.

"It's not that she's a girl," Kay says, speaking for the first time in a while. Tristan and I exchange a glance, neither of us saying anything. "It's just that I wanted to win," he continues with a sigh. "I wasn't ready to be kicked out yet."

"Everyone wants to win," Tristan says carefully.

"Aye, I know." Kay groans. Then, after a minute he asks, "Where did she even learn to fight like that?"

Tristan and I exchange another glance, while Perci only rolls his eyes.

"I think people need to stop underestimating her." My laugh is soft, but there's an edge to it.

Kay drains the rest of his ale, signalling the red-haired bar maiden for another one. She brings another round for the table, whisking away our empty mugs.

"I heard you're to fight Torr tomorrow," Graham says to me.

"Aye, I heard that as well." I nod.

I wish that was who Perci had gone against today. He would have beaten Torr easily, and it would've at least gotten him through one more round of the tournament.

But either way, he would have ended up losing in the end. Only one of us can win, and it has to be me.

Eventually, Perci and Kay get over themselves and start to enjoy the night. We're all thoroughly drunk by the time a pair of miller's daughters saunter over to our table.

One of them sits next to me, her long dark hair tossed over her shoulder, dress cut too low to be considered virtuous. She makes idle chit-chat, overtly flirting and running a finger across my chest as she leans into me.

A few months ago, I might've taken her up on her unspoken offer—hell, a few months ago, I did take her up on it. But now, the only girl I want looking at me that way is locked in a dungeon.

Heaving a sigh, I wrap my hand around hers and gently push it back toward her. Nodding toward Perci, I redirect her efforts to him and say, "He got that black eye in the tournament today." It's an apology and a peace offering because, even though we said no hard feelings, something tells me he's not holding up his end of the bargain.

"Oh, wow." She takes it in stride, dropping her chin into her hand and staring at him with an over-exaggerated pout. "That must've really hurt."

"A bit," he says, shrugging her off. His eyes dart to mine, brows furrowing, and I can't tell if he's still mad at me, if he's simply not interested, or if it's something else…but he makes no effort to keep up the conversation with her. Eventually, she turns her attention to Kay, and after a few moments, the three of them are standing and making their way toward the door, Kay throwing one arm around each sister as they go.

"Well, his night is about to get a whole lot better." Graham snorts. The four of us burst out in laughter, and he signals for another round of drinks.

THIRTY-FIVE

ARI

I groan involuntarily. Morning, it seems, has come too soon.

"Ari?" The two-tone, sing-song way Tristan says my name gives me the impression he's been trying to get my attention for a while now.

Forcing my eyes open, and pushing myself into a sitting position, I wince, clenching my teeth. My arm is stiff and throbbing, though when I pull back the bandage, the stitches look good—no sign of infection so far.

When I look at Tristan, he's still staring at my bandaged arm. He's leaning against the open cell door, arms folded across his chest. There's a deep crease between his brows, hazel eyes brimming with concern.

"Unless you have healing magic in your eyes, stop staring at my arm," I snap, but there's no venom to it.

Staring for a moment longer, he shakes his head and says, "There are only eight duels today, so no matter who you fight, it won't be easy. There's no one left at this point who's gotten here by sheer luck."

"Except maybe me."

He smirks. "Except maybe you." No part of me thinks he's doubting my skill with a blade, and we both chuckle with the jest. We both know that under normal circumstances, I could hold my own against most of the knights competing.

He hands me a skein of water and a fresh, folded shirt, turning around to let me change. I toss the bloody, dirty, torn one on the ground and finish the water in three long swallows, handing it back to him once it's empty.

"Yours is the first fight today," he says, stepping back to let me pass through. I stretch my muscles as we walk, my shoulders and neck stiff and protesting. "They dismantled three of the four rings last night, so everyone will be watching each fight from here on out."

I grunt in acknowledgement, stuffing that piece of unfortunate news down to the bottom of my list of worries.

When we get to the base of the steps, Tristan stops walking. He turns to face me, then holds a hand out between us. "May I?" he asks, eyeing my bandaged arm.

I nod and hold it out to him, wincing when he lifts my hand above my head, and again when he fully extends my arm to the side. He's slow and deliberate with his assessment, pushing and pulling and prodding, all the while the crease in his brow deepens.

"Morgana did what she could, and I'll just have to make sure I keep the sword in my other hand today."

A scowl settles across his face, made more severe by the flickering torchlight and the shadows cast upon his skin.

"She told me to come back before my duel today, so she could reapply the salve to my arm."

He nods once, but the intensity on his face never wavers.

We ascend the steps in silence, turning the opposite way as usual at the top to head toward the infirmary. We start down the next corridor in silence, too, but the growing tension is making me fidget.

"You're worried," I say, breaking the silence. "That can't be good."

"I'm not—"

"Please, don't lie to me." My voice is so quiet it doesn't even echo throughout the corridor.

Tristan turns to look at me, his hazel eyes full of concern. He nods and sighs, glancing at my arm again. "Sorry."

"There's nothing we can do now." I shrug, offering him a tight half-smile.

He eyes me for a moment, brows twitching, jaw working furiously.

"What?" I say finally, my nerves feeding off his tension.

"There *is* something you could do, though…" His words trail off, but I can fill in the blanks.

"I thought about it, I truly did." I think about it again, just for a moment—how easy it would be—and how much trouble it would get me in. "There's no way I could hide it, even if we left the bandage on." One side of my mouth lifts up in a defeated ghost of a smile. "It would be too easy to get caught up in the moment and forget. Arthur would know, I would be burned or beheaded, and then I would never get my freedom."

He nods, knowing I'm right and that there's little point in arguing. He knew before even hinting at it, but the fact that he did anyways touches my heart, warms it a little.

A morbid thought crosses my mind, and with a quick laugh, I say, "Although perhaps death would offer its own unsavoury version of freedom."

"That's not an option I'm willing to consider." He shakes his head, glaring at me. "You just have to get through this duel, and then we can go from there."

"I don't deserve your friendship," I tease.

He meets my eyes and snorts. "Is that what we are now?"

"I could go back to hating you, if you'd like?" I raise an eyebrow at him, fighting the smile that threatens to spread across my face. "By all rights, even though you're trying to help me, you should still hate me for the loss of your friends. Maybe you do—or maybe if you did, that would make it easier."

"I don't hate you," he says with a smirk, and I can see it then—how easy it would be to befriend Tristan in earnest. To share a mug full to the brim with ale at the end of a long day. To laugh over crude and outlandish stories. To spend long afternoons with a pair of blades between us, neither of us yielding to the other. To have someone to confide in, to bear witness to one another's achievements and milestones.

I can see what it would be like to truly trust someone without question.

I can see it, and then, just as easily, I watch as the notion dissipates before my eyes. No matter how this ends for me, we come from different worlds. He is bound to Camelot, and I am desperately trying to escape it.

"Earn your freedom," he says, clearing his throat as if he, too, were lost in some deep thought, "and then we'll revisit the friend thing."

The infirmary looks almost exactly as it did the night before. A few of the beds that were occupied yesterday now lay empty, but a few others have been filled in their place.

Most of the men are sleeping. It's still early in the day, and Morgana moves around the room silently, replenishing supplies, refreshing bandages, and tending to the sick and injured.

It's odd to watch her work this way. It almost feels like an intrusion into the inner workings of herself that she hides away from others. Every single one of our interactions has been barely tolerable at best and extremely uncomfortable at worst, so watching her now with an almost tender air about her is somewhat unnerving.

"Are you going to stand there and gawk at me all day, or are you going to come and sit down?" she asks without looking up at me.

Tristan bristles beside me, but I push past him and cross the room to the same bed I sat on yesterday.

Her green-gold eyes meet mine for only a second before turning to glare at Tristan. "You may go, knight," she says coldly.

"I don't think that's up to you." His voice grows closer as he comes to stand at the foot of my bed.

"I've no need of you here." She scowls, lips forming a tight, thin line. "I've enough to do around here without tripping over someone so considerably unnecessary on top of it."

She says it so flippantly, her tone dripping with such condescension and finality, that it raises my eyebrows and pulls a small, surprised breath from my lips.

Beside me, Tristan stands his ground. "I am under strict orders from—"

"Yes, knight, and I have my own orders from the princeling. Regardless of whatever he's demanded of you, you have no jurisdiction here." She practically hisses at him.

I've met dryads with less rancour than her.

"You are in my domain, seeking my help. If you do not wish to abide by my rules, then I have no time for you." Her eyes, rich and warm in colour yet entirely unfriendly in feeling, glance to me as she adds, "You may leave—both of you."

Tristan opens his mouth to snap back at her, but I place a hand on his arm, quickly interrupting him. "No, please," I say, glancing from her to him and back again.

Her jaw clenches, one eyebrow raised.

"It's okay," I say to Tristan. "I'm okay here. I'll see you after the duel."

He stares at me for a long moment. So long that I wonder if he's going to argue. His warm, forest-coloured eyes dance back and forth between my own, eyelids briefly fluttering shut as he forces a slow breath into his lungs. "Are you sure?" he asks quietly.

When I nod in response, he raises his arm, fist in front of his face, just as he did yesterday. I do the same, bumping our forearms together in an X. Mouth set into a tight line, he nods once. "I'll see you out there, then."

As soon as he's gone, Morgana's bravado falters, and I wonder if she often has to wear that armour around the knights… I wonder if they've ever tried to put her in her place, even after she's helped heal them… And I wonder if Arthur would protect her if it came down to it.

She must see the questions plainly on my face because she pulls in an agitated breath and snaps at me, "Don't look at me like that. I don't need your pity."

"I do not pity you."

Her eyes narrow, as if my admission makes her uneasy, but she must decide to take my words for truth because she busies herself gathering supplies from a nearby cupboard and arranging them on a tray at the foot of the bed.

As she unravels the bandage around my arm, she laughs under her breath. "I half expected you to heal this yourself."

"I'd rather keep my head," I reply in the same cool tone.

Her lips twitch and tighten, but she says nothing. She begins cleaning the wound, and I stare at her face while she works, marking both the resemblances and the differences between her and Arthur, wondering which of the differences set her apart from her lineage and from being a mage.

"Why do you stay?" I finally ask, curiosity getting the better of me.

Her fingers still, as does her breathing. Her eyes flick to mine, hesitant and wary.

"Why do you choose to stay here in Camelot," I clarify, "when you could live elsewhere and use your magic freely?"

"You do not know of what you speak," she says quietly, shaking her head. She quickly glances around the room, her hands dropping to her sides. "Do not speak to me of choices."

"There are other mages out there, not many, but there are some who—" She recoils as if I've struck her, and her reaction gives me pause. Hesitantly, I try again. "Merlin would be able to—"

"Merlin can rot on the other side for all I care," she hisses. Her eyes hold nothing but loathing, the sudden change causing me to physically flinch.

She returns to her work, vigorously cleaning the cut on my arm. I have to grit my teeth and dig my nails into my palms against the pain. Wordlessly, she disappears into the storage room, returning with a small jar of ointment. She twists the lid off, then hesitates.

"I've always had a passion for healing people," she says quietly. Her eyes meet mine again, and, for the first time, I catch a hint of empathy in their depths. "My mother… My mother could not be saved, and so I spend my time saving as many people as I can to make up for it."

I don't say anything. I just stare at her while she works, deciding what she will and won't share with me. She applies another generous amount of ointment to my arm, and then ties a fresh bandage around the wound.

"Arthur does not allow magic within Camelot, but I do not need it to save lives. That is why I stay," she says. Something shifts in the way she holds herself, though I can't figure out what. "For Arthur, and for Camelot."

Her eyes drift over my shoulder, and she nods once. Two knights that I don't recognise come into my line of sight, one of them nodding to the door.

"They'll escort you to the duel." There's a vacancy to her eyes now that wasn't there before, a level of detachment that doesn't sit well in my stomach.

The knight nods toward the door again, so I hop off the bed. Something uneasy settles over me with the movement, an unwelcome drop of dread unfurling in my chest, and then my arm starts to tingle, like a hot ember is fastened beneath the bandage.

THIRTY-SIX

ARI

If I had any doubts about Morgana before, I don't anymore.

I don't know what she put in the salve, but it's working fast. I can feel it coursing through my veins with each heartbeat. It might have taken the pain of the cut away…but it replaced it with a fiery, burning sensation.

I try to turn around, to find Morgana, to ask her why, but the knights shove me through the door and down the hallway. They herd me roughly toward the ring, and I stumble every step of the way.

Is this Arthur's doing? I can't help wondering.

The pair of knights all but toss me over the railing, and my eyes desperately search the crowd for anyone who can help. After only a heartbeat, I realise I'm looking for Tristan. I see him with Lancelot across the ring, leaning against the railing, both of them laughing at something Perci's said.

It immediately strikes me as odd that Perci—normally quiet and subdued, if a bit on edge—could say something to illicit such a reaction from them, but that thought is quickly overshadowed by the knowledge that there's nothing they can do to help me now.

My heart continues to sink when Bors hops the fence, a wicked grin lifting up one side of his face. Three dark red gouges mar his cheek, a small consolation to this rapidly declining situation.

My breathing begins to falter, coming in quick, shaky bursts. I can feel my heart hammering sporadically in my chest, driven more chaotic now that I know who my opponent is.

Risking a glance at my arm, I'm somehow unsurprised to see that, peeking out from beneath the bandage, darkness is seeping through my veins—black instead of blue and spreading with each thump of my heart.

Arthur never meant for me to survive this tournament; I have no doubts of that now either.

"For Arthur"—her words whisper through my head, taking on a whole new meaning—*"and for Camelot."*

If her magic doesn't kill me, Bors surely will. He's already killed another competitor.

The commander briefly goes over the rules without so much as glancing at me.

I sway on my feet, nearly losing my balance when I bend to pick up the sword. My hands are shaking so badly I almost drop it, and I have to blink repeatedly to keep Bors in focus.

Half-breaths are entering my lungs in rapid succession, and I try to push them slowly back out to ease my heart rate, but to no avail. I try to swing the sword in my hand, adjusting and readjusting my grip on the hilt, but my palm is sweaty, my wrist feels weak, and the blade drags through the dirt.

I've never been religious, but I send up a silent prayer, anyway... To the gods. To Penn. To Merlin. To anyone who will listen.

And then, the commander is backing out of the ring.

At first, Bors only stands there, taunting me.

Does he know?

Then he advances, attacking again and again.

I can barely keep the sword in my hand, let alone block and deflect his onslaught of attacks. He puts all his weight into the next attack, and it knocks me to my knees.

Of course, he knows.

Black spots creep in from the edges of my vision, my breathing now incredibly shallow, but still, I cling to that sword. It's the only thing keeping me focused—as focused as I can be, anyway.

This fight is going to end before it's even begun.

His boots appear in my line of sight, and then his sword is touching my neck. I can feel the sting of the cut before it registers that he's drawn blood, and I'm immensely grateful that it's not grounds for elimination.

He's letting the magic work its way through my system—his impossible advantage growing with every second.

He's drawn blood.

The thought hits me nearly as hard as if Bors had done so himself.

I could summon my magic.

"Yield," he snarls, voice dripping with contempt.

I can't.

I can't yield, and I can't summon my magic—both would cost me my freedom.

When I don't move, he says it again.

But I won't yield, no matter how many times or how many ways he asks.

He laughs, as if he realises this, but there's no humour to it.

He bends down so that he's crouching in front of me, blade still poised against my neck. He smiles, and it makes me wish I could crawl out of my skin. "You never stood a chance, *girl.*" He keeps his voice just low enough for me alone to hear. "You never had a hope of winning this tournament. You're going to die, if not today, then in the dungeons, cold and alone— the way all monsters deserve to die."

None of that phases me. It's what he says next that sends me into a blind rage.

"Like I said…" He laughs that humourless sound again. "You're just a weak little girl who was raised like an animal by a beast in a cave."

And, just like yesterday, I don't think. I just scream, and then I launch myself at him.

He's ready for it this time, though, and his fist collides with my face before I can even touch him. There isn't even time for me to react before the darkness pulls me down.

THIRTY-SEVEN

LANCELOT

"What's wrong with her?" I hear myself ask, unable to recall forming the question. Beside me, Tristan shifts on his feet, and I can tell that he's just as worried as I am.

"I don't know…" He shakes his head, his eyes focused intently on Ari. "She's slow…and sloppy."

"She's *too* slow." I nod, returning my attention to the ring in front of us.

She tries to swing the sword underhandedly, feigning a defensive manoeuvre, but the rotating hilt in her hand is wobbly, the tip of the sword dragging through the dirt. She's pale, even by her standards, and her breaths are shallow and uneven. She looks like she's going to fall over. Beads of sweat dot her brow, and they haven't even truly begun the match yet.

"Is she ill?" Perci asks, leaning forward to rest his arms on the perimeter fence. The fact that he's openly showing anything other than indifference towards her only adds to the horrifying thought that something's wrong with Ari.

My eyes dart around the crowd surrounding the sparring ring. For the most part, everyone's just focusing on the two of them, waiting for them to attack each other. When Bors finally advances on her, he's single-minded and ruthless, continuously forcing her to fumble and struggle to maintain her footing.

On either side of me, Tristan and Perci both inhale audibly. Again, my eyes dart around the crowd, finally landing on Arthur atop the stone dais. To his left, Guinevere's eyes are glued to Ari's wayward form, and to his right, Gawain looks wholly uninterested. But Arthur…

Arthur's face is set in its usual scowl, but somehow, it's different. There's a deep intensity to his gaze and a hard set to his mouth that turns my blood to ice in my veins.

"She needs help," I whisper.

Tristan's head snaps toward mine, his eyes desperately darting back and forth between my own.

"Look at Arthur," I continue, keeping my voice low, not wanting to be overheard.

Tristan and Perci both look at the prince, the former swearing under his breath, the latter taking half a step toward the dais. My hand wraps around Perci's forearm, and his gaze swivels to my face, eyes full of concern.

"Don't draw attention to yourself," I murmur.

Jaw clenched, it takes a moment for him to stand down. Perci's reaction confuses me, but before I can let it distract me, Tristan swears under his breath again and my head snaps back toward the ring just as Ari stumbles.

Rage courses through me, unchecked and barely contained, when the audience cheers.

She stumbles again, unable to catch herself this time. She's on her hands and knees in the dirt, trembling.

I have never liked Arthur—he is whiny and arrogant and spoiled, but most of all, he is cruel. It never dawned on me until now how truly output he is by having her here—a girl with a wild story and an even wilder temperament, though she's shown nothing of the sort since arriving.

A girl he forced to stay, no less. A girl who took the spotlight away from him, during the only thing he's ever been looking forward to.

"Perci," Tristan says with a deadly calm to his voice that I cannot fathom. "Go to Vera's and tell her we're on the way." They look at each other for an excruciatingly long moment before he nods, disappearing into the crowd a second later. "I never should have left her," Tristan murmurs under his breath, but the words don't seem like they're meant for me.

"What do we do now?" I ask nervously, shifting on my feet. "Can we interfere?"

"I don't know," he says. "I don't think so. Not without consequences."

Her wound from yesterday is bleeding through the bandages, and I wonder if she's torn the stitches. Blood slides down her arm in slow, steady streams of dark crimson.

"The moment the match is over…when Bors stops toying with her," he growls, "we get her to Vera's as fast as we can."

"Why Vera's, though?" I ask, brows furrowing. "The infirmary is right here—" My eyes slide closed, jaw clenching. Her name comes out of my mouth as little more than a groan. "Morgana."

He nods solemnly. "She would do anything for Arthur, and I'm almost positive that the castle is the last place we can take Ari for help."

"D'you reckon she was poisoned?" I ask, afraid of the answer.

"I think it's the most likely option." He nods, scrubbing a hand across his face. "Morgana had access to her yesterday and again this morning. It would have been easy enough to do with no one the wiser." Slamming a fist into the wooden boards of the fence, he grinds out in frustration, "I should have known better than to leave them alone together."

"But why?" I ask. My stomach turns and I feel as if I'm going to retch. "It doesn't make any sense."

"Because Arthur was never going to let her walk away."

She cries out, and my eyes focus on her once more. Bors has the tip of his blade resting against her throat, a thin line of blood running down her neck, and still, she clings to the blade in her hand.

Still, she refuses to yield.

He bends down so that he's on her level, a malicious smile on his face. From here, I can't make out what he says to her, but whatever it is renews the fight inside her.

Without warning, she launches herself at him, screaming in a language I don't understand. It's terrifying and haunting and beautiful all at once.

But her strength is gone, the adrenaline fading. All it takes is one well-aimed blow to the face for her to crumple to the ground beside him, sword discarded in the dirt between them.

He stands, dusting himself off, and spits on the ground beside her.

The instant rage that surges through my veins is appeased only when I realise that Tristan has already hurtled over the fence surrounding the sparring ring and is quickly making his way over to her.

I jump over the railing after him, my eyes never leaving Bors. He turns to Arthur and smirks—it's so small, such a tiny gesture that it almost goes unnoticed. When he turns to survey Tristan sliding his arms underneath her, he mutters something again and spits at their feet before walking away.

Tristan lifts her limp form easily, one arm wrapped around her back, the other beneath her knees. I help him get her over the fence, repositioning her head when it falls to the side. Already a black and purple bruise is forming on the corner of her eye, the welt beginning to puff out.

Part of me wants to ask Tristan to let me take her, but I know we don't have time for that right now.

Pushing my way through the crowd, I carve a path for Tristan and Ari to follow. We've barely cleared the town square when, she stirs, surprising us both.

"Merlin," she rasps.

Tristan's eyes find mine for a brief moment. "We're taking you to Vera's," he says calmly, though I know he cannot feel it.

She winces, and I can barely contain the urge to reach out and soothe her. "I need Merlin," she chokes out before drifting off again.

She drifts in and out as we make our way through the city. Curious eyes follow us—two frantic knights and a beaten, bloodied girl—as we weave our way through the streets of Camelot.

If she can hear us, she shows no sign of it, but Tristan and I keep up a mantra of, "It's okay. You're going to be okay. Just hold on," nonetheless.

The farther we get from the duelling ring, the more noticeable Tristan's accent becomes. The growing fear seeping into his voice makes the hair at the back of my neck stand on end. Tristan has always been steadfast and sure in every situation… If he's not now, then…

I can't let myself think about that—can't let myself dwell on the what ifs.

When we finally make it to Vera's, Perci's waiting at the front door for us, propping it open so we can pass through easily and without losing any time or momentum. The curtain to the back room is pulled aside as Vera ushers us in, pointing to the empty round table.

"What happened?" she asks, assessing Ari as I help Tristan put her down. We try to be as gentle as possible despite the full-blown tremors wracking her body.

"We think she was poisoned," Tristan says, "but we don't know for sure."

We back up to give Vera room to work.

"Who poisoned her? And how?" she demands, all business.

"Morgana."

Their eyes lock across the table, and they exchange a loaded glance.

"Ari was injured in her match yesterday. Morgana tended the wound afterward and again this morning, though it seems more likely that it happened today," Tristan says, pulling in a shaky breath. "She was fine, other than being sore and tired, when I went to get her this morning."

The mage exhales what I can only assume is a string of curses in a language I do not understand. Turning back to Ari, she pokes and prods, turning limbs this way and that as her fingers fly deftly over Ari's body, following the shadows that seem to be flowing through her veins. Her left arm is now a maze of black lines that mar pale skin, the poison slowly but undoubtedly spreading with each passing moment.

"If it's been in her system for a while, we won't have a lot of time—if we have any left at all."

"What about charcoal?" Perci asks to my surprise. He's never been one to know much about herbs and remedies.

Vera shakes her head, expelling a long breath. She rubs her forehead before turning toward the wall of dried herbs, but scanning for what, I don't know.

"Charcoal will only make her vomit; it won't counteract what's already in her bloodstream," Vera says absently. "And that's under the assumption it's something she could even vomit back up."

"Can you bleed it out of her?" Perci asks, an urgency to his voice I can't explain. "Re-open the wound in her arm and pull the toxin from her somehow?"

"Do whatever you have to do, Vera…" Tristan says, unable to tear his eyes from Ari's arm. His voice is solemn, and there's a faraway look in his eyes.

As if on cue, Ari's shaking turns to full-on convulsing. She's simultaneously sweating and shivering, barely clinging to consciousness and writhing on the table.

I feel as helpless as she looks.

"Merlin," she pants with great difficulty.

For a moment, everything seems to come to a screeching halt; the chaos is replaced with a heavy silence, reinforced only by the sudden wrath on the mage's face.

"What did she just say?" Vera's voice is so deadly calm, so at odds with the tension in her shoulders and the whiteness of her knuckles, that it sends a shudder rippling through me.

Ari's eyelids flutter open, her scared green eyes locking onto mine. Bracing my arms on either side of her shoulders to try to quell the convulsing, I shake my head, murmuring under my breath, "We don't know where he is. You'll be dead before he gets here."

She knows as well as I do the risk she's taking by asking for him, by wishing him brought here. Whether or not he is ignorant to the mages who already live in Camelot, if Arthur didn't already want her dead, he won't hesitate to kill her once he finds out she summoned Merlin to his kingdom to heal her with magic.

She shakes her head with great difficulty, lips trembling. I can see the defeat as clear as Lake Umbra in her eyes. She thinks I don't understand, but I do. I know exactly what she's asking. I know exactly what it would mean for him to save her.

"I'll return again," he'd said, voice quiet. *"I'll come back and—"*

"That's not necessary. I wish for no reminders of my old life."

The conversation I'd overheard drifts through my mind, and I wonder how she'd feel if we actually summoned Merlin. I wonder if she'd regret it afterward.

"Did she say Merlin?" The calmness of Vera's voice has gained a deadly edge, pulling me from my thoughts.

Ari's eyes drift in and out of focus, her lids fluttering, lips trembling.

"Aye," Tristan says quietly. "They have history."

Tears roll down Ari's cheeks as her eyes slide to Perci's then Tristan's, silently begging each of us to understand.

"Vera, if you won't...is he an option?" Tristan asks, his voice taking on a desperate edge. "I know what he—"

"I'll not have that heathen in my shop." Her words are a warning, one I do not wish to push. But if I don't, Ari's going to die.

Ari is going to die.

She needs Merlin because whatever Morgana did to her, it wasn't a poison of herbs or plants. It was magic, and the only way to undo magic is with magic.

"She's dying." My voice is louder than I expect it to be, ringing in my own ears, and though I will it to be strong, it still wobbles. "If you can't save her, you have to tell me how to summon him."

Ari continues to shake violently beneath my grasp. Her throat seems to struggle with the effort of swallowing, and she clutches at her shirt, her complexion paling even further.

"She can't tell me, so you must." My voice is firm, though my nerves feel fragile. "Tell me how to summon him." I'll do anything I can to save her, and if I can learn how to summon Merlin in the process, then it'll save me trouble down the road.

"I have no need for the likes of Merlin." Vera sneers, meeting my eyes with a glare and spitting the words at me with disgust. "Stand aside, knight. No one is going to die today."

I do as she asks, reluctantly moving to stand beside Tristan and Perci.

"He'll have you burned or beheaded," Tristan says, voice thick with emotion, though it sounds more like a warning than a plea to reconsider.

"I do not fear the boy king." She snorts, glancing at Tristan. "Take her hand. She's going to want you to hold that."

Ari opens her mouth to speak, but no words come out. Instead, she begins coughing so violently that blood dots her lips—red, tinged with black—dripping down the side of her mouth.

"Whatever you're going to do then," he says, taking one of Ari's hands in his and gesturing for me to return to her side and do the same with the other, "now's the time."

Tristan and Vera lock eyes again for a brief moment, and then the room erupts into a bright, golden light.

THIRTY-EIGHT

A R I

As I drift in and out of consciousness, the hateful, spiteful words from Bors echo through the back of my mind. They taunt my thoughts and plague my hazy dreams, and in the moments when the darkness loosens its hold on my subconscious, I can feel my body at war with itself.

My skin is freezing cold and burning hot at the same time. My blood feels like erratic jolts of lightning in my veins. My tongue is thick and dry in my mouth, and I can feel my body convulsing.

My thoughts are muddled, trapped somewhere between past and present.

Memories of Penn and my childhood keep drifting to the surface, snatching my attention but disappearing before I can truly get lost in them. The onslaught of images seem to weave and blur, shifting and blending as Bors' words continue to play on a loop in my head.

Finally, one memory above all the others seems to stick.

Though I can understand his apprehension now, when I was seven, it felt like a betrayal.

"She's just a girl," Bax's voice is angrier than I've ever heard it.

"She may be just a girl, *as you so crudely put it, but she still needs to know how to protect herself."*

"You have no business being here, mage." Bax has always hated Merlin,

perhaps more so than Penn.

"I am the only one who has any business being here."

"You are the one to blame for this, Merlin! That does not give you the right to treat her like an animal. She is a—"

"I know exactly what she is, knight. It would be unwise to forget your place in all this." Merlin snarls at him, and for once, Penn takes his side.

Penn never takes Merlin's side.

"There is no other way, Baxen." Penn's voice leaves no room for negotiation. "We've already looked."

"Surely, there must be something else—"

"It doesn't work that way," Merlin says, sounding as if he wished that it did.

"Are you not the most powerful mage in existence? Can you not simply use your magic to alter the cost of hers?"

"Do you think I've not already tried that? The spinners of fate have decided that it will be blood, or it will be nothing at all. The fact that she can even summon magic at such a young age is a blessing."

"Or a curse."

"Perhaps it is both. But alas, I cannot change the cost it will take from her, for I did not decide it. A great many things are within my control, but this is not one of them."

At the time, I couldn't see past my pure joy and delight to truly understand what they were arguing about.

It had taken us months to figure out how I could summon magic. On a particularly bad day of lessons with Merlin, after a tantrum born of pure frustration, I had tripped on my way back to the cave and accidentally scraped my hand. As I was picking out the bits of grass and debris mixing with the blood in my palm, I had wished for something pretty to distract me from the stinging pain, and, in doing so, I'd turned one of those blades of grass into a daisy.

I'd begun screaming so loudly that Merlin was breathless by the time he reached me a few moments later. The pride in his eyes and the grin on his face mirrored my own excitement.

I'd finally done it.

I wanted to make another flower, and then another until the whole valley was full of them.

I wanted to show Penn.

He didn't like that I wanted to learn magic, and he liked it even less that I would have to bleed to do so. But he respected my wishes; he let me learn anyway, so long as Merlin and I both promised to be careful, to never draw too much, to never let it get out of control.

But I couldn't understand why Baxen was so upset when I showed him what I had learned during his next visit. I couldn't understand why he was so against me learning how to use magic, and I couldn't understand why he hated Merlin so much.

I wanted them to be as excited as I was—Penn and Baxen. I wanted them to be proud of what I could do, but Merlin seemed to be the only one who ever was. While Penn tolerated my use of magic—accepted it, even—it was only Merlin who ever encouraged it.

More images of my childhood flash through my mind, but this time, they're all of Merlin.

The first time I summoned him—on a whim and pure luck alone—his tall frame crouching down before me, a gentle hand on each of my cheeks, the most satisfied smile on his face.

The first time he dared me to put a gnome under a sleeping spell— after it had left me paralysed—and the fiendish look on his face when I followed through without hesitation.

The first time I reversed the effects of his emotions, sending the raging thunderstorm away from the valley and out toward the mountains—his sad, broken smile disintegrating like the clouds before my eyes.

The first time he helped me rebuild the broken arm of a mountain troll that had been left behind and left for dead by its horde—reminding me that sympathy and compassion are always an option.

The memories seem to change as I get older, transforming into something deeper, something more personal as they drift through my mind.

The sorrow on his face as he wiped the tears from my eyes when Baxen did not return. The way his hand has always felt in mine, strong and reassuring. The rapid beat of his heart after I kissed him for the first time. The fear in his eyes when he awoke from the dryad's spell.

Merlin is the only one who would risk using magic in Camelot to save me. He might have left me behind, but he would never let me die.

I'm going to die.

That realisation settles in slowly among all the chaos—either Merlin will save me, or he'll reunite me with Penn.

THIRTY-NINE

ARI

The first thing I notice is the silence. The absence of sound is nearly deafening.

Taking a mental note of my body, it seems as if most of the pain has vanished from my limbs—along with the chill from my skin—though a dull, persistent ache seems to linger at the base of my skull. My breathing feels steady, if a bit slow, and my heart is no longer racing. The distant, indistinguishable murmur of voices tells me it's unlikely that I'm dead.

It seems I won't be reunited with Penn after all.

"Can you hear me?" someone asks, but I can't make out who it is. I don't even know where I am.

Forcing an eye open, I hiss at the bright sunlight filtering in through a nearby window. A flash of pain causes me to wince and squeeze my eye shut again. It takes me a moment to realise that only one of my eyes could even open, and an image of Bors' angry face darts across my thoughts. Groaning, I bring a shaky hand to gingerly touch the swollen bruise on my face, and another hiss escapes my lips.

"Easy."

My eye cracks open again, and when my gaze collides with a pair of hazel ones that vividly remind me of home—of the forest—I relax a little. When

I try to sit up, Tristan keeps a firm hand on my shoulder to stop me.

"You need to rest for a while."

"You should've let me die."

"Don't be ridiculous." He snorts, leaning back. As he pushes a deep breath from his lungs and shifts in the chair, I try to take in the unfamiliar surroundings. We're in a narrow room that consists of a bed, the chair Tristan is currently occupying, and a small table. Wherever the one door leads to, it's closed, as is the only window.

"Where are we?"

"Vera's," he says, rubbing his eyes and stretching his arms high above his head. "Her shop doubles as her home. She's downstairs with a patient, so Ector was keeping me company while we waited for you to wake."

A ginger cat I hadn't noticed—Ector, I assume—uncurls beside me, stretching and yawning widely before curling back up again.

"He's going to kill you," I murmur, letting my good eye fall closed again. "For helping me. For saving me. He'll know you intervened, and he'll punish you for it."

"All I did was escort you to a healer," he says evenly. "It's quite literally in my job description as your ward to keep you alive."

"Then you've put everyone else in danger—anyone else who helped me."

"I did what I had to do." There's an edge I can't quite place to his tone, the northern lilt creeping heavily into his words.

"And you would risk Vera's life for mine?" I ask, forcing my good eye open again to meet his. "You would risk your friend for someone who means nothing to you?"

"The only one who can risk Vera's life is Vera."

"What is that supposed to mean?"

"She's in no danger from us. Arthur won't be able to prove she or anyone else did anything without first admitting that he had you poisoned with blood magic."

I mull over his words for a moment, trying to find a weakness in the plan. If Arthur hates magic so much, it would go against everything he stands for and everything he's preached to the kingdom over the years if it were to come out that he was behind Morgana's assault on me. He would either have to publicly condemn his half-sister to death, or he would have to acknowledge that he knew about her use of magic and did nothing.

Perhaps, Vera is safe, for the time being.

Nodding, I open my mouth the same time he does, our words tripping over one another's.

"Thank you, Tristan," I say.

"Are you okay?" he asks.

We both crack a smile, and he dips his head. "No thanks necessary, m'lady."

I glare at him in earnest, and his smile deepens, so much so that it produces a dimple in his left cheek that I've never seen before.

"Are you okay?" he asks again, eyes flitting over me quickly.

"Aye." I nod. "I feel a lot better now than I did the last time I was awake."

Ector stirs as Vera bustles into the room carrying a tray with a cup and a large steaming pot. "You look horrible," she says by way of greeting.

Tristan scoots the chair back from his place at my side, and Vera sets the tray on the small table next to the bed.

"I imagine you feel about the same." She arches a dark brow at me. Helping me into a sitting position, she slowly eases me back so that I can rest against the wall for support. Pouring some of the steaming liquid into the cup, she wraps my hands around it and murmurs, "Drink this."

The room fills with the aromatic scent wafting from the steaming pot, and I do as she says, relishing the way the warmth of the tea soothes away some of the lingering aches in my bones.

"Thank you," I say. "For everything."

The look she gives me sends an involuntary shiver down my spine, but she simply says, "You're welcome."

I glance at Tristan, and the downward tilt of his mouth sets a ripple of restlessness through me.

"I know what you did for me comes at great risk," I say, swallowing down the growing unease in my chest. "I'll likely never be able to thank you enough for—"

"There's no thanks necessary, Ari." Vera glances at Tristan, and they share a look I can't even begin to understand or decipher.

"My silence, then, of course." She turns back to me, eyes narrowed in question. "I would never out you, Vera," I say hesitantly, "for using magic against Arthur's decree. I can swear it in more ways than one, if you'd like."

"I do not need your blood promises, child." She scoffs, waving a hand in my direction. "And I do not fear the boy king."

"He's not king yet," Tristan says, shifting in his chair again.

"Never mind that now," Vera chides him, refilling my cup.

The delicious, inviting smell of the tea floods my senses again, and years of steeping and brewing flowers and herbs for this very reason helps me to easily identify the scents. An unexpected knot of comfort and familiarity fills my chest. Closing my eyes, I inhale each herb, smell each flower, as she names the ingredients and their intended purposes.

"Passionflower, hops, and chamomile for sleep. Lavender and peppermint for pain, and a touch of feverfew, just in case. The side effects of magic can be nasty, especially when opposing ends of the spectrum are in effect. Do you need honey? I didn't think to add some—"

"No," I say quickly. "No, thank you. It smells wonderful."

"You should rest, then." She looks pointedly at Tristan. Nodding, he clears his throat and stands, pushing the chair into the corner.

Vera steps out for a moment, quickly returning with an armful of thick, woven blankets. She piles them at the foot of the bed and motions toward

Ector. "Don't mind him. He'll leave if you shoo him off."

"I don't mind," I assure her. "I like having company."

Nodding, she turns to Tristan. "You should return to the castle, see what you can find out. But…be careful."

He nods, the corners of his mouth turning downward again as his brow furrows. "I'll be back as soon as I can." He glances at each of us before swiftly departing.

Expelling a large sigh, Vera turns back to me one last time. "Rest, child. I'll check on you in a while."

"Thank you," I say again, drinking down the rest of my tea greedily.

"Shout if you need anything."

Settling back into the bed and pulling the blanket up to my chin, I let my eyelids slide closed and drift into a dreamless sleep.

Sometime later, the incessant, impatient sound of tapping drags me from unconsciousness.

"Are you here to agitate me, or are you just incapable of sitting still?"

"Well, aren't you pleasant when you wake up?"

"When I'm *woken* up, you mean." Cracking my good eye open, I muster as much of a glare as I can.

Perci snorts, returning the front two legs of the chair to the ground and leaning in close. "You look pretty rough."

"Aye, well, that's what happens when someone bigger than you punches you in the face."

He snorts again, leaning back so that he's balancing on the back two legs of the chair, feet propped up on the bed beside me. He's got a nasty black eye that probably rivals my own, and one of his hands is freshly bandaged.

"I'm a little surprised to see you here."

"Lancelot's duel should be underway by now, and Tristan's trying to find out anything he can about what happened earlier," he says indifferently. "We figured you should stay here for now, and that someone should be here, just in case."

"Vera's here," I counter.

"Someone who can fight, if it should come to that."

"You're a fool if you think she can't defend herself." Now, it's my turn to snort.

"Aye, well, I'm here, so deal with it."

Despite his tone, the corners of my mouth lift a little, and an awkward silence falls over us. His tapping resumes, one of his fingers rapidly thrumming against the wooden arm of the chair. Contemplating his seemingly agitated mood, and weighing it against the odds of getting him alone again, I push down my nerves and force myself to break the silence.

"Can I ask you a question?"

"You just did." He seems to sense my hesitation, his reluctance mirroring my own. After a moment, he swallows visibly and nods.

"Why do you think Arthur had me poisoned?"

His finger stops tapping, and he seems to stare at me for a moment, considering my question. His eyes narrow and grow distant, a weird mixture of curiosity and pity filling their dark brown depths. Slowly, he lowers his chair back to the ground, removing his feet from the edge of the bed and hunching forward to rest his elbows on his knees, clasping his hands in front of him.

"It just doesn't make sense that he'd let me enter the tournament only to have me poisoned a few days later," I add in a quiet rush, waiting for him to respond.

Perci glances at me briefly, nodding slightly before looking away again. His thumbs fidget with one another, absently alternating between pushing against each other and digging one nail into the pad of the other.

"I think…" he says slowly, his words trailing off. Clearing his throat, he tries again. "I think he's afraid."

"Afraid of what?"

"You." Perci's eyes find mine, and any brief notion I might've had that he'd been joking vanishes. His gaze holds nothing but sincerity, and perhaps, a hint of vulnerability.

"What reason does he have to be afraid of me?"

The seriousness in his expression changes to something far too perceptive for my liking. He arches a thick, dark brow and a ripple of doubt spreads throughout my gut, but before I can say anything, he does. "Why are you asking me this?"

"What do you mean?"

"Exactly what I said," he deadpans. "Why are you asking *me* about Arthur's motives?"

"Do you see anyone else around for me to ask?" I smirk wryly at him. In response, he simply continues to stare at me.

Pushing out a heavy sigh, I say, "Tristan is cautious in voicing his opinions, though I believe him to be a bit biased. Arthur is not the first ruler he's been sworn to, and I imagine that means he weighs and compares Arthur's actions to those of his former king—for better or worse."

Perci leans back in the chair again, silently studying me.

"Whereas Lancelot absolutely detests Arthur and has been openly hostile in his opinions of him." A humourless laugh escapes my lips. "I believe he would forswear his oath to the blood crown in a moment, if it wouldn't brand him a traitor like his father."

"But you…" I drop my gaze to the cat curled up at my side, threading my fingers through his soft, orange fur. "You seem *indifferent,* for lack of a better word."

"What makes you say that?" he asks, shifting uncomfortably. His right knee begins bouncing just as rapidly as his finger had.

"I just don't think you dislike or distrust him the way the other two do," I say, lifting my eyes to meet his again. "I'm not judging you for it, Perci. It's just something I've noticed—and I think that makes you most likely to give me an honest answer about him."

When he continues to stare at me silently, almost nervously, I add, "I don't particularly care one way or another how you feel about Arthur, it makes no difference to me."

He nods, using a hand to massage the back of his neck. "Whether you want to believe it or not—whether you can understand it or not—you threaten him, Ari." Perci's tone is quiet, guarded. "You threaten the perception of his people, the trust of his knights, and the short-sighted decrees and violent legacy that Uther left behind for Arthur to uphold." He sighs so deeply I wonder if, in some ways, he feels as bone-deep weary as I do. "And when people are scared, they lash out."

FORTY

LANCELOT

The rest of the day passes by in a bit of a blur. After Vera assured us Ari would be okay, I had to leave or risk forfeiting my duel. Distracted as I was, it was an easy enough win. The young knight accepted his defeat with a grace that some of his superiors could learn a thing or two from.

Tristan, Perci, and I had agreed that we couldn't all be seen frequenting Vera's, or it would undoubtedly give away Ari's location, so I had to force myself to stick around and watch the rest of the duels while Perci, of all people, sat by her bed.

A few hours later, Tristan appeared at my side, looking far too on edge for my liking, and shortly after sunset, Perci tracked us down in the great hall.

"How is she?" I can't keep the nerves from my voice as it cracks with each word.

"She's asleep again," he murmurs, sliding onto the bench beside Tristan.

"And Vera?" Tristan asks, glancing at him sidelong.

Perci simply nods once, and Tristan returns to his half-empty mug of ale, heaving a sigh before draining the rest.

Irritation swells in my chest. "Those aren't answers," I growl, glaring across the table at Perci.

"They're answer enough," he snaps back. His dark eyes hold a glare that must match my own because Tristan intervenes to break the tension.

"Everyone's doing the best they can, aye?"

Gritting my teeth, I drag my eyes away from Perci and focus on Tristan instead.

"Get a hold of yourself, Lance," Tristan warns. "She's in the safest place we could think of, and she's not alone."

I nod, knowing he's right. Without a way to get her out of the city, Vera's *is* the safest place for Ari to be tonight. The two of them have more than enough magic to protect themselves on their own, but together? Very little could get past them unnoticed.

If anyone other than the three of us not only can, but will, look out for Ari, it's Vera—a mage who shares a history with Tristan and seems to dislike Arthur almost as much as we do.

It dawns on me how obvious it is that Arthur was only ever playing a game—one Ari was never meant to win. The fact that Bors and Morgana were in on it only makes things worse. We have no way of knowing who else is playing the game, or what the game even is, really. No way of knowing who else we can trust, if anyone, and no way of knowing what Arthur plans to do next.

Tristan is right. She's not alone. She's safe, for now.

The only safer place she could be is with her dragon, hidden away in their cave.

A wave of shame rolls over me, a feeling that's getting harder and harder to ignore with each passing day. I'm not naive enough to believe that she's forgiven me simply because she's tolerated me lately—and I'm not ignorant enough to expect anything at all from her yet, even if she seems to have found some sort of common ground with Tristan.

A wave of jealousy surges through me, though I can't bring myself to blame either one of them.

He wasn't there. He didn't disobey her words. And he had no part in the destruction of her family. He's simply a knight who volunteered to oversee her time in the dungeons. A knight who came to Camelot by happenstance, who was neither born here nor truly belongs here—just like her.

Perci and Tristan are talking quietly opposite me, but I can't focus on anything they're saying. Instead, I lose myself thinking about all the ways our situations differ and the irrevocable ways our fates have all been intertwined.

I'm so lost in thought that I do little more than grunt in acknowledgement when they stand to leave.

Everything that's happened over the last few months replays through my mind on a continuous loop. Garreth telling us of the dragon's whereabouts and his untimely death. The arrival of the strange and intriguing girl, who looked less like a girl and more like a wraith, or a wildflower. My undeniable need to know more about her and my inability to stay away from her. The loss of her dragon and her ensuing imprisonment. Arthur allowing her to enter the tournament, only to have her poisoned.

The more I relive the events, the more I devolve into a downward spiral of guilt and emotion and the less things make sense to me. The only thing that does make sense, unfortunately, is her animosity toward me. If I had left her alone, she more than likely never would have come across another knight of Camelot.

If I had left her alone, she wouldn't be fighting for her life and her freedom.

If I had left her alone, her dragon would still be alive.

But how did Garreth know where the cave was to begin with? How did he have any idea—

Behind me, someone clears their throat.

I feel almost disoriented as I turn to find a page standing a few feet away, shifting his weight from one foot to the other, fidgeting nervously.

He can't be more than ten or eleven, and hasn't even properly grown into his uniform yet.

"Sir Lancelot," he says quickly, his voice squeaking. "The king requests an audience."

"The prince," I say with too much of an edge, not giving myself time to think better of it. "He's not king yet."

"I—yes—" he stammers, glancing anywhere but at me directly. "I was sent to retrieve you, Sir Tristan, and Sir Percival." After a brief pause, he adds, "The others are already in the throne room."

"Very well, then."

The pair of knights standing on either side of the carved black and red doors of the throne room acknowledge me with a nod as I approach. I recognise both of them and offer a greeting in return as I step over the threshold.

As always, the large throne room is dark and depressing. Though I usually find it to be a bit overwhelming, today, it seems to fit my mood.

It seems to fit Arthur's, too, if the scowl on his face is any indication. Even from across the room, I can see the wrath in his eyes, the unchecked fury boiling just beneath the surface.

The room is uncomfortably silent, and I take my time making my way to the base of the dais.

There are more knights than the last time I was in here, but far less than Ari's trial. A wave of panic washes over me as Tristan turns around to meet my gaze from the first row of benches. Beside him, sits Perci, Kay, and Graham. Sitting on the opposite side of the aisle is Bors, the commander who oversaw Ari's duel, and the two knights who escorted her to the ring.

On the far side of the dais, Guinevere and Morgana are sitting as far apart as possible while sharing the same bench. Gawain is nowhere to be found, and Arthur…

Arthur looks pissed.

"Your Highness," I say, bowing deeply as I reach the base of the dais. "You sum—"

"Where is she?" he asks, a myriad of barely contained emotions fighting for dominance in his voice, his eyes, his face.

"I beg your pardon?" I ask, glancing around the room.

"The girl—where is she?" he asks again. I open my mouth to continue the charade, but he rises from the throne with a flourish. "Where is the girl? The prisoner? The sorcerer? The *she-dragon?*" He hisses the last one through his teeth, his face turning nearly the same shade as his hair. *"Where is Ari?"*

"I imagine she's still with a healer." I shrug, glancing around the room again. "She was looking pretty worse for wear after her duel today. As far as I know, she sought medical attention afterward." I say my words carefully, only giving away enough to be considered the truth.

"Who is she with?" Arthur snaps, eyes flashing.

Tristan doesn't turn to look at me, but I can feel him tense up all the same, fear for Vera evident in the set of his shoulders.

"Apologies, Your Highness, but is she in some sort of trouble or something?" I ask, stalling for time. "She may be a prisoner, but surely, you wouldn't wish such competent kitchen help to be out of your service so quickly."

To his credit, he doesn't take the bait. He simply pulls in a slow, steadying breath.

Then another.

And another.

The ruddiness of his face begins to fade, his normal colour returning. The sheer will and absolute control he has on his temper right now is honestly impressive.

"Sir Lancelot," he says, and the forced tolerance in his tone implies just how much I've gotten under his skin. "Unless it is some secret you wish to keep from the crown, I implore you to answer the question." His nostrils flare, but it's the only sign of anger that seeps through the mask of indifference now settled onto his face.

"No secret, Your Highness." I shake my head, offering him half a smile. "She's with that healer…the one near the old mill. Her shop has those carvings on the door."

I don't have a choice. I have to tell him something, and a lie will only cause more problems. I don't name Vera outright, but I don't have to.

Camelot is big enough, but it is not that big. Arthur knows exactly of whom I speak, and Tristan's just going to have to forgive me.

The prince's eyes narrow, his mouth drawing into a thin line. "Why did you take her there?" he asks, struggling to keep the leash on his anger.

"Morgana seemed like she had her hands full with all the other injured men from the tournament, so I figured I'd try to lighten the load a little." I shrug, glancing at Morgana and offering her what I hope comes across as either an apologetic or understanding smile. "It was the first place I thought of."

"I see," Arthur says, sitting back down in his throne. He crosses one ankle over a knee, drops an arm onto the armrest, and then his chin into his hand—looking for all the world entirely bored and indifferent.

A long, heavy silence settles over us. It stretches on so long that I grow restless.

"Apologies again, Your Highness"—his eyes dart to mine with barely veiled contempt—"but is there anything else I can do for you, or…"

The words hang between us, both a question and a challenge. We both know I will not leave until I'm dismissed, but unless he intends for us to stay here all night…

For another long moment, he simply stares at me. His gaze is unflinching—unyielding—and then, as if this has been the most trivial conversation ever, he simply waves his hand in front of us.

That's a dismissal if I've ever seen one, and my fellow knights must agree. Everyone seems to spring to their feet, all as eager to get out of the throne room as I am.

I step out of the way, gesturing for Bors and his men to leave first, and end up hanging around just long enough to hear Guinevere ask Arthur if he's okay, if she can do anything, if she—

He silences her with a harsh word and a sharp glare. She takes it in stride, her curtsey mockingly low before departing out the side exit.

Tristan, Perci, and I share a quick glance before making our own exit.

"What the hell was that about?" I hiss as soon as we're clear of the throne room.

"What the hell do you think it was about?" Perci snaps, glaring at me. We follow the others down the long stone corridor before the three of us round a corner, breaking off from the rest of the knights. Once we're truly alone, Perci says, "We knew he wouldn't just let her disappear."

We walk in uncomfortable silence for a moment before Tristan says, as if he'd heard the questions racing through my mind, "He's been interrogating us one at a time for about an hour. We were nearly at the barracks before the page found us. We figured you weren't far behind us."

"What were Kay and Graham doing there? And Bors and his little pack of feral dogs?"

"Arthur summoned everyone who's come into contact with her in the last day or so once he finally realised she not only didn't return to her cell, but wasn't even in the castle." Tristan runs a hand through his already disheveled hair, pulling the tie loose and wrapping it around his wrist.

"It doesn't explain why Guinevere was there," Perci murmurs.

"Guinevere's always there," I mutter. "She's practically glued to his hip these days."

Tristan rolls his eyes but doesn't dispute my words. Perci scowls but says nothing.

We continue to walk through the halls in strained silence, the leather soles of our boots quietly thudding against the stone floor.

"I need to go to Vera's—"

"That is the last thing you need to do." Tristan snaps at me under his breath.

I bristle, surprised at both his disapproval and his dismissal. "What do you expect me to do?" I ask. My voice sounds hoarse and raw, but I can't find room in my head to be embarrassed.

"Right now, I need you not to make things worse."

Perci snorts despite the tension, but has the dignity to mutter an apology. I can't stop myself from glaring at the pair of them.

Only after we're within the safety of our room do I round on Tristan again, but before I can even speak, he says, "You charging off to the one place Arthur is surely going to keep under a hawk's watch isn't going to help Ari. It'll only confirm whatever suspicions he already has."

"I can't just leave them unprotected—"

"They are far from unprotected." The anger in his voice sets off the growing defiance laying waste to my rational thoughts.

"Do you truly believe they can fend off a dozen knights, or however many Arthur sees fit to send their way? Do you truly believe Vera will risk using magic *again* to protect them? Do you—"

"Sometimes, doing nothing is the best thing!" Tristan shouts, his eyes full of disdain. "Sometimes, not getting involved is the only way to not make things worse!"

"You can't be serious." I throw my arms up in exasperation, rolling my eyes at him.

"What do you think is going to happen if you get caught going to Vera's tonight? What do you think Arthur is going to do if he decides to send Bors after Ari and drag her back to her cell?" His hands ball into fists at his sides. His chest is heaving, and his eyes are alight with a wild fire I hadn't known him capable of possessing. Tristan is usually subdued and always steadfast. Sometimes, he's on edge but never outwardly emotional.

"I think—"

"I don't give a damn what you think." He turns, slamming his fist into the wall, effectively silencing the rest of my sentence.

Tristan and I have never come to blows. We've barely had more than an argument before, but whatever is happening right now, whatever line I can't seem to comprehend that's being drawn between us… Well, I'm relieved that he chose to hit the wall instead of me.

Tristan curses under his breath, then again, louder. He doesn't so much as wince when his fist comes away from the stones, bloody and cut up. He opens and closes his fingers reflexively before balling his hand into a tight fist again and shoving it into his pocket.

"You both need to take a step back," Perci says quietly, shifting so that he's a physical barrier between us, even though we're on opposite sides of the room. "You're both a little too invested in this situation, and losing your head isn't going to help anyone. Are we clear?"

I nod at Perci, still stunned at Tristan's outburst.

"Are we clear?" Perci asks again, his face even and unaffected as he awaits Tristan's response. After several deep breaths, Tristan nods his head, almost imperceptibly. "Good, then you need to calm down," he says to Tristan, not bothering to wait for an acknowledgement before turning back to me, "and you need to quit underestimating people. They can take care of themselves, and if they can't, we'll deal with it, if and when the time comes."

Though it sounded rhetorical, Perci still eyes both of us warily.

Tristan slumps down on his bed, deflated. He drops his head into his hands and murmurs, "She's not safe here anymore—either of them."

"You don't say," Perci snarks. His sarcasm manages to lift one side of my mouth in something that feels halfway between a grimace and a smile.

"I can't believe this is happening again." He says it so quietly I'm sure I've misheard him.

"What are you talking about?" I ask Tristan warily.

"Now that she's out of the tournament, we need to get her out of the kingdom," he says, heaving a sigh. When he lifts his head and meets my gaze, he adds, "As soon as possible."

I nod in agreement, even though he didn't answer my question.

Anguish and sorrow mix in my chest, fighting with the panic and fear and leftover nerves from this hellish day.

"My duel tomorrow…" I say after a moment.

Tristan and Perci both stare at me with one brow raised.

"I'll make sure it's one worth watching." Resolve settles into my bones, and I have to force the words out, the mere idea causing my chest to tighten. "Get her out while everyone is distracted."

FORTY-ONE

ARI

"They don't live in caves, little dragon."

"Why not?"

"Because they belong on farms."

"But they could live in a cave…"

"Have you ever seen a bird in our cave?"

I pause to think about that for a moment, tilting my head to the side and scrunching up my face. "No."

"Then why would you want to force them to live somewhere they're not used to living?"

"Because you don't fit in a tree, Penn." A dramatic sigh escapes my lips, my hands thrown out to the side for emphasis. "If we can't go to them, then we have to bring them to us."

He snorts, trying and failing to hide his amusement. "What do you want chickens for, anyway?"

"Because they lay eggs." It comes out so matter-of-factly, as if it was the most obvious thing in the world. "And then I wouldn't have to steal them from the birds in the forest."

"Where would you get them from?"

"Merlin said he could—"

A heavy sigh heaves its way from the large, crimson dragon's chest. He stares at me, his bright golden gaze intently focused upon my face. After a moment, he asks, "You really want one?"

"Or two…" I smile hesitantly at him. "I'll take care of them myself; I promise. I'll feed them and play with them and protect them from the gnomes."

"What if they run away?"

"I'll magic them to stay close."

"You shouldn't use your magic on others against their will, little dragon."

"Only to protect them," I swear.

Another heavy sigh escapes his nostrils in the form of a thick cloud of black smoke. "Fine," he says defeatedly. "But they will be your responsibility."

"Will you shut up? Honestly. You're the most annoying of the bunch. You don't need to squawk about absolutely everything." An exasperated groan leaves my lips as I glare down at the reddish-brown bird with rumpled feathers. I bare my teeth at him, and he rustles his plumage at me in defiance.

Eyeing the forest around us, I spot Olive nestled beneath a nearby bush, her white and brown flecked feathers providing her with ample camouflage in the speckled midday sun. Hazel is foraging in the underbrush, her light brown body weaving in and out of the foliage at leisure.

I sit down and lean against a thick trunk, and after a moment, Hazel comes over to inspect me. Reaching out a tentative hand, she lets me pet her for a few moments before climbing into my lap, nestling into the space between my crossed legs. "You're not nearly as annoying as your brother," I murmur, stroking the bird's head. Glancing at Olive, I add, "You're still up for debate, though."

Violet darts off into the bush, still squawking, and I can barely suppress my eye-roll. When a disgruntled shout comes from within the forest, I don't bother to get up; this is what happens every time Merlin comes to visit the cave these days, and I wouldn't be any more useful than the mage himself.

"Ari!"

Hazel looks in my direction, head cocked to the side as if she knows exactly what's going on. I raise an eyebrow at her, the corners of my lips twitching in response to Merlin's exasperation. I can hear him long before I can see him, but the ensuing laughter escapes my lips long before he comes stumbling out of the forest.

The words, "stupid," "arrogant," and "attack bird" come grumbling out of his mouth just before he comes into view, and the outrage on his face makes him look feral, which only makes me laugh harder.

"Your bird is barbaric!" he shouts, hand thrown out to the side, pointing to the forest behind him.

"He's—"

"He jumped on me!" Merlin snarls as he paces in front of me, glaring at me when I can't contain my laughter. His eyes drift around the small clearing in front of the cave, pausing for a moment at the rocky entrance before meeting my gaze again. "Where's the dragon?"

"Hiding from the birds." I snicker.

"He didn't take you with him?"

Shaking my head, I snort. "He reminded me that I begged for them for months, and that they were my burden to bear, not his. He's gone hunting to take the edge off."

The angry little bird comes stalking into the clearing, simultaneously smug and flustered. His feathers are rumpled and a little disheveled as he skirts around Merlin, giving us both a wide berth.

"What did you do to him?" I ask.

"Momentarily incapacitated him," Merlin quips. "You should have named that thing Violent, instead."

"Says the man who had to use magic to subdue a chicken."

"Just because he doesn't attack you—"

"Oh, he attacks me, too," I say with a grimace, lifting my bandaged hand up between us. "He bit me just this morning."

"See," Merlin deadpans, levelling me with an unimpressed glare. "Violent."

I don't dream of my childhood again, or the trio of chickens.

I don't dream of Penn, though I wish that I did.

I don't dream of Merlin or Baxen.

I don't dream of anything at all.

Sometime later, I know that I'm no longer sleeping by the dull ache pulsing in the back of my head, and without opening my eyes, I can tell that it's completely dark in here, which must mean it's the middle of the night.

Idly, I wonder how long it's been since Perci left. I wonder if Lancelot won his duel. I wonder if Tristan managed to learn anything about Morgana using her magic on me.

I wonder if Arthur's figured out where I am, or if he even cares at all. I wonder if he knows someone used magic to heal me. I wonder if Vera—

A small creak catches my attention. It sounds as if weight is being shifted on a plank of wood. That must be what woke me in the first place, the unexpectedness of the sound interrupting a dreamless sleep.

"Finally, you're awake."

My breath catches in my throat, unease spiking through my veins. The voice is neither comforting nor entirely unfamiliar. It has a thick, northern lilt to it—not high pitched, but distinctly female.

"Did Vera send for you?"

"She's asleep in her bed," she says evenly. "I snuck in through the garden with the mage none the wiser, though that does take some of the fun out of it." It sounds as if she's pouting.

Slowly, my eyelids flutter open—one more so than the other thanks to the swelling still marring one side of my face. It takes a moment to adjust to the dimness of the room. The only light comes from the faint glow of the moon through the singular window. Ector still sleeps soundly at my feet, undisturbed by the calmness of our voices. A calmness I do not feel on the inside.

"Arthur sent you to finish what the others could not, then?"

My eyes drift to the corner and the shadow in the chair shifts slightly. Her silent presence is both intimidating and impressive. I can't see her face in the darkness, but something gives me the impression that she's smiling all the same. Or smirking, perhaps.

"Will it hurt?" I ask quietly. Right now, I couldn't fight her off even if I wished to. I do not think Vera would hear my struggle, nor would Ector wake from his slumber if my assailant did not wish it so.

After an impossibly long silence, the she-shadow vacates the chair in the corner and soundlessly covers the four steps it takes to stand beside me. A thick cloak made of midnight continues to shroud her in darkness even after she steps into the dim light of the moon.

A hand falls to my face, a gentle and haunting caress, prefacing the imminent kiss of death that awaits me. A thumb brushes away the single tear that slides down my cheek. I hadn't even noticed as it slipped from my good eye.

Swallowing down a lump of emotion, I manage to whisper, "The prince is going to a lot of trouble to kill someone so insignificant—an outsider that barely even belongs to his kingdom."

A quick laugh escapes lips I cannot see. "Surely, you do not think me that naïve?"

When I say nothing, a soft sigh follows the retreat of the hand upon my cheek.

"Insignificant you are not, Arturia of the Dragons." She pushes the hood back from her face, revealing the last person I expected to find standing in front of me, yet, somehow, knew deep in my soul was hidden beneath the cloak. "And you are anything but an outsider."

A soft curse escapes my lips.

I can just make out her features in the dim light—determined blue eyes, a confident smirk, blonde hair, bound and braided, and half a dozen golden rings pierced through the outer ridge of one ear.

"Dragon," I correct. "There was only one."

She simply laughs, a wry twist to her mouth. "We have much to discuss before the mage wakes," Lady Guinevere says evenly.

"We have nothing to discuss," I say, not without venom. Slowly, I push myself into a sitting position, easing myself backward to lean against the wall.

"You have far more in common with me than you might think," she hisses, noting my disdain. As I rattle my brain, trying to find anything we might have in common, she continues, her mouth shifting from a sneer back to a smirk. "And you have more in common yet with the one who sent me."

"I wish to have nothing in common with the prince—"

"I never said I was working with Arthur." She takes in my furrowed expression and, after a moment, she says unapologetically, "I only let you believe so for a moment because I rather enjoy watching people squirm."

"If not Arthur, then who?"

"Someone who does not wish to see Arthur sit upon the throne," she says evenly. "Someone who also does not wish to see you dead, especially by Arthur's hand."

My mind races, trying to think of who she could be talking about, but the list seems somehow equally endless and nonexistent. Arthur has followed closely in Uther's footsteps, leading his men through kingdom after kingdom, burning farmlands and expanding Camelot's borders. His knights have been ruthless, and he has upset many people, but I don't see why any of them would care if I died by his hand.

"What is it that you want, Guinevere?" I ask warily.

"My friends call me Guin," she says.

"What is it that you want, *Guin?*"

"Exactly what I said." She keeps her tone slow and unbothered, as if I should already know the answer. "For Arthur not to sit upon the throne."

"And what is it, exactly, that you think I could do to prevent that?"

A slow, wicked sort of smile spreads across her face. "Get creative." There's a glint in her eye that unsettles me to my core.

"I could never get close enough to kill him outright," I say. Glancing down, I stare at my hands, firmly nestled in my lap, and expel a long, slow breath. "Nor do I have any desire to do so."

"He did not have to get close to you to poison you," she counters. I'm trying to place the emotion in her voice—trying to decipher her motives when she adds, "You don't have to kill him, if you don't wish to, but he simply cannot ascend to the throne on his name day."

"Why should I care who sits upon the throne of Camelot?" I ask, trying to buy myself some time to think. To understand. To fit the pieces together.

She looks almost taken aback by my question but recovers quickly. "You know very well why."

Her words strike me as if she had physically done so. I almost wish she had.

"Aren't you here to gain his hand in marriage?" My voice is little more than a whisper. "Don't you need him to become king? Why else would you have left Northumbria?"

"What I want and what I need are two very different things." She pulls in a tight breath. "Do not make the mistake of thinking they are one and the same." Glancing away for the first time since she stepped up to the side of the bed, I watch as her throat bobs when she swallows. "For the moment, I need little more than for Arthur to waste my time."

"So, you don't intend to marry him?"

"I will marry him if I must, but I have every intention of returning to my homeland when I can."

"I don't understand—"

"You don't need to," she says curtly. "What matters is that you help me prevent Arthur from claiming the throne."

"Why would you come to me?" I ask warily.

"Because none of the knights who could be tempted into treason are smart enough to get close enough to him without getting caught. Nobody in his immediate circle of people would ever be able to get away with it, and no one else would even consider it—and if they did, they'd turn me over long before they'd ever go through with it."

"If you're so willing to do what it takes to stop his ascension, then why not employ someone from your own kingdom? If not a soldier or a knight, then I'm sure you could find a sell-sword or free-lance?"

She scoffs, waving a dismissive hand in the air between us. Huffing, she plops down on the bed beside my legs, the movement jostling Ector, who simply repositions himself and goes right back to sleep.

Guinevere stays silent for a moment, her fingers tracing indistinct patterns on the blanket. "Tristan had a hard enough time convincing Arthur to let him join his ranks, and he would never do it if I asked. We only have a few days until Arthur's name day, and besides…Northumbria is more than a little preoccupied right now." Her words trail off, as if she was speaking more to herself than to me.

Clearing her throat, she rounds on me again, fresh determination etched into her features. "So, here I am, coming to you."

"I still don't get why you think I would help you?"

"Surely, you don't need me to tell you?" Her brows furrow, a deep line forming in the middle. After a moment, she says, "If Arthur were no longer on the throne, you would no longer be a prisoner of Camelot." She lets me ponder this information for a moment before adding, "But I can offer you more than that. I can offer you something better."

"There's no guarantee that whoever succeeds Arthur would let me go," I say carefully. "The first act of a new monarch is rarely to undo the last of the former."

The smile she gives me tells me that we both know a lot more than what we're saying—that we both know that, not only am I right, but that even with Arthur removed, I stand next to no chance of leaving Camelot anytime soon.

"I wish to offer you a deal," she says with the utmost confidence. An involuntary shiver rolls down my spine at both her audacity and her choice of words.

"You want me to remove Arthur from the throne." I sigh, nodding. "But, surely, whoever replaces him will not simply empty out the dungeons and set free his prisoners. You can offer me nothing truly worthy of what you ask."

She leans forward, and when the faint light of the moon peeking through the window hits her face, her smile turns feral, her eyes burning like liquid fire. "In return for displacing Arthur, we intend to give you the one thing you thought unimaginable."

FORTY-TWO

LANCELOT

I don't know how early it is, but the rhythmic sounds coming from the opposite corners of the room tell me it's early enough. Tristan is lying on his stomach, breathing deeply and evenly, while Perci lays sprawled on his back, snoring softly.

We didn't say much after Tristan's outburst last night. We didn't acknowledge that he'd lost his temper or that Perci had to mediate, and we didn't spend much time forming a plan, either. We all know our roles in what comes next. Tristan will get Ari out of Camelot while Perci keeps an eye on Arthur and I provide a duel worth everyone's time. The less details Perci and I know about what happens after, the better.

I didn't tell them I wished it was me taking her away from this place. I didn't have to. When it's safe…when enough time has passed…I'll find my way back to her. One way or another. We can leave Camelot behind us, and eventually, she'll realise I never wanted this to happen. Eventually, she'll stop blaming me. And eventually, we can move forward. Together.

But for now, it has to be Tristan. He didn't enter the tournament, and it makes sense for them to disappear together. Arthur will brand him a traitor and send the rest of us on the hunt to retrieve them. Hopefully, Perci and I can buy them some time.

Although I wish more than anything that it was me going with her today, I understand why it has to be Tristan. Perci has warmed up to her a little over the last few months, but he still only tolerates her at best. At least, Ari and Tristan have spent enough time together to have some semblance of camaraderie by now, no matter how flimsy.

I trust them with my life, and yet, it pains me to know that they aren't as invested in her safety, her future, and her well-being as I am. It makes me feel helpless.

As for Vera and any safety concerns we have for her…whatever she decides to do now is her choice. She's more than capable of taking care of herself, and if she needs to start over again…then so be it.

Heaving a sigh, I force myself to sit up, swinging my legs over the side of the bed. With only four duels set to take place today, the list of opponents will be posted at first light.

I have a good idea of who I'll end up in the ring with, and that very thought is what has me dressing quickly and sheathing my father's sword at my hip before silently slipping into the hall. Before I fully realise where I'm headed, my feet and my heart are already pulling me towards my destination.

As I make my way through the quiet streets of Camelot, I can't help thinking of my mother—of why I need to win this tournament—and what it will mean for her when I do.

I should have gone to see her before this all started. I should have made the time to go and sit with her for a while, to bring her those little lemon cakes and blueberry pies she loves so much, and to let her fuss over me as she's always done—how long my hair has grown, how little sleep I'm getting, if I'm eating enough.

I should have gone to see her before all the fuss and commotion of the tournament, Arthur's name day celebration and coronation, and whatever else comes after that. No doubt he'll grow power hungry once he's crowned king, with a renewed need to prove himself without the shadow of his father's legacy or his uncle's impulsive decisions.

It's likely he'll start another war, and who knows how long that'll last. Who knows how long it'll be until Camelot knows peace again.

I should have gone to see her while I had the time, and I should have asked her about Ari. I should've asked her why she never told me that they knew each other, and how I'd managed to go my entire childhood without meeting a girl who is possibly the only other human child to be raised in that forest.

I wonder if things could have been different had I known about her... If I had grown up with her... If I had been given the chance to meet her under different circumstances...

Would my life have turned out the same? Would I have still chosen to become a knight to try to preserve my family name? To right the wrongs done to my father? To save his legacy and to carve out a better future for myself?

Or would I have spent my life with the girl and her dragon?

Would I have grown up loving her, knowing I would do so until the day I left this earth? Would we have spent early mornings swimming in the lakes, warm afternoons getting lost in the forest, and lazy evenings counting the stars? Would we have watched the sun rise and fall each day, hand in hand, and faced the world together?

By the time I get to Vera's, it feels as if I am mourning the life we could've had.

My hand hesitates just shy of the gnarled, wooden door. The weak pre-dawn light reminds me that it's still early, and between my haste to get away from the castle and the overwhelming thoughts I had on the way here, I didn't stop to wonder if either of them would even be awake yet.

Pulling my hand back hesitantly, I turn around and lower myself to the ground, leaning my back against the door with a heavy sigh.

Again, my mind wanders to how differently things could have been— and, if I'm being honest with myself, how differently I wish they were. Whether this is a distraction method my brain is utilising to prevent me from dwelling on today's duel or not, I'm not sure, but some small, somber part of me welcomes it all the same.

As the hours tick by and the sun begins to rise, the sky changes from violet to blue, yellow to orange. Streaks of red slice through the pale clouds before the colours finally melt away into a soft, warm, cheerful hue. For once, the clouds don't look as if they hold rain or the promise of a storm.

Perhaps that's a good omen. Perhaps it means that today holds good outcomes for us all. Perhaps Ari will finally forgive me…before she leaves Camelot for good.

The thought makes my stomach turn.

Again, I wonder of the life we might've had if things hadn't gone so wrong. If Bors' never had me followed. If her dragon hadn't been killed. If she hadn't become Arthur's prisoner.

I wonder if she might've considered leaving the cave behind and eventually moved into Camelot. I wonder if we might've gotten a small house on a street much like this. I wonder if we might have gotten married and built a life together, and, one day, had children.

Or maybe she would have convinced me to return to the forest—to the freedom I knew as a child but cannot bring myself to wish for now.

Maybe we would have left all this behind.

Maybe she would have convinced Merlin to release my mother from her curse.

The longer I sit here—pining, and mourning, and wishing—the more nauseous I feel. Suddenly, the potential thought of having to face Bors in the ring today seems easier than asking Ari for forgiveness.

Or perhaps it's her rejection I'm afraid of. To wish for these lives we could have lived, only to have her throw them back in my face, unwanted…

I could not bear it.

Before I can talk myself out of it—before I can convince myself it's better to stay, to see her one more time and end up heartbroken—I force myself to stand, and then I force one foot in front of the other, heading back toward the castle, back toward the now-posted opponent list, and back toward the safety of my ignorance.

FORTY-THREE

ARI

The smell in the quaint garden behind Vera's shop is intoxicating, and though the sky has remained dry so far this morning, a light drizzle of rain has been present over the last few days, making everything smell that much more fragrant. The soil is darker, the leaves are greener, the flowers more vibrant—all in beautiful contrast to one another.

Fat little bumble bees drift lazily from flower to flower, and earthworms the size of my forearm weave their way through the stone path, leaving a trail of slime in their wake. This garden seems to be as much for purpose as it is for pleasure, and has been wholly cultivated out of love.

A row of sunflowers nearly as tall as I am line the small, open space. Within the walls of the big, golden flowers—that remind me a little too much of Penn's eyes—are several rows of valerian, stinging nettle, and feverfew. Closer to the front are lavender, three different types of sage, and wild mint that seems to have run rampant. Scattered throughout the garden, there are dozens of clusters of herbs—some that I recognise, and some that I don't. And right there, next to the door, is a small patch of the mountain variety of cornflower, a beautiful, bright, blueish-purple colour that stands out above all the others in the small garden.

It brings an unexpected wave of grief and longing to my chest. If I close my eyes, I can almost imagine that I'm back at the cave, Penn snoring like distant thunder from deep within.

Home, I correct myself. It is, or was, my *home*, not just *the cave*.

"Vera said I might find you back here." The warm, husky voice only startles me a little, but it's both friendly and a welcome distraction.

The corners of my mouth twitch upward despite everything that's happened over the last few days. As he approaches, something that's been tugging at the back of my thoughts over the last several months finally slides into place.

Tristan, I've realised, simultaneously distracts me from Penn's absence, yet also reminds me of the best parts of the companion that I lost. He's a genuinely kind and compassionate person. He's calm and steady in the face of adversity. He's gentle, honest, and effortless to be around.

Once again, I'm reminded of how easy it would be to befriend Tristan—to *really* be friends with him.

"She helped me bathe this morning," I say sheepishly. "And she even took away the swelling in my eye. But I worry that she'll grow to regret my presence here, so I figured I would spend as much time in the garden and out of her way as possible."

"You needn't worry about Bedivera," he chuckles, grinning ruefully at me. "If she wished to be rid of you, she'd simply turn you out on the street."

I've been perched upon a pile of crates for the last hour or so, and without hesitation, or seemingly a second thought, Tristan lowers himself down beside me, the two of us now squished upon the same crate.

I glimpse the fresh cuts on his knuckles and feel my brows pull together. "What happened?"

"What?" he asks, and I gesture to the hand in his lap. "Oh." Lifting it in front of us, he opens and closes his fingers. "Nothing."

"It doesn't look like nothing. It looks like it hurt." I take his hand in mine and hold my free one out between us.

He unsheathes a blade from his thigh and hands it to me wordlessly. "You don't have to—"

"Shut up."

He snorts and tips his head back against the wall. He always seems to look away when I draw blood, though I don't believe him to be squeamish. Several heartbeats later, his knuckles are smooth and tanned once more, flecked with tiny, pale scars.

I let go of his hand just as the clouds above us turn a darker shade of grey, promising the threat of rain after all. We sit in silence for a few moments, the air in the small garden turning thick and humid.

My eyes track the slow progression of a worm, and I ask, "You know her, don't you?"

"Aye."

"Is it meant to be a secret?"

"We share a homeland." He shrugs, his arm brushing against mine with the movement.

"She's Northumbrian?" I ask in disbelief. "She doesn't have the accent."

"Aye," he says again. "Though I suppose that's not truly where she's from, only where she settled. She had been there for a long time before we ever crossed paths."

I glance at him sidelong, tilting my head to one side. "Is it safe to assume you have a bit of history, then?"

"Sort of, aye." He nods. "She helped my brother learn how to use his magic—and how not to fear it." He finally turns toward me, his hazel eyes searching my face.

"Your brother is a mage?"

"He was." The corners of his mouth turn down as he nods, clearing his throat.

"You're not the first magic-wielder I've known." His voice holds the same contemplative quietness now as it did that day in the dungeon.

I chew on my bottom lip for a moment before murmuring an apology.

Shaking his head slightly, he presses his lips into a tight line. "What is it you said to me before? 'They aren't your misdoings to apologise for.'"

"What happened?" I ask carefully.

"That's a long story." He sighs, expelling a long, shaky breath. "One I will share under the darkness of night, after we've reached the bottom of several pints of ale." He absently fidgets with a worn, braided piece of leather around his left wrist, and I realise it's what he put between his teeth the day he broke his hand. I wonder if it belonged to his brother.

"Tell me what you need."

He hadn't been scared of me using my magic, only that I might not be able to stop what was happening to my body. He was calm and sure, even through the concern.

"Take a deep breath."

He was so unbothered every time I needed to take the edge off. He was never wary of it the way Perci was, eyeing my hands anytime he came to collect me.

"Let me help you."

Tristan has no fear of magic or mages, not the way most humans do. He grew up around it. He respects it.

It makes so much sense now.

"I'm sorry," I say again, because I don't know what else to say.

"Don't be." He shrugs. "You didn't know him, and it doesn't matter—there isn't anything anyone can do about it now." He looks up, swallowing visibly.

The first drops of rain begin to fall, leaving little raised bumps of flesh along my arms in their wake. Frowning at the sky, I return my attention to Tristan.

"I'm still sorry," I say, placing a hand on his arm. "Regardless of how much time may have passed or what might have happened, I know what it feels like to lose someone you loved so fiercely."

He flinches, then says, "I know you do." He scrubs a hand across his face, and his next words come out a bit hoarse. "Ari...the dragon—*Penn*...I'm so sorry."

"It doesn't matter now."

When he slides his hand over mine, the heat from his arm beneath my palm and his fingers around my own seeps into me, chasing away the chill of the morning rain. A sad smile touches his lips, there one moment and gone the next. "You remind me of him," he says quietly.

"Is that why you're doing this?" I ask. "Because of your brother?"

"Aye," he nods, tears now lining his eyes.

"Will you tell me about him?" I ask hesitantly, unsure if that will make things better or worse. His hazel eyes seem to shudder, but that sad smile returns to his lips.

"He was loud, and crude—*unrefined*, my mother would say." He releases a weak laugh, eyes losing focus with the memories. "He was passionate about everything but most of all plants. He was obsessed with learning what each plant could do—how it could help us. He was a protector, through and through. He would defend anyone who needed it, without question or hesitation."

His eyes drift up to meet mine, and I offer him a genuine smile. "He sounds like a good person."

"He was." Tristan nods absently. "I think you would've gotten along really well."

"Because we're both vulgar and have a thing for plants?" I smirk.

"Aye." He nods. "Among other things."

"I think he would be proud of you," I say, keeping my gaze steady on his. "I didn't know you before, but I think I have a decent idea of who you are now, and I think you would make him very proud, Tristan."

His lips wobble, and an errant tear slips down his cheek, but he makes no move to wipe it away.

"Will you tell me about your dragon?" he asks, then quickly catches himself. "About Penn?"

"I..." My mouth opens and closes around several different answers. "He..."

"You don't have to," Tristan says with a small shake of his head.

"No, I want to. I haven't... I don't allow myself to think about him often, because I'm afraid that, if I do, I'll fall apart. And once I fall apart, I won't be able to put myself back together again." The blatant honesty makes my chest feel hollow.

A stretch of silence falls over us as the rain picks up in intensity. Neither of us move to go inside, though, letting the cold drops fall around us. The fresh smell of wet earth mixed with the aromas of various herbs and flowers is both heady and intoxicating.

"Do you trust me?" Tristan asks after a moment. I turn to meet his gaze again, scrutinising what I see in his eyes—and what I don't. The last time he asked me that, he intentionally broke his hand so that I could siphon my magic to fix it.

For a moment, I let myself think of all the people I've trusted in my life. I don't know if it's sad or not that I can count them on one hand. Penn and Baxen are both dead. Merlin left me behind when he could've so easily taken me with him, and Lancelot... If it weren't for Lancelot, Penn would most likely still be alive.

Trusting people has cost me everything.

But this situation is nothing like either of those, and the only thing I can see in Tristan's eyes is a mix of compassion and sorrow.

"More than anyone else, I suppose," I say with a choked laugh.

His fingers tighten around my own, and I realise my hand is still on his arm. The physical contact doesn't embarrass me like I thought it might. In truth, it's refreshing.

"You can tell me about Penn if you'd like, and you can fall apart if you want. The least I can do is stay by your side while you do it."

"Why?" I whisper.

"Because it's okay to fall apart," he says, taking a deep breath. "It's okay to fall apart, even if you don't think you can put yourself back together. Don't be afraid to feel what you need to feel—to cry, and scream, and rage. To grieve, even if it seems overwhelming. It's okay to miss him." He squeezes my hand again, and that small, sad smile returns to his face. "I miss my brother every day, and I will miss him every day for the rest of my life."

Nodding, I inhale a shuddering breath. "I don't like going into the chicken coop with you. It reminds me of Penn—the way they flock to you. The way they follow you around."

"I didn't know." His voice is quiet, his hand tightening reflexively around my own.

"You couldn't have." I lean my head back against the wall. "We had chickens when I was younger. I begged Penn for months and months until he finally relented." A slow grin spreads across Tristan's face. "We had three of them, and they followed him everywhere. They trailed after him as if he'd laid them himself."

"It's kind of hard to imagine." He chuckles. "Chickens following a dragon?"

"He hated them." I exhale a laugh, fighting the smile that threatens to spread across my face. "Absolutely despised them. Honestly, sometimes, it was hard to tell who was more dramatic—him or them. But he knew they made me happy, so he tolerated them. Penn was selfless." I drop my eyes to the garden again, swallowing down a thick lump of emotion. "He was patient, and kind, and generous. He took me in and raised me when he didn't have to. He taught me anything and everything—history and languages, how to wield different weapons, what plants I could use, and how to set a snare to hunt animals. For all the things he couldn't teach me, he found someone who could. He didn't have to do any of that. He could've eaten me or left me to my own fate. He could've pawned me off or sent me back, but instead, he made sure that I could be self-sufficient… He made sure that I would survive.

"I've done so many stupid things over the years, but the dumbest thing of all was not telling him about the deal I'd made with Merlin to protect us. Maybe if I had, things would have turned out differently." The words come out hoarse, and tears blur my vision as they line my eyes. "Maybe if I had, it could have saved him."

Beside me, Tristan pulls in an audible breath. He shifts, lifting his arm in open invitation. I hesitate for only a second before leaning in and letting him wrap it around me, and for the first time in months, I let myself cry. I let myself mourn the family I lost, the parent I failed, and the dragon I loved.

Tristan lets me cry without protest or interruption, and through it all, his constant warmth acts like an anchor, tethering me to reality while my emotions finally spiral into despair.

FORTY-FOUR

ARI

By the time I've finally managed to pull myself together enough to stop the tears and slow my breathing, the storm around us is in full swing. Thunder booms overhead, lightning streaks across the sky, and though the rain is coming down in earnest, we stay huddled on the crates behind Vera's shop.

"Do they know?" I finally ask, breaking the silence. "Where you come from?"

"Aye, Lancelot and Perci do," he says, nodding. "Arthur does as well, considering I used it as a bargaining chip to let me swear fealty, though from what I can tell, surprisingly enough, he seems to have kept it to himself. If anyone else suspects, they say nothing. Most of the men just think I'm a farm boy from the northern borders of the last kingdom Camelot invaded."

"Why did you tell me?" My brows furrow. "You could have kept it a secret. It wouldn't have made any difference if I knew or not."

"Because, just as you share in my misery of having lost a loved one, I also share in the feeling of being an outsider, unable to return home. Sometimes, it's just nice to know you're not alone in something, regardless of what it is."

"I've been there before," I say quietly. "To Northumbria."

"When?"

"When I was little. Before the war started there. Penn used to fly us all over the continent, from coast to coast, over the forests, through the mountains…"

"I can't imagine what the world looks like from that high."

"Absolutely extraordinary," I breathe. He's silent for a moment, and then something shifts in him. I pull away, sitting up straight as I regard him. "What is it?"

"We don't have a lot of time left, and there are some things I need to say—some decisions we need to make."

"Okay."

He takes a deep breath, exhaling slowly through his nose. "Regardless of how you feel about him now, regardless of what happened afterward… Lancelot saved your life that day."

An uncomfortable tingling sensation spreads through my veins. This is not something we talk about, he and I. The before, the incident, the ramifications. We only ever talk about the present, the now, the daily monotony of castle servitude.

"After the first time, after we…" He hesitates, searching for the right words. "When we returned with Garreth's body and nothing to show for the loss, Bors was enraged. The only thing he cared about was revenge for Garreth, but I suspect it was mostly the glory and bragging rights for slaying a dragon that he truly sought." A shudder rolls through me with his words. "We tried to dissuade him, Lance and Perci and myself. He would get the knights riled up after a night of drinking, and he'd turn on us and accuse us of not caring or not wanting revenge for our fallen brother."

"The thing is, Garreth was Perci's brother—his real brother—and out of everyone, Perci was the most adamant about not returning to the forest." Tristan inhales and exhales several deep breaths before continuing. "None of us wanted to return. At least, I thought we didn't. We agreed that we wouldn't. We agreed to move on.

"I didn't know that Bors had his own suspicions, his own plans. I didn't know that he had assigned someone to trail us in the hopes of leading them back to the cave—to Penn. I didn't know that Lance had gone back to see you." He shakes his head almost angrily. "At all, let alone more than once. He chose days when he wasn't on duty but Perci and I were, so that we couldn't stop him or follow him."

"Instead, someone else followed him," I say under my breath.

"Aye." He nods. "He told me what happened that day, sort of. His recollection is a bit shaky, but I understand grief, and I understand how good a blade feels in your hand when it brings the justification of pain and suffering, and above all else, I understand the allure of magic.

"I don't fault you for what happened—I grieve for my friends, but I do not fault you." His eyes bore into mine with an intensity that makes me uncomfortable. "Lancelot is stupid, and rash, and doesn't think things through. Most of your assessments of him are probably correct, but he also cares deeply for those around him."

"Why are you telling me this?" The words leave my lips in a strained whisper.

"I guess I'm just trying to say that it's okay to hate him, but it's okay if you don't." He rubs the back of his neck, pinching and massaging the muscles there for a moment. "I've known Lancelot for a few years now, and I honestly believe he has nothing but good, if not often misguided, intentions. I have to believe that he never meant to hurt you, and he certainly never meant for Penn to die.

"I guess what I'm trying to say is, if you had been at the cave when Bors and the knights showed up, they wouldn't have hesitated to slay you simply for being there. It displeases Bors that you, and subsequently Lance, are able to dispute the version of the story he wishes to tell. It displeases him more that it's cost him something with Arthur." His face scrunches up a bit, and he eyes me sympathetically. "But, had Lance not been there at all, you would have died alongside Penn that day."

"You say that as if it would have been a bad thing." Despite the truth in them, the words hang uncomfortably in the air between us.

"No matter how great the pain, death is never the answer." On the surface, his words are quick and sharp, bitter with anger, but underneath, they're solemn.

"What is it that you are asking of me?"

"Nothing at all." He shakes his head, one side of his mouth lifting up in a half-smile. "I merely wished for you to understand that, for all his faults, Lancelot has a big heart, and sometimes, that gets him into trouble."

"His mouth seems to get him in trouble, too." I smirk.

"Aye." He laughs, a genuine smile spreading wide across his face, that dimple in his left cheek making a rare appearance. "That it does."

"What else?"

"It's time," he says grimly, lifting one shoulder. "Time for you to get out of Camelot and disappear."

"How do you expect me to do that?"

"We're going to use Lance's duel today as a distraction, to slip out while no one is looking."

"Where am I going?"

"Anywhere but here. We'll go somewhere far away."

"You intend to come with me?"

"Camelot is not the kingdom I hoped it to be." There's an edge to his words now. "I've started over before; I have no problem doing it again."

"You wish to be sworn to a third king?" I ask hesitantly.

"I don't need to be sworn to anyone." His hazel eyes cut to mine, a sincerity burning there that surprises me. "But if I swear myself to another heir, it'll be a worthy one."

"You simply wish to disappear, then?"

"Aye, if that is the best path."

"You'd risk Arthur finding out you helped me escape?"

"He would have to find us first." An arrogant smile lifts up one side of his mouth.

"And then what happens?" I ask, pushing for more information. "Once we've disappeared?"

"We can figure it out as we go." He shrugs. "We can go to the Western Wastelands and start over somewhere neither Camelot nor Northumbria have managed to claim a foothold yet, or south to the coast, across the Great Stone Bridge to the little village on Isle Tintagel. We could simply walk into the forest and live off the land until the day we die, or we could go out in search of an adventure and track down the Holy Grail itself." He says this as nonchalantly as if we were discussing the weather. "Or we can part ways, if that is what you wish, but whatever happens next, we can figure it out together. For now, I only want to help you get away from this place before Arthur's temper provokes him into doing something that cannot be undone."

I let his words sink in for a moment, weighing them carefully. If I leave now, I risk Arthur's wrath and his army when he finds out that I'm gone, jeopardising the lives of those who've helped me—Tristan, Lancelot, Perci, and now even Vera.

If I leave now, I'll never get another shot at fulfilling Guinevere's request. Her *bribe*.

I'm about to protest when he says, "Can I ask you something?"

"Almost anything."

"Why didn't you run?" he asks quietly, meeting my gaze intently. "That day at the river, you had several opportunities—I made sure that you did—so why are you still here?"

"Truthfully?" A humourless chuckle forces its way out of my chest. "I

thought about it. I wanted to—of course, I did—but where would I go?"
As I push out a shaky breath, my thoughts shift to Merlin, wondering if
he would still help me, even after he abandoned me. Wondering, if after
everything we've been through, he'd come through for me one more time
when I need him most.

"I don't think I can return to the only home I've ever had," I say after a
moment, "and though I have called it home for nearly two decades, that
forest is not somewhere I wish to wander aimlessly—or alone."

"You could join another kingdom," he offers.

"I did not wish to be a part of this one, let alone any other."

He snorts, chuckling to himself.

"Can I ask you something now?"

His grin widens, and tiny wrinkles form at the corners of his eyes as he
nods.

"Why did you come to Camelot?" It's not the same question, not really.
He doesn't have to tell me what happened to his brother; I only wish to
know why he chose this particular kingdom.

"I didn't have a plan when I left. I only knew that I couldn't stay where
I was." He's silent for a long time, and I peek at him out of the corner of
my eye several times before he speaks again. "I don't really know why I
came to Camelot, but I don't regret it, either."

We stare out at the garden, lost to our own thoughts.

"Destiny is a fickle thing," I murmur.

He grunts beside me. "I think I've lived my destiny already." His tone
is wistful, his laugh somber. "Now, I'm just trying to do right by those
around me."

Thunder echoes throughout the kingdom, and lightning flashes across
the sky as the rain washes away the remnants of the honesty and raw
truths laid bare between us today.

After a moment, he hops off the wooden crate. Surveying the garden for the length of a rolling boom of thunder, he finally turns his gaze on me, a warm contrast to the coldness of the morning storm. "I'll be back soon. I need to collect a few things before we go."

I nod, and he turns to leave, his body already halfway through the little door at the back of Vera's shop when I finally find my voice again. "I'm glad for having met you, Tristan." I blurt it out before I can stop myself, knowing that what comes next will likely change everything.

He pauses mid-step, leaning back to meet my gaze. A handful of emotions dance across his face before he finally settles on a curious expression, one corner of his mouth turned up hesitantly and one eyebrow arched high.

"Whatever reasons you have for leaving Northumbria," I say instead of answering his unspoken question, "I'm glad for having met you."

FORTY-FIVE

LANCELOT

"Are you ready for this?" Perci eyes me skeptically, glancing around the otherwise empty armoury. There's no one else in here besides us and Tristan; the rest of the knights are already out on duty or in the square claiming a good spot to watch the day's duels.

His lack of faith wounds me, but I keep my voice even as I tighten the straps of the leather vambraces along my forearms. "I'm not afraid of Bors."

It was announced at first light this morning that Bors and I would be the fourth and final duel today. We saw it coming—anticipated it even—and, somehow, it still managed to surprise me almost as much as it scares me. Not that I'll ever admit that to Perci.

I'm so close to winning, so close to the mere possibility of what I seek—the luxury to be able to finally do something to free my mother from her curse—that I can't bear to let myself think that I could lose something so important because of Bors. Again.

I won't lose today. Or tomorrow. Or the day after. I'm going to win the tournament and free my mother. And then I'm going to track down Ari and earn her forgiveness, one way or another. No matter how long it takes…

"You bloody well should be," Perci snaps, clearly annoyed at my indifference and, apparently, insulting lack of self-preservation.

"Well, I'm not." I force steel into my voice, my nerve, and my resolve all at the same time.

"Then you're a fool and a—"

"Enough," Tristan growls, levelling him with a glare that raises even my eyebrows. "You're not helping, Perci. You're just being a prat."

"He has no idea what he's—"

"I have every idea what I'm doing!" I shout at him, frustration getting the better of me. A harsh silence falls over the armoury, but my anger surges, and I can't help myself. "I know what I'm getting myself into, and I know exactly who I'm going up against. You don't need to keep insulting me, Perci."

His jaw clenches, but he says nothing.

"I know what I'm doing," I say again, a bit quieter this time. "Going in there afraid of Bors after what we've all seen him do in the ring, let alone on the battlefield…that doesn't increase my chances of winning. I don't have to fear him to understand him."

"Even if you understand him—his motives and what he's capable of—the stakes are so much higher now."

"They're not any higher today than they were yesterday," I lie, returning my attention to my armour. "As far as anyone is concerned, we simply dumped Ari on a healer and left with no one the wiser. Whatever Arthur thinks he knows, he has no proof."

"The fact that you're fighting Bors today proves he knows enough," Perci says indignantly.

Tristan shakes his head. "It only proves he has a theory. If something had him truly scared, he would've had Vera's door kicked down in hunt of her after he dismissed us yesterday. He knows where she is, and he knows what she can do, and, I think, for now, that's enough for him."

"How do you know he *didn't* have her door kicked in?"

"Because I was there this morning," Tristan says evenly. "If Arthur sent anyone there in the dead of the night, they did nothing."

"Why does he hate her so much, anyways?" I hear myself asking. Tristan and Perci exchange a quick, surprised glance.

"Because he fears her," Perci says finally.

Tristan nods solemnly. "He fears that she can do magic without being a mage. He fears that she slaughtered so many of his men so easily." He sighs, pinching the bridge of his nose. "I think...I think he fears the story more than the girl itself. This girl who was raised in secret by a dragon and hidden within his kingdom. He has no idea what to do with her, and because she slew six soldiers without so much as blinking an eye—*and* without using magic—he cannot let her go unchecked. He cannot simply let her wander the streets of Camelot any more than he can let her go free."

They exchange another glance, Perci's face twisting into a grimace as if he smelled something foul as he says, "But he also cannot put her through training and have her knighted, either. Bors would have her head before she ever made it that far, both out of hatred and revenge for his men. But more than that, the other knights would never trust her on the battlefield—"

"I trust her," I say without meaning to interrupt him.

"As do I." Tristan nods.

"Even so," Perci continues, "Arthur's hands are tied. If he cannot knight her, and he cannot free her...either by his own volition or that of the kingdom's, then he's in an incredibly precarious position. He may not have been as quick to take her head as some of the knights may have wanted, but if she dies, then his current problems will die with her."

"She never truly had a chance at victory. We were just too naive to see it," I snarl at him despite my anger not truly being his fault.

There's a long moment of silence between us, full of tension and buzzing energy before Tristan asks, his tone careful, "What would you have done if it had come down to the two of you?"

"What?" It takes twice as much effort to swallow down the lump forming in my throat.

"If the final duel had come down to you and Ari, what would you have done?" My stomach turns as if it can sense his next question, and I'm not confident I won't throw up all over his boots. "She already blames you for Penn's death. Would you truly take her freedom from her, too?"

"Don't say his name."

Her words flash through my mind like a bolt of lightning, the pain in her voice as clear in my head as it was that day in the town square. She's never allowed me to say his name, not once, and yet, Tristan wields it so easily—so carelessly.

Not for the first time, I wonder how close they might've become during his time as her ward. I have to resist the urge to snap at him, forcing my jealousy into something manageable before it distracts me too much. I need to focus on today's duel with Bors and making sure it lasts long enough to give them a good enough head start.

If Tristan feels so comfortable saying the dragon's name, then I have to trust that Ari feels enough ease around him to allow it, which means she's more likely to go along with the plan. Aside from winning the tournament, her being safe and far away from Camelot is the only thing that matters to me.

Whether he'd been genuinely curious, or goading me into some sort of a reaction, it doesn't matter. I take a deep breath to steady myself and ignore the implications of his question as I say, "It doesn't matter. She's no longer in the tournament, and as far as we can tell, Arthur intends to just lock her back up in the dungeons as if none of this ever happened. Vera's healed her of Morgana's death magic, the poison no longer in her system, and with it, Arthur's chance at discretely getting rid of her is now gone."

"It makes no difference what Arthur intends." Tristan smirks, but there's no humour to it. "She'll be long gone before he ever realises she's out of his reach."

FORTY-SIX

ARI

"He wants you to run, doesn't he?" Vera's arrival doesn't startle me. Neither does her question, but the fondness in which she regards Tristan, even after the hardships they've endured together, makes me feel guilty for what I must do.

"Aye." I nod, glancing at her briefly before returning my gaze to the garden.

Thunder continues to boom overhead, lightning flashing across the sky in huge bolts as the storm continues to rage on. There's a chill in the air now, a cold breeze that rustles the leaves and sends shivers down my spine. I have to rub warmth into my fingers to keep them from going numb, but I welcome it. The beautiful chaos of nature has always felt like home to me.

"Thunderstorms feel like home to me, too." One side of her mouth lifts up in a half-smile. The confusion on my face pulls a laugh from her lips—a pleasant, happy sound as she says, "I've been around a long time, child. I've grown very good at reading people."

"Where is home?" I ask tentatively, then add, "Your *real* home."

She chuckles softly before answering. "Far from here, there is a place deep within the ancient parts the forest you grew up in where my brothers and I were born. We spent most of our childhood there, venturing out only when men started to explore the innermost parts of this continent."

We fall silent again, but after a moment, she adds, "Many, many years after my brothers destroyed all the good in one another, I went north. I stayed there as the power of men rose and fell like pieces of a game, no king content with what he'd been given or what he'd managed to take. I stayed there through wars waged and kingdoms lost. I called the north home for nearly two centuries until, finally, a king decided that his problem no longer lay with men, but with magic. And when they started hunting mages, burning and beheading them, I realised I could no longer call that place home."

I shift uncomfortably on the crate, letting her words sink in.

When the last war broke out in Northumbria, had they started hunting mages? Is that what happened to Tristan's brother? A lump forms in my throat, and I can't find the courage to ask her, though I know I'll never be able to bring myself to ask Tristan. If that's what happened to his brother—burning or beheading—I would never make him talk about it just to satiate my own curiosities.

It bothers me that I didn't know this despite all of Penn's teachings about the numerous kingdoms on this continent. Although, perhaps. that was a small mercy that he and Merlin agreed upon considering the only thing they ever agreed upon was me learning magic in the first place. Perhaps they didn't want the burden of what my gift could cost me weighing on my mind if I wandered too far into hostile territory. Perhaps that's why we stopped going north anytime Penn and I set out for an adventure.

Instead of pressing Vera about it, I focus on something else she said. "Do you still see your brothers?"

"My real ones?" She snorts, a rueful smile touching her lips. "No."

"Real ones?" I ask, unsure what she means.

"All mages are brothers and sisters—beings born of magic, irrevocably tied together by the strings of fate," she says wistfully.

"How many other mages do you know?" I ask.

The words seem to hang between us for an eternity before she finally says, "All of them."

"How is that possible?"

"I have walked this earth a long time, child, and I plan to walk it a long while more. Every time a new mage is born, I can feel it." Her lips lift up in a quick, indulgent smile. "I imagine Merlin can, too."

I can only stare at her, certain I've misheard.

"I was one of the first," she says in quiet answer to my dumbfounded expression. Her eyes lose focus, as if the story in her head and heart are unfolding in the very garden before us. "There were three of us—Velho, Merlin, and myself. Three magical children born of the enchanted forest, charged with maintaining the precarious balance between order and chaos."

I turn to face her properly, full of disbelief. "Merlin is your brother?"

"Unfortunately," she says, a vein twitching in her forehead as she clenches her jaw.

"I had no idea," I whisper under my breath. "I didn't realise… I knew he was old, but I didn't know he was one of the first."

"Aye, one of the three original mages," she says bitterly.

"I know he has a bit of an unsavoury reputation, but I didn't realise you actually *knew* Merlin."

"Aye, child. I've known him for more than half a millennia." There's a bite to her words, an edge I can understand, even without context. "Merlin is a great many things, Ari, but I assure you that whatever you know about him doesn't even begin to scratch the surface."

I want to say more, to ask more—so many questions are rolling around in my head, fighting for space, begging to be asked—but the anguish and sorrow in her expression has them all dying on my lips.

"I'm sorry," I say instead.

"Whatever for?" she asks, incredulous.

"Whatever he did. Whatever part he played in destroying the goodness in Velho, whatever happened between your brothers…I'm sorry."

"It is no business of yours to make apologies for him."

"Then I'm sorry that it happened, if not for his part in it."

She places her hand on my shoulder, her fingers warm against my rain-soaked shirt. Her tone turns lighter, a wry smirk lifting up one side of her mouth. "Might I give you a piece of advice before you decide to run?" I nod, but something tells me she wasn't going to wait for an answer. "You have a big heart, Ari. You have seen many things and had many freedoms others couldn't even begin to fathom. But you have also suffered great losses, both old and new. Do not let them define you. Do not let the darkness of the world change you, and certainly do not let the monsters try to control you."

"What of the darkness and the monsters within me?" I ask quietly.

She stares at me for a long moment, her green-gold eyes full of mischief. "When it threatens to overtake you, you only have two options: give in to it and let it destroy you," she says with a wink, "or release it."

"And then what?" I whisper.

Her lips twist into something that is equal parts mischief and malice. "Forge the darkness into armour. Wield it like a blade. Let your enemies know exactly who you are and what they cannot take from you, and then pray like hell it doesn't consume you anyway."

The look in her eyes tells me everything I need to know.

She knows. She knows *everything*.

She knows, and she's telling me not to run, no matter what Tristan says. No matter what Lancelot believes is best. No matter what I risk by staying here.

"Nobody, no little prince or future king—absolutely no one will hand you your freedom. You must take it, or spend the rest of your life suffering the consequences." A deafening crack of thunder unleashes overhead, but she merely raises one eyebrow. "Do you understand?"

I'm supposed to be at Vera's, waiting for Lancelot's duel with Bors to start so that Tristan and I can escape, unnoticed. I'm supposed to be waiting for him, ready to flee—to disappear like a phantom wind. I'm supposed to be willing to risk my life, and the lives of those who've helped me. Risk Arthur's wrath, Bors' rage, and the entirety of Camelot's army hunting me down.

All for what?

So that I don't waste away, cold and alone in the dungeons of the castle? So that I don't die at the hands of Morgana's death magic, Bors' blade, or Arthur's anger? If I run, I risk losing everything that I have left. It's not much, but it's still worth fighting for.

Even on my darkest days, I did not run. Not from Penn when his temper shook the mountain, nor from Baxen when his patience grew thin. I did not run from Merlin and the foulest of his moods, nor the dryads who tried to kill us. I did not run from the cowards who slaughtered my family, nor the prince who enslaved me for my actions.

I've never run from a fight before, and I will not start now.

Not when there are other lives at stake, other people who would be hurt by my actions. Not when the only chance I have of getting the one thing I want besides my freedom requires me to stay in Camelot.

This morning, I finally allowed myself to mourn Penn—finally allowed myself to feel all the things I hadn't dared to feel since being taken prisoner. It's for that very reason, because of those tears and the level of acceptance that came with them, that I'm able to put one foot in front of the other right now.

Arthur can threaten me all he wants, but he doesn't actually hold any power over me. If he wished me dead—truly wished to kill me—he would have done so already.

The rest of it has just been theatrics.

He could have killed me the moment I set foot in the throne room, or any moment after that. He could have ordered me starved to death, beaten, or beheaded, but he didn't.

Morgana was a test; ultimately, one that I failed. That failure has now put other people at risk—something that I'm not comfortable with. Had I used my own magic to heal myself, had I been able to, he could have burned me on a pyre for it. But then he would've also had to admit to knowing I'd been poisoned in the first place, and even for me being a prisoner, that wouldn't look good for him.

And Bors…I believe Arthur is simply entertaining him, fuelling his anger and hatred of me *because he can.* It makes my blood boil—the games that he plays. And he is to rule a kingdom? He, with the temper of a woodland gnome and the malice of a dryad?

I fear for his people. Fear for the future of this kingdom. Fear for *him.*

The thought startles me, physically halting my steps, stopping me in the middle of the cobblestoned street. There's no one around, no one to question me or stare at me; they're all in the town square watching the duels. Lancelot's will be starting soon, undoubtedly the one most looked forward to today.

My feet resume their path, slowly making my way toward the ring.

Lancelot wanted me to use him as a distraction to get out, but I think it would surprise him to know that I wished to see him one more time before everything changed. Not to forgive him, but…to support him, I suppose, and his need to win in order to free his mother, in the same way he's been trying to support me since I've arrived here. I know that I don't owe him anything, but I find that some small part of me wants to give it anyway. For the boy I thought he was, before everything went wrong.

Tristan will be furious with me for lying to him—for breaking his trust. But after today, I will either be dead or free, and then it will not matter how furious he is with me. I'm supposed to be waiting for him, but this is something I have to do, and I cannot leave here until it is done.

Thunder booms so loudly overhead that it rumbles through the cobblestones. Lightning flashes across the sky and *zings* through my veins, fear and anxiety mingling with something that feels an awful lot like relief—the finality of something long overdue coming to a close.

I allow myself a moment to pull a long, slow breath in through my nose and out through my mouth. Another deep breath, then one more.

No matter what happens next, this was *my* choice.

If Arthur decides to end my life today, then I can only hope he won't have a reason to take anyone else's because of me.

I take one last deep breath, and then I follow the sounds of shouting and cheering, the sound of metal on metal, as I drift past Excalibur and head toward the fighting ring.

FORTY-SEVEN

LANCELOT

I hit the ground—hard—struggling to pull air into my lungs. Bors is fighting dirty, but since the rules are so loose on what's considered foul play...

I push myself to my hands and knees, the death-grip on my father's blade the only comfort I have. I spit a mouthful of blood and dirt on the ground between us and wipe the back of my free hand across my lips. Bors laughs loudly, a malicious joy burning bright in his eyes.

Automatically, I scan the crowd for Tristan and Perci, forcing down the disappointment building in my chest when I remember that only one of them is here.

Directly across from me, and leaning against the wooden railing of the ring, Kay catches my eye. He nods, and the cold fury on his face sends a ripple of resolve through my veins. One of his eyes is so purple it's almost black and half swollen shut. His lip is split, along with every knuckle on his left hand.

It turns out that while we were plotting Ari's hasty departure after Arthur's summons last night, Kay and Graham went to the tavern for a pint. One thing led to another, and some of Bors' low-life commanders took it upon themselves to remind Kay that not only had he recently been beaten by a girl, but exactly how weak that made a knight of the king's army look.

They're only lucky I wasn't there.

The ground thuds with Bors' quick arrival, and I glance back in his direction, digging my feet into the soft earth and forcing in a slow breath. He's growing reckless and arrogant, his swings growing wider and wilder as he basks in the cheers of the audience. His overconfidence has him assuming that, because he's knocked me down a few times, he's already won.

But that presumption is his first mistake.

His second is underestimating me and my desire to win. If I can't be the one to take Ari away from here, then nothing is going to stop me from freeing my mother.

I let him get close to me, let him think I'm still recovering, still trying to pull air into my lungs after being winded. I wait until he's too close, uncomfortably so, and then, when he arcs his sword unnecessarily high above his head for no other purpose than to be dramatic, I strike.

I drive the heel of my boot into his knee as hard as I can, only waiting a second for his body to reflexively curl inward before thrusting my fist into his face. Blood spurts from his nose, which is not only broken but split across the bridge, too.

He staggers to the ground, assessing the damage to his knee and leaving his right side wide open. If we were on the battlefield, he would already be dead. My sword would have already disembowelled him and be on its way to the next victim.

But since we're not on the battlefield—and unlike my opponent, I don't intend to kill anyone in the ring just to win—I stay my hand.

My foot connects with his torso next, and he sprawls backward in the dirt, swearing profusely.

"Yield," I snarl, the tip of my blade less than an inch from his throat.

A hushed murmur spreads through the crowd, but I ignore it. Whether they did not expect me to win, or they did not expect me to be so ruthless about injuring my captain, I cannot tell.

Bors is lying at my feet, an impressive string of curses filling the air between us. He uses his free hand to wipe some of the blood from his face, smearing it across his cheek—across the dark red scabs marring his skin. Three perfect lines left by Ari.

I let my thoughts drift to her, just for a second. Let them drift to the hope—the *need*—for her to get as far away from here as possible.

Once I've won the tournament and been given the resources to free my mother from her curse, I'll try to find her—try to do what I failed at this morning. Apologise. To earn her forgiveness. To become her friend again.

That being said, maybe she won't want to be found. Maybe, once she's out of Camelot, she'll wish to never think of the kingdom or anyone in it again. Maybe Tristan will never even tell me where she's gone.

"What are you waiting for?"

Perhaps Bors hit me harder than I realised earlier. There are no spots at the edge of my vision, no wobbly off-kilter feeling in my gut, no dull pain behind my eyes or throbbing between my brow, and yet, I could have sworn that was her just now, screaming at me, clear as day.

"Lancelot, finish him!"

Everything seems to slow to a near stop—the cheering of the crowd, the string of curses pouring out of Bors' mouth, the pounding of my heart. Even the rain seems to lighten, the clouds holding their breath as what is surely the biggest cosmic joke unfolds before me.

My eyes find hers before I even comprehend that I was looking for her, but there she is, standing next to Kay and Garreth, leaning over the edge of the fence with the fury of an entire dragon horde burning in her forest-green eyes.

It feels as if I am underwater. Panic courses through me, weighing my limbs down and restricting my lungs. I can't move. I can't breathe. I can't separate one sound from the next. I can only focus on the deafening roar in my ears, on the pressure in my chest and the fear in my veins.

"No." It comes out as a whisper but, in my heart, it's a scream.

She was meant to be free, meant to be getting as far away from this place as possible. This was our one chance to get her out. Our one chance for Tristan—*where the hell is Tristan?*

Bors has managed to recover during my distraction, although he stands on shaky legs. He's favouring his injured knee, putting all his weight on the other. Blood still pours from his nose, and already his face is turning a brilliant shade of purple where I hit him.

I glance at Arthur and immediately wish that I hadn't. I wish that Tristan had not failed in getting Ari out of Camelot, because, while I am looking at Arthur, he is looking at her. Beside him, Guinevere smiles like the she-wolf she is, equal parts devious and predatory.

"Fool." Bors spits on the ground between us, both as insult and to relieve himself of a mouthful of blood.

My attention is now divided, and he knows it—between him and the duel, Ari at the edge of the ring, and the slow descent Arthur is now making from the dais. The crowd parts hastily for him, a wave of tension rolling through the town square.

I catch the quick glance over her shoulder, the clench of her jaw, but her eyes dart back to Bors, and I begrudgingly return my attention to him. Enough is enough. This duel has gone on for far too long, and neither of us can rally the showmanship to continue toying with one another. He can barely walk, so I'm going to have to take the fight to him.

I loathe being on the offensive, loathe having to close the distance between us to make the final strike. I would much rather my opponent come to me, come into my controlled space.

But if I'm going to win *and* stand any chance of intercepting Arthur, I need to end this now. I feint left and then right, but Bors anticipates it, keeping his sword held firmly between us. I dance around him in a circle, parrying the entire time, waiting for an opening. All I need is one. One opening, one misstep, one miscalculation.

I risk a few more feints, and narrowly avoid a sword to my face, but then the opening I'm waiting for is in front of me and I seize it. He falters, just for a second, his hand angled exactly the way I need it to be, and where he hesitated, I do not.

The tip of my blade glides across the back of his hand so effortlessly it could have been butter on a hot summer day. He shrieks—an ungodly, horrible sound—and I know that I've crossed a line I cannot come back from. Tournament or not, Bors and I are about to have a whole lot of problems, because while he is most certainly still holding the sword, I don't know that he will ever do so again.

My blade has cut clean through the tendons on the back of his hand.

There's a long moment where we just stare at each other, neither of us moving. Tears of pain and rage well in his eyes as the overwhelming relief of beating him settles into my bones. His eyes drop to his hand, and before he can even grab the hilt with the other, I wrap my hand around the blade and pull it from his grasp, tossing it on the ground behind me.

The crowd erupts like thunder, cheering and applauding, shouting and whistling. Several knights hop over the wooden railing, keeping Bors on his feet as they half-carry him into the castle.

Kay and Graham are in my face, cheering and clapping me on the back, and Ari—*Ari*—is standing in front of me, the most genuine, arrogant grin spread across her face. The feeling of having her this close without all the grief and hostility, mixed with the relief and triumph of beating Bors, is nearly euphoric.

"Thank you," she says. Her tone is light, but her words feel so much heavier than they should.

"For what?"

Something shifts in her expression, turns it softer for a moment, more reminiscent of our time together before and full of something else I can't quite place. Before I can try to, it's gone again. "For beating him," she says finally.

I smile down at her, nearly dizzy with conflicting emotions but nodding all the same.

"Ah, my favourite prisoner," Arthur says, hopping over the railing with all the grace and confidence of a mountain cat. "Welcome back."

FORTY-EIGHT

A R I

"Prince Arthur," I say, matching his bravado. "I didn't realise I had gone somewhere."

His green eyes seem to pierce my soul, cold fury radiating off him in waves. "There seems to have been a brief period of time yesterday when our most renowned prisoner was unaccounted for." He's trying to bait me.

"I left the ring pretty wounded." I release a self-deprecating laugh, glancing around the ring at the others. Lancelot, Kay, and Garreth are close by, and Perci is just hopping over the railing to join us.

All of them look tense. All of them look ready for a fight.

Lancelot would defend my life if it came down to it, I have little doubts about that. Perhaps Perci would, too, or at the very least, try to intervene. I know where Kay and Garreth's loyalties lie, but at this point, it doesn't matter. I don't intend to let it get that far.

Maybe it's good that Tristan isn't here. The last thing I need is for him to do something stupid when he's only just found a home again—a kingdom to love and defend, despite its monarch.

"I didn't know seeking medical attention was against the rules of the tournament," I say, baiting the prince right back.

A quick smile lifts up one side of his mouth. "Seize her. Return the prisoner to her cell."

For a heartbeat, no one moves. My eyes dart around the ring, glancing between the knights who are meant to imprison me before meeting a pair of sapphire blue ones, full of simmering rage. Guinevere stands with white-knuckled hands clenched on the wooden railing, the same fire burning in her gaze as the night before. She nods once, almost imperceptibly.

I offer her the closest thing to a nod that I can muster before turning back to Arthur, my heart racing in my chest. Kay and Perci are closing in on either side of me now, one hand on the hilt of their swords, the other outstretched as if to grab me. At least if they're going to be the ones to take me, it won't be as bloody as if it were Bors and his commanders.

"Alternatively," I say loudly, mustering every single drop of courage I possess.

Arthur's eyes turn murderous. He takes two quick, involuntary steps forward, his anger getting the better of him.

"How about a duel?" I ask, refusing to break his stare. His eyes search mine for a moment, darting back and forth, brow furrowing. The beautiful, poisonous, evergreen colour of them speaks to something deep within my soul—something long lost, broken, and forgotten.

He says nothing for a while, he just stares, and stares, and stares. He has to swallow several times before he speaks again, jaw clenched as he asks, "What are your terms?"

I have to force myself not to smile, force myself to rein in the hesitant glee bouncing through my veins.

We both know that he cannot decline my challenge, that even though he is to be named king at week's end, he cannot let a prisoner, a murderer, and a *girl* challenge him. If he does not accept, he looks weak.

But even worse, if he accepts and loses, all hell will break loose.

"If I win, you pardon me and let me go—immediately—and I will never set foot in Camelot again." I keep my words loud and clear, ensuring anyone close to us can hear my terms. If Arthur agrees, the more witnesses I have, the better, even if he doesn't follow through with his end of the bargain. The terms of me winning are as much a promise to myself as they are a warning to both Arthur and Guinevere. "If you win, you can have whatever you want. Kill me, keep me locked in your dungeon, it doesn't matter."

His eyes squint as he tries to find the loophole, tries to assess what part of myself I've left defenceless, what miscalculation I've made that he can exploit.

But as far as I'm concerned, there isn't one. No matter what happens next, Arthur will not only look the fool, but he will not ascend to the throne of Camelot. I know what I have to do, and I am prepared to face the consequences.

For this, for what Guinevere has offered me, I would do anything. I don't dare look at her for fear of triggering suspicion in Arthur, but I will meet her terms so long as she understands mine. Those words were as much for her as they were for everyone else. If I win, I will *never* set foot in this kingdom again.

"I accept," Arthur says slowly. There's a flash of something in his eyes—agitation or resolve, maybe even anticipation.

Kay and Perci stand down immediately. I glance at each of them, just briefly, then back at Arthur. He seems dazed, his eyes unfocused as he goes about unclasping the cape fastened at his shoulders, tossing it at a page who scrambles under the railing to catch it. Arthur plucks the blood crown from his head, discarding it on the pile of crimson fabric in the young boy's hands.

The boy, to his credit, doesn't balk. He looks absolutely terrified, but he doesn't so much as flinch as the crown comes to rest in his grasp.

Arthur somehow manages to look every bit the regal heir, every bit the prince of Camelot, even without his crown. He stands tall, shoulders squared, a sneer lifting one side of his mouth.

His fingers tremble as they reach for the sword at his hip, though—such a small movement that I'm not sure anyone else even noticed it, but I did.

He draws the sword—a beautiful, impressive blade forged of the same depthless black material as his crown. It's long and slender, the hilt intricately carved. I'm calculating the advantage of range he'll have over a training sword, even as I say, "I don't have a weapon, Your Highness."

His pupils dilate slightly, his nostrils flaring. He tilts his head in Lancelot's direction without ever breaking eye contact with me.

Lancelot walks toward me, drawing his own sword—the one he'd just beaten Bors with, the one he tried to slay Penn with, the one he inherited from his father. The carved serpent pommel is warm to the touch when I take it. Instinctively, my free hand reaches up to touch the matching medallion resting against my sternum, hidden beneath my tunic.

If I die today, he'll never know.

If they take the medallion from my cold, lifeless body, will they recognise it? Will they return the heirloom to the bloodline of which it belongs?

Something tells me that's unlikely.

I should have told him. From the moment I saw the sword, and Penn's life was no longer in danger, I should have told him. Despite everything, he deserved to know the truth, and now, he may never.

"Thank you," I whisper, forcing myself to meet his worried blue eyes before refocusing my attention on Arthur.

Lancelot, Perci, Kay, Garreth, and the page all back up, retreating over the railing and to the safety of the other side. I watch them go, catching the wary look Lancelot gives Guinevere as he stands beside her, and the uneasy way Perci shifts his weight from foot to foot.

Between one heartbeat and the next, Tristan appears beside them, panting and breathless, a raging fury burning in his hazel eyes, betrayal clear on his face.

I'm sorry, I mouth to him. He shakes his head, biting back whatever retort he surely wishes to say. I tell myself that he will either forgive me or I will be dead, but, right now, it doesn't matter.

"Are we going to fight or not?" Arthur asks. Without giving me time to answer, he lunges at me, that beautiful blade ready to separate my head from my neck.

FORTY-NINE

ARI

He tries to catch me off guard, and I dodge him easily enough, though he manages to keep me on the defensive. We circle each other around the ring a few times, feeling each other out, but neither of us make anything more than a half-hearted move toward the other.

"Maybe you should reconsider?" Arthur calls, taunting me. He backs off, putting a little space between us. "It's not too late, you know." He laughs, pacing back and forth. The people in the square laugh with him, even if it is a bit hesitantly.

"I'll take my chances." I can't stop the words from coming out sharp and bitter. The idea of just giving up and returning to my cell without a fight, without another chance at getting out of here—possibly ever—is no longer an option. He's already proven that he's willing to play dirty. He had Morgana poison me to ensure that I'd lose my duel against Bors, no matter how slim the chance of victory was to begin with. There's no guarantee he'd follow through with his word in three years' time and actually release me.

His eyes cut to mine, and I can't tell if the upward tick of his lips is pride or something else. Does he truly think I'd back down now? Does he expect me to be happy remaining a prisoner?

I realise, as his gaze continues to bore into mine, that we're precisely the same height. We've never been on the same level before, so I'd never had a chance to notice. Somehow, despite the dais, the air of superiority, and the crown, I figured he was taller.

He lunges again, but this time, I'm unable to properly evade him fast enough. I manage to deflect the nearly fatal hit so that his blade slices across my arm instead of my chest. It glides across the bandage, shredding the fabric and tearing open the skin beneath once more.

A satisfied sneer spreads across his face. "Sorry, had that already begun to heal?" he quips too loudly, solely for the benefit of the audience. "Morgana does such fine work."

I can't help grunting against the fresh, sharp wave of tingles that rolls down my arm. My skin feels hot and tight, like a shock of lightning has gone through it. Blood surges down my arm, the stitches now re-opened, a new cut carved over the old one.

Clenching my teeth against a hiss of pain, I open and close my fingers a few times, testing the strength of my hand. The fist is weak and loose at best and my fingers shake when straightened, but that's fine. I can keep the sword in my right hand.

Arthur's putting on a show for the crowd—grinning and boasting and strutting about—so he's not paying attention when I lunge for him again. He must've thought the injury would stop me, but it's only slowed me down. There's too much on the line to just give up now.

His face quickly turns from arrogance to annoyance, indignation flashing in his eyes. He meets me blow for blow despite my attempt at being relentless, eager not to give him another opening. Our blades lock in a bind dangerously close to his face and he *smiles* at me.

It catches me off guard, and I physically jerk backwards at the unexpected reaction, a ripple of unease shooting down my spine at the sadistic look on his face. His foot comes up between us, connecting with my stomach in a singular kick that sends me staggering.

My back hits the ground hard, and I'm gasping, desperately trying to pull air back into my lungs. Panicked, I roll onto my stomach and manage to get shaky arms beneath me, crawling away from him to put some distance between us.

He doesn't let me get too far, though. I can hear the thump of his footsteps trailing after me across the ring, and whatever he's doing—whatever bout of showmanship and dramatic flair he's enacting for the pleasure and reactions of the crowd has them cheering and whistling once more.

I take a moment of Arthur's little display to try to even out my breathing and use the railing to pull myself up. When my eyes meet those of the person standing less than a foot away, it takes everything in me to keep it together. The cold terror staring back at me from the depths of Tristan's eyes—the ones that remind me so much of the forest, so much of home— turns my own growing fear to lead in my chest.

"I'm sorry," I breathe, turning back toward Arthur before I can allow myself to be distracted.

I've somehow managed to keep a death-grip on Lancelot's sword, and now that Arthur has made his way over to me, a sharp whining sound rings out across the town square as he slides the edge of his blade down the length of mine.

"It didn't have to be this way," he whispers over the blades, low enough for only me to hear. There's something in his voice that makes the hair at the back of my neck prickle, but it lacks the harshness I expect from him. Instead of an edge, it's more like a weight—the heaviness of an unbearable, uncrossable chasm between us, directly contrasted by the desperation glinting in his eyes. "Things could have been so different between you and I."

"Perhaps you shouldn't have locked me in a dungeon." My response is half-wheeze, pushed through gritted teeth.

He goes rigid. His pupils dilate, the black nearly swallowing the deep green entirely. "You killed six of my—"

"And they killed my dragon," I snarl. Pushing off the wooden railing, I rush him, manoeuvring our swords out from between us and throwing my face into his with as much force as I can muster. His head snaps back, and for a second, nothing happens, but then blood spurts from his nose and a foul string of curses falls from his lips. He takes one step back, then another, bringing his hand to his face and scowling at the dark red blood staining his fingers.

Black spots dance at the edge of my vision, a throbbing pain spreading across my forehead. As I lunge at him once more, I can tell that I've underestimated what head-butting him would do to me. Dizziness washes over me, completely throwing off my aim.

He blocks me easily, deflecting my next two swings. We parry for a moment, neither of us gaining any ground, and then all of a sudden, he's switched hands without my notice, the hilt of his sword now held firmly in the other hand as his dominant one connects with my face.

He punches me, his fist connecting with my jaw, and I go careening to the side, but he's there before I can fully right myself, hitting me again.

Swinging my sword both wildly and aimlessly—half in hopes of defending myself and half in hopes of getting him to back off, even a little. I only realise that I've managed to strike him when his frenzied onslaught ceases and a sharp intake of air echoes through the ring between us.

We're both panting hard, chests heaving, sweat drenching our brows. For a moment, neither of us move. We simply stare at each other, regarding the injuries we've inflicted, our blood mingling in the dirt between us, and that inescapable chasm that simultaneously tears us apart and binds us together.

Blood still trickles from his nose, and now, it oozes from the deep gash in his arm, as well. He switches his sword back to his uninjured hand, eyeing me skeptically.

Heaving a breath, I move first, breaking the bizarre stand-off between us and swinging Lancelot's sword at Arthur with all the strength I have left. His free arm snaps out toward me, his hand wrapping around my wrist with a strength that surprises me despite the injury, stopping me mid-motion. At the same time, he slams the bottom of the hilt of his sword into the back of my hand. The sharp pain mixed with the fierce grip of his fingers digging into the tendons on my arm has my hand reflexively dropping the sword, effectively disarming me.

No.

He shoves me back a step so that he can bend to retrieve Lancelot's blade, readjusting his grip on the sword held in his injured arm several times, and then he laughs—truly laughs, a loud, vicious sort of cackle. His head tips back and his whole body shakes with victorious delight, even as blood still trickles from his nose, coating his teeth.

When he finally stops—that arrogant, wicked smile upon his lips once more—he levels both swords in my direction. The blades cross just near the tips, the sharp edges but a hair's breadth from either side of my neck.

"I yield." The words are little more than a breath from my lips.

"Oh, Ari," he says, the venom in his voice prickling the hairs at the back of my neck again. "This isn't that kind of duel."

FIFTY

A R I

I knew it would most likely come to this—knew I could save it as a last-ditch effort, but still I hoped I could avoid it all the same. Guinevere's terms were simple: prevent Arthur from ascending to the throne. I had naively hoped I could best him in a duel, but if I succeed, this will still be enough to fulfil my end of the bargain.

I duck half a second before he lunges for me, sprinting the three steps to the railing and diving through the large gap in the horizontal boards, rolling sloppily into a crouch on the other side.

I don't have time to take in my surroundings, or to try to figure out if any of the people around me have friendly faces. Arthur hops the barrier as easily as he did the first time, even with a sword in each hand, and the crowd parts hastily, leaving a wide berth around us.

Dropping to the ground, I narrowly miss being decapitated, and a slow, wicked smile lifts up both sides of his mouth again. He halts to bask in the collective awe of the audience once more, ignoring the underlying tension in the square as he paces back and forth, droning on about something I cannot find the strength to focus on.

Crawling backward, I move as fast as I can, digging my fingers into the cracks between the cobblestones as I push with my heels—doing anything

I can to put some space between us.

As I move, I send up a silent prayer to the gods, to Penn, to Merlin—to anyone who will listen—for a friendly face, a moment to breathe, a reprieve from Arthur's hunt. Because that is what this has become—a hunt. If I fail now, I have no doubts that I will not see the sun rise tomorrow.

The prince whirls on me, head cocking to one side as his predatory gaze homes in on me. For every foot I gain, he takes two more until he's too close for comfort and closing the distance still.

I fling my hands out desperately behind me, searching for anything to help pull myself to my feet. Searching for something to defend myself with. But instead of a weapon, my fingers find a wall of stone, worn smooth by time.

The effort and strain on my arm as I use it to force myself up rips a cry of pain from my chest. The throbbing in my arm matches the throbbing behind my eyes and the pulsing in my veins. Leaning heavily on the mass of stone supporting me, I try to slow my breathing and calm my heart.

He walks toward me, teeth as clenched as his fists are on the swords. They're beautiful swords, I have to admit. One light, one dark. Both engraved with the tales of their lineage, and the power of their bloodlines.

If this is how I die, at least it's at the mercy of a beautiful weapon.

He lunges for me again, and I react on instinct alone. I spin, facing the wall of stones supporting me, and just as I'd hoped, it's not a wall at all.

It's a resting place.

It's a tomb.

It's Excalibur.

And it's the only chance I have of saving my life. Grabbing the hilt with my right hand, bloody and bruised, I pull with all my strength.

He's so close, almost close enough to end everything, but still, I persist. All the rage, the hurt, the betrayal, and the emptiness of the last several months crash into me, and I welcome them with open arms. For the second time today, I let all the emotions I'd been avoiding since the knights of Camelot slaughtered Penn fill me, fuel me, give me strength.

I know who I am.

I have always known.

Penn never hid it from me; he never even tried.

But the life that goes with my true name, my blood, my birthright— that was never mine. It was taken from me the night I was born, and I have never wanted it since.

I can feel Arthur closing in on me, but I will not let fear get in my way any longer. The sword moves, just a little, and relief floods through me. Wrapping my left hand around my right, I grit my teeth with the effort. A guttural scream comes from within me, a battle cry ripping through the town square like the animal that I am.

One second, the sword is buried in the stone, the next, it's in my hand, free of its ancient, ageless tomb. I do not waste another second, using the momentum of freeing it to block Arthur's death blow.

A loud clang fills the air, ringing in my ears. His eyes grow impossibly wide, lips parting in shock, and a myriad of emotions take turns flitting across his face.

Never, not once, did I assume Penn was lying. What reason would a dragon have to lie to the human child he chose to raise? What reason would he have to lie to the child he loved and claimed as his own?

But here, now, with the sound of Arthur's blades striking against Excalibur still ringing in my ears—the sound of an entirely different life, and the means to extend this one—a strange calming sensation washes over me. A sense of something else, something more—belonging, maybe—settles deep into my bones.

Without losing momentum, I use his distraction to my benefit, swinging our swords down and lifting my knee high, connecting my foot with his torso with as much force as I can muster, shoving him backwards—the way he did to me only moments ago. He hits the ground hard, a cloud of dust puffing up in his wake.

Behind him, several knights step out of the crowd, closing in on me, but I don't have any fight left in me. I release Excalibur, watching as it clatters to the ground in front of me. Prince Arthur still sits in the dirt, stunned.

"Your Highness," one of the knights says, awaiting his orders.

Another knight tries to help Arthur to his feet, but he waves him off, his astonished green gaze never leaving my face. "Seize her," he says. It comes out hoarse and broken.

They do.

Two knights grab me by the biceps, one rougher than the other, and the knight holding my injured arm makes sure not to touch the still-bleeding cut. My eyes find his at the same time that my steps falter, and I'm both surprised and relieved at the sight of the fierce hazel gaze staring back at me.

My knees give out, and Tristan catches me before I hit the ground, my strength and adrenaline now spent. Black spots creep in from the edges of my vision.

His mouth is moving, but I cannot hear what he's saying. The throbbing in my head now outweighs the throbbing in my arm. I try to pull air into my lungs, but no matter how hard I try, it's not enough.

Darkness crashes into me, pulling me under like the deepest wave.

FIFTY-ONE

LANCELOT

"Seize her."

I hadn't even realised he'd left my side, let alone made his way over to Ari, but Tristan does as Arthur commands. I'm glad one of us is with her right now, even if it's not me.

Tristan has her by the arm, helping to steady her wobbly legs, as he leads her from the square. He catches her when she stumbles, waving off the other knight, and then he's carrying her unconscious body into the castle.

I stand motionless, rooted to the spot in the middle of the square, Guinevere and Perci still on either side of me, all of us lost to our thoughts after the commotion that just unfolded. The moment Arthur levelled both swords at Ari, my heart stopped. Instinctually, I had known he wasn't going to stop until she was dead. She'd bolted like a doe being hunted, fled the ring and managed to put enough distance between them to give herself enough time to…

To pull Excalibur from the stone.

She pulled the sword from the stone.

Only an heir of Uther can pull the sword from the stone.

Everything she's said and done since the moment I met her, everything that struck me as odd or unlikely, things that didn't make sense, things that didn't add up—it all clicks into place.

She's been so careful, so incredibly careful not to let anything slip, and yet, she practically handed me her weight in clues. Clues that I either ignored or was simply too blind to see for what they were.

They hit me like waves now, an onslaught of all the pieces I should have put together months ago.

"Do you have any idea what you've done? Any of you? Do you realise that even if I don't die trying to save his life, he's going to have to kill you for coming here? For what you've done? For what you now know?" She'd been so angry, so hostile—so afraid.

And then, that first time I'd gone back to see her, something about all her questions felt off; I just couldn't figure out why. The way she'd asked them, or perhaps, the way she so desperately clung to an air indifference… as if she needed the answers not to matter.

"Which king do you serve?"

"King Uther of Camelot."

"What of his heir?"

I didn't notice before, but now, it makes total sense. All at once, the air of mystery shrouding the girl with the dragon lifts and all the pieces I couldn't connect align with perfect clarity.

"My parents are exactly where they're meant to be."

Dead. Her parents are dead…and she's known the entire time. Penn knew who she was and he raised her anyway instead of asking a king's ransom for her return.

A king's ransom that Uther never would have paid.

But all this time…she knew, and Penn knew, and…the person who brought her to him in the first place… It would've had to be someone with access to the castle, someone who could get close enough to the king and queen to not raise any suspicions.

Someone she hasn't seen in years…an advisor, perhaps. A guard or a servant. Which means there's a good chance someone else inside the castle knew who she was when she arrived, too.

Does Gawain know? He's barely tolerable of Arthur most days and rarely sober, but he'd looked her in the face the day of her trial… If she is who I think she is, how had he not recognised his own flesh and blood?

And Arthur… I have to assume that Arthur doesn't know. I have to assume that even he isn't that cruel and spiteful. If he's known this whole time, why would he lock her in the dungeon? Why not welcome her home and herald some great story of her return to the kingdom?

Whether or not he knew, Arthur nearly killed his own sister just now… and he had their half-sibling poison her with death magic yesterday.

"Morgana is Arthur's half-sister."

"Are you positive?"

She hadn't known—Ari hadn't known that Morgana was her half-sister.

A pair of guards walk up to us, but I can hardly focus on them. "Shall we escort you back to your rooms, Lady Guinevere?" one of them asks, both his voice and his stance rigid with tension.

"That's not necessary," she says coolly, placing a hand on my elbow. "I have two perfectly good escorts right here." She shouldn't be touching me—it's entirely inappropriate—but if either of the guards take notice, they say nothing.

"That's not necessary."

The words ring through my head, tugging at another memory. The dismissive way that Guinevere says it takes my mind back to that day in the kitchens, when Merlin came to see Ari.

"I wish for no reminders of my old life."

"Who else will bring you dragon's blood?" He'd been angry—at her, or at the dismissal, I don't know, but she'd been just as angry at him. For not saving the dragon, and for not getting her out of Camelot…

He knew… Merlin knows who she is, and still, he left her in Arthur's dungeon.

"I do not think you understand what I'm saying. Your eyes are already beginning to change. Your hair will not take long to follow suit."

Her eyes, which were dull and pale when she first came crashing through the trees in the forest all those months ago, are now warm and bright and evergreen. Something I hadn't even noticed until just now. *They have the same eyes.* Arthur and Ari…

My eyes latch onto Excalibur—discarded and forgotten in the dirt—then turn to the stones that held it, and my mind drifts back to another conversation we had, almost in this very spot.

"He comes from a long line of sole heirs, though there were whispers for a time that he was not the first born."

"What d'you mean?"

"For a long time, there were whispers of another born to King Uther and Queen Igraine—a daughter."

How had none of us figured it out?

"We need to move," Guinevere urges quietly, tugging on my arm and pulling me from the downward spiral of memories I'd been drowning in. "Now."

Most of Arthur's men are breaking up the crowd, forcibly sending everyone home. It doesn't matter; they all saw what transpired. They can't hide that from the entire kingdom—can't just sweep it under the rug and pretend it didn't happen.

I don't know where Arthur is or when he got up. I don't know if he's followed Tristan and Ari into the castle or sought out Morgana to bind his wounds. It unnerves me, not knowing where he is, and even more so, not knowing what's going to happen next.

Guinevere tugs on my arm again, spurring my feet into motion. Perci and I walk on either side of her, faces carved of stone. She smiles reassuringly at the people as we pass by, but even I can tell it's a flimsy facade.

"Where are we going?" I ask, ensuring that I don't look at her directly, forcing myself to mind my position and look the part that is expected of me.

"To my rooms," she murmurs through a tight smile.

Her lady-in-waiting steps into our path, unsettling me even more as she beams at us in greeting. She looks like a ray of sunshine amid the chaos; not a single hair out of place in her simple golden braid, nor a wrinkle in her pale blue dress. I think her name is Gracelynn, though I've never actually spoken to her before. She drops into a deep curtsey before Guinevere, not bothering to acknowledge Perci or myself. "Delightful weather we're having today, wouldn't you agree m'lady?"

"I would," Guinevere replies, demure despite the edge in her tone. "Though I do prefer the thunder and lightning of a good storm."

Gracelynn nods once, her easy, practiced smile never so much as wavering. She disappears back into the crowd just as quickly as she'd arrived.

"What the hell was that?" Perci demands under his breath.

"As if you boys don't have your own system of secret codes to pass messages along," Guinevere chides half-heartedly. We duck into a side entrance of the castle and drop any pretence of formality. "Ari's in trouble," she says flatly. "I can help her, but I need you to provide a distraction."

"What sort of distraction?" I ask warily.

"The less you know, the better." She must sense our unease because she sighs heavily through her nose and then adds, "You can either trust me, or you can let Arthur punish her for what she did today."

"Why would we trust you?" I snap back, unable to keep a hold on the agitation building inside me.

"Because I'm the one who asked her to do it." She shrugs, lifting one shoulder nonchalantly. "And I'm likely the only one here able to do what's necessary to help her now."

We both stare at her in shock, mouths dropping in unison. "You… what?"

"Not here, not now." She shakes her head. "I have a plan to get her out of this. Are you going to help me or not?"

Why would she ask Ari to challenge Arthur? What could Guinevere possibly have to gain from their duel? And does that mean she knew all along what I'm only putting together now? Just how many people might know Ari's true identity? And why have none of them said anything? Why have they all allowed her to be locked in a dungeon and treated like a prisoner for months?

"I know who you are and where you come from."

I thought Tristan simply meant here in Camelot. I thought he was just becoming fond of Ari—protective, even—after spending so much time with her. I'd been so distracted by my own jealousy that I never even considered there might've been more to his words… Has Tristan known all along who she is? Is that why he was so willing to be her guard? To help her train? To get her out of Camelot?

"Why are you telling us this?" Perci's quiet anger pulls me back to the present. "What's stopping us from going to the prince with word of your treason?" There's a defensiveness to his tone that I can't quite place the origin of.

She scoffs, rolling her eyes at him, before rounding on me. "Are you going to waste time questioning me, too, or can we go get Ari out of the dungeon before it's too late?"

"I don't understand. I—"

Pinching the bridge of her nose, Guinevere huffs audibly, exasperation rolling off her in waves. "Honestly, Lancelot, are you always this obtuse, or is today a particularly off day for you?"

She doesn't stick around long enough for me to answer her.

FIFTY-TWO

ARI

I don't know how long I've been out, but when I finally come to, the cold of the stone floor beneath me seeps through my clothes and soaks into my skin, chilling me to the point of shivers.

My head pounds with each beat of my heart, pulsing in my temples and behind my eyelids. My arm is throbbing, though there's a constant pressure around the wound, so I can tell that it's at least been bandaged. My stomach aches where Arthur kicked me, and my breaths come in uneven, ragged spurts that echo off the damp walls. Vaguely, I wonder if he cracked a rib.

Through the hazy fog of pain, I can make out the sound of someone else breathing, and the realisation that I'm not alone sends an uncomfortable tingle down my spine.

I open my eyes slowly, and the pain intensifies for a moment before settling again. The cell is dark and cold, the hall beyond illuminated by torchlight, as always. It's the same cell I found myself in the first time I woke up in Camelot—my home for the last several months.

"I'm a little surprised to find myself still alive," I croak out.

"I would have to disagree." Arthur snorts, and I can hear him shift where he sits against the wall beyond the iron bars that separate us. "You have proven to be rather resourceful." When I glance at him, his eyes hold nothing but contempt. "Though, I was a little surprised to learn you ever lived at all."

Some small part of me, hidden deep within the confines of my heart, has always longed to look at his face. To study his eyes and the freckles splattered across his cheeks, to see the coppery hue of his hair and the scowl carved of stone. I have never once wished to set foot inside this castle, nor this kingdom, but I have always wished to look upon his face. Just for a moment, just to see for myself and to know for sure.

Now, after everything, I wish that I'd never had such a thought.

"Sorry to disappoint you," I say, wincing as I push myself into a sitting position. He almost certainly cracked a rib. A hiss escapes my lips as my many injuries protest in tandem at the movement.

For a while, he says nothing. He does not move, nor rise, nor leave. He does not call his guards or send for his advisors. He simply sits there and stares at me.

"I imagine you have questions," I say after the silence and scrutiny become nearly unbearable.

"I have a great deal of questions, *sister*." He spits the word at me like a curse, eyes flashing. "I've just yet to decide if I care enough to hear the answers."

"If you're going to kill me anyway, then why not ask the questions?" I counter, arching an eyebrow at him. "You'll still have questions once I'm gone, but no way of getting answers."

A wide array of emotions dance across his face, but after a moment, his features settle into forced disinterest. "Did you know who you were when you first came to Camelot?"

"When your knights forcibly brought me here against my own will, you mean?" I try to match his feigned indifference but am unsuccessful. "Aye."

"How long have you known?"

"Since I was a child." I hold his stare, forcing myself not to flinch at his unrelenting gaze. "I have always known."

"How?" It sounds less like a question and more like a demand, though his questions often do.

I shrug. "It was never kept a secret from me. In fact, it was something everyone in my life made sure I was aware of—and exactly what the consequences would be if anyone ever found out."

"And yet, you came to Camelot, anyway."

"I did not choose to come to Camelot!" My shout echoes off the walls around us. The faintest clank of metal catches my attention, and it dawns on me that, just because I cannot see the guards, it doesn't mean they aren't there. Idly, I wonder if Arthur has personally chosen everyone present, to control the flow of what he no doubt deems harmful information.

"I never wanted to come here," I say, quieter. "I never intended to set foot in your kingdom."

"You forsake your birthright so freely?" he asks, completely unfazed by my outburst.

"Camelot is not my birthright, Arthur. It's yours." I sigh, shaking my head. "We may have shared many things—a bloodline, a womb, a birthday…but that does not mean what's yours is also mine, or the opposite."

"I have a hard time understanding why you wouldn't choose to return home and fulfil the role of lost princess—to reclaim what was taken from you." His chest heaves, and his words come out unsteadily.

"There is nothing to reclaim, Arthur. Camelot is not my home." I toss my hands up indignantly, wincing again as a fresh wave of pain ripples through me. "I don't know how else to explain this to you, but, up until very recently, I was rather happy with my life. I had no desire to be a princess or to help rule a kingdom. I did not wish for the life you claim was taken from me, I was content with the one I was living."

For the first time, he breaks eye contact. His gaze lowers, following his finger as it traces a pattern absently across the stone floor. After a long moment of silence, his throat bobs as he whispers, "Why you?"

I stare at him, openly confused. "Why me…what?"

"Why were *you* stolen at birth?" I can't decide if he's angry, or jealous, or something else. "Why *you* and not *us*?" he clarifies.

"That's not something I ever expect to have an answer to." I shake my head, one shoulder lifting a little.

His eyes dart back and forth between mine, searching for something more. As if he thinks I'm hiding the real answer from him, and he expects to find it hidden just under the surface.

I inhale deeply and push the air slowly from my lungs, forcing myself to smile at him, even if it's small and not entirely genuine. "Perhaps, in another life, we could have been friends."

"In another life, we could have been family." His tone is full of venom, and malice, and pain. He stands in one fluid motion, staring down at me sharply. "What am I to do with you?" he mutters, mostly to himself. "The whole kingdom saw you pull the sword from the stone. A girl raised by a dragon in a cave… Nobody even knew you existed, and yet, you pulled Uther's sword from the stone."

His words make me flinch, an echo of what Bors said earlier this week. Similar but different enough that they don't hold the same sting. Arthur doesn't wield them like an insult. To him, they're simply fact.

"That was *my* birthright," he snarls, his tone growing more sour by the second. "You stole it from me."

"You were going to kill me, and we both know it," I argue. "Surely, you did not expect me to just let you behead me in the town square to boost your ego?"

"That was my birthright!" he bellows, lunging towards the bars. His hands wrap around the iron, knuckles white. "You had no right!"

"If anyone had a right, Arthur, it was me." I drag myself to my feet so that I can look him directly in the eye. "In all technicality, pulling the sword from the stone is *our* birthright, not yours alone. Whether or not you wish it to be true, I am your sister, and I have just as much claim to the throne as you do."

He opens his mouth to continue shouting, but I hold up a hand and speak before he can. Surprisingly, he lets me.

"The difference between us is that I have only ever done what is necessary to ensure my survival. I do not want the throne. I do not want the crown. I do not even want the sword, though it is a beautiful blade." His eyes are wild and furious, but he remains silent as I continue. "You have gone to extreme lengths to get rid of me this week, yet, you were the one who demanded I stay in the first place. Think about it, Arthur. I never wanted to come here. I've known for nearly two decades where I come from and I never once stepped foot in Camelot until your knights destroyed my family."

He looks away, chest heaving, jaw working furiously. His knuckles whiten further around the bars.

"I did not come here of my own free will, and I only remained here because you decided that my punishment for vengeance was to be served within the walls of your kingdom."

"What would you have me do?" he asks through clenched teeth, dragging his gaze back to mine. The torches behind him cast eerie shadows over his face, the whispers of the flames mingling with the breathless sounds falling from his lips.

"You've made it abundantly clear that you have neither need nor want of me. Just let me go."

"I cannot do that." He shakes his head, dismissing my suggestion immediately.

"Until very recently, you didn't even know I existed, and only a few hours ago, you learned that I was even a threat to you." I sigh, the pain in my head swelling with the exertion demanded by this conversation. "Let me go and you will never see me again. I will disappear just as easily as I appeared, and no one need be the wiser."

"I knew very well that you existed, once." The words are so quiet I almost miss them.

"You did?"

"I have always known of the twin I shared a womb with, the sibling I did not get to grow up with, and the sister I did not get to serve my kingdom with." He glances at the floor, just briefly, before continuing. "I am very aware that I was left to endure our father and his reign of terror alone."

I sigh, what little energy I had upon waking now drained. "Just let me go."

He's silent for a long time, his green eyes boring into mine. "No," he says finally, "and you will address me as King Arthur from now on."

"But you're not king." My brows pull in as I assess his face, his words, his stance. "Not yet."

A slow, cruel sort of smile spreads across his face. "Not yet, indeed," he murmurs, pushing away from the bars.

"Are you going to kill me publicly, then? In front of all the people who watched me pull Excalibur from the stone?" I know it's not wise to bait him. I know it as sure as I know my own name, and yet, I can't seem to help myself.

"Almost as if you, yourself, handed me the weapon of your execution." He smirks.

"Just let me go, Arthur," I try again, knowing it's useless.

His head snaps to the side, eyes scanning the hallway as several sets of footsteps echo down the stairwell.

At first, I think he's not going to say anything else, but then he turns back, his face half hidden in shadow, and murmurs, "You said I didn't know you existed, but that's not true. I knew who you were the moment you set foot in my throne room."

"How?" I ask quietly.

"Do you truly think I do not recognise my own face?" he asks bitterly. "Do you think that because your hair was a different colour and your eyes not as bright that I would not see myself when I looked at you?"

"Nobody else—"

"Nobody else knew that you were alive," he says quietly. Angrily. "Any who did are either dead or had no real proof. It's easy to be blinded to what you do not wish to see." He sighs, raking a hand through his already disheveled hair. "That is how nobody recognised you. Years of believing that I was the only heir, your differences in appearance just subtle enough. It's quite funny if you think about it. All this time, I wished to know my sister. Wished to have those years together—playing, and fighting, and teasing. Wished for a best friend to love, to protect and defend. Someone with whom I could endure our father and mourn our mother. Someone I could rule our kingdom with. You were so close, easily within my grasp, and yet, you were infinitely out of my reach, worlds away. This whole time, I wished for a sister who never wished for me at all."

FIFTY-THREE

LANCELOT

As we come around the corner, Arthur's head snaps in our direction. The tension rolling off him is its own physical presence within the dungeon, so tangible it's nearly suffocating. When he turns back towards the cell, he speaks too quietly for me to hear.

Perci eyes me warily but says nothing. Arthur had sent a page to summon him, requesting his immediate presence in the dungeon. The boy had found us halfway between the square and Guinevere's rooms, and I'd all but refused to let Perci leave me behind.

We wait with the rest of his personal guard at the end of the hall. Tristan is standing closest to Ari's cell, just out of view, and the other knight who'd moved to grab her is nowhere in sight. Tristan's face is entirely unreadable, but whatever conversation the siblings have just had, he's undoubtedly heard it all.

With a scoff and a sneer, Arthur pushes away from the cell and stalks towards us. "I thought I made myself clear to you," he snaps in my direction. It's hard not to bristle at the ferocity in his glare and the venom in his tone. "I told you to put an end to it. To whatever misguided notions or intentions you have regarding her. I told you to let it die."

Did he know who she was, even then? Is that why he warned me to back off? Because he knew she was his sister? Because no knight is worthy of a princess, despite her not being raised that way?

I clench my jaw, ignoring the heat that spreads across my cheeks at the admonishment, forcing myself to drop his gaze and dip my chin, though I cannot bring myself to say anything.

After a moment, Arthur pivots towards Perci, and his voice takes on a lighter tone, bordering on indifference. "Stay with her until I tell you otherwise." He disappears up the stairwell without another word, personal guard in tow.

Releasing a tight breath, I chew on the insides of my cheeks to distract myself from Arthur's words. Perci and Tristan exchange a quick glance as we move to stand in front of her cell.

She's sitting on the floor, forehead resting against her knees, arms wrapped around her legs. She's shivering, and she looks pale—even for her, even in the dimness of the cell.

For a while, no one says anything. She doesn't look up at us, and I don't even know if she's aware that we're standing here.

Eventually, though it's muffled, she says, "Have you come to laugh at how horribly I've messed things up?"

I open my mouth to say something—anything to try to make her feel better—but Tristan beats me to it. "Something tells me you didn't, though." There's a hint of amusement to his voice. "Did you?"

She lifts her head, eyes slowly climbing upward to meet his. One corner of her mouth twists up, and there's a subtle sort of delight dancing in her eyes. "Depends which part we're talking about."

"You had a back-up plan." He doesn't sound accusatory, but there is something close to hurt in his voice as he crouches down in front of her cell.

"Did I miss something?" Perci asks, eyeing me skeptically over Tristan's head.

I shrug just as Ari says, "There was indeed another plan." She ignores

Perci, offering Tristan a ghost of a smile. "But, for what it's worth, I wish we could have done as you'd wanted."

Some silent moment passes between them, and a pang of jealousy courses through my veins. I wonder if I would have ever seen her again—either of them—or if they would've simply disappeared into the wind together.

"Please, tell me you're not talking about Guinevere," I say flatly, ruining their moment. "She's half-crazed, bordering on unhinged. You're insane if you think that she's actually going to help you."

"The last time someone insulted a girl in our present company, it took several grown men and fully-trained knights to sort out the situation." Tristan glances up at me over his shoulder, arching a brow. "You've just insulted two."

"I—what?" I stammer. "I didn't mean to insult Ari, but you can't mean to trust Guinevere?"

"We no longer have a choice." I don't need to be able to see his face to know that he isn't joking.

"So, you're in on it, then?" I ask Ari dubiously. "Whatever this grand plan of hers is, you know about it?"

"She truly means to help you escape, then?" Perci asks, leaning against the bars, brows pinched.

"I suppose she does, now that I've done what she's asked."

"What did she ask you to do?" I ask quietly. "Specifically."

Ari turns to face me, giving me her full attention for the first time. Her lips are drawn into a tight line, brows furrowed slightly. "I had to put Arthur in an impossible situation—I had to prevent him from becoming king," she says evenly. "So, I pulled the sword from the stone."

"So, you knew?" I demand, unable to keep the echo of betrayal from my voice. "All this time, you knew who you were?"

She doesn't even bat an eyelash. She just holds my gaze and says, "Yes."

"Did you?" She turns to Tristan.

"Aye." He nods. "From the very first day we met." He says it almost nonchalantly, and I can't help the surge of indignation that rolls through me.

"That's why you kept calling me m'lady, isn't it?"

He nods, and she laughs once, her chest quickly rising and falling with the hollow sound.

"Yes, yes, we all know who you are now," Guinevere says, stepping out of the shadows behind Perci. The air around her seems to shimmer, a metallic tang filling the air.

Perci and I both flinch, while Tristan doesn't seem the least bit affected. Ari looks taken aback, but recovers quickly. I start to ask Guinevere where she came from, but she cuts me off before I can do anything more than stutter over the first few words.

"Arthur has just set your execution for sunset, two days from now. After the final duel, but before the celebration banquet."

"All in time so he can claim his crown on our birthday with no one to oppose him," Ari says dryly.

"He can't be serious?" I demand, anger simmering just under the surface again.

"He can," Ari and Guinevere say at the same time without so much as glancing at one another.

"I had to wait for Arthur to make the announcement before I could sort out the last few pieces of the plan." Guinevere tilts her head to each side as if to crack her neck, sapphire eyes drifting shut after a particularly loud *pop*. "Now that he has, I have a plan…and a rather simple one at that."

"Of course, you do." Ari grimaces, rubbing her hands up and down her arms. I have the urge to take my shirt off to help warm her up, but I don't think it would go over well in present company.

"Just like this morning, when you and Tristan were supposed to escape"—Tristan and Ari exchange a loaded glance at her words—"we're going to use the final duel as a distraction. We can't risk doing anything before then in case he comes down to see you again before the fight. I believe he'll have you brought out right after the victor is named, while everyone is still in the square, so it'll have to be during the duel itself."

Perci makes a soft grunting sound in the back of his throat, like he's considering her plan. Arching a brow, he asks, "What of the guards?"

"Best case scenario, it'll be either or both of you," she says, gesturing between him and Tristan. "Worst case scenario, we'll have to get a little creative."

Ari snorts, her mouth twisting into a wry, mocking grin. "Define creative."

"I think you're capable of using your imagination, Arturia." Guinevere clucks her tongue, raising her eyebrows conspiratorially. Ari glares at the use of what I can only assume is her full name, but before I can take a moment to properly absorb that piece of information, Guinevere continues on. "Either way, you're going to have to trust me."

"You've already said that to me once this week." Doubt shines clearly in Ari's eyes, the first real crack in the notion of her willingly working with Guinevere.

Guinevere clicks her tongue again. "And look at what we've managed to accomplish so far."

"What exactly have you accomplished?" My eyes dart back and forth between the two *princesses* before me. I still cannot fathom the reality of Ari being a princess...let alone Arthur's sister.

"It doesn't matter," they say in unison. This time, they share a bemused half-smile, and the thought of Ari sharing anything with Guinevere makes my stomach turn.

"If you expect us to trust you, then you don't get to keep secrets," I snap.

"For once, Lancelot, just for right now, can you leave it alone?" Tristan cuts a glare at me over his shoulder before standing to face Guinevere.

"You're not going to have long before someone either notices you're gone or comes back down here."

"Wait." The anger has been growing in my chest, like the warning rumble of a coming storm, now threatening to spill over in a torrent. "Back up a second. You don't actually expect me to just go along with whatever plan she's daydreamed up, do you? You think I'm going to blindly trust her word and follow her orders and hope to the gods that everything works out?"

"Aye, right now, I do. This is neither the time nor the place, and we have far more pressing things to discuss at the moment."

"Nobody is handed blind loyalty like that, Tris. I'm sorry, but I don't know her, and I'm sure as hell not going to risk Ari's life because she—"

"Excuse me"—Ari grunts as she pushes herself to her feet, and it looks like it takes a lot out of her just to stand, let alone remain upright—"but my life is not yours to risk." I open my mouth to say something, but she continues before I can. "I've already chosen to trust Guin. I need neither your permission nor your approval to do so. Whether or not you go along with the plan is up to you."

I don't know if it's the tone she uses, or if it finally sinks in that she's been lying to me since the moment we met, but I bristle nonetheless. "Apologies, *Your Highness*, but do you truly mean to tell me that you're on a nickname level of informality with her now?"

"Don't call me that," Ari snarls, baring her teeth at me.

Guinevere merely clicks her tongue again and looks me up and down. "Girls can get a lot done when we set our differences aside," she says, with more than a hint of venom. "Now, are you going to help us, or are you going to continue being dramatic just because you have nothing better to do?"

FIFTY-FOUR

ARI

After my precarious little group of allies dispersed, most of which seem uncertain at best, I managed to get a few hours of sleep before rousing to the soft rustling of movement outside my cell. There's a brief, murmured exchange between Arthur, Perci, and Tristan, but their voices are kept low enough that it doesn't fully wake me.

Sometime later, when I manage to rouse enough to crack an eye open, Arthur's still there. He's slumped against the wall opposite my cell, legs splayed in front of him, head drooped to one side.

His words haunted my dreamless sleep, chasing me into consciousness where they continue to swirl through my mind in a haze of mixed emotions that I don't have the energy to decipher.

"This whole time, I wished for a sister who never wished for me at all."

It's both true, and yet…not.

It's not that I never wished for him—never wished to know my twin, to see his face, to hear his laugh. I knew that he existed, knew that he was here, knew that I wished to look him in the eye, at least once.

It's more that I didn't know what I might be missing. I simply didn't know any differently. For the most part, life with Penn in the forest was never lonely. If he wasn't around, Bax or Merlin or the chickens were. I was rarely *truly* alone, and never as a child.

I don't know how to mourn a life I never had. I don't know how to mourn a relationship that never got a chance to exist. Arthur is my brother by blood, but we did not share a life together. I know that I'm supposed to long for more with him, a chance to make things right, but I just don't know how to.

I don't know how to reconcile the things I know to be true with the things that I wish weren't. I don't know how to separate the brother I should've had—the one who claims he wished to have me by his side all these years—with the spiteful prince before me. The one who locked me in a dungeon and had me poisoned for entering his tournament.

I don't know if there's any point in trying.

I've managed to pull myself upright and shuffled as close to the iron bars as possible without realising I'd done so. Resting my head against the cool metal, a bar on either temple, I exhale deeply. Wrapping my hands around the bars, I sit and study Arthur.

He looks so peaceful in sleep, younger, despite only being a day shy of eighteen. There's an innocence to his face, a softness in the set of his mouth instead of a scowl. He looks nothing like the furious, indignant, entitled prince he pretends to be for his kingdom.

"When people are scared, they lash out."

Perci's words drift through my thoughts, and as if they summoned him with their unbidden arrival, he clears his throat, scaring the hell out of me. I reel back from the bars, heart pounding.

He laughs under his breath, shifting on the ground so that he's leaning against the bars of my cell instead of off to the side and out of sight. Despite the bars between us, the fact that he's comfortable sitting like this, with his back to me and his neck within reach, shows how far we've come since the first time he brought me down here.

"Didn't mean to scare you," he murmurs over his shoulder, keeping his voice low so that it doesn't wake Arthur. "Did you really think his guard would let him down here without someone close by?"

"I'm locked behind bars. What is it that you think I'm going to do to him?"

A snort is my only answer.

My lips quirk up in response, and after another moment, I ask, "How long has he been down here?"

Perci tenses, and his middle finger starts tapping against his leg, a nervous, almost unconscious habit. Eventually, he says, "A while. It's nearly dawn."

I don't know what to make of Perci being here with Arthur. He doesn't feel as strongly about him as the others—at least, not in the same way. But he knows what our plan is, and he clearly hasn't told Arthur.

I don't know that I trust Perci the same way I trust Tristan, but I want to. I want to believe that, whatever his reasons are for helping me, for keeping our plan to himself, it's not going to blow up in my face later.

"Have you slept at all?"

"Not really." He sighs. "I'll sleep when this week is over." Whether his loyalty is to Camelot or its prince, the tension in the lines of his neck and the set of his shoulders tells me how stressed he really is. Part of me wants to reach out and offer him some small bit of comfort, but I don't think he'd accept it from me.

"Something tells me that's unlikely." I almost feel guilty at the chaos that will ensue. Almost.

His finger stops tapping, and he tilts his head towards me, not enough to make eye contact but enough that I can see the grim ghost of a smile. "Aye, something tells me you're right."

On the morning of the final duel, I wake to the cold stone of the wall seeping into my back. My muscles are stiff, my shoulders are tight, and my neck is sore. I'd fallen asleep in the middle of a silent stare-down with Arthur, neither of us willing to break the silence first. Tristan and Perci had both been in the hall the last I remember, but now, all three of them are gone.

I don't want to think about the numerous ways Arthur can bring about my death if things go awry today. He suggested using Excalibur—for poetic justice, no doubt—but he's got much more than that at his disposal.

Nerves sizzle through my veins like lightning in anticipation. So much hinges on things I can't control, and if any one of them goes wrong…

A whisper of sound down the hallway catches my attention, and I press my face into the stinging cold of the bars to peer into the shadows. The half dozen torches that line the opposite side of the hall snuff out, one by one, causing the hair at the base of my neck to prickle.

The sound of footsteps echoes around the dungeon, slow and measured, coming to a stop directly in front of me. There's a soft laugh, and then blue flame erupts from Guinevere's hand, casting the dungeon in cool, dancing shadows.

Magic-blessed, that's what Elie had called it. I've heard Merlin use the term before, but I didn't know there were others…

It's not that I assumed I was the only one…to be fair, I'd never really thought about it. But with how many years it took for us to figure out how I could summon magic—all the trial and error—I just assumed I'd never cross paths with anyone else who could do what I can. That's even more rare than finding a mage to teach you in the first place.

"I do hope the midnight visits from your dear brother haven't changed anything for you," she says by way of greeting.

"Does he still intend to have me executed at sunset?"

"He does."

"Then nothing's changed."

"Well, not nothing…" She glances over her shoulder as if she expects someone to be waiting in the shadows. Where the guards are—or Tristan or Perci, for that matter—I don't know.

"I don't smell the tang of you *popping* in here like last time, so how did you get down here? And who taught you how to wield magic, for that matter?"

"Smoke and mirrors." An impish grin lifts one side of her mouth as she answers the first question, ignoring the second. "I have my own methods of moving about the castle undetected, but I also had my lady-in-waiting help with a distraction upstairs."

A pit of dread begins to form in my chest. A last minute change of plans is not what I expected, although, perhaps I should have. I can't help wondering if it's going to end up being a trap. The thought of how horribly—and how easily—this could all go wrong sends that knot of dread spreading throughout my body until it threatens to consume me.

When I don't respond, she sighs impatiently. "Time is very much of the essence, and you and I still have much to discuss now that we've found ourselves alone again."

"I did what you asked." My breathing comes out unevenly; the mix of nerves and dread have left me feeling off-kilter and a little lightheaded.

"You know of what I speak, Arturia." Her fingers twitch, and the flame in her palm flickers unsteadily for a moment. Her sapphire eyes are turned luminescent by the fire, but I can still see the usual mix of ferocity, hunger, and determination in them. Her golden hair is woven into a simple braid that falls down her back, and she's wearing the same black outfit as the night she snuck into my room at Vera's—a loose tunic, fitted pants, knee-high boots, and a cloak to conceal what the rest does not.

"Aye, you're rather full of bold promises—ones I do not think you can follow through with." It proves no small feat to keep my voice from wobbling, whether from anger, or doubt, or unwelcome hope, I cannot tell.

"As you said, I believe you've already upheld your end of the bargain." Her smile is wolfish. "In pulling the sword from the stone, you've indefinitely disrupted his plans for a coronation, whether or not he believes it to be true."

"Then free me from this prison and consider us even."

"You," she continues, as if I hadn't spoken at all, "the daughter who never lived, only to resurface at the last moment possible… An unforeseen player on the board, yet, somehow, fully aware of the game itself. Impressive, really."

"I never intended to come to Camelot. I never wanted anything to do with this life."

"That may be so, and yet, here you are anyway."

"Nobody knows," I say, shaking my head back and forth, slowly at first then gaining in speed. "Nobody will believe it. A trick, they will say. A sham. *Magic.*"

"Enough people of importance know, and many more would believe it," she counters, an unwelcome honesty in her words. "Many do not wish to see Arthur sit atop that throne. Many more wish for a new bloodline altogether."

"Then give them one," I hiss. "I do not wish to usurp him!" She opens her mouth to speak, but I interrupt her before she can say anything. "If you say that's the best reason to put me on the throne, then that makes you cruel. To force someone into a life they never wanted just because you don't like the current option… I refuse."

"Despite your reservations regarding the crown, I do think you'd make a rather refreshing ruler."

"A refreshing ruler, or an indebted ally?"

The flame pulses in her hand, and a slow smile spreads across her face again, lifting up each side of her mouth in earnest. "Why not both?"

"Enough," I snap. "I never actually agreed to help you so you owe me nothing, and even if I had, I do not believe you can fulfil your end of the bargain. Do not mock me further simply to humour yourself. Either get me out of here, or get out of my sight, but either way, let's be done with this."

"What would it take for you to believe me?" she asks, tilting her head to one side. "For you to put faith in my words?

"Why don't you tell me what proof you have to back up your claims, and I'll tell you what else I require to know before I consider an agreement?" I grind the words out through clenched teeth.

"What do you know of resurrection spells?" she asks darkly.

"I think you mean necromancy," I reply evenly. If she's waiting to see me squirm, I will not give her the satisfaction.

"They are not one and the same, Arturia"—she shakes her head—"though, I understand how you might think so."

Inhaling deeply, I push the air out slowly before speaking again. "I know that it's dark magic—blood magic—and not the sort that I'd ever wield. The price for that kind of magic is much more than I am willing to pay."

"You have paid steep prices for magic before," she retorts, arching a brow.

"Yes, when the sacrifice of using that much magic was worth the cost!" I snap, unable to regain my composure. "When it meant saving a life!"

"What makes this any different?" she challenges, one shoulder lifting in question.

"I—because this isn't saving a life that you speak of, Guinevere, it's—"

"It's returning something to the realm of the living. Giving life back to that which has lost it. Regardless of circumstance, the subject would indeed be alive." Her tone sharpens ever so slightly.

"You've done it before." My voice is quiet and shaky, but it poses no question. Even before she answers, a chill slides down my spine, settling over my body like a weight.

"Aye." She dips her head ever so slightly.

"What more do you want from me? I've told you I won't do it." I have to force air into my lungs, force my mind to stop spinning at the implication she's just made—the atrocity she's just admitted to.

"I want to get you out of this cell," she says, eyes sweeping around the small, cold space, "as payment for fulfilling your end of the deal— intentionally or otherwise."

"And?"

"And then we can sort out the details once we're no longer in this gods forsaken castle."

The only sound in the dungeon is the flickering flame upon her hand and the shallow breaths between us. We stare at each other for a long, tense moment.

"I don't trust you," I say finally. "Not on this."

"We both know that you don't really have a choice."

"Speaking of trust, where's Tristan?" I had hoped that he would be here by now, but whether Guinevere's distraction has held him up, or something else... "Why did you come alone?" My voice betrays me by shaking.

"Don't worry about that right now. It's time to go." The lock on my cell door pops open and clangs to the ground, echoing loudly.

"Where is Tristan?" I demand.

"Currently, he's with that old mage of his, unharmed and ill-informed. But if you continue to test my patience, I cannot say that will last very long."

My eyes fall shut as I weigh my options. Just like last time, Tristan was supposed to accompany me today, and despite the change in plans, I cannot risk something happening to him because of me. Guinevere's still offering me a way out, and I have to take it.

"Will you tell him?" I ask, slowly lifting my eyes to meet her gaze. "That I didn't...that I wasn't..."

"Yes, yes, I'll tell your little knight that it wasn't your choice to leave him." She waves a hand in the air between us, pursing her lips. "I'll tell him where you've gone, Ari, but know that the last thing you'll want is for him to follow after you."

"You're not taking me to the forest, then?"

"No, I'm not." She offers me her hand. My gaze drops to her outstretched palm, to the smooth surface of her skin, and I can't help wondering what price she must pay to wield magic.

Instead, I ask again, "Who taught you?"

"Taught me what?" she asks coyly.

"To travel like that. I've never been able to figure it out."

"Take my hand and find out."

Her reluctance to answer the question makes me uneasy. Something in my gut turns sour, and my breathing quickens as her smile deepens.

Knowing I have no choice, I place my hand in hers. The air around us shimmers and distorts, and there's a suffocating pressure in my chest before my knees give out and the cell around me fades away.

FIFTY-FIVE

LANCELOT

Arthur stands at the centre of the stone dais looking every bit the king he intends to be, despite Ari and Guinevere's notions of that no longer being possible.

Instead of the usual rumpled, unkempt look he graces us with shortly after rolling out of bed, today, he wears a well-fitted jacket of the deepest onyx with the most intricate crimson stitching, pressed black pants tucked into polished black boots, and the blood crown sitting atop his head—a stark reminder of what is to come.

Behind him, the lord regent and the royal advisor are also in their best finery, both of them wearing beautifully embroidered jackets in Camelot's customary black and red. The royal guards stationed at the foot of the dais all wear black, with Camelot's sigil stitched across the front in crimson— one crown on top of another with a sword through their centres.

Two blood crowns, one for the king and one for his heir, with Excalibur down the middle to symbolise the once and future kings of Camelot and the sword that binds them.

Two blood crowns, I realise, *for two blood heirs. One for each twin.*

Every one of them on and around the dais looks the part of unity and conformity that Arthur expects of his subjects—openly daring anyone to challenge his claim to the throne. Though Excalibur is no longer in the centre of the town square, it's also not strapped to his back, either.

Guinevere, thankfully, is nowhere to be seen. Hopefully, that means she is making her way to the dungeon to fulfil her part of the plan.

Arthur gives another grand speech before the tournament's final duel, though this one does not mention either of his parents. He also doesn't encourage any of the children to pull Excalibur from the stone—not that they could—lest it remind them of what happened only two days ago. He gives a half-hearted thank you to the entertainers and the vendors, and then he motions to the archery targets on either side of the square.

He calls a knight named Benjimin to the dais, awarding him a finely hand-crafted long bow and a quiver of two dozen beautifully carved white oak arrows for hitting the most bulls-eyes at the farthest range. Part of me wonders if it would have even been a competition if Tristan had chosen to participate.

"May your arrow always strike true," Arthur says to Benjimin, a tight grin touching his lips.

The knight takes the bow and quiver, bowing deeply. "Thank you, Your Highness."

"And now, the moment you've all been waiting for," Arthur says, rubbing his hands together. A hush settles over the crowd, a thick ripple of tension settling over the square like a blanket.

"One hundred and twenty-eight brave men entered the tournament, but only two remain. One hundred and twenty-six matches over the last six days, but only one left." Arthur pauses for a moment, soaking in the attention of his captive audience. "Whosoever should win today's duel will not only be given the title of King's Champion but also granted one wish—anything within my power to give. This tournament has not been for the faint of heart. Many men have been injured this week, and I fear both of our competitors today stand a high chance of enduring the same fate."

I have to stop myself from snorting in derision at his continued blatant avoidance of anything related to Ari. Ignoring the fact that she declared and earned her way halfway through the tournament before he had her poisoned, unleashed Bors upon her, and then nearly killed her himself.

It's also interesting that he chose to ignore mentioning that Bors fatally wounded one of his opponents.

I grip the hilt of my father's sword, the only thing I have left of him, eyeing the carved pommel—a serpent eating its own tail. *That which does not kill you can only make you stronger.*

"You good, Lance?" Perci asks, leaning against the wooden railing beside me.

"Aye," I murmur, nodding without looking at him.

"You've got this," he says, nudging my elbow with his own.

"Aye." I nod again, a smile I don't feel tugging at one side of my mouth. "Have you seen Tristan?" I glance up at him, tuning out the remnants of Arthur's speech. His lips tighten into a thin line, and he gives me a knowing look. The only confirmation I need.

"He's good, Perc," I say quietly, changing the subject and nodding to Bors' second in command across the ring.

Sir Lucan is younger than Bors by nearly a decade, but his ruthlessness and ambition both in training and in battle afterward earned him his rank. He and Tristan went through training together, becoming quick allies—Tristan an outsider nobody had heard of, and Lucan a farm boy who hadn't spent much time inside the walls of Camelot until he was drafted for training.

He looks so much like Tristan in this moment that it unsettles me. Tall and lean, with dark hair that reaches his shoulders, hastily tied in a knot at the back of his head. Most of the men they went through training with keep their hair longer, tying back half or all of it when they're on duty or going to battle.

But while most of their brothers went on to varying ranks, Tristan made a name for himself as an unparalleled archer, and Lucan worked his way up to second in command. Absently, I wonder if he'll be getting a promotion one way or another after the tournament is over, considering the unlikelihood of Bors ever holding a sword again, much less leading an army.

Despite how well Lucan and Tristan got along during training, his proximity to Bors was ultimately what lead to the wedge between them and the leading factor in the decision to leave him out of our close-knit little group.

"He's good," Perci agrees under his breath, "but so are you."

"Thanks, Perci." This time, the smirk that lifts one side of my mouth is genuine.

I've tracked Lucan's fights all week, admiring the easy wins he's managed to attain. I can only hope he doesn't feel the need to settle a score on Bors' behalf.

Arthur steps down from the dais, making his way through the parting crowd towards the ring. He stays firmly on the outside this time but motions for Lucan and myself to enter the ring, waiting for us to hop over the railing and take up positions on our respective sides.

"Sir Lucan," he says, nodding in his direction. "Sir Lancelot." He glances in mine. "May you both maintain your honour and integrity throughout this duel, and may the best knight win."

The crowd cheers, shouting and clapping, but we both drown it out, the lethal calm of an impending battle settling over us.

One of the first things they teach you in training is how to block out distractions. It doesn't always work, but on the battlefield, it can be the difference between life and death. Pulling a slow, steadying breath in through my nose and pushing it back out through my mouth, I shift my weight on my feet, bending my knees.

Our eyes meet across the ring, and Lucan smiles, dipping his head once in acknowledgement.

With honour, then—not revenge.

"You may begin," Arthur says with wicked delight.

FIFTY-SIX

LANCELOT

The roar of the crowd is deafening—the chanting, and screaming, and whistling, and clapping. It's overwhelming, sending me into a bit of sensory overload as my heartbeat struggles to even out. My breathing is shallow and laboured, and my fingers still tingle with nervous energy.

Lucan wipes a hand across his face, smearing the blood where my fist split the skin just above his eyebrow. He stretches and flexes his left hand, rotating his wrist a couple of times, biting back a wince.

Using my thumb to probe the cut on my lip, I grunt in acknowledgement as he makes his way over to me. He stoops down to pick up my sword along the way, testing the weight of it with his sprained wrist. Again, he tries to hold back his wince. Three more steps and he's extending his good hand, offering to help me to my feet.

I take it without hesitation, keeping my weight on my uninjured leg. The weight of the fight feels like lead in my stomach.

"If you had won," Lucan asks quietly, barely audible over the commotion of the crowd, "what would you have asked for?" He offers me my sword, and I sheath it at my side, not bothering to wipe the blood from the blade. I'll do it later.

"Time," I say just as quietly. "Time away, to help my mother."

"Where is she?" Our attention snaps to the other side of the ring—to Arthur. The quiet rage in his voice sends a chill down my spine.

I can hear it over my own ragged breaths and Lucan's deep, heavy ones beside me. The crowd has begun to calm down, but his voice is like the cracking whip of thunder before the lightning strikes—his face pure rage, masked with a stillness like the calm before the storm.

A knight in training—a rookie named Erec—stands barely two paces to Arthur's left, bent in a deep bow. His unruly blond hair, cheeks full of freckles, and quick smile normally maintain his boyish charm, but, right now, he looks terrified, that innocence replaced with fear and self-preservation.

He looks as terrified as I feel.

Dread uncoils like a tornado in my chest, panic rumbling through my veins. I force myself to breathe slowly, willing my features to remain neutral.

"How much time?" Lucan says, turning back to me, only half-interested in the conversation now.

"I don't know." I shrug, looking at him sidelong. "It doesn't matter now."

Erec says something too quiet for me to hear, but the reddening of Arthur's face tells me all I need to know. I turn to face Lucan fully before Arthur can make eye contact with me, out of fear of my expression giving anything away.

"Bors named me captain during his recovery," Lucan says slowly, his brows pulling in slightly. "At the very least, I can give you a month."

"Why?" I ask before I can think better of it.

"Because you fought like hell today, and because you're a good man," he says evenly. "You may have had your differences with Bors, but loyalty isn't given freely, it's earned, and if I want your loyalty, then I have to be willing to do something for you in return."

My eyebrows lift higher with each word, but I find myself nodding and saying, "Thank you."

"You fought well today. Have you ever considered becoming a commander? Leading your own men one day?"

I stare at him for a moment, searching his face for any sign of a joke or a trap. Satisfied that he's merely asking a question, I say honestly, "That depends."

"On?"

"How long you'll stay captain."

"Well, then, you had better find her!" Arthur screams at the young knight, his rage silencing the crowd and putting an abrupt end to our conversation.

Slowly, as if it takes a great deal of restraint and control, Arthur manages to collect himself. His eyes seek out every knight within his immediate proximity and then he says, loud enough for the entirety of the square to hear but without raising his voice very much at all, "I want every inch of this kingdom searched—every home, every shop, every stable. I want the prisoner found and returned to me immediately. Use whatever precautions necessary but leave her alive. If she is not found within the walls of Camelot, then turn your searches to the farmlands beyond—to every village and every town. Do not stop until you find her. Anyone found aiding her will meet a fate worse than death."

The crowd seems to be holding its breath, but nobody moves. Everyone glances at the people around them, but nobody dares to say anything.

Lucan meets my eyes, raising his eyebrows quickly before turning to signal the rest of the knights to follow suit. "You heard the prince," he shouts to the square. "The hunt is on, boys."

And just like that, any thought I had of camaraderie, any hope of him being better than Bors, dissolves into thin air.

FIFTY-SEVEN

ARI

Emptying the meagre contents of my stomach, I retch until nothing but bile comes up, dry heaving when even that is gone. My head spins, and my blood feels like shards of glass in my veins. This is almost worse than being poisoned by Morgana's magic.

"Hello, Ari."

The shards turn to ice in my veins.

"You have got to be kidding me." Glaring at Guinevere, I take pleasure in finding her in much the same state as myself, despite it being her magic that brought us here. "This is who taught you magic?" I ask, throwing my hand in his direction. "This is who you're working with?"

I should have seen it coming.

I should have known better.

"I figured you wouldn't come if I told you who it was," she pants, wiping the back of her hand across her mouth.

"Why are you even sick when you gallivant around the castle this way?"

"Around the castle, yes. Across the country, no." She rolls her eyes, pushing herself to her feet. "It takes a lot out of a human to travel that sort of distance, let alone to take someone with you."

"Don't be angry with her. I knew you'd never agree if I asked you myself."

"I wonder why?" I shout, turning my rage towards Merlin. "You weren't willing to help me before, so why should I believe you're genuine now? I *begged* you to take me from the castle, begged you to set me free. I offered to make you a deal. I would have paid anything—*anything*. I told you to name your price, and still, you left me behind!"

"It pains me to say this, Ari, but you were exactly where I needed you to be," he says quietly, seemingly unaffected by my outburst.

"Excuse me?" I reel back as if he's struck me. Perhaps if he had, I'm sure it would feel like less of a betrayal than what he just admitted. "What did you just say?"

"I needed you to be in Camelot." He meets my glare unflinchingly. "I had to leave you behind, Ari, and for that, I am truly sorry."

He left me there, for months, because he *wanted to*. Because he *needed me to be there.* I can't decide it I want to continue screaming at him, shove my fist down his throat, or gouge my hand open and hurl every last drop of my magic at him.

The rage and betrayal coursing through me threaten to overtake me, and I have to force myself to take in our surroundings to distract myself. We're so far away from Camelot, I wouldn't be able to walk back, even if I tried—not that I'd want to get back to Camelot, necessarily, but the only place I would go is even farther.

In front of us, the white cliffs that drop into a sheer plunge towards the ocean take my breath away, just like they did the first time I saw them from atop Penn's back. We had soared over the water and climbed straight up, past the grassy ledge of land beyond and high into the clouds, circling back to glide along the beautiful, white crags for miles. Wind whipped my hair in every direction, stinging my skin and eyes, fat tears prickling at the corners.

The same wind assaults me now, and I relish the feeling, welcoming the onslaught of memories.

Turning back to Merlin, I ask, "Why didn't it work?" My voice is so quiet, the wind nearly carries it away.

He stares at me for a long moment, his green-gold eyes full of sadness and tinged with reluctance.

"Why didn't it work, Merlin?" I ask again, louder this time, as the anger seeps back into me, fighting the numbness creeping in from the cold wind—the numbness from months spent in that cell. The numbness of being abandoned. The numbness of losing Penn. "When I tried to summon you the day they slaughtered him, why didn't it work?"

Again, he only stares at me.

Unable to meet his gaze any longer, I focus on the rise and fall of his chest, counting the breaths going in and out of his lungs. When I get to twenty, I can't hold my accusation in anymore. "You were already there, weren't you?" My eyes blur over with tears before they fall freely down my cheeks. My knees grow weak, and I slowly sink back down to the ground. "I couldn't summon you because you were already there."

A sob hitches in my throat, and I have to fist my fingers into the thick grass to ground myself, to keep me steady. "You were there…you were in the forest…you could have stopped them…" My eyes drift to his face, furiously trying to blink back the tears. "You could have saved him."

"I wasn't willing to pay the price of resurrection without the other pieces in place first," he says quietly. "We have much to—"

"If you had stopped them, you wouldn't have had to pay the price at all!" I shout at him, my voice hoarse and thick with emotion.

At least, he has the decency to look ashamed.

I swear at him, a violent string of every insulting word and name I can think of in every language I can speak. He stands there and takes it, letting me pour my anger, and hatred, and betrayal into every word I hurl at him. Eventually, his face changes from remorse to indifference, and when I finish, he merely holds my gaze, one dark brow raised.

"Impressive." He smirks, then asks, "Are you finished?"

"I have barely begun—"

"Do you wish to see Penn again or not?"

His interruption stops me in my tracks, his words leashing the rage that I could not. "I will not pay the price of necromancy," I say through gritted teeth. "I already told her that."

He crouches in front of me so that our eyes are level. "I am not asking you to pay the price of *resurrection*. I—"

"All magic has a price."

"And I will pay it, Ari." He stares intently at me, and something lurches in my chest. Something that still hungers for the life we used to share.

"No." I shake my head, tears still falling down my cheeks. "I don't want any part of this. I don't want to owe you anything more than I already do. I'm done, Merlin. I am done making deals with you. I am done with you."

"Then consider us even," he says, resigned. "Consider this payment for concealing the cave—"

"*For concealing the…*" The words are little more than a breath between my lips before the anger takes over once more. "You promised to hide the cave and they found us anyways! You promised protection and Penn still died!"

"Ari, just listen, please," Guinevere says, a desperate edge to her voice. I'd almost forgotten she was here.

"No. There's nothing you can say will change—"

"It'll change everything, I promise." She exhales a bone-weary sound. Now that we're out of the dungeon, I can see the exhaustion in her features, the purple smudges beneath her eyes, the sag to her shoulders.

"Your promises mean nothing to me." Guinevere and Merlin exchange a wary glance and I add, "Either of you."

"After everything we've been through, Ari, you wound me." There's a flicker in his eyes, an emotion I can't quite place, but it's gone before I've barely noticed it at all. Some small part of me believes there is truth to his words.

"After everything we've been through," I spit back at him, "I expected more from you."

"Ari—"

"Why didn't you tell me about Baxen?" He reels back, but he isn't quick enough to mask his emotions this time. "You knew, didn't you? You just thought I'd never find out. You thought that I'd continue to assume he left me, never questioning why, so that I would be solely dependent on you as my tutor." I laugh. It sounds callous and depraved. "What else have you lied about and kept hidden from me over the years?" I demand, knowing he won't answer me. "What else have you manipulated to best serve you, everyone else be damned?"

A gust kicks up, pulling more hair from my braid and lashing the strands across my face. A shiver rolls down my spine, the wind off the ocean cold against my bare arms.

His silence, and the magnitude of his betrayal, are what finally quell my rage. It dissipates, almost as if it were never there at all, and in its place is a void, devouring everything I thought I knew, everything I thought I could trust between us, and everything I ever felt for him.

Even though I am finally free of Arthur, and finally free of Camelot, I feel neither joy nor relief. Where I should be grateful, all I feel is nothing. All I feel is empty.

"You don't need me for anything," I say when I can no longer stand the silence. "Arthur has little chance of making it onto the throne now that I've pulled Excalibur from the stone. The people can revolt, or whatever it is they intend to do. You got me out of that cell, payment fulfilled. I don't want to make any more deals. I'm done," I say again. My voice sounds almost as hollow as my chest feels.

Merlin clears his throat softly. "You do, Ari. You and I both know you want what I can offer you. You've always wanted what I could offer you, with or without Penn's blessing." The double entendre to his words stings, and a mixture of guilt and resentment tug faintly at my heart before the void can swallow them up again.

"Do not speak his name like you were friends." I bare my teeth at him. Much to my dismay, the words come out sounding as much like a warning as they do a plea.

"Let me fix it," he says, reaching a hand out into the space between us—reaching for me. "Let me bring him back for you."

"Why?" I lean away from his touch, and something shifts in his face—a quick furrow of his brow and clench of his jaw that tell me what I need to know. A small, humourless laugh escapes my lips. "What is it you need me to do for you, Merlin?"

His mouth opens and closes half a dozen times, but no words come out.

"Don't add insult to injury," I say, shaking my head at him. "Don't pretend you're doing this for me. You want something from me, you just don't want to ask for it until I've already agreed to your terms."

He stares at me for a long time, his gaze darting back and forth between mine. Sable black hair sticks up at all angles atop his head, windblown and curling slightly around his ears. His normally tanned skin is pale, which is at odds with the warmth of the season. He looks as young as he did the day we met, and not for the first time, I wonder if he's truly immortal or if it's merely an illusion.

"I need you to retrieve something for me," he says finally, deciding the only way he stands a chance at getting what he wants is by being honest.

"Can Guinevere not do your bidding for you?" I throw a glare in her direction, and she leers back at me.

"Alas, she needs to stay in Camelot to oversee things there," he says with a sigh. "There is only you, and if you succeed, then I will bring him back for you."

"I thought the deal was Penn in exchange for keeping Arthur from the crown?" A sound of derision forces its way from my throat as I scowl at Guinevere. "So, it was all just a lie, then? Pretty words to get me in a position to do what you really wanted. What do you even gain from me helping him?"

Again, they exchange a wary look and I can't help but laugh. "Let me guess, you owe him something, and this was a way to pay up?"

"I told you I was working with someone," Guinevere says dryly. "It's not my fault you made the same mistake of trusting him."

What a mistake it had been.

"And if I say no?"

She shrugs nonchalantly. "Arthur will hunt you through every forest, over every mountain, across every river. He will hunt you from one coast to another, leaving no stone unturned until he finds you."

"Is that a threat?" I snarl at her, hands clenching at my sides. Rage starts to seep back into my veins, and I welcome the trail of fire it leaves in its wake.

"It's a fact," she snaps. "Agreeing to this gives you somewhere to be while he exhausts his resources for a while." Her sapphire eyes burn with an intensity I'd admire, if only I didn't detest her so much. "It gives you somewhere to be while we ensure that he sends his men on a wild goose chase."

Sighing, I turn my attention back to Merlin. "What is it you need me to do?"

"I need you to seek out Nhimue and retrieve the sword in the lake," he says evenly. "Do that, and I will bring back the dragon for you."

FIFTY-EIGHT

ARI

Merlin lives in a small stone hut with a thatched roof, nestled against the base of a mountain. The ocean lies to the east, the ancient forest to the west. A well-cared-for garden sits along the side of the house, and ivy crawls around the front door. It's far simpler and more modest than I ever expected it to be.

The interior is clean and tidy and sparsely furnished. The only thing he has in abundance is books. Books on magic, and spells, and charms. Books on creatures, and history, and war. Books in every language—some that I recognise, some that I don't. These are the books that he's been bringing me for years to fill in the gaps in what Penn and Bax had been teaching me.

Merlin claimed he wanted to give me a chance to rest after everything that's happened, and we've been here for nearly two days now. Being injured, poisoned, and nearly beheaded after months of sleeping in a cell and minimal magic use has definitely taken a toll on my body.

Not to mention losing Penn, learning that Bax has been dead for nearly a decade, and finally coming face-to-face with my twin after eighteen years. I'm exhausted, to say the least, and yet, due to the light shed on Merlin's recent betrayals, this is the last place I want to be.

"Go away, Merlin," I groan before he can even rap his knuckles against the wood. Even if I hadn't heard his footsteps on the floorboards, I can feel the tension radiating off him like a coming storm.

After Guinevere brought me to Merlin, the rest of my eighteenth name day passed with little to no fuss. I awoke the next morning to find a single pink peony in perfect bloom waiting for me, but I neither put it in water, nor bothered to enchant it. My eyes catch on the half-dead flower now, noticing the dulling colour, shrivelling petals, and wilting leaves.

"Ari, please." There's a soft *thud* that reverberates through the door and into my spine. I locked myself in here shortly after arriving, refusing to let him in. He may have wanted me to rest, but I think he just wanted a chance to apologise—to tell whatever story he thought would earn my forgiveness.

"Can we just talk?" Merlin sighs, and his words come through the door a little muffled.

"I have nothing to say to you." My arms are wrapped around my knees, chin resting atop them.

"Just let me explain."

"I don't want to hear whatever elaborate story you're about to spin for me. You can give me answers, or you can go away."

"Ask me anything." There's the tiniest bit of pressure against the door, pushing against my back, and it sounds as if he's sliding down to mirror the way I'm sitting.

I don't know where to start, so I pick somewhere in the middle, somewhere relatively safe. I pick something I already know the answer to, just to test him. "Are you truly five hundred years old?"

"What does age matter to an immortal?" There's an arrogance to his tone, bordering on mockery. It's exactly the way I expect him to answer, though it's not an answer in itself.

"It matters to me."

"But does it change anything?" he asks, almost hesitantly. "You knew what I was. You knew what I could do. You knew I was older than you… it shouldn't matter exactly how old I am when every decision about us was made by you."

"How do I know that it was, though? How do I know that you didn't manipulate every situation just to get what you wanted?"

"Do you truly believe I would do that to you?"

"I don't know," I say, disappointment flooding through me when I realise that it's the truth.

"Yes, Ari." His sigh is weary and bone-deep. "I've been here for more than five hundred years, and I will be here for five hundred more. A thousand, maybe. Until something strong enough comes along and ends this existence for me."

We're silent for a moment, and I glance around his bedroom. A simple bed big enough for two with a large wooden chest at the end. A small table in the corner with a stack of books, a candle, and a half-dead flower—that's all that's in here. "I don't mean for this to sound offensive, but if you've been here for hundreds of years, why aren't you, like, the king of everything? Why don't you live in a castle or something? Why haven't you…I don't know…accumulated more?"

His deep laugh rumbles through the door, but there's little humour in it. "It took me a long time to realise that wanting more than what you have only creates problems. I did want more—more power, more magic, more *everything.*" He lets the silence stretch on for a while before continuing. "I was king of these lands long before a crown ever sat upon any man's head…and then I lost everything. After that, there didn't seem like much point to wanting anymore."

My head tips back against the wood, and a heavy breath pushes its way from my chest. It's an evasive answer, but it still feels as if it holds truth to it, so I switch to something else. "Why are you working with Guinevere?

How does she fit in to all this?"

"Guinevere is but a means to an end. She is nothing more than a loophole and a back-up plan."

"I wouldn't let her know how irrelevant you deem her to be." I snort, and he laughs in earnest this time, lightening the mood a little.

"Why did I need to stop Arthur from ascending?"

"Because no one deserves to sit atop that throne but you," he says without hesitation, as if that was the question he'd been waiting for.

"You can't possibly believe I want it, in fact, you *know* that I don't."

"Not yet, perhaps."

"Merlin, I—"

"I've told you a hundred times, dear Ari. There isn't anything I wouldn't give you. There's nothing that I wouldn't do for you, including securing you a throne—especially if that throne happens to be your birthright."

"Have you learned nothing? You just admitted that wanting more cost you everything." Tears line my eyes, but I refuse to wipe them away. "I have nothing more to give, Merlin, nothing more to lose. Certainly not for a kingdom I want no part of."

"Wanting more *did* cost me everything—but it brought me to you," he says solemnly. "I've never had to ask you to trust me before, but I'll beg you to do so now."

I have to swallow down the lump in my throat before I can say anything. "How can I trust you after you betrayed me? You let them murder Penn, and then you let them take me prisoner—you left me behind!"

His tone turns pleading as the first crack of thunder goes off overhead. "You have to trust that I know what I'm doing, Ari, trust that I'm going to take care of you. Everything that I've done has been for a reason—for *us*."

Rain starts to fall in torrents outside, and I have to press my ear against the door to hear him over the sound. Opening the door and letting him in would be easier, but I'm afraid he would take that as a sign of forgiveness, and I'm not ready for that yet.

"I've waited a long time for you, Ari—for someone to be able to stand me long enough to put the broken pieces of my soul back together. For you to hold the jagged edges of my heart in your hands and not flinch when they cut you. To not run away when I lash out, to simply accept me for me. That's all I've ever wanted."

His tone turns somber, and I can hear the thunder rumble across the sky and echo through the mountains just as clearly as I can hear the emotions in his voice that he's fighting to keep at bay. "All those days of teaching you magic, all those afternoons spent rolling around on the forest floor… every deal we made, every promise we spoke…I meant it all."

"I don't know how to give you what you want." My voice is raw and hoarse, barely audible above the storm now raging outside. "I don't know how to move past the way I feel." I don't know how to bridge the void in my chest to get back to the way things were. Reasons or not, he left Penn for dead, and then he abandoned me.

"Let me make things right," he says softly. "Let me fix this."

Pulling a steadying breath into my lungs, I force it back out slowly, repeating the process a few more times. I don't have the energy to decipher how I feel about Merlin right now, or his declarations, but I can shift my focus to something I can control. I can worry about what comes next.

"If I get you the sword, you'll bring Penn back? Just like that?"

There's a weighted pause, as if he'd been hoping for forgiveness, or acceptance, or some sort of declaration back, but after a moment, he simply says, "Yes."

"It can't be that easy."

"It can, and it is. Retrieve the sword and I'll bring back your dragon." He shifts on the other side of the door, the wood pressing into me again, and then he says, "Everything will go back to normal, you'll see."

Again, my eyes drift to the flower wilting in the corner. It's the same flower he gave me the first time we met, and every birthday since. "*A pretty pink peony for a pretty little princess.*"

"I've waited a dozen lifetimes for you," he says, the vehemence in his voice sending a shiver down my spine. "I'm not going to lose you now."

"I can't just forget everything you've done…" The reluctance in my tone sounds flimsy, even to me.

"Give it time, Ari," he says slowly. "You'll forgive me. You always do."

FIFTY-NINE

ARI

Lake Umbra looms before me. The water is nearly black and shows nothing of what waits within. Little more than a faint shadow of the surrounding forest reflects off the surface, the sun having not yet risen above the tree line to show off the beautiful blue hue of the lake—the same blue of Lancelot's eyes.

The irony isn't lost on me that this part of my journey will end here, where everything began for him. This journey caused by his actions, by his inability to leave me alone, that has now found me at the whims of both his mother and his namesake.

The morning mist swirls through the trees at the water's edge, shrouding the forest in a vale of mystery. Had I not dreamt of this place for years, I might be uncomfortable. Had I not been here before, I might be afraid— but Nhimue is not my enemy.

The handful of times I've been here before, Penn was always with me. Today, I sit on the shore alone.

This morning, Merlin *popped* over to the cave and collected some items I'd need for this journey. My hands began to tremble at the mere thought of having to return for my things, and without me having to ask, he simply disappeared and reappeared a few moments later with an armful of my belongings in his grasp.

Now, I wear the soft, fitted black pants, worn leather boots, and loose tunic he brought, and a travelling cloak that helps to conceal several daggers hidden beneath my clothes. My hair is braided down the length of my spine, wisps of loose tendrils catching on the faint morning breeze.

The natural red colour is slowly starting to seep back into the strands after months without dragon's blood in my system. Vera hadn't been able to procure it, after all, regardless of her original assurances, but it's probably for the best, anyway. My identity is no longer a secret, and therefore, the leaching of colour is no longer necessary. I haven't used enough magic for the side effects to be unmanageable—the headaches little more than a dull throb—so, luckily, the absence of dragon's blood hasn't been as dire as I'd thought it would be.

After what feels like an eternity, a ripple in the centre of the lake appears. It spreads and grows until the nymph emerges, gliding through the water effortlessly towards me as I rise to greet her.

Her long, colourless hair flows past her feet, swirling in the water behind her. "Arturia," she says by way of greeting.

"Nhimue," I reply in kind.

"It has been a long time." She smiles, and though it's ethereal, it doesn't quite reach her eyes. The pearly hue of her skin is pale in the dim light of dawn. The scales across her brow hold the faintest hint of blue.

"It has, indeed."

"I'm sorry about Penn. He will be missed among our kind." His name falls so easily from her lips that it sends a jolt of shock through my veins. It shouldn't—they had no ill will towards one another—but still, it startles me.

I don't know what to say to that, so I say nothing at all.

She gestures to the sandy bank, and we sit down next to one another. Her toes dig into the sand beneath the water's edge as she leans back on her hands, regarding the lake.

"If rumours are to be believed, you managed to achieve your birthright and pull the sword from the stone, yet, I do not see Excalibur with you now."

"I don't have it," I say with a shake of my head. "It's in Camelot with Arthur."

"You may not have it now, but you will." She shifts her feet, and the movement sends ripples spreading across the surface of the lake.

"I have no intention of returning to Camelot and challenging Arthur for a sword."

"Your intentions don't matter, Arturia. The sword *is* yours."

My eyebrows furrow, half-a-dozen questions poised on my tongue, but she continues on without giving me the chance to voice any of them. "The current possession of Excalibur matters little, for it is a different sword you're after now."

"Aye, apparently."

She smirks at my tone, shaking her head just a little. "I can grant you access to that side of the lake, but the sword will not be easy to come by."

"Define access," I say warily.

Her eyes narrow in a mixture of surprise and disbelief. "Did Merlin not tell you of where it rests?" she asks hesitantly.

"No, not really. He only said to seek you out and retrieve the sword in the lake, but I assumed that simply meant swimming to the bottom—"

She makes a sound of indignation in the back of her throat, and I have to laugh. *Of course, he didn't tell me any real details, because he knew I'd say no.* Expelling a long sigh, I ask, "What can you tell me about the sword?"

"The Bone Sword belonged to the first king."

"The first king?"

"Your father is the ninth Uther of his bloodline. The sword you seek belonged to the first and, arguably, the most cunning."

I let her words sink in, the enormity of the task at hand washing over me. How am I ever going to find the sword of someone who's been dead for hundreds of years?

"He made an arrangement with your dragon," she says curiously. "Did you know?"

My head whips towards her, my eyes searching her own desperately. "The first Uther knew Penn?"

"Indeed." She nods, her mouth set in a smug slant. "Every Uther has known him."

"I don't understand." My brows pull together, head shaking back and forth.

"He was a new king to a new land with many enemies. He struck a bargain with the fiercest creature he could find—an oath of protection and fealty against those who sought to usurp him." She looks across the lake almost wistfully, as if she's remembering it first-hand. "Half the kingdom's gold in return for the dragon's protection."

"I never knew," I whisper.

"Every Uther made the same bargain, the same blood oath. Every one until your father."

"He wouldn't pay?" I ask, unsurprised.

"He would not. The war was long over, and he did not believe in further indebting himself or his kingdom to a dragon—to a being of magic."

I knew his hatred of magic ran deep. I heard stories over the years of those who dared to use it in his kingdom and the gruesome end they faced, and it brings me a small kernel of joy at how resentful he would be to know that one of his children, a daughter no less, had spent many years indebting herself to a mage, raised by the very dragon he refused.

My chest tightens, and a solitary tear slides down my cheek as one of the unknown pieces of my origin clicks into place. After Bax stole me away from the castle, he brought me to Penn—to the one place he knew my father would never find me. To the one place, and the one creature, who would protect me from him at all costs.

"Why did Penn stay?" I ask, unable to hide the wobble in my voice. "Why didn't we just go far away from here?" I don't know that I expect her to have an answer, but when she does, it doesn't surprise me.

"That cave had been his home for many, many years," she says softly. "And I think he wanted you to have the option to go home, if ever you wanted—or needed—it."

I release a shuddering breath and wipe the tears from my eyes.

We sit on the sandy bank, staring out at the infinite depths of Lake Umbra. I notice once again that her feet never leave the water—something I knew, yet hadn't really understood—and it hits me with shocking clarity exactly what this curse has cost her.

It makes me want to retch, to purge my stomach, as if Guinevere had hurled us halfway across the country again. To be confined to this lake— this prison—for who knows how long… I've never asked Merlin about his other bargains, but I can't help wondering if what she traded for this was worth the price.

"I met your son," I blurt out before thinking better of it.

Nhimue merely blinks at me in surprise.

"You managed to hear rumours of what I've done, but not that it was your son who forced me down that path to begin with?"

"It's been a while since I've spoken with my son," she says, tilting her head to the side as she ignores my question in favour of her own. "Tell me, how did he come to find himself so entwined with your fate?"

"He and his friends took it upon themselves to try to slay Penn and steal his gold." I cannot tell if it's my words or my tone that startle her more.

"Surely, he didn't—"

"He did, and they nearly succeeded. After that, he simply couldn't help himself. He kept returning to the forest—even after I told him not to— and eventually he was followed. More knights returned, and this time they did succeed. Lancelot is a good part of the reason Penn is dead.”

When her gaze meets mine, it’s full of both disbelief and apprehension.

Heaving a sigh, I clear my throat before adding, “Despite all that, he also had a hand in helping me escape Camelot.”

Dropping her eyes, she nods slightly, the movement small and distracted. A heavy silence falls over us until she finally says, “It’s time,” just as the sun begins to shine through the trees on the distant shore. “I will take you into the lake now.”

“What happens then?”

A wry smile lifts up one side of her mouth. “You swim like your life depends on it, and you do not stop until you reach the other side.”

“What does that mean?” I ask, but she doesn’t answer.

We stand in unison, and she laces her fingers through mine, squeezing my hand gently.

“I’m afraid,” I whisper, my eyes locked on the lake before us.

“We will go together.” She squeezes my hand again. “I will go with you to the other side, and I will be here waiting when you return with the sword.”

“How do I get back?” A drop of panic spreads through my gut. My heartbeat picks up, and my breathing turns shallow. “How will you know when I’m ready to come back?”

“It is my lake, Ari. I will know when you try to return.”

“What’s waiting on the other side?” I ask, hesitant and wary.

Her mouth twists into an attempted smile, her eyes losing focus for a moment. “The realm on the other side of this lake is not one of the living—and only for those with magic in their veins.”

I’ll tell him where you’ve gone, Ari, but know that the last thing you’ll want is for him to follow after you.” Guinevere was right about that, at least—not that Tristan would be able to, even if he wanted to.

“But I—”

“You can wield magic, Ari. That’s all it takes,” Nhimue says. “On the other side of this lake is the afterlife for the magic folk.”

“How did Uther get the Bone Sword to the other side?” I ask, brows furrowing.

“He gave it to me, and I took it there myself. Those without magic cannot cross between the barrier, and I thought it best to leave it someplace where very few people would be able to find it again.”

“Why would you help him?”

“Because he swore to make my son a knight, regardless of his heritage.”

At least, he kept his word.

“Are you ready?”

Pulling in a slow, steadying breath, I nod.

We walk into the lake hand in hand, the water lapping at our feet, welcoming us into its depths. It’s neither cold nor warm; the only thing I feel at all is the resistance of the water itself as it moves around us. When our shoulders are submerged under the surface, she turns to me, an easy, reassuring confidence in her features. “Deep breath.”

I do as she says, treading in a slow circle to scan the entirety of the shoreline. I don’t know why I’m searching for him; I know without a shadow of a doubt that he isn’t here. Merlin will not step out of the shadows to offer me one final farewell before I undertake this task for him. He will not risk Nhimue’s wrath to see me off—he who bound her to this lake.

My eyes find hers again, and in the brightness of the sun, I can see they’re the same shade of blue as Lancelot’s. Guilt bubbles in my chest. I should have returned his father’s medallion to him a long time ago. Now, it feels heavy around my neck, as if it intends to drag me down into the lake and keep me there.

“Together,” she says softly, drawing my attention back to her.

Her head slips below the surface, and then she’s pulling me down into the dark shadowy depths of Lake Umbra. So far down that the pressure threatens to explode in my ears and behind my eyes. Until there is no more air left in my lungs, no more strength left in my limbs. Surely, she is just dragging me at this point—carrying me farther and farther into the darkness of her domain.

It's so dark, so infinitely and endlessly dark, that I cannot even see my own hand in front of my face.

After what feels like an eternity, the pressure begins to ease, and after a moment more, we burst through the surface. Clean, crisp air assaults my lungs as she drags me to the shore, supporting the entirety of my water-logged body. I cough and splutter and choke up more water than should be possible, even after she deposits me on the edge of Lake Umbra.

Except, that it's not Lake Umbra anymore.

"Welcome to the other side," she says grimly.

"It looks…gloomy."

"Things are not the same in this realm, Arturia. I would not linger any longer than is necessary." She grimaces, and a ripple of unease spreads through my chest. "Find the sword and return to our realm."

With those final words, she slips back under the surface, leaving me alone on the rocky shore.

SIXTY

LANCELOT

I stay hidden in the shade of an ancient, gnarled oak tree long after they've submerged. Like two wraiths gliding effortlessly through the water, hand in hand, with only a moment's hesitation. With one slow scan of the shoreline, Ari's eyes pass right over me before the pair of them slip beneath the surface.

I came to see my mother, to tell her about the tournament and all that has happened in the last while, but when I spotted Ari on the shore next to her, I froze. I believed she was alive, but knowing it and seeing it are two very different things, and I hadn't found the ability to make my limbs move—or the courage to go to her—before they left this realm together.

I stay beneath the heavy canopy of the tree long after the ripples of their departure have dissipated, and long after the warmth of the sun has replaced the morning mist. Long after it crossed the sky and dipped below the tree line again, setting the forest on fire with a rich, golden hue, the last wisps of blue now faded and the sky a stark mix of blood red and burnt orange.

A cold, heavy pit of dread has been growing in my gut all day. Twisting and turning, writhing with fear and anxiety for what comes next. For where she has to go. For what she might have to do. Wondering if she'll come back. Hoping and praying that she does. Regardless of how things were left between us, I refuse to accept any other alternative.

When the ripples start in the centre of the lake again, my nerves settle just a little. My mother rises to the surface and makes her way towards the shore, a kind and welcoming smile lighting up her face at the sight of me.

"Why do you look so troubled?" she asks, tilting her head to the side. "She will be back."

"You can't know that." I shake my head. "She shouldn't have gone alone."

"There is nothing either of us could have done to stop her. You could not have joined her, and I could not have stayed with her." She releases a small sigh, and we settle together on the sandy edge of the water.

"Couldn't you have stayed on the other side?" I ask, annoyed at the petulance in my voice. "In case she needs you?"

"I may watch her from the shores in that world just as I watch you from the shores in this one," she says calmly, "but I am still bound by the laws of magic, no matter which realm I am in."

We sit in silence for a while, the sun sinking lower and lower behind the trees. The golden hour has come and gone, fading into the murky yellow and deep purple of twilight.

"Is there anyone who could have gone to the other side with her?" I ask quietly, not entirely sure I want to hear the answer.

Without hesitation, my mother says, "Yes, although not many, and certainly none she could trust."

"Merlin?" I ask warily.

"Yes," she says again, "but any who cross through my lake need my permission to do so. On both sides."

"Or something to use against you," I counter, glowering at the water.

"Or something to use against me," she repeats absently.

We fall into another silence, neither uncomfortable nor unwelcome.

"Will time pass differently for her there?" I ask finally.

"Many things will be different for her there," she says, turning to look at me sidelong. "Though we cannot know the extent of it until she returns."

"When she comes back…I fear the Camelot she left behind will not be the one she returns to."

"You are probably right," my mother says softly. Nothing ominous or foreboding about it, just a simple truth. "But I have no fears that you will be the same."

It's my turn to look at her sidelong now. "I've made so many mistakes—"

"I have watched you grow into the person you are today, little knight, and not without your fair share of difficulties. You are steadfast and true, strong and loyal. No matter how long this part of her journey takes, I do not fear that you will be any different when she returns."

That may be so, but how different will she be?

By the time I make it back to Camelot, the moon is high in the sky, though well passed its apex. I deposit Willow, now well-worked and in need of a good rest, with a sack of grain and a pile of fresh hay. Riding for hours has left my leg throbbing, even with the herb-packed sutures and tight bindings to support the deep cut left by Lucan during our duel.

The walk to Vera's is both far and inconvenient from the stables, mixing with the constant pain in my leg to turn my mood more foul with every step. They'll have been waiting for me for a while now, but I don't care.

I rap my knuckles against the front door of Vera's shop, right below the carved crescent moon, entering without waiting for someone to answer. Low voices murmur beyond the black curtain that separates the front half of her shop from the back, the dim flicker of candles visible around the edges of the fabric.

It takes me a moment to collect myself, to calm my thoughts and steady my breathing. I watched Ari disappear into Lake Umbra—watched her dip below the surface and enter another realm entirely without knowing if she would ever come back. There are so many things I should have said to her… so many things I wanted to ask her…so many things I still wished to know.

And now, the only thing that I do know—the only thing that I can cling to—is the hope that my mother was right, and that she will, in fact, return. To this realm, to this kingdom, and, one way or another, to me.

Beyond the curtain, I can make out the deep, northern lilt of Tristan's voice and the sarcastic edge of Perci's. He laughs at something, and then a third voice murmurs a response, and unease spreads through my veins like ice, freezing me to the spot. Last I heard, Vera wasn't going to be here tonight.

That same voice speaks again, louder this time—female and distinctly Northumbrian—and yet, not the voice of the mage who lives here. My feet carry me forward, spurred on by the disbelief coursing through me. As I shove the curtain aside, three sets of eyes lift to meet mine—two that I expected and one I did not.

My eyes lock onto the pair of deep, fiery blue ones. "Lady Guinevere," I force through clenched teeth. "What a surprise."

A slow, impish grin lifts up one side of her mouth.

"Tristan," I say, not taking my eyes off the wolf in the pretty dress— that's what he once called her, and yet, even after all her lies and trickery, here they sit together. "A word?"

"Leave it alone, Lance." He sighs, dropping his elbows onto the round, gnarled table. "Just come in and have a seat. We can—"

"She betrayed us," I snap, tossing my hand in her direction but turning my anger on him.

"Aye, she did, and there's nothing we can do about it, is there?"

"How can you sit here with her after she lied to us?"

"Lancelot—" Perci tries to intervene, but I don't let him.

"It was *her* plan!" I don't even try to keep the disgust from my tone. "She lied to us and then she took Ari to Merlin, of all—"

"Actually"—Guinevere clucks her tongue disapprovingly—"if you want to be specific, I took her some*where,* not to some*one.* He was there, don't get me wrong, but I couldn't have just whisked us to wherever he was in that moment. It was a predetermined location," she says nonchalantly, studying her nails. "If you're going to gather the troops to take me down, at least get the facts straight."

"You're not helping," Perci murmurs.

"Oh, I'm going to do more than gather the troops," I snarl at her.

Tristan stands so abruptly that his stool falls, clattering to the floor behind him. "Enough! You're not going to get anywhere by screaming at everyone just because you're upset. We're all upset, Lance. We're all angry. Do not make the mistake of thinking you're the only one who cares about Ari." His hands are splayed out on the table in front of him, and without intending to, my gaze drops to his knuckles. Where I thought I would see scabs, still healing from the last time he lost his temper, I only see the faintest hint of scars.

"Aye, Guinevere lied, but she's also helping ensure that Arthur sends his men to all the wrong places looking for Ari."

"What is this, Tristan? Why are you defending her? Because she's from Northumbria?" I throw my arms out to either side, chest heaving. "You're supposed to be my brother. You're supposed to be on my side."

"My brother is dead, Lancelot. I owe you nothing."

I take an involuntary step backward, flinching as if he'd punched me. The tension in the room grows palpable, and it takes me a moment to find my voice again. "We're supposed to trust each other, Tris, but you've been keeping secrets for months—years, apparently," I add bitterly. I didn't even know that he had a brother, let alone that he was dead, but I can't contain the animosity writhing in my chest.

"Her true identity was not my secret to tell," Tristan says quietly, ignoring my jab and bending to pick up the stool. He sits back down, propping his elbows on the table again and dropping his chin onto his fists. "You make everything so black and white, but the world doesn't work that way, Lancelot. Not everything can be that simple."

"Nothing about this is simple." I laugh—I can't help it. "I was there the day you swore fealty to Camelot—to your *brothers*, by blood or by choice. I don't know what's going on, or why you continue to trust her, but you can't have it both ways, Tristan. You can't be loyal to both kingdoms—to both crowns."

"That's not fair. You know that I'm not."

Perci clears his throat, catching everyone's attention. "Our plan never would have worked, Lance," he says evenly, unaffected by anyone's outbursts. I glance around the table, scowling when I find Guinevere's gaze already fixed on me.

"It wasn't *our* plan, it was *hers*," I have to correct him through gritted teeth. "Of course, it wouldn't have worked because she had another plan that didn't include us."

"Lancelot, just stop for a moment—just long enough to actually consider the likelihood that we would've succeeded." Perci sighs, pinching the bridge of his nose. "There is no way that using your duel would've served as enough of a distraction. We all heard the order Arthur gave when he found out she was missing—he wanted every inch of Camelot searched, and he will continue to extend that search until she's found. It was only a matter of time until he sent knights to scour her cave and anywhere else they might have gone. He wouldn't have stopped until he found her. Do you honestly think there was anywhere safe enough that Tristan could have taken her with such little time?"

To his credit, Tristan looks torn—annoyed, angry, and something else

I can't quite place—but it does nothing to quell the emotions rolling around in my chest.

"Then why not clue us in on your plans?" I ask Guinevere. "You know we wanted to get her out of Camelot, so if you had a way to do it and somewhere safe to take her, why not just tell us?"

She snorts, rolling her eyes and clicking her tongue. It sends a fresh wave of fury through my body.

"First of all, just like Ari and Tristan, I don't owe you anything, least of all the inner workings of my plans." I open my mouth, but she continues on as if she couldn't care less about anything I might say. "Second of all, the first thing Arthur did after you lost your duel—my condolences, by the way—was barge into my rooms demanding to know where I'd been and what I knew of the prisoner. Had I not been retching my guts up from a second trip across the country in just as many hours, he never would have believed I had nothing to do with it. Arthur doesn't trust me." She in no way sounds like she's sympathetic of my loss, and her smug tone makes my lip curl.

"I don't blame him," I say under my breath, but she continues on as if I haven't spoken at all.

"His next step, as you can assume, would've been to haul you into his throne room and interrogate you on her whereabouts—just like last time. Had you known where she was, he could have tortured it out of you. Had you given him my name, I would be in that dungeon cell right now, if not dead for my acts of treason. So, I sent him on a wild goose chase instead, sharing with him just enough of the truth to keep him busy."

"He's not foolish enough to put you—"

"He's precisely that foolish," she snaps. "He is a child, and he is rash and hot-headed and he would stop at nothing to get what he wants. More than one of those dungeon cells will end up claiming someone before this is over."

"You still should have told me." I sneer.

"You're such a child!" Guinevere shouts, returning my glare. "Why are you so obsessed with Ari, anyway? She's nothing to you. She's not your family or your lover…she's barely even your friend. Why do you care where she is so long as she got out?"

"It's not about who she is to me." I shake my head and it takes great effort to keep my voice from rising again. "It's about the fact that she thinks I single-handedly ruined her life, and I didn't get a chance to set that right—to make it up to her."

"You didn't get a chance to earn her forgiveness," Guinevere says with an eye-roll. "There's a difference, and quite honestly, she doesn't owe you a damn thing, least of all forgiveness for the death of her dragon."

We stare at each other for a moment, Guinevere meeting my glare unflinchingly.

"You better hope you know what you're doing," I say finally.

"I got her out of Camelot, didn't I? She's in good hands with Merlin."

"All you did was change the hands of the monster. Merlin is no better than Arthur, and you'd be wise to remember that."

Guinevere snorts, shaking her head. "You don't know a damn thing about Merlin or the princess." Guinevere wields the title like both a weapon and an insult.

Shaking my head, I stand to leave.

"Where are you going?" Perci protests.

"I want no part of this—whatever this sham of an alliance is."

"Lancelot, wait."

"Sorry, Perc. But I'm not just going to sit here and pretend I'm fine with this," I say, shaking my head. "Don't say I didn't warn you when this blows up in your face and you realise you were wrong to trust her."

I've already got the curtain drawn back and one foot out of Vera's kitchen before Perci asks for a second time, "Where are you going?"

"Ari's gone, and I don't know when she'll be back. As far as I'm concerned, we're done here. I have other things that need my attention until she returns."

"Like what?" Guinevere huffs, her tone mocking. "What could you possibly have to do that's more important than keeping Arthur misinformed?"

"You can clearly handle the prince without me." I snort, laughing gruffly. "I have a curse to break."

EPILOGUE

ARI

SIX WEEKS LATER

Panic surges through me like wildfire, and a dizzying sort of numbness spreads through my body as I flee. Everything else fades away as I half-run, half-stumble through the forest, my focus narrowing on the path before me.

The blinding pain in my arm threatens to consume me; the arrow protruding from either side of my forearm burns where it tore through the muscles and now sits wedged between the bones. My hand is shaking, spasming violently.

I can hear them shouting behind me, though I cannot make out what they're saying, and I dare not stop to try. The Bone Sword is clutched to my chest, my uninjured arm wrapped around it with an iron grip.

Velho screams—a sound of pure rage—and I flinch, unbounded fear sliding down my spine and slithering through my veins.

The arrow snags on an old pine tree as I push past it, and a violent hiss escapes my lips. The pain in my arm is so momentarily overwhelming that all other thoughts elude me. One moment, I am propelling myself through the forest as fast as my wounded body can carry me, the next, I'm free-falling to the ground.

I slide through dirt and pine needles, over roots and rocks. Remnants of the forest floor coat the inside of my mouth, mixed with the metallic tang of blood. There is no air in my lungs, and the ability to pull any in seems to have evaded me.

Lia comes crashing through the trees right behind me, a colourful string of curses flying from her mouth. She stoops down, grabbing the discarded sword with one hand and sliding the other beneath my good arm. Hoisting me to my feet, and shouldering the bulk of my weight, she drags me forward, barely losing any momentum at all.

"Don't stop," she grunts in my ear. "You can't stop."

I try to nod.

I try to steady my shallow breaths.

I try to swallow down the remnants of blood and dirt—try to see past the spots at the edge of my vision, to focus on anything other than the unrelenting pain in my arm.

Footsteps rapidly approach behind us, and Lia all but shoves me down the path towards the lake, thrusting the Bone Sword into my shaky arms.

Isa bursts through the trees, and we all sag with relief—short-lived by the angry screams of Velho fast approaching.

"Go!" Isa shouts. "I'll hold him off for as long as I can."

"I can't ask you to—"

"Move!" Lia yells, ignoring my protests. Once again, her arm slides under my own, and she hurtles us down the path towards the beach. "How do you summon her?" she asks urgently, eyes scanning the lake as it comes into view.

"I don't know." I grunt with the effort of staying upright. "She said she'd know when I was ready to come back."

She snarls in my ear. "Stupid, cryptic nymphs."

A blast of heat hits us from behind, and we turn in time to see a massive wall of fire go up between the trees.

"That's going to cost him…a lot," she murmurs, more to herself than to me.

"Death magic." Isa had laughed when he told me. *"Because using it quite literally kills me."*

"He made his choice," I remind her. She cuts me a cold glare, but it doesn't faze me any more now than it did the first time she turned those olive green eyes on me. She turns us back towards the lake, but I step out from her support and hold my arm between us. "You need to pull it out."

She nods once, snapping the flight feathers off and then yanking the broken arrow shaft from my forearm before either of us can think better of it. I scream, and she tears off a piece of her tunic—my tunic—hastily tying it around the gushing wound. I clutch it to the Bone Sword, holding it as tight as I can to my chest.

"Where is your stupid water nymph?" she growls, scanning the surface again.

"I don't know," I whimper, shaking my head.

We make our way across the rocky beach, Lia stopping at the edge of the water as I continue into it. The icy coldness seeps into my boots and into my bones.

Isa joins us, all but crashing into Lia as he breaks through the tree line. He looks exhausted; creating that fire wall had to have taken up most of the energy he had left. Sliding his bow over his shoulder and nocking an arrow, he takes up a defensive stance between me and the forest. Beside him, Lia pulls two double-edged daggers from her belt.

The wall of fire is still holding strong, but no one is stronger than Velho, and it will not take him long to catch up to us.

"Where is she?" Lia shouts again, and the panic in her voice shatters what's left of my frazzled nerves. Tears well in her eyes, mirroring the ones that blur my own.

Six weeks was all we were given. It was never going to be enough, but if we both die now, there is nowhere else for us to go. There is no other afterlife for us to find each other again.

My feet move of their own volition, taking a step towards her, but I force myself to stop. If I go to her now, I do not know that I will have the strength to leave.

Her brows pull together, her mouth turned down at the corners, but her eyes—full of fight and determination and sheer spite—dip to the Bone Sword, still clutched to my chest. No, not the sword, but my arm—to the blood coating my skin, seeping through the makeshift bandage.

Pulling my damaged arm away from my chest, I let the blood run to my fingers, let it pool in my shaky palm. As soon as my hand is coated in the sticky, crimson liquid, I plunge it into the water, digging my fingers into the muddy ground beneath, chanting his name over and over and over again.

A lifeline. A desperate plea. A Hail Mary.

Merlin.

Merlin.

Merlin.

THE STORY CONTINUES IN...

HEIR OF SPITE AND FURY

Scan the QR code below to sign up for my newsletter
and receive a bonus scene from this book.

ACKNOWLEDGEMENTS

First and foremost, I want to thank Evan for all your love, patience, and enthusiasm over the years—you've been my number one cheerleader during this entire journey, but thank you most of all for being my best friend and for being a wonderful father to our son. And thank you to the little boy who doesn't quite understand what I've been doing, but usually lets me work without distraction anyway.

To Molly; my beautiful, wonderful Milky Way. Your unconditional friendship and support over the years has been an absolute godsend, and your honesty, advice, and encouragement in pursuing this career has been unparalleled. And for all the extras you've done for this book—the cover, the formatting, and the countless hours spent talking me off ledges, through plot holes, and planning for later books—thank you always and for everything.

To my beta readers—your thoughts, opinions, and feedback have proved invaluable. A huge thanks to Molly and Whitney for all of your wonderful insights, to Nika and Nico for your unparalleled enthusiasm, and a special thanks to Tess for being Lancelot's number one hater, literally from the very first draft—your passion for his downfall has been a delight.

Thank you to my mom for never doubting that I could do this, even though I originally told you I was going to write a book almost ten years ago. To my brother, my go-to plant guy who's more than happy to give me far more information than is necessary whenever I ask about them "for research." And to Irene, who has consistently said "I can't wait to read it" for the last five years.

Last, but certainly not least, I'd like to thank **you** for picking up this book and coming on this debut journey with me. This story started out as a NaNoWriMo project in 2017, was shelved several times in lieu of other projects, and has changed drastically over the years but ultimately remained the story I needed to tell most.

ABOUT THE AUTHOR

ALISHA is a Canadian author who lives close to the Alberta Rockies, spends more time buying books than reading them, and enjoys listening to songs on repeat. She's a mom to a sassy little four-year-old, two rescue pups, and several dozen plants. She's a mood reader (who refuses to DNF, no matter how many years it takes), devoted Monster drinker, and Shrek reference enthusiast.

Find her online at:
WWW.ALISHAWOOD.COM
@authoralishawood on Instagram and TikTok

9 781738 332212